PRAISE FOR *DASHBOARD ELVIS IS DEAD*

'I loved this book. It covers decades, continents and a wide cast of brilliant characters, all with seemingly impossible depth ... sharp dialogue, vivid descriptions and sideways views of the world ... If you want a book that combines brilliant writing with loads of action against a backdrop of well-known real events, *Dashboard Elvis is Dead* is a great pick' Katie Allen

'David F. Ross has written a rich and rewarding novel that takes in the culture and social history of both Scotland and the USA, beautifully weaving stories together over decades before bringing them together in a manner which is devastating ... proves that David F. Ross is only getting better. And considering his body of work that's some achievement' Alistair Braidwood, *Scots Whay Hae*

'Gripping, gritty and gloriously written, David F. Ross captures characters, places and moods like few other writers. A real talent; a triumph of a novel' Martin Geissler

'A mesmerising road trip through the America of Kerouac, Warhol and Reagan. *Dashboard Elvis* may be dead, but this book is full of vibrant, authentic, colourful life' Stuart Cosgrove

'This is an ambitious, sweeping novel. The intertwined stories draw you in, asking fundamental questions about fact and fiction. Taut and gritty, *Dashboard Elvis Is Dead* interrogates truth, and pulses with life' Donna McLean

'A masterclass in transatlantic intertwining storytelling from one of Scotland's finest writers' Derek Steel

'A dazzling, time-hopping patchwork of pop and politics, sewn together with wit and compassion' Kirstin Innes

'With a rawness and sensitivity that is visceral, this is another extraordinary novel from David Ross' Random Things through My Letterbox

'A stunning piece of historical and contemporary fiction. Nothing I can say can do it justice. Just read it and you'll know what I mean' From Belgium with Booklove

'It's great when a book surprises you. This is a story with a punch, clouded by memory and regret' The Bookbag

'Simply a brilliant debut novel' John Niven

'Powerful and punchy, with well placed, darker-than-dark humour' LoveReading

'As warm and authentic as Roddy Doyle at his very best' Nick Quantrill

'A solid gold hit of a book!' Colin McCredie

'Full of comedy, pathos and great tunes' Hardeep Singh Kohli

'Dark, hilarious, funny and heart-breaking all at the same time' Muriel Gray

'Just brilliant' Bobby Bluebell

Dashboard Elvis Is Dead

ABOUT THE AUTHOR

David F. Ross was born in Glasgow in 1964. His debut novel, *The Last Days of Disco,* was long-listed for the Authors' Club Best First Novel Award, and received exceptional critical acclaim, as did the other two books in the Disco Days Trilogy – *The Rise & Fall of the Miraculous Vespas* and *The Man Who Loved Islands*.

His most recent book, *There's Only One Danny Garvey*, topped several Best of the Year lists and was shortlisted for the Saltire Scottish Fiction Book of the Year 2021.

He is a regular contributor to *Nutmeg Magazine* and in 2020 he wrote the screenplay for the film *Miraculous*, based on his novel. Follow David on Twitter @dfr10 and his website: davidfross.co.uk.

Other books by David F. Ross,
available from Orenda Books

The Disco Days Trilogy:
The Last Days of Disco
The Rise & Fall of the Miraculous Vespas
The Man Who Loved Islands

Welcome to the Heady Heights
There's Only One Danny Garvey

Dashboard Elvis Is Dead

DAVID F. ROSS

**ORENDA
BOOKS**

Orenda Books
16 Carson Road
West Dulwich
London SE21 8HU
www.orendabooks.co.uk

First published in the United Kingdom by Orenda Books, 2022
Copyright © David F. Ross, 2022

A catalogue record for this book is available from the British Library.

ISBN 978-1-914585-40-1
eISBN 978-1-914585-41-8

Typeset in Garamond by typesetter.org.uk

Printed and bound by CPI Group (UK) Ltd, Croydon CR0 4YY

*For sales and distribution, please contact info@orendabooks.co.uk or visit
www.orendabooks.co.uk.*

For Nadia. Your independent spirit is the soul of this.

And for Jude and Jamie,
and those they encountered along the way.

'The story is not in the words; it's in the struggle.'
 —Paul Auster, *The New York Trilogy*

'Everybody has their own America ... a fantasy America that they think is out there ... pieced together from scenes in movies and music and lines from books.'
 —Andy Warhol

YES!

8th October 2014

The word is written in chalk on a small, wall-mounted blackboard behind the hotel's tiny reception desk. It sits under four other words: *Thought for the day*. I look at it intently, moving closer.

YES!

The exclamation mark is less obvious than the letters. It could be mistaken for a crack in the surface. As if letters and punctuation were put there by different people and at separate times. The power of – or comfort in – positive thinking? Defiance in the face of defeat? From my brief time in the city, I understand these to be indigenous Glaswegian traits.

Have a nice day, I hear from behind me.

Impersonal platitudes. A gift to the world from America, my homeland. No need for a response, and it doesn't receive one from me. The young concierge then asks, Have you *had* a nice day? and another hotel guest ignores his act. He needs a new scriptwriter.

The lobby doors swoosh apart. On the outside, the cold is like a mugger. It rushes me. Steals my breath. It takes minutes for my respiratory rate to recover. I've been in colder places than this. Much colder. It's a reminder of how unprepared I am. It is October. I'm primed for incessant rain, sapping the soul. But this cold is unexpectedly raw. A grey pallor coats Buchanan Street, the city's public spine. The atmosphere somber. Almost devoid of color. Heavy-clad people, angled into the wind's bitterness, collars up, heads down. In a hurry. Sensing the cloudburst that is threatening to migrate from the west. I attribute this feeling to the aftermath of the brutal referendum. Three weeks ago, Scotland voted to remain part of the United Kingdom. This city houses the highest percentage of the losers.

I observe the monochromatic urban tapestry. It is my one recognised talent. I lift the lens. *Point, focus and…*

Click: Two old men drop crumbs as a determined band of pigeons congregate around their feet.

Click: A young, tattooed couple kiss aggressively in a sheltered doorway. Consumed by – and consuming – each other. Each has a dog tied to their ankle by its lead. The ugly beasts sit obediently, heads turned outwards. Sentinel gargoyles, guarding the wet embrace.

Click: A woman with a young child looks up into the rain and points at a shiny, black statue of a man on a horse. The statue is wearing a traffic cone. As is the horse. The child appears uninterested.

Click: A tall, monolithic building draped in a vast banner. The words *PEOPLE MAKE GLASGOW* on a shocking backdrop of pink bursting out of the grey.

Click: An enthusiastic busker murders a familiar song. Only its chorus identifies the victim. *All I need is an independent state of mind,* he croaks. The song, once obscure, now as universally identifiable with its country of origin as whisky, tartan and an Australian actor with his face painted saltire blue. Of late, this song has descended from hopeful anthem for the 'early days of a better nation', to a lament for a lost opportunity. As I can personally testify, it is a song for all seasons. I'm drawn to the busker not just because of the song. But also because of the gaudy, gold-framed, Elvis-style shades that conceal his eyes. I shudder at the cracked lens, visible when I zoom in to his haggard face. It immediately reminds me of Matt back in 1983. Poor, fucked-up Matt.

The busker drags the refrain out for far longer than in the original song. He's enjoying an audience of one. I wait for him to finish before advancing. The open guitar case in front of him has a few coins in it. I suspect he contributed most of them to encourage others. But I've taken his picture and his downward glances confirm that there's a price to pay. He smiles broadly. Yellowing incisors frame a tunnel-like gap where the front ones used to be.

I applaud and reach into a deep pocket to pull out a note. It's a twenty. Far more than the performance deserved.

Fuck sake! The busker sighs. Twenty quid? Ah've nae change, hen.

He's unwilling to give up the coins, but I don't want them anyway. I put up a palm and his blotched, reddened face lights up.

Cheers, missus. Ye'll be rewarded in Heaven, ya wee stoater, ye. He might be high.

I lift the camera and click some more. Capturing a truth. Getting my money's worth. The busker poses like a professional boxer. His head covered by a dirty white sweatshirt hood. He pulls back his coat to reveal a large *YES* written across the shirt underneath. He draws a finger under the word, underlining that he was one of the 45% minority. It briefly occurs to me that he could be the musician behind the once-famous song. The battered, pockmarked skin suggests he is certainly old enough. I smile at the ridiculousness of the notion; at the fantastical odds that such a coincidence would represent.

For hours I've been documenting the people who make this famous Victorian city what it is. Recording the transition of a country as its identity changes. It's not why I'm here though. Not really. I arrived in Glasgow months ago, searching for several elusive people who might still be here.

The cold has diminished, replaced by a drizzling dampness that must gnaw at the bones of the old. It's the type of rain that nags like toothache. That seeps into the pores over weeks rather than drenches a surface in minutes. I long for the warmth of the sun. It's been thirty years, but I still miss the Texas heat, if little else about my birthplace.

The light is leaving. Sodium paints glittering patterns in puddles until vehicles spray them. The scurrying citizens avoid them instinctively, tuned in to the rhythm. But I'm caught. Doused by a bus I didn't see coming, like I'm a Jackson Pollock canvas. But my attention is caught by a gallery of posters on the other side of the junction. Lights change. The traffic halts. And I cross with the multitude. Ten posters in a row; the same smiling woman. Each poster daubed with graffiti. Scribbled penises drip onto her face on seven. Teeth blacked out on four. *FREEDOM*, in speech bubbles for all ten, but six of those have the word *FUCK* added above by a different hand.

The ten posters reflect in their own ways the outcome of the vote. The smiling woman is Anna Mason. One of the slippery people from my past. She is now the rising political star of the Scottish National Party. Their recent loss may yet be her gain. I had hoped to interview her about her plans for her future and about her tumultuous past. But Anna has closed that down. The song defiantly sung by the street busker earlier connects us – emotionally, but financially too. So, I'm waiting. Sometimes doing nothing is best – it allows circumstance to step in and deliver what we seek.

Yes?

A medium Americano please?

The barista looks up sharply. The drawl, no doubt.

Tae sit in?

Yeah. Thanks.

Milk wi' that?

No. No thanks.

Anythin' else?

No. That's it. Thank you.

I'm forced to pay with a card. The busker's twenty was the only currency I had. It's a busy establishment. Bustling with activity. Backgrounding the hubbub, I detect the sounds of inoffensive Americana: middle-of-the-road music from my teenage years. Given that much of my free time here has been spent contemplating that period of my life, and the people I shared it with, I welcome the serendipity. It comforts me.

There is a free table at the window. I drape my saturated coat around the thick industrial radiator next to my seat. Steam visibly rises from it. I've only just opened my notepad when an old woman catches my eye. Raindrops drip from her horn-rimmed spectacles. As she removes them, she looks directly at me, and I can't help thinking that her motherly look provokes the words that I scribble on the pad:

I landed at Momma Em's sprawling Ingleside home in the summer of 1983, after the life-changing trauma of Matt's brain injury.

Momma Em was a warm, assertive Donna Reed sort – a mom to many children she hadn't birthed. But not to me. I wanted her to take me into her family. To treat me like the other kids instead of a hired hand. To be the mom that I'd wanted Delphine to be – but that she never could. But there was a distance between us. Momma Em didn't entirely trust me, and perhaps that explains why I reacted the way I did after the fire that disfigured Rabbit.

I'm approaching this endeavor in reverse order. Where the journalist records and then transcribes, I find myself writing arbitrary sentences, then committing my memories to tape, using these notes as cues. My professional writing process has always been rigidly structured. The spoken word gives me the freedom to improvise.

The old woman struggles with a tray containing a pot of tea, a cup, and a large piece of cake on a plate. Her bag hangs from a meaty forearm by its frayed straps. Perhaps acting as ballast. As the old woman sails closer, she seems to nod, smile, and wink at the same time, and in doing so, she reminds me again of Momma Em. The similarity recalls a notion I've long held on to: that coincidences might simply be fate's suggestions.

Haw, hen, is it aw'right if ah sit doon here, next tae ye? says the old woman.

I'm sorry? I reply.

It's the rapid delivery that confuses me. I'm still adjusting to it.

Whit for? Whit've ye done? she says.

Uh ... I'm sorry. I didn't hear you properly.

Yer spare seat, hen. Anybody usin' it?

Before I can answer, the tray is down, and the bag has colonized the seat.

Ah, no. Please, I say.

Her bag is moved to the floor. The old woman drops onto the seat. She sighs with relief.

Thanks, lovely. This weather, eh? Bloody burst ye. There's a guy doon Argyle Street buildin' a big bliddy ark. An' folk aw lined up tae buy tickets for it.

She cackles. She pours her tea. Three heaped spoonfuls of sugar disappear below the surface. She stirs determinedly while looking around herself. Then, just as I begin writing:

So where are ye fae, hen, f'ye dinnae mind me askin'? That accent's no' Govan anyroads, eh?

The undulating rhythm of the woman's speech is captivating. Listening to Glaswegians in full flow is like being blindfold on a rollercoaster: exciting, life-affirming, and a little bit scary all at the same time. I slowly close the notepad, preparing to respond. But by time I look up again, the old woman is already elsewhere.

How ye, Sadie, hen?

Aye, no' bad Eileen, says a doppelganger. She shakes the water from a small umbrella as she strolls towards us. She looks quizzically at me.

Did ah hear right ... your Charlie's wife's back? Sadie asks.

Naw, says Eileen. Who did ye hear that fae? She tuts. That wee midden's long gone. Robbed him blind when he went inside, the bitch. Aye, good riddance tae bad rubbish. He's been put through enough. Tryin' tae get himsel' sorted oot.

That's good. Tell him ah'm askin' efter him.

A nod of Eileen's head suffices. Eileen pats my knee. The touch jolts me. She leans forwards, stern-faced, as if she is about to accuse me of something.

This lovely lassie's just gie'd me her spare seat. She's no' fae Glesga, are ye hen? Eileen's speech has slowed, allowing me to understand it better, but the exaggerated annunciation has me feeling like an imbecile.

No, I'm from the States ... Texas, originally.

Ooh, lovely, says Sadie. John Wayne an' Red Adair an' they chewy chocolate bars that stuck tae yer wallies, 'member them?

Uh...

Eileen laughs at my puzzlement. She points at me to reinforce it.

D'ye know, ah walked in an' ah wis thinkin' that her skin looked far too tanned tae be fae 'roon here.

I suddenly stiffen. I'm primed for a slight, but none comes. Sadie guffaws at her friend's observation. It's a loud, hearty look-at-me type of laugh. I imagine it being forged in a large family where loudness was rewarded with attention. Maybe *I* should have been louder?

The old women laugh on together. It doesn't feel like a continuation of the previous laugh. It doesn't seem to be prompted by anything else though. Just two old friends laughing contentedly at nothing.

See ye at the Gala, th'night, Sadie?

Ye will, that. Must be about ma turn wi' they numbers. Huvnae won big since Moses wis a wean!

Both women laugh again. Sadie walks away to join the queue at the counter. Eileen opens her newspaper. She leans to one side and whispers to me out the side of her mouth, as if we are Cold War spies passing a secret.

Poor Sadie, her man died a fortnight ago.

Oh. I'm not quite sure of what else to say. That's dreadful, I eventually add.

Aye, she mumbles. He wis a right bastart though, so nae great loss, ah suppose. Still, ye'd miss a gammy leg wi' gangrene if it got cut off, eh?

I check my phone. No messages. My plans for the next few days depend on one. I resist the urge to look at Twitter. I put the phone back in my pocket and reopen my notebook, and as I do so, the café's hubbub simmers down for a moment, and I hear it: 'She's Gone', prodding at me from the coffee shop's speakers. It's funny how you remember summers by the records you heard; and two records stood out during 1983 – that tumultuous year when everything changed for me. There was 'She's Gone' and Laurie Anderson's 'O Superman'. Neither were released that year, but I've come to associate them with it. With AJ Carter. I start writing:

Years later, rereading my journal entries, I am surprised at how dispassionate they are. I had diarized AJ's killing in the same way. As if I was emotionally removed. As if it wasn't my school. As if it hadn't taken place on the sports field on which I'd competed. As if he wasn't my – I couldn't write it then and I still struggle to – boyfriend.

...Yeah, I thought I'd reminisce some more. That's all this is, right?

It's hard to concentrate. I've become aware of the old woman mouthing the headlines that she's reading.

Ach, pish, says Eileen.

That is not one of the headlines.

Pish, she repeats.

Is everything alright? I ask her.

Whit's that, hen? she asks, perhaps realizing that she's been louder than she intended. Aw, it's nothin', love. Bloody lottery numbers. Fifteen quid a week for ower twenty year. Sweet F.A. She sighs. Christ, if ah'd just saved aw that money, *ah* could've done a Shirley Valentine, an' left that useless toerag behind!

Glaswegian women like Eileen seem happy to laugh at their own misfortune.

Then a punchline with an acerbic edge:

Freedom, eh?

Eileen folds her newspaper. She pours more tea. She takes the teabag from the pot. She squeezes it tightly against the cup. She wraps it in a tissue. She puts it in her bag.

Minutes pass, me writing, the old woman staring quietly out of the window. Driving rain now pounds the pavement. An older man moves into the view, framed by the wooden window surround, noticeable because of his struggle against the rain, and against the general direction of the other pedestrians. He appears to trip over something. He's down. The old woman rises immediately. She, Sadie and two others are outside in a flash. Like geriatric Avengers. I watch them tending to their fallen, sodden comrade without a thought that I should be out there helping them. My first instinct is always to observe. The rest of Eileen's cake has gone. It resurfaces outside in the hand of the old man. The old woman lifted it so deftly, I didn't even notice.

The group returns. The old man's lips are laced with chocolate. His eyes are glazed. He may not have tripped over anything physical.

Daft aul' goat, says the old woman. She's back in the seat next to me.

Is he alright? I ask.

Ach aye. He went doon there as if he'd been shot by a sniper. Ah saw him clutchin' his chest. Ah thought it wis his heart.

She slurps at the cold tea.

He had his fags in the top pocket an' he wis tryin' tae save them fae gettin' squashed.

A loud cackle accompanies a shake of her head.

Aye, even when we're pished, we never forget about life's priorities, eh?

I smile. I watch her gather her things. And then I return to the page.

Larry. Poor Larry. Larry told good stories.

Listen, hen, ah'll need tae go. Get *his* tea oan. Nice chattin' tae ye. Eileen stands. Ye away somewhere nice, yersel?

Eh, well … I'm not too sure. I have a meeting at Petershill Drive.

Having been set to leave, the old woman sits down again.

Aye? Ye need tae watch yersel' up at they Red Road flats, hen. It's no' the nicest ae places. Ma boy's oot that way. He's no' had his troubles tae seek, like. Eileen leans in closer. Whit's yer business up there?

She won't go until I elaborate, it's clear. I find it disconcerting to be discussing something so personal with a stranger. I wish I'd simply said *no* or invented something.

I'm here to catch up with someone I haven't seen in a very long time.

I surprise myself.

If they'll see me, that is, I add.

Yes!

I look at the old woman. The old woman winks and glances downwards.

Yes? she says again; this time inquisitively.

I look down at the page. I had written the word several times without being aware of it; like a tableau of absent-minded doodles.

Is it yer fella? Ye got a man up they towers? Did he propose? Is that who yer writin' tae? Is it a love letter? Is *that* whit yer writin'?

Her questions rip into me like I'm in the dock. But then she softens:

That's awfy … romantic, hen.

Ah, no. No, that's not what I'm writing. I stutter.

A polygraph chart of this conversation would resemble an outline of the Grand Canyon.

I don't know what this is, I admit.

There are few blank pages remaining in my notebook, and this is volume number twelve.

The old woman tilts her head. The old woman touches my knee. Again. Once again, I flinch.

Yes, says Eileen. She's giving me the answer to the question she thinks is troubling me.

If only more ae *us* had said yes. She tuts.

What's the worst that could happen? Trust yersel, love. Ye'll dae fine.

The old woman stands. Smiles.

Cheerio, darlin', she says. Aw the best wi' waitin' for yer man.

The old woman opens the door. She leans forwards to bolster herself against the angular rain. And then she's gone. Another one of these fleeting encounters that I always attach so much significance to. I'm left wondering whether the old woman will give our conversation a further thought. As she heads home, or later today, or next week, or in a year's time.

Ah wonder if that American lassie ever did say Yes?

I pick up my phone. The call rings out. Once again. I am politely encouraged to leave a message by an anonymous female voice.

Hi. It's me again. I'm sorry for leaving so many messages, but I really want to see you once before I go back to the States.

There's a gap. All she'll hear is my breathing. I'm not sure what else to say, especially if this is my last chance. I don't want to plead. I simply say,

Yes. I do.

PART ONE:

1983 – The Land of the Free

A State of Independence (1)

by Judithea Montgomery

Humble, TX. Yes. It wasn't always bad.

1: My favorite dungarees. The white sneakers I found when I was nine. **Yes.** And my *Starsky & Hutch* T-shirt. **Oh. Yes.** 2: The big rusting skillet *everything* was cooked in. 3: Sizzling catfish from the fishing trips to Lake Houston. *Hmm.* **Yes.** 4: The clouds of cigar smoke mixing with the meat smoke (when Larry's money stretched far enough for both). **Yes.** 5: Gonzales. The belligerent beer-drinking hound that hated everybody. (Gonzales – or Gonzo – was Larry's dog. I tried to poison him, and he bit me. He liked me after that.) 6: The fresh paint from Ed White's new fence. 7: The taste of the Cognac. *Hmm.* **Yes.** Like the best maple syrup ever made. Dripping slowly down my twelve-year-old throat. The burn from it. **Yes, yes.** Replacing my *take* with Larry's after-shave. Hoping (in vain) it would make Momma sick because she'd made Larry ground me. 8: The nights when Larry tended bar. 9: 'O Superman'. Playing it incessantly. Ha Ha Ha Ha Ha Ha Ha Ha Ha Ha Ha Ha Ha Ha Ha Ha Ha Ha Ha. It droned, and drove Momma crazy in the days before I left. Ha Ha Ha Ha Ha Ha Ha Ha Ha Ha Ha Ha Ha Ha Ha Ha Ha Ha Ha Ha. 10: *When love is gone, there is always justice / and when justice is gone, there is always force / and when force is gone, there is always Mom.* 11: The thick gasoline smells of the trailer park. Dirty engine parts everywhere. Oily puddles. 12: Interstate 69: The Greyhound to Houston with stolen money and second-hand roller skates. **Yes.** 13: And Adam John Carter. Hmm. Mutual attraction. **Yes.** AJ. *Yes!* 14:

'*I love you.*' '*I love you, too.*' 15: Me, fifteen years old, and *three* of the bases. *Hmm.* The solid feel of him. **Yes.** 16: Ice cubes and homemade piercings. **Yes.** 17: The fake ID. The Lyons Park drive-in. **Yes.** 18: Popcorn. Soda spilling, and *An Officer and a Gentleman.* 19: The last night. The last, lingering, probing kiss. *Hmm.* **Yes.** 20: To the memory of AJ Carter. **Yes.**

If the truth of any situation is merely how we choose to memorialize it, then it's surely important to commemorate the good things.

The darkness, when it descended, it descended on the whole town.
  Not just on me.
  But that's not how it felt.
  It felt like it was mine, alone.

4th June 1983:

It is my birthday. Sweet sixteen. Delphine Toussaint, my mom, has allowed me to stay home from school. Larry is driving a car to Dallas for his boss. So Momma wants some company, I guess. She is in a good mood. Sober too. That will make it particularly memorable. We sit on the porch. We laugh about Gonzo chasing a rabbit. And Gonzo's fat hairy ass getting jammed in a gap in Ed White's fence.

Aw Jeez, Jude, Ed wails. I'm gonna have to paint that again now!

But even he can't prevent a smile at our big, dumb dog's attempts to free himself. Mom and I shake so hard at this. That rare type of uncontrollable laughter where you can't even speak. Your jaws ache. Tears fall, but they're the good kind for once. I'm going to pee my pants if my pelvic muscles lose control too.

Ed is a new neighbor. He came around and introduced himself when he moved in. He seems nice. The others around and across from us aren't nice. *Uppity niggers,* I've heard whispered when out doing circuits. Mom's boyfriend Larry ... Larry Espinosa, a Mexican, is guilty by association. We have two paid jobs in our house: Larry's, at the bar, and my weekend shifts at the local store. That is so unusual around here by itself it would attract opprobrium, but the even bigger issue for many of our neighbors is that I'm at Humble High School on an athletics scholarship. One of my grade-school coaches had gotten a job there and recommended me for one of a two-student program. My previous school still bore the old signs that segregated the public restrooms and the drinking fountains, yet this poor white-trash community we call home fixates on our limited social privilege because we aren't white.

We come inside. We sit on the sofa. My mom in her regular place, me on an arm. We eat ice cream. We watch an old movie. I am happy.

And then the darkness comes. Stability gives way to confusion. Joy interrupted by tragedy.

Sirens screaming past isn't news. Only a month past, Al Havens took a shotgun and fired it at his neighbor over a disputed bet. The sirens were loud then too. They only stopped when Al Havens was dead. He'd tried to give himself up, Larry said, but the cops shot him anyway. Just to be sure. That happens a lot in our community. Doubt rarely benefits the Black locals. Thirty-eight people dead in five years, usually following domestic altercations. But this cacophony is different. It is something out of the ordinary. Something remarkable. By mid-afternoon, the sirens have escalated into an unhinged orchestra of chaos. Something big is happening downtown. A large fire, maybe. Or a multiple RTA on the highway. We remain sure that it is something accidental.

A month earlier:

It begins innocuously enough. Larry gets a call. He is always getting a call. This time, he's to collect a set of expensive golf clubs and drive them over to the new course. The one that just opened, out west of the airport. Momma is days into a withdrawal temper, so I go with Larry, just to get out of her range.

Jack designed it, but I'm sure Lee helped him, Larry says, like Jack and Lee are his drinking buddies from the bar. It seems strange to me that Larry can get so excited and animated about a course they'd never let someone like him play. Larry is never happier than when scuttling practice shots off the Texas hardpan over the trees behind us. Golf is his dream. Larry has a fertile imagination. If you keep quiet and out of sight, you can hear him addressing the ball. Commentating in the third person. He's part of a three-ball with Nicklaus and Trevino. Trevino is Larry's hero. Trevino is a professional Mexican. Larry is a real Mexican. Trevino was dirt poor once. Larry is dirt poor still. Trevino can play the new course. He is an acceptable outsider. He's overcome his poverty, like it was a disease. He has been cleansed. Larry isn't cleansed.

Never thought I'd ever get the chance, he says as we drive up Farrell Road. He is referring to seeing the course, not playing it.

The turning is on us before we know it. And the turning is tight. A sharp right into a dense tree belt. No signs. The rich white people it has been created for don't want it to be easy to find. A few twisted bends later and we reach the gatehouse. Metal capitals on the imposing gates read: *THE LOCHINVAR GOLF CLUB*. The place has a Scottish heritage. As do I. On a plate under that: *Private Members Only*. Two guards come out. One tall, one small. Stetsons tilted forwards. Both holstering weapons. Anticipating trouble. Right hands held higher than lefts. Both wandering around the car. Eyes darting around the inside like they've observed the cops doing. Aspiring to be someone more powerful.

Help you, sir? asks the taller guard. He speaks to Larry but looks at me. My eyes are level with the butt of his revolver. It has worn black tape wrapped around it.

I'm here for Mr Oliver, says Larry.

Which one? asks the taller guard.

Uh ... Drayton, Larry replies. He hesitates as if unfamiliar with his boss's first name.

Which *one*? stresses the smaller guard. Larry looks puzzled.

Senior or junior? The patience of the taller guard is being stretched.

Hmm. Senior, I guess. The taller guard opens a hand and wafts it, exhorting Larry to continue with our purpose.

I have the clubs ... in the trunk. The golf clubs. Mister Oliver's clubs, says Larry.

His nervousness is obvious.

Mister Drayton *Senior*, Larry adds.

The taller guard looks at the smaller guard.

He, uh, asked me to bring them to him, says Larry. Finally.

Wait here, says the taller guard.

Wait there, echoes the smaller guard, pointing to a *there* as his superior speaks into a walkie-talkie. A few nods of the head. Another glance at me. Then a shake.

Okay, *you* go through. Someone will meet you at the top of the drive. Don't get out of the car, says the taller guard.

His smaller colleague removes his hat. He rubs a stubby hand across an aggressive crew cut. He heads back to the gatehouse and then the gates open slowly.

Not her, says the taller guard. He is standing in front of the car. She stays here.

Larry shrugs at me as the car pulls away through the gates and into the verdant nirvana of his fantasy. The taller and smaller cuckoos retreat into their timber-paneled clock house. And I am left. Sat cross-legged on the roadside in the blistering sunshine.

❦

I don't see him approaching. I have lost all sense of time passing. Larry seems to have been gone hours.

Hi, he says.

I stare up at him. The sun is directly behind him. At first, I can't see anything but his muscular outline.

I've seen you around Humble High, he says. You run track, don't you? I'm AJ.

My eyes adjust and I know him. Adam John Carter. *AJ* in bold university-style font on the deepest-blue shirt. He is a star high-school quarterback. From the celebrated team. The golden generation. He and his father, the politician Devlin Carter, have been successfully courted by the Houston Cougars. I know some of this. It is big Humble High School news. AJ Carter won't know anything of me. Not even my name. Just perhaps that I run sprints in the school track team two grades below him. We were both awarded a sports medal on the same day over a year ago. Were positioned at opposite ends of a wide-framed group photograph. Delphine didn't purchase a copy when she had the chance, but the original still hangs in the school's large public foyer. He can't have remembered me from that day.

It's Jude, right?

I look down. My store name badge? Nope. I don't have it. I can't believe it. How can he know?

Yeah, I stutter. Unsure of myself.

Are you okay out here? he asks.

This is not a place for the likes of me.

Uh ... yeah. Sure. Thanks. I have to wait here for my, uh ... for Larry. Um, he's my momma's... I tail off because AJ Carter can't possibly be interested in my reasons for being here. He shakes his head.

I hate this club an' their stupid rules, he says. Do you want to sit in my car? He nods over his shoulder towards the vehicle.

Mister Carter? The taller guard emerges from the timber gate-house. He advances toward us. Perhaps he's concerned that I present a threat to the young white sportsman almost a foot taller than me. Are you okay, sir? The taller guard presses his concern. Just doing his job.

AJ Carter smiles knowingly at me as he opens the passenger-side door.

The expensive golf clubs Larry is transporting to the Lochinvar Golf Club are a gift from Larry's boss to Devlin Carter, for his son, AJ. Larry's boss is repaying a favor with this gift. Devlin Carter's favorite son has been summoned to accept the gift in person. And to be paraded in front of his father's golf-club fraternity before heading to the University of Houston in the fall. AJ Carter doesn't want to be here.

You look a bit … lost, he says. He laughs. I do too.

I could drive you back, if you'd like, he says. You could tell me more about you?

He is polite. And his interest seems genuine. But what is there to tell? I am a watcher. Constantly on the periphery of things. A loner. Tall, flat-chested. Invisibly asexual. I have few friends, since access to Humble High School for someone like me isn't a birth right. I don't really fit anywhere, other than on the athletics field.

I am wary about who I trust. I might be open to someone in the halls one week, the next week they might use the 'N' word. Or I'll overhear low-level locker-room jealousy that my speed across the track is down to genetics. Centuries of practice borne of running away from the white man. Those who speak and act this way probably don't consider themselves to be racists – and are most likely parroting opinions that they've grown up around. They might even come to consider their younger selves as just stupid, thoughtless kids being obnoxious to each other. Drilling down deep for a reaction. But it does happen. And it hurts. And that word, *nigger*, it has never lost its power to cut deep and right to the bone. To demean and isolate. I've learned to be detached.

The gates open. Larry drives the car through them. He pulls up next to the taller guard. I see Larry leaning over, and then the taller guard points at AJ Carter's Chevrolet.

Thanks, I say. I better go.

Where are you goin' for spring break? he asks.

It takes me so much by surprise that I lie without even thinking.

Uh, San Francisco, I tell him.

If only. Perhaps someday.

Cool. I'm just headin' back to Fort Liquordale, he says. He flicks the head of a plastic Elvis Presley figure on the dashboard. It smiles back at us, legs spread, finger pointing. The figure's head bobbles and wobbles. He flicks it again and Elvis falls over, the adhesive on the base giving way.

That'll be me, he says, and then, *Uh-huh-huh!* He laughs and then seems embarrassed because I don't.

I should go, I say. Again.

I'll see you in school? he says. Upturned at the end. He is asking my permission.

Yeah, I say. You will.

My face is flushed. I'm not sure what to make of his attention.

Larry hadn't gotten out of the car further up the drive. He hadn't even made it to the members' car park. Security was tight because there were VIPs visiting. A second gatehouse, with two more diligent guards – that was as far into the hallowed grounds as Larry was permitted to go. He didn't get to see the course, or the clubhouse.

No teamsters. No trailer trash. And most definitely no Black – or even mixed-race – females. Unless they merely strive to keep the place clean. And as for Mexicans? Well, there can only be one Lee Trevino. He wouldn't be exceptional, otherwise, would he?

Our drive home is conducted in silence.

I sit on our rotting timber porch every day, watching Larry dig up the early-season bug larvae. Occasionally I read, but I do little else. I think about AJ Carter a lot during the Easter vacation. I think about his freedom and contrast it with my own. Confined to this trailer park complex surrounded by people who never go anywhere. I hate this seasonal imprisonment. My subjugation. I imagine him on the Florida beaches. Playing volleyball in his shorts with his friends. Laughing. Letting off steam. Getting school and exams out of his system. Getting wildly drunk and the wild, drunken dancing afterwards. Having unprotected sex in convenient roadside motels. Sowing oats. Recharging as only the children of means are permitted to. Maybe even getting arrested. Things to brag about during the comfortable life that stretches out in front of him like a wide, open interstate highway. I think about him spending more money in one hedonistic week than Mom and Larry can spend on food in eight. Thinking about him like this gives me a panicked trembling in the pit of my belly. And it aches this time. Because, despite the unlikeliness of common ground, despite my ordinariness, his remarkableness – despite everything, I like him.

I see AJ Carter six times in the week following the return to school. I can't say I was looking for him specifically, but in a student population of over two thousand, that seems too coincidental.

Strangely, given the significance I've attached to everything since, I can't recall the lead-up to our first date. The precise words. Whether he stumbled over them nervously or delivered them with the assured confidence of a popular prom king. Much of the weeks that followed has been blanked out. Like a protective cover has been thrown over them to preserve them as sacred.

We've been hanging out in the shadows for a couple of weeks. Just the two of us. No-one else. We take the Greyhound into Houston. AJ's idea. He wants to go to the new skate park. Devlin Carter doesn't approve of skateboarding, fearing what injury could do to his son's varsity prospects. Devlin Carter – a Republican senator, no less – wouldn't approve of me. I would cause a different type of injury.

No-one knows where we are. We decide to go roller-skating instead. I don't have my own roller-skates. AJ gives me roller-skates. He says he has stolen them. But I suspect he bought them. I'm sure he is sparing me any embarrassment. It's sweet, both the gift and the lie. I find it endearing.

What type of music do you like? he asks on the bus.

We are slowly edging past the initial attraction.

Not sure, I say, giggling. I like Stevie Nicks. I like Hall & Oates.

Really?

You'd expect me to like somethin' a bit less ... Ivy League white boy? I am chiding him. But not really.

No, no ... um, that's not what I meant.

His pale cheeks blush.

Like Marvin Gaye? Or maybe James Brown, or... And then he starts singing.

People sat in seats in front turn around with looks of bemusement. Then disgust. He sings louder.

More passengers turn. A ripple effect that washes up to the driver's seat. I glimpse the driver looking in the mirror. AJ stands. He looks down at me. A hand on his chest, the other waving freely before his hips swivel, and he points like the dashboard Elvis from his car. He serenades me as the people at the front of the bus frown their disapproval of us, the white quarterback and his racially indeterminate female companion.

She's gone, she's gone
Oh I, oh I ... I better learn how to face it.

He sings louder. It's amazing the unshakeable self-confidence that a secure future can breed. I blush. But it is exhilarating. We don't reach Houston. The driver puts us off his bus at Kinwood. We walk home. Ten miles or so. Laughing, skipping, me on AJ's back. Him briefly on mine before we topple over. We ignore the protesting horns from cars as they pass us. We repeat the 'ha' breathing sound from 'O Superman' for almost thirty minutes. It is the best day I can ever remember having.

4th June 1983:

2.25pm.
Momma goes outside. She stands on the trailer's porch.
No sign of smoke, I hear her say.
Then a more distant voice yells: Somethin' goin' down at the High School.
But it's a statement, not speculation.

2.50pm
We take Gonzo and walk. Some people run. Our pace naturally quickens. Everyone is heading in the same direction. And those that aren't stand and stare towards the high school. I see old women at the five-and-dime hold trembling hands over their open mouths. The shockwaves have rippled this far already, it seems.

3.30pm
Oh my God! screams one woman repeatedly. Those poor boys! she manages to yell before being helped away from the police cordon. A large group has gathered. The road down to the school gates is now blocked. The insistent wail of the sirens has been supplemented by the buzz-buzzing of the overhead media helicopters. Flying low and competing for the shot.
What happened? asks my mom. No-one answers her.

3.45pm

Well, Christ Jee-sus! The radio's sayin' eleven of 'em. Eleven of those boys. All gone. Dear God in Heaven.

The man who says this is on his knees. Tears stream down both cheeks. He stands and calls on his Lord and punctuates the calls with awful high-pitched yelling noises. It's as if he is possessed, like many who crutch religion often seem. Three women and another man run to him. He collapses as they reach him. Momma leads me away. Further to our right, on the other side of the stream near the school fence, a large group of students are hugging and crying. Paramedics tend to them. Beyond them, another cluster. And further round, on the edge of the tree belt, another. Each much larger in size than the previous.

It's the football team! I hear another man's voice in the distance.

He's shot the fucking football team! shouts the man.

It is my birthday. Sweet fucking sixteen. Life – and all its challenges – stretches out in front of me.

Their bodies aren't yet cold. There is widespread support for the bereaved in the wake of yet another mass shooting. But nothing will change. Devlin Carter's Republican colleagues rally around the Second Amendment like it was the Alamo. Death has descended on Humble, and a compliant media is on hand to capture it. The death of an American dream. The right-leaning side of the dream. The one where an individual can achieve anything they want in life regardless of their race, religion, gender, or sexuality, so long as they are prepared to work hard enough to achieve it. The all-white American Dream that *does* go better with Coke. That *does* star Natalie Woods and Steve McQueen or Bullwinkle and Julia. That *does* come with a Jim Webb theme tune sung by Glen Campbell or The Rare Earth. *The Suppression That Will*

Always Be Televised. There's your commercial tagline, middle America.

I live alongside those who are conveniently brushed out of sight. Those individuals who can't – or won't – work hard enough. And those who might hold down multiple minimum-wage jobs and still can't dream of ever owning their own home. Those forced to pay unreasonable rents for sub-standard properties. Those whose greatest hope in life is that they never fall ill. Those with a hand permanently out for welfare. That's my community. That's our immediate neighbors: the ones who despise Delphine and Larry because the mixed-races are somehow worse than Black people.

Although I'm aware from first-hand experience of the gulf between those who have and those who have not, I remain naïve about the restrictions my ethnicity, my background and my gender will impose on my future. The continuing fortune of the scholarship relies on maintaining a certain performance level on the field. The middle-class teenagers I share the classroom with do not have that pressure. Our deprived little part of Humble, where the trailer-trash kids live, sees none of the oil money that Reagan's early presidency was built on. There is none of the palpable optimism that sustains Houston and Dallas – the boom cities that are gaining international capitalist attention.

14th June 1983:

AJ's funeral is the eighth of the fourteen. His receives the most coverage. An unstoppable outpouring of grief for the school's star quarterback. I enter at the back of the vast, modernist Christian Church, with its vaulting concave timbers rising to a peak like it is the mould for an upturned boat's hull. I sit in the rear pew. The closest position to a side exit. Those in front and to the side of me have leathery skin, artificially ripened by the sun that shines right-eously on condos down in the Florida Keys. My natural brown tone is lighter. Yet I am still their inverse, their opposite in every conceivable way. An older, paler Ruby Bridges, freed from the canvas of Norman Rockwell's *The Problem We All Live With*. I listen to the praise and the celebration and the regrets, and observe the restrained public grief politely expressed for a young, promising life taken far too soon. I don't recognize the eulogized *him*.

The death of an American Dream, says the minister. God-fearing Republican heads nod in agreement; the young man they are burying today was the epitome of their own American Dream. He represented their truth. The canvas onto which they painted their own vicarious ambitions. They grieve for themselves. Less for him. 'From the Depths of Woe' rings out enthusiastically, despite the doleful context. They exhort their Lord to turn a gracious ear. They lament their loss – a glorious young man with his whole adulthood ahead of him has been ripped from them. They acknowledge that no man can glory in God's sight. And no-one is blaming God, for theirs is a God this congregation sees in their own likeness and not the other way around, and to apportion blame to God would be to acknowledge that He had forsaken them and the money that had built this House. It wasn't an act of God that caused Timothy Allen Rennick to drive to his high school that May afternoon. To park up near the sports field. To advance towards his former team-mates and to fire bullets indiscriminately from an automatic rifle into their huddled bodies.

Those numbers. Twelve eighteen-year-old football players and two coaches, neither yet thirty years of age. Nobody can comprehend why he did it. What could've caused a good, white Christian boy from a good, white Christian family to act so savagely. To behave like an unprincipled savage. The sense of disbelief clogs the humid summer air, irritating everyone like a pesticide dusted over the entire city.

The savage is still alive. Leniency – perhaps even argued for by some of the people in this room – may yet save this privileged young man from a death-row gurney. Leniency can help them to understand what drove him to it, this barbarian brutality. Had he been Black, it would be easier for them to understand. Had he been Black, he'd be dead already. No need for trained negotiators to talk a Black boy down. *The death of an American Dream*, says the minister. Again, but slower. Underlining it as if this short life only makes sense when summed up by hyperbole. So much was expected of AJ Carter. He was destined for success in every aspect of his life. But the subject of this awful sermon is a different AJ Carter. The AJ I briefly knew didn't want his life's achievements to have been handed to him on a silver platter. My version of him didn't want to go to the University of Houston. Didn't want to study law. Didn't want to follow his daddy and his grandaddy into Grand Old Party political circles. And didn't want to spend conspiratorial whisky weekends with the likes of Larry's boss over at the Lochinvar.

The AJ Carter I briefly knew wanted to escape from a life mapped out by others. He wanted to hit the road, *Jack*. To travel America and then keep going when America ran out. He talked of Kerouac. Of Allen Ginsberg. Of Bob Dylan. What did I know of the life, the love, the personal desires, and the cinemascope wishes that they sparked in him? At sixteen, I barely knew these names. But I came to appreciate what they represented for him. Freedom. And independence. The twin pillars of a dream that America denies so many of its own people. Everybody has their own version of the American Dream. Paradoxically, escaping the one painted at his funeral service was the kernel of AJ Carter's. And gradually, as the darkness lifted, it became mine. That was his legacy.

The loss experienced by those who surrounded me in that church on that awful day in 1983 must have been immeasurable. None of them knew who I was, or why I was there, or how I could have known their boy so intimately. But I understood their grief.

I just didn't understand my own. His body left the building to the southern, plinky-plod piano death march of Elvis Presley's 'Amazing Grace'.

Yes, I too was blind but now I see.

The Ballad of the Band (1)

by David F. Ross

Why do we write about anything? I ask myself that question regularly, and not just in the dark hours when words dance on the periphery of my imagination but like truculent children, refuse to co-operate. Writing is a chore. Words that should fit together like Japanese tenon joints jar like ill-fitting false teeth. I get up and I move away. I change position. Cigarettes and alcohol. Anything to kick-start a bit of creativity. I try to fool myself. *No-one will read these words, in any case.* But that doesn't work. I remind myself that any writing is only about the writer. I hope that universal truth will alleviate the burden of imminent criticism. *It's about me. My truth. My perspective.* If the point of writing is for the writer to determine who they are, to express that in ways that are unique, then who gives a fuck if *nobody* gives a fuck?

I once authored a work entitled 'Ballad of the Band'. It's undoubtedly what you know me for – if my name does ring any bells, that is. Immediately prior to it being published in a fashionable UK magazine, I was a young, aspiring writer. I'd had a few inconsequential pieces placed here and about; nowhere of note. But like many who write, I was struggling. In much the way I've described above. Struggling to find the point in writing anything at all. I imagined what else I could do with the ridiculous amounts of time it absorbed. Building a wall. Fixing a leaking tap. Digging a fucking hole, only to fill it in again once dug. Anything else but sit for days in front of twenty-six letters that I couldn't drill into meaningful composition.

Writing became an unrewarding habit that was affecting my fragile mental health. I read the work of others, searching for inspiration, but found only desolation in the knowledge that where they soared with angels, I stumbled and tripped. Writing didn't provide me with a means of making a living. But I didn't need a career – in writing, or in anything else. My late father was a musician. A relatively unknown one, his singular contribution to popular culture was the part-composition of a song, which, while not specifically about Christmas, has become a staple of the festive season. From the end of October to the start of Hogmanay, you'll hear it hundreds, if not thousands, of times. From street buskers to department stores, hairdressing salons to television adverts. It's everywhere. It will drive you mad. You can't escape from it. Unless you kill yourself.

Most people intent on suicide and drawn to a river, throw themselves from a bridge spanning it. My father couldn't swim. He hated the thought of being in open water throughout his life. His dry body was found, twenty feet *above* the Clyde, hanging from the City Union Bridge in the early hours of 1 January, 1978. There were other factors involved. It wasn't solely attributed to the song. The day after my sixteenth birthday, my mother, having fulfilled the terms of the job as she saw it, left us. My father never got over this. Any guilt he had over his own failings he deftly transferred to me. He spent the rest of his life reminding me that he had remained when his opportunities to escape had been plentiful. I've neither seen nor heard from my mother since the day she walked out. There's nothing quite like parental abandonment to reinforce a lifetime of low self-worth.

I tell you all this only to provide stipendiary context. As his only child, I have, since the early eighties, been the beneficiary of substantial annual royalties – primarily from the version of my father's song recorded by Elvis Presley – which provide me with a high level of financial security. It allows me to spend far more time in the Cayman Islands than I should, given my personal preference for a Scotland independent from the ties that bind it to an outdated Union.

Perhaps it would've been different if financial necessity propelled my artistic purpose. As it was, I was on the verge of giving up writing; this tortuous, unforgiving vocation. Admitting defeat. Acknowledging that I'd never compose anything that mattered to someone else. That I'd never produce prose that offered any understanding of what it was to be human. This acknowledgement was a rejection far more painful than the hundreds that came from uninterested editors or blasé agents. The knife to the heart of the would-be writer is always self-inflicted. The sudden realisation of the gulf to be bridged between a modicum of untutored talent and the aspiration to be a 'real writer'. It was as wide as the Atlantic crossing I was making when fate intervened.

Sometimes, doing nothing is the best way for circumstance to deliver what we need.

In the late summer of 1983, I was returning to Glasgow, via a protracted route that required stops in San Francisco and London. For reasons that are unimportant, I flew economy despite my means, and I found myself seated next to an agitated young man. Even with the dark glasses and the cap pulled low, there was a familiarity to him. His right arm was heavily bandaged and, although not in a plaster cast so far as I could see, a sling suggested a broken bone. As our flight left California, I introduced myself, asking if I could help him with a packet of peanuts he was struggling to open. Initially reticent, he soon gave way, and I sensed that he wanted to get something off his chest. To relieve himself of a great burden. As I mentioned earlier, I knew something of burdensome weights. So, I encouraged him.

His name was Jamie Hewitt. He was – or had been – the guitarist and songwriter in a popular music group named The Hyptones. I hadn't heard of the band back then. You'll think me hypocritical but popular music was of little interest to me. I didn't need to enjoy listening to it to benefit from those who did. But over the course of several hours, Jamie Hewitt's story sparked something inside me. Like a pilot light suddenly igniting the burners on a gas boiler that has lain cold for months, ideas, phrases ... whole paragraphs were suddenly screaming to be written, prompted by his story of fatal fame, and by the ticket stub and the blurred Polaroid photograph that he showed me, and let me keep.

He was telling me a truth, but not, I suspected, *the* truth. But what is the truth of any situation, other than our own perception of it? In the weeks that followed our brief meeting, I wrote around his rollercoaster exposition. I wrote to explore the complex relationship between fact and fiction. And I wrote about failure. Mine, as much as his.

A State of Independence (2)

It has been a month since the shooting, and something inside me has irrevocably changed. But I'm not sure what it is or what it could mean. So, I run, hoping that an answer will emerge out of the dusty haze.

I run a regular circuit that's approximately four hundred meters, my best distance: from the porch, down Viscount, then a turn just before the old water tower. Past the Hudsons' place, and their shabby yard – full, year-round, with gaudy, unlit Christmas decorations. Back up Wisteria and around the unkempt thorn bushes that bullies throw weaker children into, just for the fun of it. My skin has been scarred on more than one occasion. Finally, round the open corner that doubles as a makeshift baseball diamond for the kids whose parents can't afford Little League. Beyond this, I've often found myself getting lost – not fully concentrating.

I'm not long back from one of these runs. Heart rate still dropping back to its normal resting state. It's summer, blistering sunshine. Perpetually dusty and hazy.

A middle-aged woman pushes a stroller loaded with bags. Four small children swarm around her. I don't recognize any of them. But that's not unusual given the sprawling nature of this characterless encampment. Suddenly she stops and rushes back out of my frame of vision. There is cursing and a commotion off to my left. I can't see the cause of it, but the ruckus is drawing attention from numerous onlookers. Three of the children turn to look too; but the smallest continues to toddle on, a fat diaper forcing the jerky side-to-side movement. I watch him – although I can't be entirely sure it's a boy – drift slowly into the middle of the dirt track, and the path of an oncoming station wagon.

Old brakes squeal and a gruff, an impatient 'Git tha' fucken kid outta the road!' comes from inside the cab. In slow motion, the unattended stroller tips backwards. The bags spill and a milk carton bursts, leaking across the dirt. Those sitting on their decks or standing by smoking look left and right as if watching a Billie Jean King rally at Indian Wells. To one side, the indiscriminate shouting and swearing continues. To the other, the toddler over-balances too, slumping into a mud puddle. The middle-aged woman re-enters my view. The station wagon makes an exagger-ated maneuver and in doing so, clips the edge of our fence. This brings Gonzo running. The middle-aged woman continues her cursing and gesticulating. She ignores her children, including the partly submerged one. She angrily picks up the pram. She reas-sembles the bags it was transporting. The milk carton is left, spilt and useless. On command, the tallest child rights the littlest one and then leads them, yelling and hollering, away towards the end of our road. Gonzo starts barking. He clears the fence, meaning I must get up and bring him back or Larry will yell at me. The mutt has gone beyond the line of the trees. I see a man, drunk and lying in the dust. Gonzo strolls out of the bushes. The dog looks at me and then wanders over to the man and sniffs him. The dog pisses on him. The dog saunters back. He laps at the milky puddle for a while and then returns. His dripping wet mouth nuzzles at my hand. The man doesn't move.

None of this is unusual. Scenes such as this pass for entertain-ment in our hidden-away corner of the Lone Star State. But the thought of revisiting this humdrum scene daily for the rest of my life is the catalyst – the kick in the ass that propels me westwards, like a frontiers(wo)man, towards something different. Hopefully better – but different will be enough.

High School finishes early out of respect for the dead. The media circus eventually moves on to the next communal outpour-ing of grief. Accompanied by yet another robust NRA defense. I note in my journal that Humble High School's massacre is one of three fatal shootings in the United States that month. A complete coincidence, but two of them occur on the same day. Only two hundred miles away, in Dallas, the Lake Highlands High School cafeteria manager is robbed at gunpoint as she counts the day's takings. After wrongly assuming she has triggered an alarm, Billy Conn Gardner – a thirty-nine-year-old white man – shoots her and takes $1,600 from the register. In Brentwood, New York, Robert Wickes returns to the East Junior High School that he has been fired from. His intention is to exact revenge on a fifteen-year-old student. A physical fight with the student was the reason for the termination of his employment. Wickes – another white man in his late thirties – enters the school dressed in camouflage fatigues armed with a semi-automatic rifle and over one hundred rounds of ammunition. The student and the school principal survive their serious gunshot injuries. Wickes releases seventeen hostages during a nine-hour standoff, before shooting himself in the head. He dies later in hospital. Democrats say Black, Republicans say white. Nothing changes.

I go indoors to watch the drunk man lying in the dirt from my bedroom window. There is a clear view of him from here. He just lays there in the road. No-one bothers him or about him. I watch for over an hour. Engrossed by the sight, but hoping he'll be collected, nonetheless. When I eventually get too bored, I turn away and look in the mirror fixed to the back of the door. I look at my hands. I turn them over and investigate the tiny cut scars all the way up each forearm. I look older than I am. My height helps with that. I pick up the fake ID that AJ got me. It will come in useful.

I decide to leave. High school *and* Humble. Abandon my relatives. Jump ship. AJ Carter's brief sojourn in my life might have been for a purpose: to turn me by the shoulders and point me away from these forgotten hinterlands – where I was born, where I'd grown up. And where I'd surely die after living a life as desperate and unfulfilled as Delphine, my mom's.

'Let's be lovers, we'll marry our fortunes together. I've got some real estate here in my bag,' he said to me during a hot, sticky, breathless night at the drive-in. Not his words, obviously, but convincingly offered as if they were. Afterwards, I whispered that I loved him. It wouldn't have mattered if he hadn't said it back because it was the idea of him that I was in love with. His restless, energetic spirit. His dreams of adventure. My love was a love of an idealized America; the one where the roads were connections to different cultures and experiences, not barriers to them. Chances to spread my wings and venture further and further from home until the very concept of home was eradicated and I didn't have one anymore. I want to feel *at* home everywhere and belong nowhere. To absorb the cultural and creative variety of my country and become a more tolerant person. What could better represent freedom than that?

Other than westwards, I have no idea where I'll go. Or what I'll do when I eventually get there. But I know there must be more life worth living out there than listening to my mom moan about her stories. More than the daily middle-aged aggravation that happens beyond the weed-ridden dirt and the rusting motorcycle parts that comprise our front lawn. And much more than witnessing Delphine and Larry's relationship slowly disintegrate because habit is all that holds it together. It wasn't always so. I recall some happier times, if not many. But I was much smaller then. And happier times in a child's life are often stage-managed by unhappy adults.

I pick up my canvas travel bag and empty the dusty track shoes and clothes from inside. I pack my other clothes into it. The ones that will accompany me. I aim to take little in the way of belongings. A new beginning should be just that: a clean slate. But I do dwell on my books. My childhood often felt like an open prison, the confinement being lack of opportunity, rather than razor-wire fences or brick walls. I did what many prisoners in solitary do: I read. I occasionally did shopping for an elderly, house-bound woman from around the corner. She'd pay me in Louisa May Allcotts or Laura Inglis Wilders. I pick a favorite from each and pack them in a side pocket of my rucksack.

I take down the posters that are pinned to my wall. I fold them up and put them in a drawer, all except the *LIFE* magazine cover with the Vietnam soldiers on it. I sit on my bed staring at this reproduction of a photograph that has been pinned to my wall for longer that I can remember. One time, Delphine seemed to be on the cusp of capitulating to my need to know more. She rummaged around in a drawer. She handed me the magazine. Under the headline 'Our Forgotten Wounded' the page was split in two: the bottom half was a grainy black-and-white picture of battered bodies lying, seemingly forgotten, in a Stateside hospital. The top half was a different photograph of a group of US troops on the Cambodian front. At the bottom right, the date: May 22, 1970. Delphine pointed to the top picture. The middle of it. To the one young soldier not facing the camera. His shoulder was wrapped in a dirty bandage, as the others stood around him, topless, laughing, joking around.

That's your daddy on the cover there, she said. Head bowed and whispering. That's Jimmy.

That was it. All she'd ever said about him to me.

I put the picture of my fake dad in my canvas bag. I hide the bag under my bed. It's there, ready, for when I am.

A week later, an argument kicks off in an adjacent room. A letter is the cause this time. It has been a fertile period for arguments. Larry has stopped getting calls. He is around the house more often, crowding my mom and getting on her nerves. The TV is on, and loudly. The words of the argument can't be deciphered, but I suspect I am getting trashed. The sound of glass breaking signals the end. I take the letter out of my pocket. It's from Edgar Vane, the owner of the store where I work. I reread the details of the disciplinary process I'm now subject to, before screwing it up into a ball and throwing it at a bin. It has caused enough trouble already.

I had been reprimanded for doing what I believed was right. I'd packed empty boxes on the shelves and taken all full packs of ammunition back to the storeroom and concealed them behind the full-height freezers. And I'd price-marked the remaining label stocks up by around one thousand per cent. It was never destined to go down in history as a pinnacle of anti-gun protests, but it mattered to me. That it didn't to Delphine was the final straw.

The morning before I leave, I hear the screen door closing. Unusual, since it is always propped open by the broken rocking chair with the missing rocker. Larry comes out. He sits on the step next to me. He is forced to shade his eyes as he looks at me. A twisted awning above us won't do the job.

Damn, I need to get that fixed, he says.

If Delphine had a buck for every time he promised to fix something, she would've been with someone else.

She don't mean it, y'know? Those words.

This confirms my suspicions about the reason for last night's fight.

She really cares for you, Jude. It's just that... He tails off.

He stares up at the broken awning. Fixing that will be a breeze compared to fixing us.

Ev'rytime somethin' like this happens, she feels helpless. She can't cope with it, girl, he says.

I'm a convenient excuse, I say.

He sighs in response.

When do they say you can go back? he asks.

Where? I reply, as if I didn't know.

To the store, he says. He is becoming annoyed.

Dunno. Month, six weeks, I guess.

Well, that's not too bad, s'pose. Give everyone a time to cool off, he reasons.

Larry takes off his cap and with the heel of the same hand, wipes the dripping sweat from his forehead. We watch three dogs fight over a piece of stolen meat one of them has dropped. If he becomes aware of it in time, Gonzo will be wading into them very shortly.

The letter says the manager doesn't wanna involve the cops, so that's somethin', Jude, he says.

I don't respond.

Jude? That's good, no?

What's good about it, Larry? Mr Vane made a big show of sendin' flowers and condolences to the families while movin' the ammunition displays closer to the front door.

It is my turn to be annoyed.

For God's sake, girl, that's just business. Independence Day was comin', says Larry.

He is defending someone else now. But I can tell his heart isn't in it.

Jesus, Larry, Independence Day is just for rich white folks with land.

Larry laughs, and it feels like he is mocking me. Strange how the gun has become the symbol of good, to be protected at all costs.

He's ... *God*, some of them don't even have gravestones yet. I take the stand Edgar Vane should've taken an' I'm the one that gets suspended? Tell me, huh, what's so fucking good about that, Larry? I yell.

I can tell he thinks me immature, not principled.

Hey ... watch the cussin', girl! I might not be your blood, but I deserve a bit more respect than you give out.

I'm not goin' back there, I say.

My arms fold to underline my decision. Neither of us knows what to say next. Larry isn't my pa, but my mom has delegated any disciplinary action to him. He is uncomfortable with the responsibility. And I've become convinced that with me gone, I'll be setting both of us free. Not for the first time, he's been placed in a difficult position. Mom is mad at me for losing the weekly income – the circumstances surrounding my suspension aren't of interest to her. She just wants me to plead with the store manager to get my job back. Larry knows hell will freeze over before that happens. And in that moment, I know it's time to go. Maybe Larry won't hang around watching Delphine wither away, abusing him as she declines.

Why you still with her? I say, nodding to the shutter door.

What's that got to do with all this? he replies.

Larry is a soft man. Kind-hearted and non-confrontational. I am trying his immeasurable patience.

It's got everything to do with it. I'm her daughter. I'm stuck in this shitpile because she wouldn't ever move us. Why couldn't you make her see?

Larry looks away. I imagine the truth hurts him.

You're a sucker, Larry, I tell him. Her punchbag. Who respects a punchbag?

Larry stands up and heads back inside.

Poor Larry. Why did I say that to him?

Fuck. Fuck. Fuck. *Fuck!*

He comes back outside. There is no indication why he'd gone inside other than to get away from me. He remains standing.

After your daddy died, I was there for your mamma. She needed someone, an' no-one else was around. She couldn't function, girl. I gave up everythin' for her, to be with her ... to love her. *And* you.

Larry turns away from me. He looks to his right and points. I don't know why or at what.

An' I've never regretted it. Even now when she's bitter an' hateful an' sick an' not thinkin' straight, he says.

His lip trembles like a child's owning up to a lie.

I still remember the tender woman I fell in love with. She's still in there. She might be slippin' away a little bit at a time ... but nothin' can take from how I feel.

Larry looks pitiful. His big, hulking frame now permanently stooped at the shoulders. A compliant farm horse yoked to a plough, spending day after day dragging it along the same furrows in the blistering Texas heat.

I need to go to work, he says hesitantly, and it dawns on me why he was pointing. His escape. The bar, not the golf course of his dreams. Where he meets other people temporarily escaping their own drudgeries. Misery loves company. I've made him leave for a shift that doesn't begin for another three hours.

I'm s—

But he's gone. Around back. I hear the sputtering of the old engine. His pride and joy, that old noisy Triumph.

An' anyways, no-one's keepin' you locked up here, Jude, he says as he comes back into view.

Larry, I'm sorry.

But my name has been a period. The conversation is over. The engine revs and he won't have heard my apology. Won't have detected the genuine regret that prompted it.

Shit!

I watch him accelerate until the rear wheel's dust cloud obscures him and he fades into the haze. Like he was never even here.

The three adults in my early life could not have become president. The statistical unlikelihood apart, this firm foundation of the American Dream had been denied them by Article Two, Clause Five of the United States Constitution. Delphine was born in Port-au-Prince. And Jimmy Montgomery – my natural father – was born in Glasgow, Scotland. For reasons known only to Delphine, I carry *his* name, not hers.

Jimmy was born out of wedlock. To escape her violent Catholic father and her three bloodthirsty brothers, Jimmy's mother and his Protestant father ran. They got married. They ran further. To

Liverpool, before sailing to what they imagined would be their promised land.

Larry – as previously described – is Mexican.

All three were immigrants, desperate people trying to escape their past and to begin a new future in this land of perceived freedoms. What is it about this country that calls out to the disenfranchised like Greek sirens? What do they believe will make them different from everybody else making the journey?

Almost all of what I know of my mother's early life came from Larry. The best time to catch him was after he'd poured himself a large Charro Negro, returning to his seat with several more of the bottles. A carefully planted rhetorical question from me and he'd be off, glancing backwards occasionally for fear of being caught. My shortened name, Larry explained, came not from my momma's fond abbreviation, but from Beatles-fan Jimmy. How much Larry embroidered to encourage sympathy for my mom was difficult to determine. Questioning Delphine was pointless. She treated such questions like an FBI interrogation. Her eyes would shift uneasily around the room. Checking for available escape routes.

There's little worth in diggin' over the rubble, she'd say. Nothing of comfort for her to be found in the wasteland, is what she meant.

In 1958, Delphine's father, Auguste Toussaint, uprooted his family – he had two wives and five children – to escape the infested slums of Haiti. He spent everything he had for standing room on a retired shrimping trawler. One wife didn't survive the crossing to the USA.

Florida was the land of opportunity for many desperate Haitians. It captured the American Dream perfectly. State and nation exuded confidence and optimism in 1958. The Soviets may have launched Sputnik into orbit the previous year. But Florida had Cape Canaveral. America had the right stuff. A man would prosper in Florida, Auguste must've reckoned.

How many men like Auguste imagined that the early days of

the space program must reap results that would one day benefit them? Larry Espinosa did. He told me so. He watched Neil Armstrong's first steps with his own father, and felt that change was *gonna* come. That space exploration would eventually eradicate poverty. Larry's father, an immigrant himself, living in poverty in the barrio, still believed in the American spirit – in hard work and upward mobility, in the idea of the West as some kind of frontier. Like many, he saw space as an extension of that – just a bit further out west. Larry talked of how gullible everyone was back then. Peaceful Civil Rights protests were descending into violence, yet no-one was pointing out that while Whitey was being sent to the moon, the Government was neglecting the marginalized non-white population.

Auguste quickly discovered that prosperity didn't extend into Miami's Little Haiti community – otherwise known as Lemon City. It proved to be as lawless and violent – and lacking in opportunity – as his Caribbean birthplace. A man had to make his own fortune. This was something Auguste Toussaint would have come to understand just as much as Devlin Carter did. Regardless of social status, this was – and remains – the American way.

Delphine's school years, limited though they were, took place amongst the many illegals of Lemon City. Delphine was the fourth of five sisters. And daughters were of little use to Auguste. He'd learned the tricks of the burglary trade from his own father. But he lamented the lack of a son – someone he could use to break into the small, enclosed spaces that he often encountered. He took his frustrations out on the girls. He laid into them with a big leather belt. Delphine always kept her skin covered up. But one time, when she was coming out the bathroom, her towel slipped. I saw the meshwork of raised scars and welts. I would've been about fourteen. And I knew, without Larry's confirmation, that Auguste favored the buckle end.

Once, when I was little, Larry, intoxicated and uninhibited, let slip that the family's westward flight was the consequence of

Auguste having killed a man in a New Orleans knife fight. Later, in a Baton Rouge juke joint, Auguste settled a gambling debt by selling Mabel, one of Delphine's older sisters. A week after this transaction, Mabel threw herself from the roof of a four-story building. The family moved on again before Auguste's creditors could claim recompense for their damaged goods.

The Toussaint clan landed in Lake Charles, Louisiana, in the mid-sixties, Auguste's wanton and opportunistic lawlessness seemingly the reason for a decade spent largely on the move. Or more accurately, on the run. In Lake Charles, Eloise, my grandmother, disappeared. My mom never saw her again. Auguste left the youngest sister – Larry didn't have a name for her – tied to a telephone pole outside an Episcopal Church. Delphine never saw her younger sister again either. At the age of sixteen, my mom was without two sisters and a mother. Her two remaining older sisters, similarly nameless, found work and lodging in a Cajun lounge bar frequented by offshore drillers, tool pushers and roughnecks. It was managed by a raucous couple from Lafayette who spoke only in Louisiana French.

One steaming hot evening, Auguste pitched up, Delphine in tow, to pick up his cut of their pay checks. His mood was dark and desperate. Alcohol had been taken. Strong, cheap 'shine, according to Larry. Auguste's daughters were working their shifts. One waiting tables while the other entertained, singing from a low stage. Neither had money for their father. An argument started amid the hot mudbugs and the whirling zydeco music. Auguste was dragged outside after punching his eldest child. Three men took him around the side of the bar. Auguste was a fighter. He wouldn't back away without getting what he came for. But the odds weren't with him. With Delphine watching from the corner of the main street, her father was dead before his black beard hit the desert-dry dirt.

Delphine was taken in by the bar owners. She cleaned the bar. She lived in the same small upstairs room as her sisters. Three years later, a lively group of young beatniks visited the bar. Jimmy Montgomery was amongst them. He returned regularly, and often on his own. Jimmy and Delphine hooked up, and – Larry didn't dwell or expand on this period – six months later, in the summer of 1967, I was born. I recall nothing of the brief time Jimmy Montgomery was in my life. I have no way of knowing whether he and Delphine were even briefly happy. Whether he remained with her out of a sense of duty, or whether he wanted to. In my time in Humble, Delphine never entertained talk of Jimmy Montgomery. She didn't feel the need to look backwards.

Jimmy Montgomery was a victim of the indiscriminate 1969 Vietnam draft, where young American men were conscripted to fight according to a lottery. If your number came out first, you were sent to war. If luck shone on you – as it often did on the privileged – you might never have to leave your family.

Jimmy Montgomery died in June 1970. He was killed in Vietnam two weeks before the end of his tour. He was twenty-one years old.

Larry Espinosa told a good story.

24th July 1983:

I can't sleep. But I lie awake thinking about Jimmy Montgomery and AJ Carter. I think about whether the bullets that ripped into both killed them instantly. About whether they'd both lain dying. Knowing that death was upon them. About what their final thoughts might've been. Whether, selfishly, those thoughts had been about me. Nothing was said last night. Larry knows I am leaving, and it follows that my mom does too.

I look out my window at the stillness. Sunlight filters through the phalanx of live oaks that shade the yards in our street. I tighten up the neck of the rucksack. I pull on my sneakers. I creep through to the main room. Delphine and Larry are asleep in the claustro-phobic space, facing opposite directions. A splinter of early-morning light cuts across their stomachs. Soon it will creep up the covers and surely waken them. I open a drawer as carefully as I can. Watching for signs of movement, I twist the lid off the jar, squeeze a hand in and take the wrap of cash. I close the drawer, making it squeak. Larry rolls over. His eyes briefly open. He sees me. He wears a disappointed look. Like there would be a different outcome. Like our relationship wouldn't end this way. He sighs. He closes his eyes and then rolls back to his original position. I walk to the kitchen. I open the fridge door and rummage around. I lift a milk bottle and roll it gently across my brow. I find a cheese sandwich I prepared the day before, pre-empting my last meal here. I bite into it and enjoy the coolness on my tongue. I shut the tall fridge door and my mom is standing on the other side of it.

Jesus, Momma, I say. I didn't hear her approach. She hands me an envelope. It is taped at the adhesive seal.

Open it later, she says.

And then there is a long silence that neither of us know how to fill. Eventually, she looks at me like she hasn't in a very long time. She smiles.

We make all these decisions, Jude, but who knows if they are ever for the best, she says.

And then she turns and returns to the room she and Larry sleep in. She closes the door behind her.

For most of my life, we've been rivals for the attentions of a ghost, my momma and me.

There was this one time, when I was around ten. I got involved in a stupid fight with two other girls. I didn't start the fight, but by the time it got broken up, it seemed like I was the aggressor. One of the girls had fallen backwards and hit her head on the side-walk. I was sent home. I didn't go home though. My mom was in a real funk. Impossible to talk to, and even harder to live with. I went to the Humble High Sports Field – the same one recently bedecked with wilting mourning flowers – and I sat on the bleachers until it started to get dark. When I did go home, Delphine was on the porch as I approached. Ranting like a demented ship's captain suddenly seeing the jagged rocks. She was drunk and scary and hateful, Larry trying in vain to haul her back inside. She screamed at me, and at the watching audience, not making much in the way of sense. Inside though, the one phrase that stuck: <u>YOU'RE JUST A FAILED ABORTION.</u>

I wrote that one down in my journal. Capitalized and underlined. She apologized for it a few days later, but a point had been made, and nothing was really the same again.

One of those decisions, and who knew if they were ever for the best.

I take one last look around the room. This home has been too small for the three of us for some time. I glance at the fading framed photograph of my mom and Larry. It was taken years ago. The picture captures them happy. Perhaps they can be again. Maybe Larry will stay. I open the door gingerly. And then the fly leaf. And I leave them to the rest of their lives.

I look down. Gonzo is chained to the corner post of the porch. His muscularity is pronounced in the half-light. If the notion took him, he could probably drag the immobile structure and all its contents with him. His massive head turns. I give him the remainder of my sandwich. My parting gift to him. He inhales it and lays down again. I walk away. Through this dense and claustrophobic maze of dented, disheveled aluminum and timber boxes. I walk on. And I don't look back.

My Dearest Delphine,
Hope you and the little one are keeping well. Both of you are in my thoughts all the time. The day when I can be back home and we can resume our lives as a family is what's keeping me going. I

really want us to get married, Delph. I know we talked about it before, and you weren't sure, but I am. We can have a great life together. I know we can.

This last week we have been preparing for an onslaught, and last night it rained down on us. Honey, I was never so scared in my life. The noise from the mortars is enough to drive a person crazy. We finally thought it was over, but then we got warning of a ground attack which, lucky for us, never came. I only have a few weeks to go now before I can come home, but the VC are really putting a big push on so it's going to be tough. That's why I wanted to write and to propose to you again, I guess.

Delph, I was so surprised last night to see that the men here were willing to risk their own lives to save a buddy's. It really makes you have faith in people again. Despite the heavy shelling, we didn't lose a single man. I hope I don't ever have to go through what we did last night but I'm beginning to think someone up there is looking after me. Determined to make sure I make it home to you and our little baby Jude.

I take our picture out quite often and just stare at it, because to see this beautiful little girl we made makes this terrible place bearable. I am thinking of her always.

All my love,
Jimmy

As well as fifty dollars, the envelope contains this faded, hand-written letter. A paperclip holds it alongside a tattered black-and-white photograph. There are small tears on the folded edges of both, but the words on the grubby paper are still legible. Jimmy Montgomery's penmanship was notable, certainly when compared to mine. There are no errors. The words hint at an articulate man, sure of his feelings, or one prepared to practice getting his message exactly right. That image of him amid his band of brothers. His fair hair and fairer skin. The ingredients that made me brown and not Black. Laughing and joking in the jungle humidity and filled with the hope that death didn't seem inevitable. The photograph is the original of the *LIFE* magazine cover photograph that has been pinned to the wall above my bed all these years. I don't know who took the picture. I only know that the picture recorded the photographer's truth. I didn't appreciate that it also haunted Delphine's truth. It makes me cry. For Delphine, for Jimmy, and for myself. Little kids move on quickly. They have no sense of past, or future. Only present. And since Jimmy hadn't been present for months, there was nothing for me to miss.

The reason it has always mattered to me to find out more about my mom, her daddy, Jimmy Montgomery, even Larry Espinosa, God bless him, was that it would give me an identity. A history. A reason for being. An understanding of what makes me *me*. Something to say in response to the hundreds of times I've been asked 'what are you?' Not 'who are you?' What. It was always *what*. That tall, weird, oddly colored girl that no-one properly remembers when they look back through the yearbooks. The one for whom 'what are you?' was a regular social opener. The mix of my race is obvious, but the origins of it aren't. And this seems to matter to people.

I stand at the corner. The Greyhound that will take me first to Dallas, and then further west, is boarding across the way. I blow kisses into the hazy morning's gentle southern breeze. A kiss to the memory of Jimmy Montgomery. A kiss to the memory of AJ Carter. God rest their young souls. A sudden guilt rises in me that both died to set me free. I shiver, like their fingers have gripped my shoulders. Had Timothy Allen Rennick stayed home and turned the gun on himself that morning, I'd most certainly be remaining here in Humble. But there would have been no shared future with AJ Carter. Too much was riding on his investiture as a captain of the universe. We'd have inevitably drifted apart. We'd have had a summer at most. His family wouldn't even have known about my existence. I'd have stumbled through the remainder of my high-school years. Maybe gone to a community college. Back with my tail between my legs working at Edgar Vane's store for a dollar fifty an hour. AJ Carter and, to a lesser extent, Jimmy Montgomery changed the trajectory of my life by becoming statistics.

My tribute to them: *I bought a pack of cigarettes and Mrs Wagner pies and walked off to look for America.* I've inherited something important from Delphine Toussaint: there is little point in looking backwards. The moment to be free has arrived.

The Ballad of the Band (2)

24th July 1983:

One of the most hotly tipped new bands in Britain are stood in line. But on this occasion, they are not waiting to receive unemployment benefit. They are at Glasgow Airport, observing the sanctioned queue-jumping of the first-class passengers with a mix of envy and disdain.

'One ae these days, that'll be us,' says Reef Malcolm, the singer, nodding towards the privileged few.

'Fucken hope no,' says Bingo McAllister, the bass player. 'Every one ae them looks like they've been caught in an explosion at a paint factory.' Reef laughs at this. 'It's weird how rich folk have got nae taste, eh?'

Oxfam have provided everything the band are currently wearing for their first trip to America. The total cost of clothing the four members in coordinated black amounts to £33.50.

'I'm changing my name. Stateside, like,' Chic announces. Chic Chalmers is the band's drummer.

'*Stateside*?' Bingo remarks.

'Tae whit?' asks Reef.

'Chad.'

'Chad? Ya fucken balloon. What for?' Jamie Hewitt's irritation is bubbling to the surface. The guitarist and remaining founder member of The Hyptones is not in a good mood.

'Well, Chic Hyptone ... it sounds like a fucken procedure that wealthy coffin-dodgers pay for on the BUPA.' Bingo pats the head of her rhythm-section partner. 'Good for you, mate,' she says. 'Never mind that miserable cunt.'

'Aye, but keepin' the surname tae,' says Chic. 'Just like the

Ramones did. Fae now on, it's Hyptone, *Chad* Hyptone. Please tae meet ye ladies.'

The drummer smiles broadly. He continues tapping out an irritating rhythm on his suitcase with his ever-present sticks, a form of Morse Code torture for Jamie.

'Jesus Christ, Chic, gonnae gie that up? It's like bein' out wi' a hyperactive toddler,' says Jamie.

The drummer ignores him and drums on. As they wait in the long check-in queue, it's obvious who is most excited about their upcoming US tour dates. And who is least. Seymour Stein is waiting for them in San Francisco, potentially lining up a lucrative recording deal with his Sire Records label. There is a lot riding on this trip.

'The fuck's up wi' you, man?' says Reef.

Jamie ignores the question, just as he did five days previously when Reef last asked it – in response to Jamie saying he wasn't coming to America.

There are several reasons why Jamie Hewitt is apprehensive about this short showcase tour of Arizona and California. The band's third single has recently been released to substantial acclaim in the fashionable music weeklies. It's currently sitting in the high thirties of the UK charts. The Hyptones are firm favourites of John Peel and Kid Jensen, having recorded recent Radio One sessions for both. But this eighteen-day jaunt to America has, in Jamie's opinion, been far too hastily and haphazardly organised. Two warm-up gigs in England have been warmly reviewed, but unknown to the others, Jamie is concealing a developing anxiety about live performance. All four experience pre-gig nerves to some extent. To combat them, Reef gets stoned, Bingo gets drunk, and Chic ... well, God only knew what Chic gets high on. But for Jamie a serious stage fright is escalating, and artificial stimulants only make it worse. And if that isn't enough, Anna*fucking*belle, his unshakeably loyal girlfriend, has blagged a place on the tour as the official photographer. Although the real reason she's here

– the reason why no-one has contested her presence – is that Ronnie Mason, Anna*fucking*belle's gangster father, is funding the tour.

Anna*fucking*belle. The AFB. Omnipresent. Like a second skin. An irritation that no amount of calamine lotion can salve. A few months earlier, the first time AFB travelled with the band, a Bulgarian concierge in their London hotel had registered her name firstly as Hambel, and then Hannibal. Four daft young Glaswegians mocked her relentlessly. They laughed at her. Jamie more so than the other three in the band.

'Jesus Christ, it's Anna *fucking* Belle. It's not difficult,' she had eventually yelled across the desk. Her rage was overtaken by embarrassment. But Anna*fucking*belle she has been ever since. She has had little choice but to warm to the name, convincing herself it's stuck because she is not to be messed with. Although she is privately grateful that now only the abbreviation is used.

Jamie's head dips again as he sees her returning from the toilets. She says little, self-conscious perhaps, in the band's working-class gang environment, of her formal diction, honed in the privileged halls of an Edinburgh private school. She makes little attempt to participate. She is an observer; a watcher constantly on the periphery, and that sets Jamie even more on edge. She is a constant reminder of the Mason obligation; the hefty concrete ball to which he is chained. If only he had finished with her before Christmas, as he'd intended. Before the hype around the group had begun. Before her brother had taken his own life. Before it would've been considered heartless. Jamie Hewitt is a fucking coward, and that's a cold reality he can't outrun.

The line of impatient people edges forward again. Jamie stares back at the terminal doors. His blood pressure is rising. Chic leans around him unseen and flicks the ear of a small, restless boy in front of them. The boy turns sharply and, sizing him up, kicks Jamie's shin.

At the tail end of the line, several adults and children are pushed to one side amid breathless 'excuse me's' and an 'ah'm wi' them up there'.

'Where the hell've you been?' Reef asks.

Kenny McFadden, the band's manager arrives, already sweating and red-faced.

'An' whit in the name ae Christ are you wearin'?' asks Bingo. 'We agreed on the black.'

Kenny looks down. He sports an emerald-green tracksuit. AFB slips her dark glasses down, shielding her eyes from its brightness.

'Taxi broke doon on the bloody M8. Had tae clamber across the three lanes,' says Kenny.

'At least the traffic would've seen ye,' says Chic.

'Aye. Ah've got a splittin' headache just looking at ye,' says Bingo.

'Beat it, the lot ae ye'se. Comfortable for travellin' in.'

'So's a Lear Jet,' says Reef.

'Bugger off. Ye'se are no' The Rolling Stones yet.' Kenny reaches into the fat leather pouch stretched around his middle. 'Right here, the passports.' He flicks open a page and hands them to their respective owners. 'Visas aw sorted. Finally. Whit a fucken palaver that was.' Kenny doesn't let on that he was advised not to bother with visas because the process was hugely complex. 'AFB, you got yer ain, hen?'

'Got it, Kenny. Right here.' She'd have had everything packed and organised from the minute the tour was confirmed. She loops an arm through Jamie's before he can stop her.

'Next over here, please?' A voice calls them to attention.

'Hope she asks my name,' says AFB, fishing for a smile from someone.

All six advance towards the smiley check-in girl.

'Are you travelling as a group?'

Reef is dazzled by the radiance of the young woman's smile. 'Too right we are, hen. We're The Hyptones. An' we're goin' tae the top ae the fucken pops!'

❦

The miserable guitarist stares out at the shiny, wet tarmac of Glasgow Airport. Loud, uncontrolled children run around, crashing into anything that gets in their way. It's like watching a tiny, human demolition derby. If vasectomies were suddenly to be made available pre-flight, he is certain most of the males waiting in the lounge would be behind him in the queue for one. *These noisy brats can't possibly be travelling to Newark.* Other international flights to Majorca, Alicante and Faro are the more likely family destinations. At least he'll be saved that. Only Chic, the biggest child here, will be left to contend with. Hopefully, the cunt's batteries will drain and he'll sleep through the flight, leaving everyone else in peace.

Jamie's negativity about this whole trip is exacerbated by fears about his beloved acoustic guitar. It should've been on the plane with him. He'd pleaded with the check-in attendant, telling her the guitar was just a hobby, naively hoping it would change her mind.

'I'm sorry, sir, it's a very full flight today. You'll have to check it in.'

Jamie watched the precious cargo disappear onto the belt with a worrying thud.

The love of Jamie's life is this Fender Villager twelve-string Natural. It is a thing of absolute beauty. Made in 1965 and, according to the brash cockney muso selling it, used by Gene Clark to scope out the psychedelic peaks and dips of 'Eight Miles High'. Jamie bought the guitar based on that impressive lie alone. The Hyptones songs began life as unrelated chords strummed absent-mindedly on it, until he properly introduced them to each other. Warm, honeyed melodies and little phrases poured from the instrument like it was describing his very heart and soul. Ideas became riffs that became songs that sounded full without the need for much else besides the guitar. And now he has been parted from it. He'd rather have had the guitar sitting next to him on the plane than AFB.

To compound this latest misery, his boarding pass is for a middle seat. A last hope that they would all be located separately vanished along with the guitar. With the case packed off to the hold, and an update advising that the flight is going to be delayed by two hours, Jamie hasn't spoken a word to anyone since his cigarette lighter set off the beeper going through the security check.

The flight is finally called.

'Right, Hendrix, chocks away, son,' says McFadden.

Jamie glowers at him.

They watch the rest of the band climb the airline steps. Their restless excitement is plain for all to see. Airplane travel is new to all of them. Except AFB, of course. As Jamie and AFB are welcomed at the entrance of the plane, Chic is led back from first-class to economy, head bowed, like James Brown being escorted from The Apollo stage, ostensibly for his own good. Jamie sees the flight attendant patiently smiling. He knows she's already thinking the same thing as him: *My God, stuck in an enclosed space with this absolute tube for six and a half hours...*

Kenny, Bingo and Reef are seated at the rear of the plane. Jamie spots the empty row in front of them.

'I'm by the window,' says AFB.

Jamie tuts. It means that he'll be sandwiched between her and Chic. Both drooling as they snore, using his shoulders as pillows. *Fuck!*

Several people are still attempting to cram large bags into overpacked overhead bins. Some of the bags look even bigger and more unwieldy than his guitar case. Jamie reaches their row. AFB sits, leaving him to store her carry-on bags. He opens the hatch above and a box falls out, hitting his head. Kenny, Bingo and Reef laugh like drunk hyenas.

'Should've got up off yer arse when ah telt ye tae,' says Kenny. *Smug bastard.*

'If yer no' fast, yer last, sunshine.'

Jamie opens other doors. All are packed full, like a winning game of Tetris.

'Fuck sake.'

'Sir, can you please take your seat. The captain is about to push back.'

Jamie turns, ready to fire off a salvo, before realising the steward is talking to Chic. The hyperactive drummer has made a second attempt on the first-class cabin.

'Aye, God loves a trier, son,' says Kenny.

'Whoa, whit's that smell?' Reef sniffs the air around him. He looks accusingly at Kenny, who shrugs. On his other side, Bingo is asleep.

'Honestly, whit *is* that? Smells like a school janny's sick mop.' Reef reaches over the seat and slaps his song-writing partner lightly on the back of the head.

'Have you farted?'

'Get fucked,' says Jamie.

'Je-*sus*!' Kenny stands. 'He's just takin' the piss. You need tae get wi' the fucken programme, son. This is the big break for us, crackin' the American market.'

'For fuck's sake, Kenny, listen tae yerself,' says Jamie.

'Just think ae it as a paid holiday, then,' says Kenny. 'Without the wages, like.'

'Aye. An' fucken cheer up, ya torn-faced bastart,' adds Reef. 'It's like bein' on holiday wi' Joy Division.' Reef's smile is intoxicating. It is easy to see why the music journalists fawn over him. He possesses the charisma that all lead singers need. The sense that something magical and memorable will happen when he's around.

'Come oan, Jamie, son,' says Kenny. 'Ye know ye want tae.'

'Bring me sunshine ... all the while...'

'Christ Almighty. Three straight weeks ae this bollocks,' says Jamie.

For the final two hours of the American Airlines flight across the Atlantic, Jamie Hewitt sleeps, unaware that a guitar case bearing his name is gliding around an otherwise empty baggage carousel in Amsterdam's Schiphol Airport.

A State of Independence (3)

I sit, window seat, driver's side, on the cramped bus. I'm careful to sit closer to the rear than the front. Extreme heat and a temperamental air-con system could be the spark for some deep-seated, deeply southern aggression. No point in offering it an easy target. I've paid $13 for the single-journey ticket to downtown Dallas. It isn't my intended destination, merely a stopping point. One of many, I assume, where I'll take stock, recalibrate, and then go again. Naively, I figure I have the rest of my life to adjust.

The silver Greyhound rattles onto the Gulf Expressway by Calhoun Road. I catch sight of the University of Houston sports fields. I imagine AJ Carter being carried shoulder high by his grateful new team-mates after a phenomenal first season. Then propelled towards the drafts as a young, star quarterback pick. And then Jimmy Montgomery vaults into the scenario from his sweaty, stinking foxhole.

I reach into my bag for paper and a pen. Ruminations on the word 'draft':

Essentially the same process. Intended to apply a sense of fairness and equality to the selections, but for totally different purposes and with opposite outcomes.

I scribble these notes in the journal that will document my adventures on the road.

Getting well beyond Houston's limits is a new experience for me. The bus hits Interstate 45 with a few warnings from the driver that we'll be arriving at our destination late. A series of temporary road closures ahead will extend our journey from just under five hours to just over seven. The heat rises, inside and out.

We travel through an anonymous landscape on arrow-straight roads where no change in character is witnessed for hours. The country's open vastness amazes me. Reinforces my insignificance. The interminable green of fertile farming land. It looks untamed and rugged. I anticipated white houses, sunlit silos, boisterous lumber yards, and freshly ironed Stars and Stripes hanging from every flagpole. Huge oil derricks swooping down like metal flamingos on the horizon. But there is nothing of that in the expanses between metropolitan areas. The only rhythm is from the wires, gently dipping and cresting between each telegraph pole as if describing a pattern of breathing. A mellow, resting-phase electrocardiogram of the communications they carry.

Gradually, the green subsides. The low-rise, industrial brown takes over. The blink-and-you'd-miss-them cities of Wilmer and Hutchins indicate that we must only be thirty minutes or so from the terminus. The driver announces these places as cities, but they're the same faded small towns as every other enclave the bus passes through. I am headed west, and to the bright lights of San Francisco. I begin to appreciate now that I'll witness familiar dead-end lives in the spaces between.

I leave the putrid locker-room stench of the bus. I gulp in the fresh Dallas air like it is the water from an oasis.

Hi. Larry? Is that you? Yeah, it's me, Jude, I say.

I told him I'd check in regularly, and here I am, fulfilling that obligation on my first full day as a runaway. As soon as he picked up, I felt foolish and immature. Like he knows this telephone call is to give *me* some reassurance rather than them. But whether I just want to let them know I'm safe, or whether my safety is in knowing they will always be a call away, I can't honestly say.

Uh. Um, yeah. Uh-huh, Jude. Yeah, where are you? he stammers.

Larry sounds drunk. Or hungover. It's early evening. He can't just have gotten up.

I'm in downtown Dallas, I say. Gonna get a burger then catch the night bus, I tell him.

There's a pause. It's as if he's on the other side of the world and there's a delay, rather than there being only three hundred miles between us.

Uh, hmm. Yeah. Okay, he says.

Are you drunk? I ask him.

Um. No. nope. Just ... well, y'know, he says.

But I don't. Larry rarely drinks during the week, and only gets drunk on the weekends. He is permanently on call, like a specialist surgeon waiting for his pager to beep. Or a butler, waiting for a master's summons.

You workin' later? I ask him.

Um. No, not tonight. Got some days, uh, off. He sighs deeply. Look, Jude, I gotta go. Your momma's asleep. I don't, um ... don't wanna wake her,' he says.

It is as if he is being held at gunpoint, forced to read words that someone else has written for him.

I'll let her know you called, and, uh, that you're fine. Um. Bye.

And with that, the line goes dead as abruptly as if a brown dust storm has zipped through the Houston County plains, laying waste to those dipping and cresting wires and the poles that hold them.

The Ballad of the Band (3)

Kenny McFadden is panicking. He can't get hold of the band's American agent, and the band are asking searching questions that he can't answer. There is no-one at the airport to meet them. No man in a peaked cap holding a professionally printed card reading 'Hyptones'. And to top it all, Kenny has just informed the disgruntled group that their transfer across the vast plains of America from New York to San Francisco, where the tour ends, will be by coach. Kenny was advised by their UK agent to purchase an American Airlines special-offer ticket for the band. It would have been an open ticket costing $500 each, permitting them to fly anywhere in the country, and as many times as they wanted during a thirty-day period. But Kenny wanted to see the country. He's a postman from Drumchapel, for Christ's sake – this might be the only chance he gets. Kenny puts more coins in the payphone. He dials one more time. Norm, the US agent, picks up.

'Holy fuck, pal, whit's the score?'

He listens to Norm's explanation.

'Well, Norm, no-one's fucken here, son,' Kenny yells into the receiver. He doesn't wait for the response before lying: 'We did land on time, man ... ah'm bloody tellin' ye.' Kenny looks around. 'An' some ae the luggage is missin' tae.'

He listens to Norm's explanation, repeated like it's playing on a loop. He sees the band striding along the concourse towards him. He wipes his brow with a paper hankie that immediately disintegrates.

'Ah suppose so. But get him tae put a shift on, eh? It's like we've landed oan the surface ae the sun here.' Kenny puts the receiver down.

'Whit's the script, Kendo?' says Reef.

'He says thirty minutes ... an hour tops.'

'Fuck sake,' Jamie moans.

'Let's go back inside. There's an Irish bar in there,' says Reef. 'They've maybe got a jukebox. Come on, eh? Mair time tae drink. Anybody got some dollars?'

Everyone looks at AFB.

She rolls her eyes dramatically. 'Okay, I suppose I'll get these then,' she says.

Two hours later, they emerge into the airless humidity of a New Jersey heatwave.

'Jesus Christ, Kenny, look at this.' Jamie knows he is being unreasonable, but it's getting too much for him. The disorganisation of the tour. The lost guitar. The claustrophobia of the last six hours. The ever-present Anna*fucking*Belle. The searing cauldron. All working in tandem to ratchet his anxiety levels sky high. The misspelt name on their driver's card is just another big laugh to everyone else, but to Jamie, *THE HYPED-TONES* comes a little too close to the truth.

'Ach, it's a joke, man,' says Kenny, finally realising what the guitarist is referring to. 'Ah told them tae write that ... for a laugh, like.'

Jamie glares at the band's manager. Two and half hours after their plane landed, Scotland's most hotly tipped group wheel their trollies across the shaded forecourt. A second suited driver stands by a black limousine, springing into action when he spots his colleague behind the group.

'You guys must be da Hyped—'

'Hyptones, aye. That's us,' Kenny sharply interjects.

'Good. Let's get youse outta here, and over da river then,' says the driver indignantly, his accent redolent of every Mafia-movie conversation his passengers have ever heard, and perhaps suggesting he might drop them in the Hudson River instead of taking them over it.

'Get in,' the driver commands Chic, who is dallying. He is taking multiple pictures of yellow cabs.

'Aye, aw'right, big man,' Chic shouts. His ears are still blocked from the descent. A shovel-sized hand on his shoulder pushes him into the back of the vehicle.

'I'm Chad,' says the booming voice from the front. 'Welcome to Noo Joisey.'

'Jesus fuck,' shouts a dejected Chic. 'First dude ye meet an' the cunt's a Chad.'

The limousine takes the I-95 north. It's 9.00pm and the traffic is still heavy and loudly protesting the slow progress. The band's heads rotate rapidly, convinced that they've glimpsed the Empire State Building or the Statue of Liberty or, unfeasibly, Giants Stadium. Signs for Hoboken and Asbury Park are met with sudden renditions of 'Come Fly With Me' and 'Born To Run' by an upbeat and excited Reef.

'D'ye think folk'll ever see a sign for Dennistoun, an' think ae us?' he asks.

'Naw, no' Dennistoun,' says Kenny. 'Barlinnie mibbe, but no' Dennistoun.'

Reef laughs. 'Jailhouse rockers,' he says. Even Jamie manages a smile.

'Holy fuck. Get a look at that.' Chic rolls the window down for them to see more clearly. New York Chad mutters something vaguely threatening. The evening humidity hits them all, reminding them that they aren't in Glasgow anymore.

'Wow,' says AFB.

Jamie's eyes widen. Reef's mouth gapes open. The Manhattan skyline sparkles briefly in front of them before the car dips down into the Holland Tunnel and the world's most iconic backdrop disappears.

'We've arrived, boys,' says Kenny McFadden triumphantly. 'This is the first tartan invasion ae the United fucken States!'

♥

'Ah'm no' goin'. You'se go. Ah'm knackered.'

Jamie feels the traumatic loss of his prize Fender is reason enough to get him out of this pointless late-night meeting with Seymour Stein. The others are excited about going out. Only AFB is caught between loyalties. Eventually, Jamie offers her the free pass she craves. As official tour photographer, she'll be heading to Danceteria with three-quarters of The Hyptones to record an impromptu audience with the unpredictable boss of Sire Records.

'It's like a kid was let loose wi' too much Lego.' Bingo's earlier take on the skyscrapers of Midtown Manhattan is less a reflection on urban design and more about their logic-defying proportions. Looking straight up, watching the summits appear to move out-wards, makes her nauseous. Amid the comparatively low-rise, Lower West Side structures of Chelsea, the Scottish contingent feel far more comfortable. There is something almost Glaswegian about the rigour of the brownstone tenements and their accentu-ated cornices, the grid-iron street planning, the cobbled lanes and side streets, and the vertical emphasis of window patterns. Only the snakes-and-ladders black-iron fire escapes face-fixed to every façade are unfamiliar.

It's past midnight and the city is living up to its reputation. It is too hot and sticky to sleep, in any case. The streets are jammed with yellow vehicles, all honking and jostling for the slightest opening. Danceteria on West 23rd Street is only three blocks away from the Chelsea Hotel, where they've left their belligerent guitarist, but it takes them more than thirty minutes to get through the congestion. It would've been far quicker to walk.

Reef's eagerness to find out what Seymour Stein is like receives only a head tilt and a shrug from their latest chauffeur. Julio works for the boss. He doesn't answer questions about him. And in any case, it appears that Julio speaks little English. Julio pulls up immediately outside the club's inauspicious entrance. It certainly doesn't look the epicentre of cool that has been anticipated.

'It's a wee bit like Night Moves, eh?' says Reef. They are being ushered past a long queue of cool, young cats stretching down the street. Representatives of various tribes. Hip-hop dudes, punks, goths, hipsters, new-romantic types, all waiting patiently to be granted entry.

'Y'all must be The Heptones,' says a louche young man wearing leather trousers, a red bandana, and a black top hat. He draws a line through their name on his guest list clipboard. 'I'm Hoaui ... H.O.A.U.I. Welcome to NYC, my young friends. Anythin' you need, anythin' you want, you'll find it right here at The Danceteria.' Hoaui the doorman then switches from Southern affectation into Bowery street punk. 'The Top Cat is waitin' for ya. This muthafucken goddess, right here, will escort you upstairs.' He clicks his fingers, and an elfin girl with short blonde hair, who has been staffing the cloakroom to Houai's left, appears at Reef's side.

'Hi,' she says. Cool. Cherubic. Edgy. Like a combination of Marilyn Monroe and Tinker Bell. 'Follow me.'

Kenny McFadden notices the tiny girl with the delicate bone structure, the pronounced eye make-up and the mass of bangles loop her arm through the singer's. *Jesus, another groupie*, he thinks. Eventually, they all head straight for Reef.

'You're in room 467, son,' Stanley, the old porter, informs Jamie once the others have gone. In the rickety, ramshackle lift on the way up, Stanley adds, 'you know that's the room where Sid killed Nancy, right?' The lift travels three floors but slowly enough for Stanley to expand on his highly implausible relationship with the doomed Sex Pistol.

Jamie knows enough about the Chelsea Hotel's mythology to recognise it as a lie; an attempt by the old boy to secure a bigger tip. It is almost certainly what he tells every guest, no matter what room they are in. Well, this isn't the Plaza, Jamie isn't Sinatra, and this lying old cunt can whistle for it. Even if there was any cash in it, Jamie's wallet would be staying closed.

Room 467 is around one hundred square feet of fuck all. A cracked sink in one corner. A box of drawers in another, positioned so close to the foot of the bed that the lowest two can't fully open. A bare bulb hangs off-centre, as if the room was once bigger. Stanley flicks the switch.

'Hmm. Yeah. Be back to ya shortly with a fresh bulb,' says the old porter, when nothing happens.

When he's alone, Jamie fires his shoe into the corner of the room. The blinking neon across the street provides the only illumination, but he still sees – and hears – several cockroaches scurrying for cover.

'For fuck's sake!'

Norm, the mysterious agent Kenny has hooked up with for this tour, is responsible for booking the Chelsea Hotel. A well-intended gesture, one that Kenny hoped would finally kick Jamie out of the depressed dwam he has been in. After all, this is the place where Brendan Behan and Dylan Thomas saw out their last days. Where Leonard Cohen and Bob Dylan wrote songs that were amongst Jamie's firm favourites. How could the petulant young guitarist and songwriter not be inspired by spending time breathing in the lingering essence of Kerouac, Ginsberg, Warhol, and Arthur Miller?

Jamie can't sleep. His brain is overheating with uneasy thoughts about the weeks ahead. He leaves the room and wanders the hallways. Grunts and squeaks and thuds and creaks sound. The building's fabric complaining and expanding in the stifling heat. He finds himself standing outside room 100. He ponders the state of mind of the doomed Sex Pistol. Was it an accident, a consequence of their uncontrollable cravings for heroin? Had Nancy pushed him too far the previous night? Was Sid different from the quiet young man Stanley has described; the shy one who never gave him any trouble, until that October morning almost five years prior, when he calmly called down to the front desk, asking for Stanley to come and help get a knife out of his girlfriend's stomach.

Jamie cups an ear to the door. Exhausted, he hears the faint sounds of a couple arguing. He pulls back sharply, shudders, and backs down the dimly lit corridor. One of the voices was his.

Danceteria is a vertical city. A creative cauldron. Climbing up through four levels of loud, crackling atmosphere, each of them different and more diverse than the last. AFB's camera is being put to good use. In one room, there is a punky live group playing to an energetic audience. The band members blending into a mono-chrome set. Jumpy video playback is screened onto the stage. On another floor, Philadelphia soul mixes seamlessly with scratchy hip-hop in a sweat-soaked melting pot. On another, a form of in-terpretive dance takes place against a street-art backdrop with beautifully precise murals being spray-painted as elastic per-formers twist themselves into unfeasible shapes.

The coat-check girl points here and about, throwing around vivid names like Bambaataa, Ziggy Flatiron, Jellybean and John Sex. AFB captures exaggerated poses from unprompted subjects. Eventually, the young Scots are led to the top floor. The coat-check girl sashays past a wildly dressed assembly of cool cats, air-kissing some and high-fiving others. They laud her like she's Joan of Arc and they're her troops. The Scottish visitors follow her to the far side of the room and into the court of an older man.

This must be Seymour, thinks Kenny. He looks old enough to be everyone else's grandad. Kenny immediately feels a bit less out of place seeing Seymour's beige zip-up jacket, his baggy, pleated brown cords and his unremarkable shirt. He looks like he should be hoovering up a pie and a pint at The Horseshoe Bar, rather than white lines at Manhattan's artiest, hippest club.

'Boys, boys. So fucking great to finally see you over here. I'm a big fan, you all know that?' Seymour Stein's immediate enthusiasm is obvious. 'I see you've all met Madonna.'

'Jeez, that's her da?' Chic says to Reef. 'She looks nuthin' like him.'

'Ma*donna!*' Reef shouts into Chic's ear.

'Aw, right. Efter the wee fitba-player. Got ye.'

'Get yer fucken ears cleaned out, Chic,' says Reef. 'Sorry about that, hen.'

'I've just signed this little dynamo to Sire Records. She's the real deal. She's going to be a superstar,' says Seymour Stein. 'D'you guys know ... I was in the hospital, a cardiac ward for Chrissake. I was lying there, recovering from a heart attack, hooked up to a goddam drip and *she* just waltzes right in. Straight into my bedroom, almost straddles the bed, and says, "Look, just tell me what I have to do to get a fucking record deal in this town!"'

'Seymour, stop it,' says Madonna.

'She charmed the fucking pants off me,' says Seymour. '"Don't worry, kid, you've got a deal," I told her.' Seymour Stein winks at Reef. He puts a beefy arm around the tiny girl and pulls her so close that she almost disappears into the folds of his clothing.

'This fucking kid has bigger balls than you four put together.' Seymour Stein's tone changes. The beaming smile remains but suddenly his words are a challenge laid down to The Hyptones. 'How much do you want it, eh, Reef?'

'Ah want it, Mr Stein. Ah *really* want it,' says Reef. It is instinctive. Caught up in the exhilarating vibe and the descending jetlag. He is immediately glad Jamie isn't here, as he'd never tire of telling Reef how much of a bell-end he'd sounded.

'Well, that's good, son. I'm glad to hear it. I need to know that we aren't just wasting each other's time here. I'm certain we'll get on just dandy.' The record-company boss looks beyond the group lined up in front of him. 'By the way, where's Jamie?'

'Ach, that dopey cunt's just a wank—'

'He's, em, back at the hotel, Seymour,' Kenny interrupts Chic. 'He got this massive riff in his head, y'know? Right on the plane. He wanted tae get it down before it vanished. "It's a bit like Marquee Moon," he said. "A total bastardin' killer."'

'That's why I love these guys, Maddie,' said Seymour. 'They never stop.'

'"*You've a wild imagination, should have lower expectations...*"' Seymour sings.

'That's your song?' says Madonna. 'You wrote that?'

'Aye,' says Reef. 'Well, Jamie ... ach, aye. Ah did.' *Fuck it, he's not here*, thinks Reef. She moves closer to him again. AFB snaps away.

'"*All I need is an independent state of mind.*" I fucking love that song,' says Seymour Stein.

It's impossible not to get caught up in Seymour Stein's entertaining wake. He signed The Ramones. Talking Heads. He knows everyone worth knowing, and no-one, it seemed, has a negative word to say about him. Reef and Jamie started The Hyptones determined to succeed on their own terms, but Reef knows that isn't going to be possible. Sauchiehall Street is full of buskers once similarly determined to break the music industry's rules. To succeed on their own terms. Reef doesn't want to be a contender. He wants it all, he can't deny it. And in the pursuit of that, what's wrong with having someone with the industry heft of Seymour Stein in your corner?

'Boys, the band are just coming on. I want you to watch them and listen to them. I really fucking dig them too,' says Seymour. 'You'll like them. They'll be on the bill with you in San Francisco. I'm just gonna have a few words up on the roof with your manager.'

The three Hyptones move closer to the stage. AFB isn't sure whether to stay with them or follow Seymour and Madonna as they escort Kenny out.

'Hi,' says the band's singer. 'We're Love Tractor, we're from Athens, Georgia, and this is something called "Highland Sweetheart".'

❧

There is just too much choice. And too much choice isn't always a good thing. Tomato, onion, olive, cucumber, beets. Feta cheese. Swiss and American cheese. Pepperoncini with Greek dressing. Ham, turkey, tuna. Boiled egg. All Reef wants is a bacon sandwich.

'Just get us one ae they rolls wi' the hole in it.' He points to a bagel.

'And what filling, sir?' asks the assistant.

'Ach, fuck knows. Egg ... an' some ae that stuff,' says Reef, pointing to a tray of pastrami. 'You want anythin'?'

'Naw,' says Jamie. 'Ah'm no' hungry, mate.'

Outside, steam rises from subway grates. Yellow cabs still jostle like dodgems. Sirens pitch above the congested bustle. Reef feels like an extra in an episode of *Kojak*.

'What a place, man, eh?'

'S'aw'right, ah suppose,' says Jamie. They are sitting on a steep flight of steps across the street from the hotel.

'Jamie, what's the score wi' you, man? What's goin' on?' This inertia needs arresting. Jamie's darkening mood is dragging everyone down. It's threatening their entire future as a band. If he wants to be a solo artist, he should at least have the stomach to tell the rest of them. 'Look, mate—'

'When did ye'se get back?' Jamie says this calmly, cutting across the singer, but Reef knows it means when did *he* get back. The others returned when Danceteria closed. Reef didn't. In fact, he hasn't even been to his room in the Chelsea yet. He is put on the back foot. Like a husband being interrogated by an aggravated spouse after an impromptu night out on the lash. They are young men. They are in a band, in the greatest city on Earth, being courted by music moguls. They are supposed to be out all night, sky high on coke, balls deep in groupies. It's part of the job description, isn't it?

'Dunno when they aw left. Fucken Chic was doin' my box in.'

'Usual state ae affairs, then.'

'Aye. Daft cunt. He comes up tae me an' shouts right in my ear, "Reef, there's a fucken lassie in the men's bogs ... says she'll suck me off for ten bucks." Well? I said tae him. "She's no' ma type, man," he says. Chic, it's a fucken blow-job, no' a blood transfusion. "True enough," he says, then heads right back in there. That was the last I saw ae him.'

'Serve him right if it wis a bloke in the drag.'

'Aye, true.' Reef laughs.

'So, whit about you, then?' Jamie asks.

'Ah went out wi' Seymour, this wee lassie called Madonna, an' a few ae her mates fae the club. He was showin' her off.'

'Who?'

'Madonna. Seymour reckons she's gonna be absolutely massive.'

'Ye should've shagged her then. Phoned the *Sun*. Get rich an' famous the easy way.'

'How dae ye know ah didnae?' Reef smiles.

'Intuition.' Jamie winks. He pulls the singer's hand towards his mouth and takes a tiny bite of the bagel.

'The Danceteria shut at 4.00am, but we grabbed a cab an' went tae this mental place in Brooklyn that stayed open right through.' Between bites, Reef mumbles the names of the fantastic new songs he heard. The creative ideas they prompted in him. 'Ye'd have fucken loved it, J.' He is reaching out. Trying to re-establish a connection. The Jamie Hewitt who formed the Hyptones with him would've loved last night's experiences. The mercurial guitarist who wrote the words *and* music for 'Independent State of Mind' would've soaked up the sweltering ambience, wringing every ounce of inspiration from the sounds he'd heard. *This* Jamie Hewitt, though ... this miserable bastard sat next to him? Reef often feels Jamie is two separate people rolled into one.

'What's happenin', Jamie?'

Jamie rubs his face. Thinks about the words. Reconsiders them. Runs nicotine-stained fingers through bedraggled hair. Blows out air like a beach ball that has been stabbed.

'Ah don't know, mate,' says Jamie. He doesn't have the energy to front it out. He looks fragile to Reef. Smaller, somehow, like he has shrunk since arriving on American soil.

'Ah'm absolutely shattered aw the time. Can't remember the last time ah was able tae sleep for longer than an hour or so. Ah just feel completely done in.' Reef hooks an arm around his friend's shoulder. 'Fucken hallucinatin' last night.'

'It'll be fine, mate. We just need a bit ae time tae absorb the attention. A lot's happened since the single went intae the charts. It's only natural that we're aw a bit frayed at the edges.'

'You're no', though,' says Jamie. Reef fears that his friend is on the verge of tears. 'You seem tae be takin' it aw in yer stride.'

'Aye, well, six months ago, ah wis fucken labourin', man. Wheelin' bricks in a rusty barrow across narrow planks, three storeys up. Ye think ah want tae go back tae that mental high-wire act?'

'That's no' what ah meant,' says Jamie. 'It's too much pressure, at times. The tourin', the writin'. Ah never wanted aw this, man. Ah was happy just makin' music wi' ma mates. Ah'm no' like you, Reef. Ah dinnae have the same confidence. An' as for havin' Anna at my side every fucken minute ae the day.'

'Christ, Jamie, fucken man up an' dump her then. We'll no' need her da's money soon. After San Francisco, an' we get the deal signed up wi' Sire, we can fire her. And Kenny. Even "Bruce an' Rick", if ye want? Remember, Jamie, you an' me are The Hyptones. We're the only ones that matter.'

'That's my point. It aw comes down tae you an' me. Writin' the songs. Dealin' wi' the record company. Makin' aw the decisions.

Checkin' everythin's bein' done right. Ah never wanted the business side ae it, an' Kenny's fucken useless. We're totally out ae our depth here, Reef.'

'We'll sort it aw when we get back hame. Until then, let's just enjoy the fucken ride, man.'

A silence descends. Reef uses it to finish his breakfast.

'Come on then, tell me what Seymour Stein's like. Chic said he thought he was a bit queer.'

'On the basis ae what?' asks Reef.

'Said he kept leaning in an' whisperin' stuff in his ear, an' that,' says Jamie.

'What kinda stuff?'

'He wasn't sure. He still cannae hear right,' says Jamie.

'Daft bastard,' says Reef. 'Did ye see him jammin' the end ae that drumstick right intae his lug? Bingo told him tae keep pushin' until he hit somethin'. Ah'm surprised it didnae come right out the other side.'

They both laugh.

'He's definitely no' gay, though,' says Reef. 'The big man.'

'Voice ae experience?' Jamie mumbles.

'Whit?'

'C'mon,' says Jamie. He stands and stretches on the steps. 'We better get back. The next leg ae the Wacky Races is about tae start.'

A State of Independence (4)

A Greyhound official confirms the departure time of the bus to San Francisco. It will take forty-one hours and almost all my money. To pass the time until departure I'm drawn, like a tourist, to Dealey Plaza. I hadn't appreciated how central it is – to the city, and, well, to this country's recent history. It's an eerily quiet place, as you might expect. People flank the Grassy Knoll. People wander, gazing here and there. Looking dazed. Searching for something. As if their understanding of this pivotal point in our history might somehow become clearer. A car backfires in the distance, shocking all around me. Heads noticeably dip, including mine. Even those – like me – born in the downdraught seem hypnotized by the weighty symbolism. A generation on, and this oddly shaped mound holds so much power.

I leave the place understanding that the prevalent sound of this country is gunfire. The smell of it, nitroglycerin.

As if I need reminding.

I board the night bus to San Francisco. I sit in a similar seat as on the previous journey – in the centre on the left-hand side. A middle-aged white man makes to sit next to me. I lift my head and although not yet dark, the reading light above catches my face. He seems to reconsider and slumps into the seat in front, tutting as he does so. There will be a lot of this ahead.

When I arrive in San Francisco, I will have two options. Mary-Lou Wagner – my fellow Humble High scholarship recipient – now lives in the Bay area. While not exactly close, we've kept in touch regarding our track achievements – of which she has many, while mine are few. Her invite was of the open kind that people often recklessly offer, hoping it will never be acted on. I have her address, and on the same piece of paper, the words, 'and if you're ever passing through Daly City...' Well, Mary-Lou, I reason, we can finally retire that ellipsis.

The other option is far less simple, and probably the real reason I chose San Francisco as my destination. In a recent moment of unguarded weakness, Larry let slip that a woman he believed to be Delphine's older sister was living in San Francisco. He didn't divulge how he had come to this understanding. I immediately pressed him on it. Naturally, he clammed up.

Don't tell your momma, he said.

Tell her what? I asked him. You've told me nothin'.

She's the singer, he said, that's it. And then, as he left for the safety of the interior, he said: and her name is Happyness.

I smile at the thought of finding Happyness in San Francisco, acknowledging that it's been my goal all along. Larry's truncated tale of a mysterious aunt escaping the poverty of her small-town existence and living the glamorous life in a big city demonstrated that there was a route out for me too.

7.15pm. The Greyhound pulls out of Commerce Street. The bus takes a left and then another, and we are on Elm. Following the route of the motorcade. Moving past the location where, twenty years earlier, gunshots changed the direction of an entire country. We pull away past it slowly. Almost respectfully.

Then up right and onto the Stemmons Freeway. Over the Trinity River and west on I-30 towards Fort Worth. The hours in Dallas, though brief, are sobering. The impact of the decision I have made begins to hit home. Whether I have registered how America's loss of something here matches my own loss of innocence, or whether I'm just daunted, I feel suddenly small. I curl up on the seat and, fighting back tears, stare out at the anonymous scrub until the darkness comes.

❧

'Abilene. Next stop, Abilene.'

The announcement wakes me. I glance at my watch. Press the button. 11.10pm. The Greyhound veers off the interstate. It drops sharply down into a small terminus. The single-story block is surrounded by take-out food outlets. Oscar's Mexican, Raising Cane's Chicken Fingers, Cracker Barrel's Old Country Store, and a Wendy's. All open. All empty. No-one gets off. No-one gets on. We wait for fifteen minutes before departing.

Interstate 20 is one of the longest in the country. It runs east-west through four states. Near its western source, it trickles around and through a list of destitute, one-horse towns, each indistinguishable from the last: Sweetwater. Roscoe. Loraine. Colorado City. Westbrook. Big Spring. Odessa Midland. When the I-20 touches any built-up communities, the Greyhound route skirts the peripheries, bypassing any areas of variety or interest. These towns are the forgotten backwaters that elected Ronald Reagan two years earlier, only to experience the worst of his brutal taxation policies as his priorities shifted.

I have dozed some, on and off, so I'd be hard-pressed to say how many on the coach began the journey with me. But if the passenger cohort leaving Houston was overwhelmingly white, our progress west gradually sees the ethnicities become more diverse.

The I-20 narrows and becomes the I-10. An hour later, we reach Van Horn, where we stop. It is 5.30am. The sun is still partially concealed behind the serrated outline of the Guadalupe Mountains. It's to be a hot one, I've been cheerfully informed by an old couple sat across from me. Mid-thirties in the shade, they'd said. A new driver takes over. A muscular, sallow-skinned man with oily black hair held in place by a hairnet. His shirt sleeves are rolled past huge biceps, each of which is inked with a beautiful collage of tattoos illustrating his love for 'Rosalita'. He turns and the back seam of his uniform looks sure to split under the stress of containing the terrain within. He says hello to us, his passengers, with a deep, rumbling voice. Only I reply, and then feel silly for having done so. Five new travelers join us. All alone, it appears from their seat selections, although choices are now limited as the bus nears capacity.

The last of the five approaches me. A Black man, handsome in a Lionel Richie way. He is perspiring and breathing as if he's just been running. He wears expensive-looking, too-tight clothes ill-suited for the heat. He moves up the aisle. His eyes flit between me and the empty seat next to me.

Sit down here next to ya, sweet cheeks? he says.

His voice is coarse. Rinsed over decades by smoke and liquor and sounding like it has talked its way out of and into many dangerous situations. I visualize Auguste Toussaint, and it shivers me. He lifts my bag from the seat before I can. He puts it in the aisle by his side. Where I can't see it.

My bag, please? I say to him.

Bet you didn't buy a ticket for the bag though, did ya? he responds.

I don't know what to say. I say nothing.

Nah ... didn't think so, he says.

He takes a flannel from an inside pocket and dabs his brow with it.

No matter, though. No harm done, sweet, he says.

He reaches down. He lifts my bag up. I reach for it. He suddenly pulls it away again. Taunting me, like he was a bully at the school I've left behind. He laughs.

No harm done, he repeats.

No harm. When he finally returns it, I keep the bag on my lap, covering my bare legs. I look away, out to the far distance as the bus heads west. Towards the last remnants of my home state. And the US-Mexican border in front of us. Time passes, but not quickly enough.

You one of the sisters? he asks.

It's the Black equivalent of 'what are you'? He moves his head forwards and looks me up and down. Examining my origins.

Black momma, white daddy, I'm guessing, he says.

I say nothing. He takes this as confirmation.

I knew it, he says. If your daddy was a brother ... well, hmm. No confusion then, lil' sis.

The older couple across the passageway look over.

Mind *your* business, he tells them quietly. And they do.

So, where ya headed, darlin'?

I continue to ignore the man. I wish I'd remembered my Walkman. Easier to avoid unwanted conversations with head-phones on. I avoided many when I was on the track team. People perhaps assuming I was *in the zone,* preparing for a race. Focused on the starter's gun. Blocking out all unwanted interruptions.

Block out all unwanted interruptions. I mouth these words, eyes shut. Dorothy, imagining she was somewhere else. But not home. Not back in Humble. I keep my eyes closed. I hear his newspaper rustle. I feel it touching my bare legs as he occupies more than his own seat. The stench of a cheap cologne hits my nostrils. I didn't notice it before he took his leather jacket off.

You travellin' alone, girl? he asks.

I detect the changing tone. Again, his question goes un-answered. This raises an irritation in him, and he asks it again. More forcefully this time.

Look it, I'm jus' tryin' to be nice, here ... to pass time, he says.

There's an undercurrent of anger. Slight, but unmistakable. Eyes still closed. I hear him sigh. I feel him touch my knee.

Folks need a bit of company ... long journey like this.

I'm shaking.

Please don't touch my leg, mister, I say under my breath.

Ain't nothin', he says.

He is leaning in, voice low and threatening now. Too close to me. I look away again. Out the window, willing it to stop.

What's your probl— AARGHH! Mutha*fucker*!

I get a fright. He leaps out of his seat. I see steam rising from a deep-brown stain that is spreading across the crotch of his grey pants.

The middle-aged man in front has emptied a cup.

Nigga, you gonna fucking die!

Other passengers turn, staring. A few of them rise. No more than this, just enough to satisfy themselves that they would've acted. Enough to garnish their account when retelling it. The bus driver hits the brakes. My forehead crashes against the seat in front. The Black man in the too-tight clothes falls forwards, sliding in the aisle. The middle-aged white man lands on top of him. The bus driver advances towards us. I notice a small club in his left hand.

Fuck *you*! says the Black man in the too-tight clothes.

Oh, says the middle-aged white man. As he raises himself, his knee goes down heavily on the stain between the Black man's legs.

Ah'm so, *so* sorry ... *brother*.

You, Pissed Pants. Get up, says the driver. Now, go sit your fat ass down ... way down there, at th' front where ah can keep a close eye.

The Black man in the too-tight pants hesitates.

It's that or you're gettin' off right here, says the driver.

We're in the middle of nowhere.

MOVE ... FUCKO! Said as velvet-voiced as Barry White but laced with the rich possibility of ruthless violence. The Black man weighs up his options. The driver is bigger, and he is holding a club. The Black man retreats, for now, forgetting his jacket.

This Greyhound bus, unlike some of its predecessors, doesn't judge race. Doesn't prioritize privilege. Doesn't respect class. Its driver has spoken. His bus. His rules. The Black man in the too-tight pants glares at the middle-aged white man and then at me. He reluctantly moves to the front. I mouth 'thank you' to the middle-aged white man, who responds with an accusatory frown.

A sign reads *EL PASO 10 MILES*. My fingers probe inside the jacket belonging to the Black man with the stained pants. The older couple across the passageway who informed me of the hot day ahead are deep in conversation. They don't notice me removing the wallet. They may not have objected even if they had.

The Ballad of the Band (4)

The band walk seven blocks in the blistering July heat of a Manhattan morning. Stanley – who wasn't the Chelsea Hotel's busboy, but its versatile owner – has provided directions. Kenny attempts to convert them into a map but has inadvertently drawn a symbol that resembles a Swastika. After heading east on 25th Street when they should've been heading west on 19th, he throws it away. Supplementary directions solicited from locals finally get the entourage to their destination: a used-car lot on a vacant corner block.

A large, battered silver transit van parked on its own waits at the rear of the lot. Jamie sighs. There are side doors but no windows in the rear. The faded words *PRIVATE AMBULANCE* can be seen on its side despite at least one attempt to have scraped them off.

'Jesus Christ.' Resigned and forlorn, an earlier appeal from Reef for Jamie to conceal his despair dilutes the aggression.

A small, fat Hispanic man emerges from the rear of the van. He is holding a card with *HIPTEENS BAND* written on it.

'Ye've got tae be kiddin', Kenny,' says Reef.

'Rock an' fucken roll, eh Kenny?' says Jamie.

Kenny's heart sinks. 'Norm, ya fucken bastard,' he mutters.

'Senor?'

'Eh, aye. That's me. Ah'm the *senor* ... Kenny. Kenny McFadden.'

'Jesus,' says Jesus Castro, the driver. He rubs his hand under an armpit before extending it towards Kenny.

'Are you takin' us, then?' Kenny asks.

'*Perdon, no hablo ingles*,' said Jesus, apologetically.

'Fucken cosmic,' says Jamie.

❦

Given that all planned engagements are on the West Coast, it now seems ridiculous that The Hyptones' management didn't organise an internal flight. Kenny has delegated all transport decisions to Norm, a man whose surname he doesn't even know – he told the band it was Epstein, in the hope that it would sound convincing – and who he's never met in person, despite his claims. He's only ever spoken to him on the telephone, after Max Mojo, the Miraculous Vespas' manager, had recommended the American. But Norm came good with the Seymour Stein introduction. And Seymour had done his homework. He knew all about The Hyptones. He loved the first three singles. He saw them as a mix of The Undertones, whom he'd signed, and Orange Juice, whom he hopes to.

Norm is also Jesus Castro's agent. Jesus is an out-of-work, out-of-condition, bit-part actor. Norm's plan is for Jesus to transport them due west across ten states, reaching Phoenix, Arizona, and the band's first proper American gig. Jesus will then head home to Tijuana. The Phoenix date is a warm-up for the real tester: the showcase event at the I-Beam in Haight-Ashbury, in front of Seymour and his A&R colleagues from Sire. The journey will take three days. It will mean Jesus driving for approximately twelve hours for each of them. The band will spend their $5-a-day allowance on Chicken McNuggets and share three to a room in cheap flophouses. An in-store record signing in Missouri and a planned college-radio interview when they reach Albuquerque are the only punctuation marks. It is going to be a very long week. Curiously, the absurdity of driving across a continent in a converted hearse, chauffeured by an extra from *The Good, the Bad and the Ugly* named Jesus Castro lifts their spirits.

Reef nudges Bingo. She turns, quizzical.

'D'ye think that is?' he asks. He motions towards the van's dusty dashboard. The white flared trouser legs of a plastic figure, glued to the pitted leather. Rosary beads dangle from its ankles. Above a thick black belt, its body is missing.

'It's maybe a sign,' says Bingo.

'Ae whit?' says Reef.

'That we're gonnae die in this fucken van,' says Jamie. 'Dismembered by a mad-eyed cunt called Jesus.'

Reef nudges him and eventually they both laugh.

'By the time, ah get tae Phoenix, ah'll be stinkin', Reef sings,

'Ye'll find ma heid in a noose, hangin' fae a door,' Jamie adds.

They cackle like children, and it feels, briefly, like it did back in the early days. When they were a band of brothers, up against the record machine and everyone in it. When a look or a nod of the head was all the communication they needed. When they had the gang mentality that propels all great young bands. AFB snaps them and giggles, and Jamie, despite himself, is beginning to relax.

A State of Independence (5)

El Paso is a scheduled stop. It arrives at an opportune time. The halt coincides with another flurry of activity surrounding the angry Black man with the stained gray pants that are too tight for his thighs. The fracas spills out onto the steaming tarmac, and I disembark unnoticed with my belongings. I watch a three-way fistfight develop between a white man dressed for business, a Black man dressed for the Vegas nightspots and a Hispanic public servant. Two nearby cops spring into action. They initially assume the Hispanic driver to be the aggressor. I sit on a bench watching the subsequent reactions. The re-setting of the expected stereotypes. The angry Black man with the stained gray pants is loaded into the back of the patrol car. The middle-aged white man receives a handshake. The driver calms himself sufficiently to get back behind the wheel. And when the dust settles, I'm in a foreign place, on the very edge of Texas. I'm sat on a bench, weighing up a new range of potential options, having departed the Greyhound bus earlier than anticipated. I wait for a long time. Conscious of the sudden freedom to make decisions without consultation. And then I get up. I walk. Westwards, in the direction I am drawn to.

I follow the highway for miles. Not directionless, I'd hasten. I picked up a guidebook at the bus halt. My ticket to San Francisco is still valid. I can always catch another Greyhound later. The $177 I stole from the wallet of the Black man with the stained gray pants has bought me time. I don't want to relinquish it just yet. I walk along the edge of the TX-375 loop road. It's 10.00am and the prediction from the elderly couple across the aisle from me on the bus is landing. It is indeed going to be a hot one. The elevated stretches of the road offer a panorama of ramshackle, colorful, often derelict single-story boxes that recall our small part of

Humble. Nothing separates Ciudad Juarez on the southern side of the narrow Rio Grande River from El Paso on the American side. The tense confluence of cultures, of identities, of ambitions, that you might imagine existing on a major international border is conspicuously absent. People traverse the bridge over the glistening water in both directions. They carry little more than bulging plastic bags. They are simply crossing from one country to the next for supplies, it seems. Others stand on the dusty banks. Fishing with thin wires and rods fashioned from sticks.

I walk further still, until the midday heat becomes too much to bear. I reach the point on the guide's map that I had circled while sat contemplating on the bench. I stand on what I consider to be the intersection of three states and two countries. A broken fence, a dam across the narrowest part of the Rio Grande, a small white obelisk, and an unruly grove of trees. A landmark location where cultures and ambitions collide. I imagine spinning a top and heading in the direction that it faces when it comes to a stop. Is that independence?

Emboldened, I find a cheap motel, as tatty as the degenerating slums of Felipe Ángeles it overlooks. The wages – or winnings – of the man with the gray stained pants could've bought me two weeks here. But I pay for three days. And for three days, cocooned in florid drapes, a worn patterned carpet and an unmatching quilt, I do little other than eat trashy food, watch television, listen to the small transistor radio I've brought with me, and masturbate regularly to the idea of AJ Carter. To the wondrous thought of him fucking me in this convenient roadside motel. As if we were on spring break. Us as anonymous equals. Jimmy Montgomery looking down on us from his place, pinned on the wall over the bedhead. His presence a comfort as well as a psychosexual barb. He skirts around the edges of my impressionable subconscious. My shame. My guilt.

Thinking back now to those three days, I remember reasoning that true independence is simply the freedom to fuck up on my own terms.

I write copiously. Desperate to capture my experiences as I am experiencing them, for fear that they might somehow evaporate in the heat and be lost to me. Pen in hand, I reflect on the incident with the man on the bus:

What have I taken from this? The Black man saw me as fair game because, to him, I looked Black. And the white man only defended me because, to him, I looked white. Black people live in a world where white people make all the rules. But not everything is about race all the time. Perhaps AJ and I were put off the bus to Houston because we were just being loud and annoying to the other passengers.

It's unnervingly quiet. It takes two full days for me to acknowledge this stopover as a line being drawn in the Texan sand. It delineates the before from the after. On the third morning, early, I venture out. I leave the key. I am not coming back. I head west. I walk the bleached concrete sidewalk. I follow the line of the curious, yellowed brick walls until they stop and become chainlink fencing along a line of railroad tracks. I walk, letting the arrow-straight road lead me somewhere. The far distance is hazy. I'm not sure how far I've walked but the disorderly clutter of structures has thinned out. Suburban to industrial to agricultural. Vehicles pass more sporadically, but at faster speeds. I'm close to the city limits, and a decision impends. After a time, I reach a gas station sitting in an open plain. Beside it is a Laundromat. Who would wash their clothes in this remote location? I don't know. The windows of the laundry are boarded up in any case. I go around back and use the rest room. Just across from it, a small concrete shelter waits patiently for its function to be fulfilled. Buses stop here.

A hot-water faucet has been left turned on. The water runs cold though. Perspiration slicks my face, neck, and shoulders. I soak a paper towel, take off my cap and douse my head.

I study my reflection in a cracked mirror:

Hi, I'm Jude, and I'm headed to San Francisco to make my fortune, I repeat.

I laugh between variations of tone: downbeat trepidation. Infectious enthusiasm. Wide-eyed naivete. Steely confidence. My fortune dependent on untested judgement and resourcefulness. There is no bin to dispose of the spent towel. I open the closet door. Two bloodied, inflated tampons float in the bowl. I disturb a little, brown, scaly lizard. It scuttles out from behind the pan, stops and jerks its head in my direction before springing away across the tiles. I follow it out of the restrooms and am suddenly surprised at the ferocity of the heat, despite having just walked for miles in it. The orchestra of crickets is the loudest it's been since I left home.

Cars and trucks motor pass, paying no notice. I walk towards the store and open the door. No-one is minding the counter. Not visibly at least. I look around the inside of the store. Every surface is lined floor to roof with roadside market tat that only desultory tourists would be tempted by. Sweat-shop rodeo shirts with the president's grinning face screen-printed on them. Bandanas advertised by a Hispanic model wearing one as a mask, and little else. Gigantic El Paso-branded Stetsons. And, improbably, a full rack of pastel-colored baggage.

I pick up a pair of gold-framed mirror shades. I lift a cuddly toy lizard. And then I spot a plastic dashboard Elvis Presley. I shudder and my throat tightens. It's Vegas-era Elvis, smiling, pointing, white-suited, flared legs apart, just like AJ's. I pick him up.

Help ya there, miss? A suspicious edge to the question. Not kindly.

I turn sharply. I drop the Elvis Presley. An old storekeeper has appeared behind the counter. It isn't clear where he has come from. There doesn't seem to be a back room. He must've been ducked down behind the counter for some reason.

No. I'm just looking at these, I reply.

Your folks out front? he asks. He looks towards an empty forecourt.

I'm nineteen, I say, stumbling over the response. It doesn't answer the question, and I've said it in a manner that only someone who wasn't nineteen would.

Don't have folks. I'm on my own, I say, recomposing.

There are security cameras here, jus' so ya know, he says.

I look around. I can't see any.

Well, I'll feel real safe then, won't I? I say.

The old man tuts. He ducks out of sight, like he has fallen through a trapdoor.

Mister, when's the next bus to Phoenix? I shout after him.

Uh, about an hour ... maybe two, he grunts, still concealed.

A tiny shelf holding three cameras catches my eye. I craved a camera to record my adventures but couldn't spare the cash – not until my encounter with the man in the grey stained pants. I pick up the Polaroid and a pack of film and examine them, searching for a price. I glance back over at a display of potato chips. The old man resurfaces. He peers at me. I hold the camera up and smile broadly.

A convertible screeches into the gas station. Music is playing loudly from the radio. A young man and woman jump out over the doors. They begin dancing energetically. Separately. I look over at the old man. He watches, bemused, like me, as the couple gyrate to their own uncoordinated rhythm. I can only laugh at their joyous abandonment. The radio's song ends, and both skip over to the shop, bursting through the door.

Well, howdy y'all ... ah'm Clyde, an' this here fine, fine young woman is Bonnie, says the young man, sing-song-style.

Under the influence of something, it seems certain. The old storekeeper stands at his till. He looks edgy. I smile nervously. The sassy young woman winks at me. She smiles, all gleaming white teeth and dimples deep enough to lose a fingertip in. She is wearing a tight red blouse and a short, black leather skirt. Kitten heels. Fifties movie-star hair, jet black. Her young man complements her. All in black: T-shirt, jeans, and boots. An exaggerated pompadour extends his height to easily over six foot.

...An' we're here to repatriate, brother ... *Hoo Wee*, the young man in black yells.

He suddenly pulls a gun from behind him.

I gasp. And the three hear me. My smile vanishes. The young woman approaches me. She puts an arm around me.

...To repatriate the ill-gotten gains of Exxon an' deliver them back to the poor, the needy ... those famous huddled masses, my comrade brother, says the young man.

He points the handgun at the old storekeeper.

Will you help me – help me an' the beautiful Ms Bonnie here in our selfless act of wealth redistribution? What say you, old-timer? asks the young man.

His lips pucker, blowing a kiss to the young woman, who pulls me tighter to her.

Rise up with fists, sir! I beseech you, the young man adds.

Don't want no trouble, son. This is my store. Not Exxon's, says the old storekeeper. I can see him shaking.

Wealth redistribution, you say? Nice touch, Clyde, says the young woman, still looking at me.

Why, thank ya kindly, Ms Bonnie. The Lord God Almighty, Johnny Cash, well, he thanks you too, he says, bowing theatrically.

I have a ... um, a security camera, stutters the old man.

That's good, ole' man. Send the tape to the oil polluters, the capitalists, Ronnie Ray-*gun*, Kiss-ass Kissinger, the NRA, and the Ku Klux Klan. Demand compensation from all of 'em, says the young man.

And then:

He doesn't, I say. Have security cameras, I mean, I add, and I don't know why I do. Please don't shoot him, I say to them.

The young man smiles at the young woman. I feel her shrug. He winks at me. He lifts the handgun. And my respiratory rate escalates. He keeps the gun pointed at the old storekeeper. Walks calmly to the till. Reaches over. Opens it. And empties it. If the old storekeeper has a shotgun under the counter, he has decided not to reach for it.

Take it, says the young woman. She is talking to me, looking at the camera and film in my hand.

I don't have to. I have money to pay for it, I say, between breathless spasms.

But where's the excitement in that, cutes? All property is theft anyway, she says softly.

Her voice calms me. Charms me. And I did steal the money, after all.

I suppose it is, I say.

We smile. There is a connection. I feel it. I bend down. The smiling dashboard Elvis is coming too.

So how about you come ride along with us, sweetie? We're having a blast – and you can join if you want. Where you headed, anyway? she asks.

After a tiny pause, I say, Same place as you, I guess.

Everything is goin' to be fantastic, she says. And I believe her.

The young woman laughs and cuddles me. AJ Carter had cuddled me. I can't remember Delphine ever cuddling me. I hold the camera and pick up more film cassettes and take them.

Thank you, sir. The oppressed victims of Ronnie's Reaganomics are forever in your debt. Take the rest of this fine day off, says the young man.

He nods to his partner. Let's blow, Batgirl, he says.

Right behind ya, Kemo-Sabay. I'm takin' this one, she says, pulling me behind her. A little hostage to our fortune! she yells.

The young man looks back and laughs.

Sure thing, sweetness. You're the boss, he says. He grabs a cheap Mickey Mouse watch from a stand near the door.

We rush out. I'm carried along with their exuberance, criminal though it is. I look back through the open door. The old store-keeper watches us leave as he reaches for a telephone.

I jump in the back, and my abductors and I speed away. Onto Interstate 10, through the hazy desert landscape on another flat, straight road until, looking backwards through the dust, I no longer see the gas station. I'm already very different from how I was before.

The Ballad of the Band (5)

AFB shuffles around in the van's back seat. Normally shy and reserved in the band's presence, she now tuts loudly and regularly and melodramatically. She is writing in a notebook. She has been asking searching questions of Kenny McFadden, about the band's expenditure mainly. Kenny increasingly feels like he's under investigation – several of her questions appear to be asking the same thing but with different words. Trying to catch him out, he suspects. It won't be difficult.

Jamie Hewitt is two rows in front. He's absent-mindedly strumming a battered acoustic guitar picked up at a Tulsa flea market. Reef sits opposite him, writing. Chic is in the middle row, fidgeting, along with Bingo who, unsurprisingly is asleep. Kenny is up front, smoking weed with Jesus Castro. The vehicle's radio remains off. Other than AFB interrogating Kenny McFadden for a spell, no-one has spoken since leaving Jefferson City six hours ago.

Jamie's temporary optimism evaporated as soon as they reached the Missouri state capital. The in-store signing session was a disaster. Copies of the single hadn't been delivered to the record store. The manager, on medical leave of absence, had forgotten to tell his staff about the band's arrival. And no-one contacted the local radio stations to plug the event. So no-one turned up. On leaving the store, Jamie spotted a poster – *IN STORE APPEARANCE TODAY BY ENGLISH BAND, THE HYPETEENS* – hastily written in felt pen by an embarrassed young store assistant an hour before the shop closed. To temper his aggravation that night Bingo gave her single room to Jamie and joined the men in their cramped quarters. Jesus Castro, as ever, slept in the van. It now smelt like he'd died in it too.

'Whit a great country, man, eh?' Chic breaks the long silence. He is reading a *MAD* magazine. The cover celebrates Charles Darwin's birthday with a cartoon illustrating Ronald Reagan as the third stage in the evolution of man – toothy, gormless, holding a club fashioned from an animal bone. 'President's a fucken movie star, for Christ's sake. Imagine Joan Collins bein' our prime minister, an' no' that torn-faced, blue-rinsed cow Thatcher?' Chic's wide-eyed wonder isn't being shared.

'Reagan's a cunt, Chic,' says Reef. 'He should've stayed a fucken movie star. He's got that daft, big, goofy face, like he's everybody's favourite Granda.'

'The irony about that cover is Republicans dinnae believe in evolution. Everythin's part ae a divine plan,' Jamie adds. 'What a load ae shite ... an' these stupid redneck fucks lap it up. Aye, whit a country, right enough.'

'Boy, you've changed yer tune. Ah've mind when ye'se couldnae wait tae get out here,' says Kenny.

'Aye, well that wis before. We're here now, an' it's full ae gun-totin' Jesus freaks,' says Jamie.

'Ah just meant that havin' a film star or a pop star as a prime minister would be cool, naw?' says Chico.

'Naw,' says Reef.

'If ye've got total fucken belief that God'll protect you an' yer rich, white family fae immigrants wi' nae faith or belief, then why the fuck dae ye need a shed full ae automatic rifles?' says Jamie. 'An' how can ye believe in God an' Christian values ae forgiveness and repentance, an' still send coloured folk tae the death penalty in their fucken thousands?'

'Holy fuck,' protests Chic. 'Ah wis just...' He tails off. 'Dae they have the death penalty where we're goin'?'

'Only for irritatin' drummers wi' single-figure IQs,' says Jamie.

'Fuck that,' says Chic. 'Ah'd beat the death row anyway.'

'How?' asks Kenny.

'Ah'd get an ever-lastin' gobstopper for ma last meal.'

The laughter stirs Bingo. She yawns.

'Jesus Christ, wish there had been a bus wi' beds an' that in it.' Bingo has been asleep for hours. She waits for a response and when none is forthcoming: 'What did ah miss?'

Kenny McFadden takes Bingo's intervention as an opportunity to lift the mood. 'Look, why don't we go an' see somethin'? A touristy kinda thing, ye know?' He is holding on to less-than-welcome news, given to him by Seymour Stein in Manhattan. He needs to find – or manufacture – the right time to release it.

'Like what?' says Bingo.

'Well, ah picked this up back in Tulsa?'

'VD?' says Chic.

'Naw, *this,* ya diddy.' Kenny holds up a leaflet advertising the Route 66 Museum. 'Come on, we've no' done anythin' like that yet. An' we're goin' past the bloody thing anyway.'

'Where is it?' asks Bingo.

'A wee place ... Clinton.' No-one responds. 'It's known as America's Mother Road. It's one ae the most famous routes in the United States. It originally ran fae Chicago, Illinois, through Missouri, Kansas, Oklahoma, Texas, New Mexico, *and* Arizona before terminatin' in Santa Monica in Los Angeles County, California, coverin' a total ae 2,448 miles.' Kenny's enthusiasm isn't matched by his compatriots. 'They're plannin' tae decommission it soon. Glad we're gettin' tae see it while we still can. Come on, let's go, eh?'

'We dinnae need tae now. You've telt us aw there is tae know,' says Jamie.

'Aye, fuck it, let's go,' says Reef. 'We can stock up on booze an' smokes tae, while we're there.'

'There's the sign,' says Kenny. 'A couple ae miles, just.'

'Thank fuck,' says Reef. 'Haven't had a shite for about a week.

Aw that junk food, man. Ah'm backed up further than an M74 pile-up on Glesga Fair Monday.'

Bingo laughs.

'Hey, dinnae fucken laugh, Bingo. That's how Elvis Presley died. If ah don't come out ae the museum bogs within the hour, send the National Guard in.'

'Fuck that,' says Jamie. 'We'll send flowers tae yer maw, but that's it.'

'Sup wi' you, Chico?' asks Bingo.

'Got the shakes,' he replies. 'Mibbe somethin' ah've ate.'

'Well, if yer gonnae spew, dinnae dae it in here,' Kenny warns him.

Jesus Castro parks the van. The doors open and all spill out, yawning, stretching, and squinting into the strong sunlight. All except Chic. He remains inside in the shade.

'Just you'se go on,' he tells them. 'Ah need a bit ae air. Leave the door open, eh?'

Thirty minutes later, when the Scottish tourists return to the van, Chic is on his knees behind it. He's vomiting violently and loudly.

'Jesus, mate, are ye aw'right?' asks Bingo.

'Ah dunno,' replies the drummer.

'Hey, who's been in my bag?' asks AFB.

No-one responds. Chic gradually raises a shaking hand.

'What the fuck, Chic?' she screams.

Jamie and Reef look inside the van. AFB holds a small transparent plastic bag with trembling fingers. It contains an amount of fine, dirty-grey powder.

'For fuck's sake, Anna. Is that drugs?' says Jamie.

'No.' AFB is crying now. 'It's Brian!'

'What?' asks Bingo.

'Brian who?' asks Kenny.

'Brian *Mason* ... yer *brother*, Brian?' says Jamie.

'He always wanted to see America,' she sobs.

'No' like this though, surely,' says Reef.

AFB can't speak. Jamie stares at the bag in her hand. Chic snorts, back on his feet.

'Christ, what was that stuff?' he asks.

Jamie grabs him by the shoulders. 'Chic, you fucken moron! Did you snort some ae that ... some ae *him*?'

'D'ye mean, *him*?'

'That wis Brian. His ashes,' Jamie screams, inches from his face.

'Eh? How the fuck...?' Chic pauses to vomit again. 'How the fuck wis ah meant tae know, eh? It wis pitch-dark in there.'

Jamie is now being held back by Kenny McFadden, restraining him by the arms. But Jamie's forehead jerks forwards and catches Chic on the bridge of the nose.

'Fucking Brian, man!' yells Jamie. He is almost in tears too.

'Aw God,' Chic splutters.

'God must've been drunk when he made you, son,' says Kenny.

'Jamie, come on, mate,' pleads Reef. He helps the manager draw the irate guitarist further back from the stricken drummer.

AFB comes out of the van. She is distraught. No-one knows what to say to her. Jamie, still raging, follows her back into the museum.

'What were ye dain', Chic, rummaging in the lassie's handbag? What were ye lookin' for?' Reef asks him, once a degree of calm returns.

'Ye know how Seymour's crew dealt out they wraps back in New York. Ah heard AFB tell Bingo that she'd take the bags but she wisnae takin' any ae the coke.'

'Aye. So?'

'Well, ah just wanted a wee boost. Needed somethin' tae take the edge off. Ye know whit it's like, Reef.' Chic sniffed and rubbed his nose. 'Ah didnae think she'd mind. I had a hunt. Found the bag. Had a wee toot.'

'Ya fucken clown, ye.'

'It wis only when the ... aw that grit shot up ma beak that ah knew it wisnae the goods.' Chic looks at Reef shaking his head in disgust. 'Reef, how wis ah supposed tae know?' he says, again.

'Ye could've asked her first,' says Reef.

'D'ye think it'll dae me any harm?' asks Chic.

'Ah fucken hope so,' Reef replies.

'Where is that absolute plank?' asks Jamie, when he and AFB finally return.

'Over there,' says Reef. He nods in the direction of a telephone box. 'Ah telt him aw they wee bits ae bone an' dental fillings gettin' rammed up his nasal cavity might kill him. He's phonin' his maw. She works at the Royal.'

'Aye, that'll help. She's a cleaner,' says Jamie. 'Hope it does fucken kill him, though. Save me the bother.'

AFB hears him and bursts into tears again.

'Ach, sorry, Anna hen,' says Reef.

Chic returns.

'What did she think?' asks Bingo.

'Dunno,' Chic replies. 'By the time she'd finished tellin' me aw about ma da fallin' out a windae, the pips went an' ah got cut off.'

'Right, let's get outta here,' says Kenny. 'What a bloody shambles.'

'Sorry, hen,' says Chic, sheepishly.

Chic might be a hardman but he'd still shite himself if the AFB raised the potential of a Ronnie Mason sanction.

AFB turns away from him.

Hours have passed since they left the museum. Hours of driving through flat, characterless nothing. The van drives past a series of billboards advertising everything from washing powder, ammunition, Marlboro cigarettes, *The Johnny Carson Show* and then finally, one for KMCR-FM, Maricopa County Radio. Another board poses the rhetorical question: *What Is the Meaning of Life?*

'Whit *is* the meaning ae life?' ponders Chic.

'Life is sufferin', says Kenny.

'Whit?' asks Chic, puzzled.

'...In silence,' adds Kenny.

'Whit does that mean?' asks Chic.

'It means shut the fuck up, because we're aw fucken sufferin' wi havin' tae listen tae you.' Even Kenny McFadden's endless patience has reached its limit.

Bingo stretches out a leg. Her boot connecting accidentally with AFB's head.

'Sorry, pal.'

It's the final straw.

'SORRY?' AFB screams. 'Fucking *sorry*? You don't know the meaning of the fucking word, you arrogant bastards. I've put up with all your moods, your determination to ignore me completely ... the relentless, horrendous farting ... and for what? To get repeatedly kicked in the fucking head inside this sweltering, stinking tank. I've had it with all of you. This is mental fucking torture. You are nothing but a bunch of horrible ... cunts!' She is crying again. 'I don't deserve this. I just don't fucking deserve it. Brian didn't deserve this.'

It's the most any of them have heard her say in months. AFB is inconsolable, her face concealed in her hands. The embarrassed males – even Jesus Castro, eyes darting between the road and the back – stare at Jamie, with inappropriate 'fuck sake, control your woman' looks. He blushes but says nothing.

'Erm, we nearly there yet?' asks Chic.

AFB's sobbing continues, getting louder and more hopeless.

'Aye ... Kenny, this is pish. Is it still fucken July?' says Reef.

'Gie it up, eh? We've only been on the road again for a couple ae hours.' Kenny is torn. They should really pull over and make sure AFB is alright. But since Jamie is making no such demands, he feels that it isn't really his concern.

AFB's sobbing gets louder. Reef kicks Jamie's foot and nods silently at her when he looks up. Jamie continues strumming the acoustic guitar.

'Have a word, eh?'

'Leave it, aw'right?'

'She's fucken devastated, mate,' Reef whispers.

'Ah said keep out ae it, okay?' Jamie has no obvious right to be irritated, but that isn't stopping him. 'Ah'm totally fucken bored wi' this aw'ready.'

'Whit d'ye mean? The sparkling repartee?'

Jamie sniggers at Reef's sarcasm. Tempers are slowing rising once again.

'We've been oan the road for less than a week, man,' Reef continues. 'The record's sellin'. The English gigs were aw good. Ye said so yerself. We're actually gettin' somewhere.' Reef is almost pleading now. He, if not the others, is aware of the pivotal point the band had reached.

'Christ, have a listen tae yersel, Reef. There wis nae cunt fae the record label tae meet us at the airport. The "luxury coach" we were supposed tae be gettin' is a fucken plasterer's van wi' nae proper seats in it. Ah lost a guitar, an' fuck knows where it is now. Probably havin' a better time than us though.' Jamie glances at AFB. 'We should've stayed in Scotland. The only thing we're gettin' ower here is fucken dehydrated. An' sick ae the sight ae each other.'

'Jesus fuck, Jamie. Ye have tae put in the effort – the fucken miles, man. Nae such thing as overnight successes in music nowadays, is there?'

'Joe Dolce?' mutters Chic. But no-one is listening to him anymore.

'You sound just like *him*.' Jamie nods at Kenny McFadden.

'At least he's no' actin' the prick every minute ae the fucken day!' shouts Reef.

'Fuck off!'

'Naw, *you* fuck off!' yells Reef, a finger pointing at the guitarist's face from less than an inch away.

Jamie lifts the wooden guitar and, with limited space for a proper backswing, jabs it at Reef's head. The body cracks into the singer's nose. Blood immediately spurts. Chic launches himself at Jamie, swinging a fist that connects with Bingo's jaw on its way round. Jesus Castro hits the brakes, propelling Chic backwards, his forehead making a dull thump on Jamie's mouth.

AFB cries. 'I wanna go home,' she wails between sobs.

'Erm,' says Kenny McFadden. 'That's us here.'

A State of Independence (6)

The two of them are intoxicating. They are named Matt and Brandy. Surnames are extraneous. Unnecessary branding, they say. A convention for others too scared to live as if every day was their last. I know nothing else about them. I am too reserved to ask more during our first day together.

Everything needed for a life on the road is packed into the trunk of their car. I spend that night in their tent. Matt pitches it just beyond the public trails of Catalina State Park. He finds a concealed spot in the scrubland foothills of Mount Lemmon. He makes a fire and cooks a chicken – bought, not stolen or caught. We drink beer. I don't like the taste. They promise me it will get better as I become accustomed to it. I lay on a blanket, another wrapped around me, my rucksack for a pillow. I sleep until the sound of them outside wakes me. Through the weave of the blanket, I watch them have sex in silhouette. Uninhibited, and unconcerned about being observed. I see her legs coil around his. His large, stiff cock edging closer until she can reach a hand down and guide it into her. Their movements are slow and hypnotic. Almost balletic. Not jerking or urgent.

I wake as the sun comes up. I can't see them. I can't be entirely sure I haven't dreamt it. Wondering if everything in the last month has been a dream. The button of my denim shorts is open. The zip is down. I'm wet between my thighs.

I'm still circling places on my map. We cruise the I-10 westwards past Marana. Onwards to Red Rock. Matt driving, a long tattooed right arm snaking around Brandy. Me in behind them. Like a little family of three, care-free and on vacation. Matt is lively and excited. He spots an isolated call box. We pull over. Matt jumps the car door again and goes to make a call.

Are you guys on the run? I ask Brandy.

Everybody's runnin' from somethin', Jude, she says. Y'know, it's not real, any of this ... not really.

B-but the gun... I stammer. Brandy laughs. She gently touches my forearm.

It's not even full, she says.

What d'you mean? I ask.

She doesn't answer me.

Who's he callin'? I ask.

Jeez, kid, so many questions. I dunno. He's a law to himself. I'm just caught, dragged along in his wake. Brandy laughs. It's excitin' though, y'know?

Yeah, I say, because it is. To feel this alive for the first time ever. Or at least since those days with AJ.

Where you from, Brandy?

Ain't where we're from that matters, it's where the road takes us, that's all. An' those we encounter along the way.

She smiles at me, but sensing my puzzlement she adds, San Francisco.

You're a long way from home too, I say.

More than you'll ever know, sweetie, she says.

What about Matt?

Him? She laughs again, He's from everywhere ... an' no place at all.

Where did you meet him?

Strangest thing, hon ... It was only three years ago, but I can't remember.

That's a long time, I say.

No, it isn't. Not really, she says. But this last year... She gently shakes her head.

A relationship takes three years to catch, she says. It's just a romantic comedy before that. It's like he's been with me – some-where deep inside me – forever. Like all the shit before him just don't matter anymore, she says.

We watch Matt burst from the call box.

And then she says: *Bein' with someone and then not bein' with them is the only way to measure time.*

And I write it down in my journal right there and then, exactly how she phrased it because it sounds important and profound, and because I think it might give meaning to AJ Carter's impact on my life.

Matt runs back smiling. He jumps into the car, again without opening the door.

What you been doin', babe? asks Brandy, coyly.

Somethin' important, he says. You'll see.

Matt turns the ignition, and we drive off. We drive with the radio on, and music that I like is playing. The radio DJ talks excitedly, and Matt turns the volume up. I notice him glance down regularly at the stolen cartoon watch on his wrist.

He taps the head of the wobbling figure on the dashboard. The one I stole from the gas station. And then he sings, country-style:

Well, ah don't care if it rains or freezes,
long as we have our plastic Elvis,
Ridin' on the dashboard of our car,
Through all trials an' tribulations,
we will travel every nation,
With our plastic Elvis we'll go far.

Brandy giggles as he finishes his improvised chorus.

Let's go to the West Coast. I wanna swim in the sea, says Matt.

Yeah, okay, babe, says Brandy.

I ain't ever seen the sea. Wanna see if it's that emerald-green color they say it is, says Matt. He looks at the watch again.

Okay, now. Shhh! Matt turns the volume right up.

...And next up, an oldie goin' right out there to a cool young dude an' his gal on their sweet way to Vegas. You're listening to Dave

Diamond on KMCR-FM, Maricopa County Radio, and this is for Brandy, a personal request from Matt ... will you marry him, Brandy?

Brandy puts her hands over her mouth. It looks like she'll cry.

This is for you two lovebirds ... it's Looking Glass, with 'Brandy, You're a Fine Girl', an' I bet you are.

Yeah. she is crying now.

Anything. Yes! I'm yours. WOOOOOOAH! she screams.

Brandy leans over Matt, and he almost can't see the road ahead of him and we nearly run right off into the dirt as he whoops and hollers. I laugh too and clap my hands in the back. I feel more comfortable in the company of these two strangers than anyone else I've ever met, other than AJ Carter.

I love ya, Batgirl! says Matt.

And I love you too, Kit-Kat. Always an' forever, says Brandy.

Always an' forever, he repeats.

She kisses him.

Jeez ... pull over if you're gonna do that. I don't wanna die right here in the back of this shit-wagon 'cos you two are makin' out doin' a hundred on the highway.

The DJ interrupts their embrace.

Yeah, that was supercool. Golden luck be with you two young hep cats. Now KMCR-FM are always ten-high when a hot new young band from England hit town. The Hyptones will be wailin' at the Rodeo Razzle Club out in Chandler tomorrow evenin'. They're jam hot an' they dropped in for a cool Dave Diamond chitter-chatter. First though, let's listen to their latest...

There is something immediate about the song that then plays on the radio. I can't put my finger on it. It isn't the type of music I know or have heard much of before. The sound has a grace and radiance to it. The song is wistful and fragile. At odds with the bluster of most American chart music. But it's the mellifluous guitar and the lyrics that grab me:

Love hearts on the glass, dripping condensation
Your wild imagination, my lower expectation
A habit hard to break, becomes an obligation
Think of better times, but just leave me on my own

I've never heard this song before, but these words seem so familiar.

Here's a new future, the birth of a dream
No division, dysfunction ... I'm starting again.
New words on the window, positive themes
YES, YES, YES, we're done. Leave me on my own

All I want is, an independent state of mind.
All I need is, an independent state of mind.
You can give me, an independent state of mind.

One listen and it's lodged in my mind forever.

Hey, who is this? I ask Brandy and Matt.

Dunno ... but they sound *trés* cool, says Matt.

The DJ provides the answer:

The Hyptones there with 'Independent State of Mind'. An' they'll be doin' two shows at Rodeo Razzle Club, Altamont Street, Downtown Chandler...

I really, really like this song, I say.

Hey, we should go, stop off in Phoenix. Celebrate. Baby? says Brandy.

Can we ... please? I've never been to a concert before, I say, excitedly.

Anythin' for my girls, says Matt.

The Ballad of the Band (6)

'Fellas, what happened?' says Dave Diamond, laughing. 'You guys look like you ran into the Incredible Hulk right outside.'

'Somethin' like that, aye,' mumbles Reef, still dabbing the blood from his nose.

'Ha, ha, yeah.' Dave Diamond honks a fake laugh. 'Whatta great record though. Tell me, Reef, what's it about?'

'Ye better ask him. He wrote it.' Reef thumbs at Jamie, whose tongue probes at the space where a front tooth used to be. Jamie's head dips. Dave Diamond glances down at his notes.

'Well, Jimmy, what can you tell the KMCR-FM listeners about the song?'

'It's about bein' sick tae the back teeth of folk that stifle the life outta ye, day in day out.'

'Gie's peace, eh?' mutters Reef.

'Ah, yeah, that's really beautiful, man … Now spill the beans, you good-lookin' fellas must have chicks throwin' themselves at you over here. Are you bein' hit on? How determined are the groupies? Is it hard to find romance in a band?'

'It is for him,' says Jamie.

Dave Diamond laughs nervously. A producer is making throat-cutting gestures through the glass.

'Now, you boys are all tight, yeah? Best buddies since forever, I've been told. So, let's see … Who's the messiest in the band?' asks Dave Diamond.

'Me,' says Chic.

'An' who eats the most?'

'That'd be me anaw, Diamond Dave,' says Chic. 'An' ah'll save ye a bit ae time, pal … before ye ask, ah've got the biggest knob tae.'

'Uh, um, uh-huh … Let's talk about influences, Reef. If folks come down to the Razzle Rodeo for the gig, what type of sounds can they expect?'

'It's pretty much the three B's,' says Reef, trying to rescue something from the ashes. 'The Byrds, The Beatles and the Buffalo Springfield. What else is there?'

'Well, that sounds right up my boulevard, dude,' says the radio DJ. 'I'll be there,' he lies, 'an' y'all should be too. That's The Hyptones … the start of the second UK Beat Invasion. Comin' right atcha from Chandler, Phoenix. Tomorrow evening at 6.00pm an' then again at 10.00. I'm Dave Diamond and this is KMCR-FM, Maricopa County Radio. Don't go away, we'll be right back after the messages.'

The Razzle Rodeo Club Incident

29th July 1983:

Jesus Castro drives the van on the dusty road towards the very
end of everyone's tether. The absence of food from last night's
motel stay is the latest trigger. The only sound – faintly heard,
against the noise of the engine – is from the radio.
They pass an old, battered sign that reads:
*WELCOME TO PHOENIX: POPULATION 620,000.
PLEASE DRIVE CAREFULLY.*
'Hey ... hey, you'se, listen. It's us. IT'S US!' Kenny McFadden
turns the radio dial clockwise.
'*...The Hyptones from England hit town. They'll be jammin' at the
Rodeo Razzle Club, Altamont Street, out on Chandler in a couple
of hours. Matinee show, an' adults-only later. Pay on the door, so
don't miss em'. They're gonna be massive. This is their latest...*'
'Independent State of Mind' plays through the van speaker. It
sounds tinny and under-produced in the context, but Kenny
McFadden turns to see a smile cross everyone's lips. Even AFB's.
'Fucken diddy thinks Glesga's a place in England!' says Chic.
'Ach, who cares. You thought Mexico was in Texas, ya balloon,'
says Reef.
Jesus Castro turns to Kenny and sniggers. '*Maldito idiota*,' he says.
'Aye,' Kenny replies.
'Hey, is Razzle no' a scud magazine here tae?' asks Chic.
'Mibbe Hugh Hefner'll be there,' says Reef.
'Don't talk pish,' says Jamie with a lisp due to the air whistling
through the gap in his mouth. 'It'll be a fucken cattle-ridin'

redneck joint. Jist oor target audience, eh?'
'Haw son, ya miserable bastart, ye. Take a break fae yersel, eh?
Yer song's oan American radio. Ye should be fucken ecstatic,'
says Kenny.
And Jamie has no smart comeback because Kenny McFadden is
right. But the thought of going onstage in front of any size of
crowd fills the guitarist with dread. He feels the bile and the
painkillers rising from his stomach.
'It's maybe a scud club for coos or sheep,' says Bingo.
'Haw, eh? Stoatin',' says Chic.
'It'll be full ae Aberdeen supporters then. We'll be fine,' says Reef.

Matt pulls the car in across the road from the Razzle Rodeo
Club. I'm in the passenger seat. Brandy is in the back. I flick the
mirror down for a final look at Brandy's work. Her make-up application makes me look much older than I am. I barely
recognize myself. We get out. It's 8.00pm. Humid. I'm sat on
the car fender. There are people in the street. And a long line of
motorcycles parked outside the club, sentry-style. Like they are
guarding it. Or blocking entry to it.
Altamont Street is full of activity, not all of it I'd anticipated.
Over to my left, down a dark, narrow side street, a small neon
sign sparks to life. The blue illuminates two figures. I catch sight
of a woman on her knees in front of a fat guy in a capped-sleeve
T-shirt. His jeans are pulled down to his thighs. She has his
cock in her hand. She turns slowly and catches my gaze. The
guy's hand turns her head back and she begins sucking him off.
Matt is talking to four people at the entrance to the club. Brandy
is smoking a cigarette. She has wandered over to a trashcan about
fifty yards away from the car. And I'm left. Momentarily alone. A
voyeur to this sex act that I can't drag my eyes from. It's private
and transactional, and seems non-threatening, yet it's happening

in the open air and without the protagonists caring much about
being observed. I lift my camera and point and...
Don't.
A voice from behind me. An unusual accent.
Ah dinnae think ye should be takin' pictures ae that.
It's a young man's voice. He speaks like someone in a hurry. Too
quickly for me to differentiate the words from the spaces
between them. But his intervention embarrasses me. Because of
how immature it makes me feel.
Ah just mean that ye should be careful, hen. That guy might no'
be happy about it, he says, but slower this time.
Jamie!
A shout from across the street.
Another soundcheck, son. Let's go.
The young man in front of me shrugs. He looks desperately sad.
His eyes are glazed, and his pupils are large. His lip is bleeding.
He wanders across the street, a half-empty bottle of Jack Daniels
in his hand, barely stopping for cars whose drivers sound their
annoyance at him. I glance down the narrow side street. The
neon remains on, flickering. But there's no-one under it.

'This set'll be better,' says Kenny.
The matinee show consisted of six people standing in front of the
stage, Jamie Hewitt playing guitar sitting down and with his back to
them. There were problems with the sound, and four songs into the
set, a mechanical bull in the far corner got activated, making more
noise than the band. AFB took photographs but has decided to sit
the evening show out, returning to the motel. Kenny appears to be
basing his latest optimistic observation solely on the increased
numbers now occupying the venue. But the tension is palpable.
Inside, the bar is a riot of activity: vibrant, gaudy neon and denim
clothing. Beige leather booths line the perimeter. Reef detects an air

of danger and violence. Maybe the band should embrace it. There's no such thing as bad publicity, right?

Jamie's anxiety is neutralising the alcohol he has deployed to fight it. He sees the young girl with the camera from outside, sitting with two others at a booth closest to his amp. He decides to focus on her. To try to block out everything else and just get through it. There is nothing left in his stomach. He is empty. He notices an argument breaking out between men playing pool in a far corner.

Matt goes to the bar. I watch him being jostled by obese men with long beards, wearing cowboy hats indoors. The band from the radio seem ill-suited to this audience. The one closest to me, with the guitar, is the one from the sidewalk who stopped me taking the picture. I see him looking at me. Staring intently. Like I'm the only one here. It's a bit unnerving.

I'm goin' to the restroom, I say to Brandy.

Okay, honey, she replies. She smiles sweetly; still surfing the natural high.

I get up, and walking across the front of the stage, I get knocked against a speaker by men in search of a fight. Violence is in the air.

Ye aw'right, there, hen? asks the guitarist. His delivery slower and clearer, but too quiet against the hubbub.

I can't quite hear you, everythin's a bit too loud, I say. He leans closer and into my ear, says: What's your name?

Ah ... it's Jude. Jude Montgomery, I reply.

He bends down to plug in a guitar pedal.

Can I take *your* picture? I ask him.

Fuck it ... aye. Fire ahead, he says. He smiles and adds a condition: If I can take yours.

I press the button. The flash pops and, slowly, a wet picture emerges from its base. I shake the card vigorously to dry it as he takes the camera from me. He takes a picture without looking through the lens. He keeps the photo and hands me my camera.

Ah need tae go. Thanks, he says.

I continue to the bathroom, ducking between the bodies, blowing on the picture. Waiting until the image of him develops.

'Right. We set?' says Reef. Kenny gives a thumbs-up from behind the sound desk. A fight breaks out near the entrance doors. A group of young, punky kids have wrestled their way in, and they are at the centre of it. The temperature is rising, and the bar's pitiful management staff seem unable to douse it. Punches are thrown but the commotion quells quickly. The young punks push their way closer to the stage. The males are wearing as much colourful make-up as the female contingent they outnumber by three to one. Jamie watches the young girl with the camera return from the bathroom. When she passes in front of him, he nods to Reef, who begins: 'Aw'right Phoenix ... we're The fucken Hyptones an' you'se cunts should spend more time listenin' tae us an' Lou Reed, an' less time shaggin' tae Foreigner an' Meat Loaf. One, two, three, four!'

Chic hits the skins, Bingo's bass kicks in and Jamie's guitar begins to shimmer. He hasn't taken his eyes off the young girl with the camera. Trying, as best he can, to block out everyone and everything else and just get through this next hour intact.

I saw you, says Brandy into my ear. She nudges me and laughs.
What? I shout.
Watching him. That guitarist. *Hey Mom, this is my new
boyfriend ... he's SOOOOO dreamy,* she sings, sarcastically. Just
loud enough for me to hear.
I laugh at her. Embarrassed.
Oh stop.
I stand on the booth's leather seats. I try to get a better view for
another picture. He's still looking straight at me. And there's
those words again:

Love hearts on the glass, dripping condensation
Your wild imagination, my lowered expectation
A habit hard to break, becomes an obligation
Think of better times, but just leave me on my own
A sad situation, a desperate generation
(An independent state of mind)
And we're different now. Opposite directions
(An independent state of mind)
Anger turns to hate, violence from frustration
Denied the chance to speak, protesting my opinion
There is another way. Remove your cruel objections
Give in to temptation, and leave me on my own

This night feels special. These words are reaching right into my
soul. I'm different now.

A sad situation, a desperate generation
(An independent state of mind)
And we're different now. Opposite directions
(An independent state of mind)

🖤

> *'Here's a new future, the birth of a dream*
> *No division, dysfunction ... I'm starting again.*
> *New words on the window, positive themes...'*

Reef is a great singer; Jamie has always known that. And here he is, thousands of miles from home, proving it to a heaving bar erupting with agitated rednecks.

> *'YES, YES, YES, we're fucking done. Leave me on my own.'*

Sensitive and compelling. Jamie feels like he is hearing the words differently. For the first time, they seem to be speaking directly to him too.

> *'A sad situation, a desperate generation*
> *(An independent state of mind)*
> *And we're different now. Opposite directions*
> *(An independent state of mind)'*

Jamie plays like a tonne weight has been lifted from his shoulders.

> *'All I want is, an independent state of mind.*
> *All I need is, an independent state of mind.*
> *You can give me, an independent state of mind.'*

Where earlier there was confusion, now there is clarity. The end is in sight.

I stand on the table. The top of my head touching the ceiling. My hair sticks to it, it's so hot inside. Perspiration drips from the lacquered wooden panels. I snap more pictures. Matt is taking too long. He should've been back by now. I look for him near the bar. I see Matt and I see him being pushed by two men who are next to him. I watch the bartender lean over aggressively. I see Matt tense and bring out the gun. He points it and I see what looks like a jet of water hitting the barman's face. Above the noise, a woman screams. A thrown bottle crashes against the mirror behind the counter. Matt turns and looks for us. And he

sees us. And even though the bar is packed and there's chaos
everywhere, I can see that goofy, toothy smile. Brandy can see it
too. We're both up on the table. The band is playing loud, and
there is Matt. The Joker. Always messing around. He smiles at
us, and my God, how beautiful he is. Frozen in time. Until the
bartender's baseball bat hits his head and puts him down.

The band play on but Reef has stopped singing. He sees fights
breaking out in all corners of the bar. More than just the initial
skirmishes. They develop into a full-on bar brawl, with chairs
and bottles being launched in all directions. Something thin
and metallic whirls past Reef, narrowly missing him. He turns
to see it embedded in the drum riser; the black, twisted end of
an iron crowbar.
Reef signals to the band and sound desk, a thumbs-down followed by a chopping hand slice. It's over.
Chic dives for cover. Bingo drops her bass. Reef pulls her with
him offstage. Jamie sees the young girl he's been watching get
pulled down from the booth table by her hair. Her friend is
screaming and trying to get from the booth across the floor in
front of stage, but the melee prevents her from doing so. Jamie
jumps from the stage to the booth, arms outstretched and...

...I see the blade. I see it glinting. Despite the mayhem. Despite
the pain coming from my scalp. I see it. Unusual for a fight to
involve a knife. A gun, yes. I'd expect that. Everyone in the bar
probably has one. There are even old Western-style rifles
mounted above the gantry. But a knife seems oddly out of place.
The band's guitarist reaches out to me, and the blade sweeps
upwards simultaneously. I cry out, shocked. I hear him crying

out too. He slumps down under the booth's table. I look for Brandy. I can't see her. But the cops are here. Outflanked, currently, but an indication that the riot will end soon. I'm conscious of the camera. Of the pictures. Grasped tightly. Cooler air rushes in from somewhere to the left of me. Before I'm aware of how it's happened, I'm outside. The flickering of blue neon is overhead. It's the narrow side street of the earlier liaison.

So soon after it began, it suddenly feels like the end.

'Holy shite ... that wis fucken mental, man!' Chic is the only one who speaks. Everyone else looks at him, open-mouthed, not able to take in what has just happened.

'Everybody aw'right?' asks Kenny McFadden.

The band members examine themselves for blood and damage.

'Haud on, where's Jamie?' asks Bingo.

They are standing in a tiny store cupboard. Kenny has swivelled two metal beer kegs across the door.

'Whit ye lookin' at me for?' says Reef.

'You're the fucken leader, that's why,' shouts Chic. 'You gie'd the skedaddle signal.'

'He mibbe didnae see it,' said Kenny.

'So, whit ... ye think he's still out there strummin'?' says Reef.

'Don't talk shite. Ah didnae mean that,' says Kenny.

'Fuck sake. Shift they fucken barrels. Ah'll go an' look for him.'

Before they can, the door takes a thud from outside.

'You'se in there?' It's Jamie.

They move the kegs and open the door. Jamie has taken his jacket off and wrapped it around his arm.

'Ah think ah might need a doctor,' he says. He steps into the light of the storeroom.

'How?' asks Kenny.

Jamie's face is white as he holds his hand up. There's blood everywhere and a substantial layer of flesh on his right forearm is loose and ripped open.

'Ah fuck, son,' says Kenny McFadden.

Jamie Hewitt collapses.

Reef Malcolm catches him.

Bingo McAllister screams.

Chic Chalmers vomits.

And that is the end of the band.

A State of Independence (7)

Finally, I see her. Stumbling out of the club's main entrance. Somehow she avoids the violence that has spilled out onto the street. The motorcycles are on their sides. Knocked over like a line of bowling-alley skittles. Police sirens sound from neighboring roads. Squad cars appear at the bar. Screeching to a halt from the opposite ends of Altamont Street.

I can't leave him, I can't! Brandy screams. Yanking at her hair in pained helplessness.

We have to go, Brandy ... The cops are everywhere. We need to...

NO! she yells.

We can't go back. We gotta get ... I open the driver's side door and push her inside. She is hysterical.

I wanna be with Matt. Leave me. HERE! Leave m—

I force her head down as more patrol cars pass us. There's no reason for them to detain us, but I don't know what else to do. I push her over, across the front seat, and take the keys from her. She opens the door and jumps out.

Brandy. NO! I shout after her.

She runs back to the bar, and I run after her. She won't be stopped. I reach her and drag her away and towards the quieter door in the narrow side street. We look inside. A full-scale riot is under way. The redneck bikers are clubbing everyone in sight. Brandy, slight as she is, disappears. Through a blur of kicking legs and swinging arms and battered bodies, I see her. A shock of movie-tone Technicolor that doesn't belong here. She drags Matt up, and although he seems lifeless, somehow she gets him to his feet. I run in and help her get him to the door. Through the door. Into the narrow side street. Shuffling him to the car. Blood pours from his head. Through the wet blackness of his disheveled hair, I feel it. Sticky. Thick. Warm. I see it on my left hand. In my right, I hold the keys. I glance in the rear-view mirror of the convertible. Brandy is wailing in the back. Holding him. If he's breathing, he isn't conscious. Her pink top is spattered with the blood from his head wound. Hesitantly, given my lack of experience behind the wheel, I pull away. She pleads with him. Cradles him. Our fallen leader. The end of our little, short-lived Camelot. Fortunately, Larry taught me the basics in a car with a stick shift, and although this one crunches its anger at me, the noisy chaos behind us masks my inexperience.

I haven't been driving long before we hit the interstate and darkness. I see a billboard. There are words written on it. As we get closer, I make them out:

WHAT IS THE MEANING OF LIFE?

I pull the car off the highway and park it behind the cover of the billboard.

Brandy jumps out. She screams, and I look back, fearful. He sprawls across the rear seat. Blood is everywhere. Brandy lies in the road, pulling at her hair. I get out and shout at her. Slap her face repeatedly.

We need to get him to the ER, I shout. Brandy! Now. Or he'll die.

And instantly she stops. She stands. She takes the keys from me and gets in the car.

Get in, she commands.

And I do.

We drive. Something digs in my ribs. I reach into a pocket. It's the Polaroid of the guitarist in the band. In the picture, he is smiling.

After the Razzle Rodeo Club incident, we drove. Simply to get as far from Altamont Street as possible. Matt and Brandy had robbed gas stations and liquor stores. Brandy was convinced the cops would see them as the instigators of the riot and would be on our tail. We reached Wickenburg, a small town in Maricopa County. There was a local all-night medical center, located next door to a motel. I remained out of sight.

Brandy persuaded the doctors that Matt had been randomly attacked. He was stabilized, assessed, and then taken to an Intensive Care Unit. Because the hematoma could've enlarged, he wasn't taken into the operating theater for a few days. Brandy talked of a measure called the Glasgow Coma Scale. I couldn't believe it. His head injury was evaluated as moderate. His chances of recovery rated as 50:50 at best. I wondered just how much money Matt and Brandy had accumulated. Because his treatment wasn't cheap and she paid for it – and our residence in the motel – with cash. But I didn't ask searching questions. And then we moved, the three of us. Here. To a low-rent apartment on – ironically – Frontier Street.

More than any other emotion, guilt can change a person. You'd think I would've said sorry and goodbye, and carried on my way to California, wouldn't you? But I stayed – to help Brandy, to look after Matt. Why? you might ask. It was simple: they needed me, and I hadn't felt needed before.

Each of us has our role, and very quickly we settle into a simple routine. Matt's only role is to give us a purpose. Brandy earns from a waitressing job that offers flexibility and as many hours as we can manage. I take care of Matt while she's out. I spend any free time in a small local library just across the street from the apartment, picking out books to read to Matt. Books, I now appreciate, that only reinforce what he has lost.

Our initial optimism wanes. Those first few weeks it feels like every day brings a tiny improvement. But it's an illusion. The only change is in our growing acceptance of a situation we aren't in control of. And that, ultimately, isn't positive. Two months pass. Each week brings greater challenges, not fewer. Brandy is like a caged animal. Desperate to be free. She doesn't wear commitment well, especially in these confined circumstances. But she can't leave. We argue regularly. About the little things primarily. And gradually, I no longer feel needed. Selfish though it sounds, I feel taken advantage of. It's like I'm back in Humble. Something needs to give. We both know it. Perhaps even poor Matt does too.

I'm sat on the edge of a single bed. Matt is propped up in front of me. He can't eat by himself. I'm feeding him from a spoon. He grips my small, plastic dashboard Elvis as if summoning enough strength to rub it would grant him three wishes and a way out of this purgatory. Unusually for Arizona in the fall, it's raining heavily outside. It's a tiny space. Cold, and closing in on us. But I can't complain about anything. I wanted to go to that redneck bar. I wanted to see the band. I wanted to absorb the vibrancy of these two people – wanted some of it to rub off on me. But now I feel trapped again. A carer for a lifeless man whose eyes plead for a pillow to end the torture. I'm now further away than ever from the big-city dreams I'd fostered. Resigned to reflecting on the fateful circumstances that brought me ... *us*, to this place. I desperately want to get out of here.

The front door opens. The interruption drags me back to the situation. I haven't been paying attention. The food has spilt. It dribbles off Matt's chin. It falls onto his T-shirt.

B ... that you? I shout, needlessly. I scrape away the evidence.

Yeah. Only me. Sorry to disappoint, she replies. She comes into the room. She smiles warmly at both of us.

Hey, handsome, she says. She leans over and kisses Matt's forehead.

How's he been? she asks, as she does every day when returning from her shift.

Well, we watched some *Captain Kangaroo*, an' then we read *On the Road*. An' then we listened to some music. Didn't we, Matt?

And I'm talking to him like he is an infant. Because that's what he's been reduced to. An immobile six-foot infant. And every time we do this, every time she comes home still hoping for the tiniest sign of a change for the better, a little bit more of her dies inside.

But there's something different about her today. I see it – or imagine it – in a glance she throws my way.

I interpret this as a signal that 'three's a crowd, and you're out', although I know that wouldn't be her intention. And even though it's secretly what I want, it feels like I'm being robbed of the opportunity to decide what's best for me.

Help me in the kitchen, Jude? she says. I follow her through to the little side room.

Jude, I'm gonna drive you to San Francisco. We'll go the day after next. Mrs Forde will come in an' stay with Matt till I get back, she says.

Angry and embarrassed that I've somehow become an additional burden to her, my immaturity shows.

What are you talkin' about? I'm not leavin' you, I say, stunned at the suggestion.

We can't keep doin' this. This ain't no life for you, girl. You need to go back to school, Jude. I don't want you makin' the same mistakes I did, she insists.

What if I already have? I shout.

Jude, keep your voice down, she says calmly.

You can't look after Matt on your own, I tell her.

I can. He's my responsibility. I'm startin' a different job soon. Workin' better hours. A lot more money. I can pay for regular care for us. *Proper* care, she says. You need to live your life ... be happy.

Tears are forming in my eyes. When I was back in Humble, I

never expected happiness. Until AJ Carter came along, I never anticipated life being joyous, or exciting, or dangerous, or magnificently unpredictable. And then Brandy and Matt materialized and in a few spectacular days I knew it was all those things and more.

I just want to be like you, I say. And the tears flow, for that admission alone.

She puts her arms around me and pulls me close.

You're better than me, Jude. Much better, she whispers.

I just want stability, I say, sobbing.

How is this stable? she asks.

I have no answer to give.

There's somethin' more than this for you. You're gonna go stay with Momma Em. She'll look after you, she says.

Momma Em was Brandy's foster parent during the period of her life before she hit the road. Before Matt. Her name has been raised regularly in the weeks leading up to this point. It's now apparent that Brandy's decision is final. Despite this...

No! I yell.

YES! Jude. You need to listen to me now.

If that's it, then I'd be as well off back in Humble, I say.

No. Don't ever look backwards. Go to Em's place. I'm telling you.

I'll fucking decide. You're not my...

Your what? Your mom? No. No, Jude, I'm not, but that's what you need.

She's becoming angry. Struggling to keep her voice low for Matt's sake.

I don't want you here no more. I can't fend for Matt *and* you at the same time. An' he's my priority, she says.

And that's the end of it. She goes into the bathroom, slamming the door behind her. I'm left staring through the doorway at Matt.

There's a massive difference between moving forward and moving on.

The following day, we leave. It is still raining. I sit, petulantly, in the back, jabbing the dashboard Elvis into my thigh. I took it from Matt when Brandy wasn't looking, convincing myself that it's to remember him by. But I'm punishing him. If I can't have *them*, Matt can't have the Elvis.

Brandy drives, ignoring my melodramatic sighs. It takes us thirteen hours. We pass through more anonymous, dull, monochrome industrial wastelands, improved only by the white dusting of an unseasonal snowfall. And we pass through colorful neon-lit nightlife, buzzing with activity, happy faces outside, people enjoying life.

We reach Ingleside, and the most recent house the teenaged Brandy lived in, and even though it's dark, and she should be in bed, I meet little Rabbit. She runs towards me, excited to show me two teeth that she has wrapped in a cotton pad. And, despite my desultory mood, I'm immediately entranced.

PART TWO:

Jamie – Down and Out in Glasgow and London

God, grant me the serenity to accept the things I cannot change.
The courage to change the things I can.
And the wisdom to know the difference.

1

Hello. My name is Jamie. And I'm a cunt!

This won't come as a shock. I suspect you know it by now. And, let me warn you, it gets worse before it gets better. I've *always* been a cunt. When the opportunity to act differently has presented itself, I've always chosen the way of the cunt. Can there be salvation for the *absolute* cunt? Well, I certainly hope so. Otherwise, all of this is pointless; this reaching into the darkness of the soul to see if there's anything worth salvaging. The point, I've been told, of committing it to paper is for me to start to confront the consequences of my cuntishness. Nothing more.

Thanks to David F. Ross – another monumental cunt – you may think you know the facts surrounding the demise of my band, The Hyptones. You don't. Well, not all of them. The violent end of the American tour was described faithfully, but the underlying tensions, while charted, were not fully explained.

His piece about the band stimulated the following confessional, and there is a certain irony to this that only he and I are party to.

I instigated the carnage at the Razzle Rodeo Club. Between the matinee and the evening slot, Kenny McFadden revealed to me that our showcase gig in San Francisco at the end of that horrendous jaunt across hundreds of miles of sweet fuck all was going to feature us and four other bands. A 'battle of the bands' competition with a Seymour Stein-sanctioned record deal going to the winner. A talent show, boys ... *Opportunity fucking Knocks*.

We'd only been in America for a week, and we were sick of the sight of each other. We hadn't properly rehearsed. And I was para-lysed with an anxiety that I couldn't control. I couldn't cope. I couldn't deal with the pressure. I just wanted to be home, back in Glasgow. For the madness to stop immediately.

The Razzle Rodeo Club was a disaster waiting to happen. The end of the band was coming. I guess I thought I'd just be helping it along. We were about to go on. When no-one was looking, I threw a bottle from behind one of the amps into the aggravated crowd, a weird mix of fucking hillbilly bikers and these young, punky kids. The resulting chaos may have happened anyway, but my action was the spark that ignited it.

I remember a young girl being nice to me. I remember her taking my photograph. I remember a big guy in a fucking denim waistcoat and a Stetson dragging her down from a table and across the front of the stage by her hair. I remember swinging my guitar and her being free of him. I remember looking at my arm. The blood. The ripped flesh. The exposed tendons. After that, every-thing remains clouded in an opioid blur.

The band continued on to San Francisco. Bingo told me later that Kenny McFadden took a cab to the Amoeba Records store in Haight-Ashbury, desperately searching for a guitarist who could fill in for me. The cheeky bastard. He came up short. The Hyptones had no choice but to pull out of the gig that could've changed our lives. It's hardly surprising they blamed me for the misfortunes that followed. Our money had run out. Kenny McFadden bought a plane ticket with what we had left and flew home on his own. The others had to wait, sleeping in Jesus Castro's van until Ronnie Mason sorted their airfares from Glasgow.

My expensive stay in a Phoenix hospital lasted a week. I was discharged following surgery to reconnect the severed flexor tendons. My fingers and wrist were placed in a bent position to keep tension off the repair. A tight boxer's dressing and a plastic splint would maintain the shape for three months. Another surgery, I was warned, would be likely once back home in Scotland. I didn't get it. Didn't see the point. My strumming hand had no movement. There would be no more guitar sounds, jangly or otherwise, for the foreseeable future.

I also found myself in San Francisco. That's not an acknowledgement of some personal enlightenment; I just don't recall getting there from the hospital almost a fortnight after the rest of the band had flown home. I had flight tickets. I had money, which, once again, thanks to Annabelle's dad, had been wired to us. I had Ronnie Mason's daughter with me, and we had time to kill. As if I had emerged from a period of amnesia, I suddenly had a different relationship with the Masons.

2

Reef concocted this wild, romantic story that fate had brought him and me together. I went along with it – that he'd randomly broken into a house in Dennistoun, had seen my Fender Jaguar copy propped up against an armchair and, rather than stealing it, had threaded a note through the strings:

I'M GETTING A BAND TOGETHER. YOU IN?

The apocryphal tale concluded with me calling the telephone number on the flipside, and him paying for the damage to the back door he'd jemmied.

Had this been true, my da would've killed him, resurrected him, and then fucking killed him all over again. But it was a cool story, and when the records started selling, the *NME* and *Melody Maker* and *Sounds*, and all the others, lapped it up.

The facts were a bit less interesting. And contained a truth I wanted to remain buried.

Brian Mason was Annabelle's wee brother. The Hyptones was Brian Mason's band. He started it. But that later became too awkward for Reef to admit. Brian and I played youth football together in the late seventies. We weren't particularly friendly, initially, but as I started to drift towards music and away from football, he recognised a kindred spirit and drifted with me. We bonded over The Velvet Underground, The Monkees, The Dramatics, Curtis Mayfield. Elmore Leonard, Jack Kerouac. *Dog Day Afternoon*. American counterculture. Even then, we were always looking west.

We should fucken jam a wee bit. See where it leads, he said.

So, we did. We hung about. Heading into Glasgow city centre on the bus. Stealing Penguin Classics from the bookshops, strings from the guitar shops, sleeves from the record shops. If I wanted cool clothes, Brian would go into Flip and come out with a pair of stolen jeans under the ones he had on when he went in. We stole golf balls from Greaves Sports even though neither of us played the game. We sold them to those who did. It was exciting. He was good to be around back then. Brian Mason made me feel that anything was possible.

Brian lived in the posh houses over in Mount Vernon. We spent weeks on end at his house. Watching old music videos on his da's VCR. Strumming away to rare records we played on the Dansette in his room. Me eyeing up his gorgeous sister, Annabelle, any chance that I could get.

There was this one beautiful summer night; one of those evenings when you become convinced the sun won't ever set. It'll just hang around the periphery of the horizon, hiding for a bit, and then burst back into life in an hour or so. We were lying on the eighteenth fairway at Sandyhills. Smoking grass. Drinking the Buckfast monks' sickly tonic wine. Staring straight up at a velvet purple sky, peppered with thousands of tiny diamond studs, sparkling away just for us.

Wish ah could move away fae here, Brian said.

Aw aye? Where tae? I asked him.

Ah'd be aw'right in Norway, he said. Ye know, livin' in that eternal sunshine where aw these notions ae night an' day lose their meanin'.

Jesus, that's fucken deep, I said.

Aw ower the world, cunts are bein' characterised by stress an' depression. They're basically fucken trapped by the clock. Ah want tae be in a time-free zone where ah can live ma life tae suit maself.

In Norway? I said.

Aye, he answered. Whit's wrong wi' Norway?

Would it no' be pitch-black for the other six months ae the year? I said.

Get tae fuck wi' yer negativity, he said, laughing. Bottle-half-empty bastart, ye!

I remember him there, on his back strumming this little melody. A phrase forming from a series of alternating major-seventh chords. Then being extended out into the depth of the universe: 'a melancholic interpretation of a world that is simultaneously beautiful and impossibly sad.' He used those words. I wrote them down when I got home.

Jamie, ye need tae up yer expectations, mate, he gently sang. Dae ye believe in God? he asked me.

A *Norse* god? Aye, ah think ah'm startin' tae, I said, staring out at the vastness of space above us, high on ounces of the East End's best underground weed, internal wiring warming from the alcohol glow, the gentle sounds coming from this simple instrument tugging my heart out of my chest.

Ah don't, said Brian.

He was denying the Almighty.

But the devil, on the other hand ... that cunt's the real deal, man.

I laughed so abruptly that it brought on hiccups that took over an hour to shake. He lifted himself up. He reached into his jacket and pulled out a rolled-up bar towel. Inside it was a small syringe and a rusty teaspoon.

Want a hit? he asked.

Naw, I said.

A fear of injections triggered by a traumatic visit to an impatient dentist has persisted from early childhood to the present day.

He's workin' me fae behind, he said. The devil's in control ae the plunger.

Whit, yer gettin' rammed up the shitter fae a big scaly cock?

Aye. Sold ma arse tae him years ago, he said.

He reclined. Slowly, slow-motion slow, down onto his back.

Aw, fuck, man. It's total fucken magic, Jamie, he said, his speech slowing too. A million fucken pin-prick sensations aw...

Ah'm makin' a list, I told him. The Satanic orchestra. Aw the bams fae round here that've flogged their souls tae the big man for a wee taste ae the fire in the veins. You'll be at the top ae it, I told him. I looked at him. His eyes were closed. Mouth slightly open.

I'd heard of the Masons. Everyone in the East End had. 'See him, he's in the Masons' was a jibe regularly aimed at a referee making unfair decisions in football matches against our team. But one time, early in my first season in the squad, I heard an opponent shout 'See him, he's one ae the Masons' when a fight on the pitch was about to break out with Brian at the centre of it. The warning was as effective at dispersing the aggro as a water cannon. Space cleared around Brian, and I immediately knew who he was. The son of Ronnie Mason. A man who'd allegedly had a fourteen-year-old kid kneecapped for scratching his Bentley with a bike pedal.

Thankfully, Brian's da was never around in those first months, when we were trying to get the band going. But then he was, and the atmosphere changed. Colder than the Arctic. I reckoned Ronnie had been inside and just got out, but I didn't ask. His da was in 'the business', Brian told me. He left it at that. So, when Ronnie was at large we steered clear of his place. I missed seeing Annabelle. But Brian was more relaxed over at mine. We mucked about with the guitars in my room at nights. Practising, getting better. Learning from each other, and from our records. We were composing lovely, intricate melodies and chord sequences. Becoming more confident and assured. Brian scribbling unusually pained but beautiful words. Lines and lines of poetry on sheets and sheets of paper. Both of us just waiting for the musical alchemy to make them soar.

The Hyptones, he said. That's a fucken great name, int'it?

Aye, suppose, I said.

Like a proper, gallus beat combo, he laughed.

That antiquated tone of his.

Beat combo? I replied. Get a listen tae yerself.

But that was us. We were off and running. A partnership of equals. Those friendships that we make in our teenage years, they often come to define us. It may not seem like it at the time, but, if we are lucky, we gravitate towards people who reflect how we see our better selves. We move from the confines of a primary-school environment into the expansion of a secondary-school one. It's daunting and exciting at the same time. We crave security and identity. We forage about, looking for those who share common ground – football, music, clothes, haircuts. But attraction comes down to one thing: we look for us, but a better, cooler, more confident version. One without the flaws, the insecurities, the inherited fuck-ups learned from our fucked-up parents. I identified a better self in Brian Mason. I loved him, and for a time in fourth year, thought I was *in* love with him.

Chico Chalmers and I went to the same school. Everybody knew Chico, or Chic as he preferred to be called. He was a legendary joyrider, sparking cars from the age of fourteen. Despite his widespread infamy, Chic was never caught. He'd set fire to a chemistry classroom by dropping a large slice of potassium metal into 45ml of concentrated hydrochloric acid. The story made the front page of the *Daily Record* and Chico became famous locally for an STV News interview in which he claimed an elderly teacher had written '45' and not '15' on the blackboard.

Ah was simply followin' orders, he said, straight-faced, straight down the camera lens and into the nation's living rooms. We'd all left school years earlier, but I recalled that, during a spell of detention in my final year, I found out that Chic had a drum kit.

Chic was pals with Billie McAllister. Billie had a reputation around Dennistoun for being harder than reinforced concrete. She was a karate black belt. She'd been in bands, and our paths had crossed a few times, as often happens with youngsters trying to do their thing around a local music scene. She collected the cards at the Gala Bingo. I sent her a note via my mam on one of her Wednesday nights. Intrigued, Billie turned up at my place late one night. She brought Chic Chalmers. I called Brian. He came round. We kicked it around a bit, unplugged. We had a go at the Velvets' 'What Goes On'. Three of us knew it, and Chic picked it up instinctively. Tapping it out on a metal biscuit tin. And just like that, we had a four-piece band.

Brian played his sister a couple of early songs we'd taped. His was a winsome sigh of a singing voice, and I was far too shy for vocal duties.

Jesus, get a singer, she said. You need one.

Annabelle told her friend Cheryl Malcolm about the band. Cheryl volunteered Keith, her brother.

Anythin' tae get him off the Bob Hope, she pleaded.

Cheryl dragged her reluctant brother to a cheap rehearsal room Billie had found. Keith was bored shitless and desperate to be anywhere else but he eventually agreed to sing for us. To get Cheryl off his case, I suspect. But he did this amazing version of 'Queen Bitch'. Hairs were rising on the back of my neck, let me tell you. We pleaded; he relaxed a bit. And then Keith – whose mates called him Reefer Madness – was in. Chic shortened it to Reef. And everybody liked him. He had a magnetism. He could – when the mood took him, as when doing the Bowie song – command a room. He had physical presence and, strangely for a dopehead, ambition too. So we had a good singer who, it transpired, could compose interesting, provocative lyrics about subjects as diverse as the Velvet Revolution, Three Mile Island, or Sid and Nancy at the Chelsea Hotel.

Our first proper gig was an end-of-term thing at Whitehill Secondary School in 1981. To his delight, Chic got apprehended while bringing in the gear. A teacher recognised him and presumed he was there to steal it. We were good on that first night. Scraping the edge of 'great' on others. People were regularly talking about us in those terms. It was our relatives and their pals after the early gigs, admittedly, but once we started to get opportunities on the West of Scotland pub circuit, a loyal following grew. I was seeing the same faces in front of us at The Spaghetti Factory, The Rock Garden, and Strathclyde University, and when we supported The Wake at Henry Wood Hall. But always, at every gig, there was Annabelle. And it eventually dawned on me that I was the reason for that, not Brian.

3

Kenny McFadden became the band's manager before we knew we needed one. Kenny coached the football team where Brian Mason and I first met aged fifteen. Kenny was a good coach. Where other youth coaches built a team with the tallest, most aggressive players at the back hoofing it forwards, Kenny stuck to ideas about possession and passing. He was ahead of his time in that regard. Kenny wasn't that much older than us. Ten years or so. That was unusual in the mid-seventies. Every football coach I encountered back then was a fat, balding, middle-aged drunk with a sergeant-major attitude and a belief that training was only about fitness. Kenny McFadden was different. He'd played the game in the juniors, and he understood how to explain the finer points of it to others. We liked him. And we trusted him. And a couple of years later, when Brian was after advice about organising gigs and equipment, Kenny seemed like the obvious person to ask for help.

At the start of the eighties, everything was looking up. Our music was good and getting better. Annabelle and I had hooked up properly. But right from the off, the relationship was a demanding one. Annabelle expected a level of commitment I couldn't provide. We fell out often. But the making-up sex was great, and regular. I remember one time. It was October 1981. I'd stood her up at a café on the night of my birthday. Brian had tickets for The Clash at the Apollo, and there was only going to be one winner. I hadn't told her. Wrongly assumed Brian had. We argued the following day, and then I took mushrooms and she let me fuck her against the cold slab of a Victorian gravestone, high, on the slopes of the Necropolis. Apology accepted.

I've never been the type to walk down the street with a spring in my step. Contentment has never been my middle name, you'll understand. But around this time, I was happy. Or happier. Life – even the argumentative parts of it – was good. Kenny was making plans. Always making plans. It didn't matter that he rarely delivered on them. We all got swept up in his boundless optimism.

There were signs though. I can see that now. I didn't then. I just thought Brian was increasingly full of shite, something we were all prone to at that age. I recall one night. We were in my room, listening to *The Idiot* on repeat. Him, staring out the window up into the darkness. I could see his right arm twitching. Fingers clicking incessantly. He needed a fix but knew my room was totally off limits. He'd curbed the spiking, at least in my presence. But his body was betraying him.

Jesus, that fucken music sounds like a car alarm goin' off, he said.

What – Iggy? I asked.

He was hearing something different from me.

Aye. It's squeal-squeal-squealin' right intae my brain, he said.

He started thumping his temple with the fingers that had been clicking. Every other part of his body was motionless. The only movement was the arm and the fingers and their impact on his head. I laughed at him.

Sit doon, maggot brain, I said. Ye're freakin' me out, man.

Ah cannae, he said.

Why no'?

Got tae be somewhere.

Where?

Ah'm waitin'.

Waitin' for what?

No' whit ... who?

Who the fuck are ye waitin' for then? Yer man.

His name's Death, he said.

I laughed again. Was it a bit from a new *Young Ones* episode that I'd missed? Something that depressive Neil had moaned about from last Friday. Just before Vyvyan had rattled a frying pan into the back of the hippy's skull.

Ah'm waitin' for death, Brian said, but louder. Not by ma own hand though. Ah want some other cunt tae dae it. You, mibbe.

Me? I said. Ye want me tae murder ye?

That'd be *ultra* cool, he said.

Tae get killed? I said, sniggering, which wasn't helping his mood. What's cool about that, Bri?

He wasn't amused by my reaction.

An' then you're at ma funeral. Haudin' a cord. Lowerin' me doon intae the hole.

Fuck sake, mate, lay off they fucken narcotics, eh? I said. Anyway, thought you'd be headed for the furnace wi' the rest ae us.

Ah want buried. Wi' the worms burrowin' right intae ma cortex.

Christ Almighty. Why?

Dunno. Fucken gone anyway, in't ye? he said.

Aye, well, you're totally fucken gone, ya mad bastard.

He was stock-still, apart from the rapidly clicking fingers. Still gazing out at the sky, like he was searching for the mothership that his uncontrolled digits were summoning.

The mystery, he said.

Only fucken mystery around here is you, ya fucken weirdo, I said.

It'll be unsolved, he said. An open case.

Ye've obviously thought this through, I said.

The Idiot hit the run-offs. The idiot next to me kept on, breathlessly angry now.

You an' me. John an' Paul, right? Lennon kills McCartney. In a fit ae fucken jealousy. He wants aw the credit. No' content wi' sharin' the genius. John helps tae bury Paul, then John tops himsel'. Blows his brains out. He cannae cope wi' the guilt. That's what's fucken cool, man, he said. Tae be remembered like that. Doomed brothers.

You're a bizarre dude, I told him.

Aye, he said. An' you're a cunt!

Checkmate.

Reef and I were growing closer. We'd become the new partnership. Although Reef took the band seriously, he was less intense, less unpredictable than Brian. Easier to read. And to be with. I'd sketch out jangly guitar lines and capture them on C-30 cassettes. He'd take them and work out lyrics. And then we'd present them as rough ideas to the band. Chic and Bingo would pick it up quickly. Bingo played intuitively. Nothing phased her. Despite his bombastic attitude to everything else, Chic was a subtle drummer in the Charlie Watts mould. His da won the drumkit in an *Evening Times* competition years earlier and sold it to Chic. He learned rhythms by listening to his sister's *Let It Bleed* LP. We did a passable cover of 'Gimme Shelter', at Chic's insistence, as the last song of every gig.

Brian became quieter in the band's company; but ever more

volatile when it was just him and me. He didn't participate in band discussions. Missed rehearsals regularly. The addictions were taking hold of him. Transforming him. Ruining him. Eventually, we didn't need two guitarists. I'd adapted to play lead and rhythm chords simultaneously. We were merely accommodating Brian. I was constantly making excuses for his explosive moods. Time passed; he no longer fit. A square peg; aggressive and abusive. I felt guilty – still do, naturally – about Brian being edged out. The band was his, truthfully, but by the end he was on a different, darker planet from the rest of us.

Brian fought with me over the money Ronnie had given Annabelle to help us out. Brian didn't want the band to accept anything from his dad, but the rest of us had nothing. A handout for proper rehearsal space and better equipment wasn't easy to turn down, regardless of where Brian claimed it had come from. Everything came to a head when Ronnie's money funded a demo session recorded at The Hellfire Club that led to our debut single being pressed and distributed by a struggling Glasgow independent label that owed Ronnie favours.

It's no' fucken happenin', said Brian.

Beggars an' choosers, we told him.

Fuck the lot ae ye'se then, he shouted.

There was pushing and shoving, just like football players squaring up to each other, but stopping short of any real violence. We had fractured though. The needle and the damage done.

Ah want ma notebooks back, he yelled, referring to those old reams of paper and the poetic words they bore.

Roll them up an' fucken smoke them, ya junkie, I said to him. They were total shite, anyway, I lied.

Ah fucken will, he said.

And the whole point of the argument was lost.

Brian called everyone a cunt, then, before storming out, spat in my face for good measure. I let it pass. Collateral damage. It was over and done with.

He phoned that night, from a call box. And he reversed the charges. Not to apologise. To accuse me of having stolen everything from him, leaving him with nothing. He made no sense. Buzzed from all the junk he was spiking into his arms. It would've been better if I'd said nothing in response. But instead, I said:

Cheer up, mate. Jesus, things could be a helluva lot worse. Ye could be a Rangers supporter tae.

He didn't appreciate the logic, but from the outside looking in, it's so obviously true. Unless you're being strapped into the chair and the metal plate is being fixed to your shaved skull before a charge shocks the life out of you, then yes, someone else will always be worse off.

Fucken cunt, ye! he said. You better watch yersel.

A week later, Brian moved out of his family's house in Mount Vernon. Or was thrown out, depending on whether you believed him or Annabelle. He moved into this filthy Bridgeton squat saturated with opiates and their abusers, and with items of his sister's stolen jewellery riding on his hip.

As I said, I felt bad about the way it ended. Except, it hadn't ended.

4

August 1982. The Hyptones debut single, funded by Ronnie Mason, was released. Annabelle made it clear to us that her father's support was conditional on Brian having no access to the finances.

Fine by me, I told her.

This arrangement put my girlfriend in charge of the meagre band accounts. Despite the proliferation of 'she wears the trousers' piss-taking from the others, all seemed content with this arrangement. Especially since Annabelle had promised them a weekly subsistence if the record took off.

The single secured airplays – thanks to Reef pounding the

streets with flyers and posting cassettes to local and national radio stations, rather than any acuity on Kenny McFadden's part. We got swept along in the buzz created in Glasgow by Postcard Records, and that was all fine. Our stock rose. The gigs multiplied. Fifteen pounds a week per band member became the established remuneration. We became a slick touring unit, with Kenny McFadden organising and driving us further afield. We had also constructed a bombastic set. Musically aggressive, lyrically sharp. It brought more favourable attention. Wider appreciation. And then, three weeks before Christmas, Brian Mason resurfaced.

How's it goin', lads ... Bingo?

The high-pitched, drawn-out gallus drawl of the Glasgow smackhead; as unexpected as it was unwelcome. I turned sharply and there he was, fidgeting and toe-tapping in front of the Tiffany's stage, acoustic guitar draped down his back, tied to him by a piece of frayed blue rope. No-one knew what to say. Eventually Bingo:

You aw'right, Brian? What's happenin', man?

Where'll ah plug in? said Brian.

We're done, mate, I said.

We were almost finished with the soundcheck. But that wasn't what I meant.

Nae problem, pal, said Brian.

The tone betrayed the false bravado. He was zooming. Eyes like kaleidoscopes. Unrecognisable from the shy fifteen-year-old he once was.

When are we oan then, J? Brian clambered awkwardly onto the high stage.

The guitar strap broke. The instrument fell and the neck split. He seemed unconcerned. I could see anxious looks coming from the burly road crew working for the headliners.

Is he wi' you? A thick Dublin accent from the midst of them.

Aye, said Brian, in response. Ah'm in The Hyptones. In fact, ah *am* The fucken Hyptones, in't that right, ya cunts?'

The mask slipped. The mood shifted. Brian was here for aggro, or retribution, or both; the drugs coursing around his system providing him with armour against the coming attack. Helpfully, or unhelpfully, depending on the perspective, the rest of the band decided to leave me to deal with Brian. Kenny McFadden was, once again, absent at a time I needed him most.

Brian, mate, fuck sake ... look at the state ae ye, I said. Ye need tae get yerself sorted. Cleaned up, mate. Maybe then ye can come back.

I hoped this olive branch would temper the inevitable on-slaught.

Sorted? he countered, arms out, open and inviting attack. Ah'm totally fucken sorted, pal. This is ma fucken band, mate. *Mine!* The Hyptones, eh? Ma songs. Aw those lyrics, ya cunt ... mine ... Ma da's dodgy fucken cash proppin' it aw up. Whit else needs sortin'?

Another guitar got lifted from its stand. Thick black strap un-strapped, Brian readied himself to swing it. I weighed up the options of letting him. And of it connecting. How sore might that be? What damage would it do? Would our band be dropped from our major hometown gig supporting Irish wonder boys U2? That night would be the biggest crowd we'd played to yet. A massive op-portunity for us. Wasted though he was, Brian knew that too. That's why he'd shown his desperate face. It might come down to money eventually, I figured, but for now it was just a battle of wills.

Fuck it. Just take the punishment. I owed him that at least. Despite it being his own doing, his fall from the band's grace didn't sit easily with me. If it came to it, I could explain it away as a minor falling-out between former friends. Musical differences happened all the time. In the end, Lennon didn't have to kill McCartney. He just needed to walk out on him.

You're done, Brian, I told him. Yer no' in the band anymore. You're a fucken liability an' we cannae have that now.

Now that we're getting somewhere is what I meant.

That you talkin'? he said. Or fucken Yoko?

What d'ye mean by that?

You fucken know, ya cunt. She's pullin' yer strings, ma cow ae a sister.

Gie's peace, Brian, I said. I moved closer to him. But only to limit the backlift. He didn't swing the guitar though. The fake swagger went out of him. He looked deflated. Resigned. As if a lever inside him had switched his status from 'wired' to 'withdrawn'. He calmly reached into a pocket. And then, just when it seemed the storm had passed, he pulled out what I thought, in the late afternoon gloom of the unlit Tiffany's stage, was a knife. Instinctively, I headbutted him. Hard. Caught him on the bridge of the nose. The bone cracked loudly. Blood spurted from the burst. Heroin had consumed his bulk, leaving little but skin and sinew. Brian went down, backwards, and easily. Into Chic's drumkit. A foot going through the floor tom. An arm sending a high-hat careering across the stage.

What the fuck's goin' on here? I heard from behind me.

This cunt's just pulled a fucken chib, I shouted.

Breathless. Disbelieving. Brian clawed himself up. The roadies rushed in, tattooed fists and steel capped boots laying into him, putting him down again. His pitiful face stared up at me. As three of the crew bundled him out, my only thought was, *Thank fuck I won't have to see him again.*

I stood on something. I looked down, and it glinted as I rolled it with the sole of my shoe. It wasn't a blade. It was a ballpoint pen. My da's inscribed silver pen. I'd handed it to Brian three years earlier in my room. He'd written pages of lyrics with it. He'd kept the pen. For luck, he said. I kept the words and the music he'd written with it.

Three days later, the stupid bastard was dead.

He'd gone back to Mount Vernon. He must've watched everybody leaving and broke in when no-one was home. He ran a bath. Injected the smack. Washed it down with a carafe of Pomagne. And fucking drowned himself. Ironic, since we'd both previously confessed that drowning was our biggest fear. A sodden handwritten note was found on the bathroom floor. The ink had run, rendering most of the words illegible. Apart from the final sentence:

That's one soul less on yer fiery list, ya cunt!

When Annabelle told me this, my first thought was to ask what a carafe was. I followed that by quizzing her on how long they had been out, since running a bath at our house took about three hours. Everything about it screamed middle-class indulgence, I told her.

The night before the funeral I had a dream. In it, though Brian was slight by the end, I strained under the weight of the coffin as we carried him into a chapel. And then again as we lifted him off the wooden runners at the grave. The heavy box determined to push me down into the soft turf. Then, a hand on my shoulder. Ronnie's. Standing immediately to my right. Sensing my struggle but not comprehending the root of it. We lowered Brian into the ground. Close family were preparing to recall fonder memories and recollections of whatever joy he brought them during his twenty-one years. I was cord seven. The melancholic minor seventh. Neither happy, nor sad. Ultimately relieved.

Forget him, son, said Ronnie. He was a cunt ae a boy. Better off dead. You're aw that matters now.

I looked around but only the two of us were left. Everyone else had gone. Ronnie handed me a spade and the two of us filled the hole with soil as torrential rain that could strip a tattoo from your skin turned the grave's edge to thick mud, our ankles sinking down and disappearing into it, and me screaming:

Yer a long time starin' at the lid, Brian, ya cunt!

I borrowed a suit from Kenny McFadden for the actual funeral. Turned up the trouser legs and safety-pinned the side panels to make it fit better. Reef fabricated an excuse, which I had to pass to Annabelle. Bingo and Chic showed up for the buffet. The service was well attended by the great and the good and the debtors and the creditors who orbited Ronnie Mason's world. There was nothing revealed about Brian that I didn't already know: talented, young, determined. A great young footballer and promising musician. The world at his feet. Taken from us far too early, etc, etc.

He'd have fucking hated the false piety. The daft cunt took *himself* from us, after all. And I was ashamed because, despite the intolerable pain it was causing my girlfriend, I was glad he had. It was one less explosive distraction. One less aggravating obstruction. One less soul on my fiery list.

The regret I was sure I could deal with. Like all bad things, it would surely pass.

5

A week or so after the Razzle Club fiasco, Annabelle and I reached San Francisco, and I won money on an unexpected Giants victory over the L.A. Dodgers. I didn't understand baseball, the structure of the innings or the player positions. But there was a winner and a loser, and that was enough for me to speculate on.

Annabelle and I spent the time and the unexpected cash boost on getting married. I can't confirm or deny if I was the instigator or not, but that doesn't matter. The reasons I did this aren't complicated: everyone had gone home. She'd stuck with me – despite my mistreatment of her. After what I'd done to her brother, committing to her just seemed like the right thing to do.

I remember that time in California as being an all-too briefly happy one. Annabelle looked beautiful, which to be fair to her, she did most of the time anyway, and without effort. And I felt like a hulking weight had been surgically removed from my shoulders. The painkiller buzz must have been a big contributor to the positive view I took on our future life together, a young, newlywed couple in our early twenties. We had no income, no obvious future direction to speak of, but for me at least, the benefit of no impending band commitments. The American dream was over for The Hyptones. Seymour Stein's admiring gaze had settled on the winners of the talent contest, a group called Love Tractor from the American South.

With no organised marketing effort to sustain it, 'Independent State of Mind' dropped like a stone out of the UK charts. The media had no interest in our disastrous trek across North America. We'd held off on signing a deal for an album, hoping to return triumphant from the States, stimulating a lucrative bidding war amongst the majors. The possibility of that had gone. I was in no rush to head back home, but with no possibility of extending our visas, the only option was booking one-way tickets on the first available flight out of San Francisco. The last two seats available. Annabelle and I separated by the length of the plane. The honeymoon very much over, I didn't even consider asking if the man seated next to me would be prepared to swap with my new wife. I often ponder the trajectory our lives might have taken if he had agreed to.

6

Inky? Jesus Christ, it's difficult to know where to start.

His name is Innes. He is my older brother. Everybody called him Inky, going right back to his primary-school days. Only our ma stuck with 'Innes' when talking to, or about, him. My da used the nickname warmly. We had different fathers but mine preferred the son that wasn't biologically his. I had no problem with this. My da was a bastard who bequeathed me nothing other than his selfish, bad-tempered belligerence. And his love of the bookies. Inky was my relentlessly optimistic, bottle-half-full counterpoint. White to my black. But I didn't resent him one iota. I envied him his sunny disposition. I loved him.

As we grew from children into men, Inky became more assured. More self-reliant. More certain about the future he wanted. I think it was this quality more than any other that endeared him to my da. He was less trouble than I was.

Ah'm gonnae be a fireman, he'd said.

It was during a Christmas Day dinner in the early seventies. The fire engine he'd been given that morning was in front of him.

An' what about you, son? our ma asked me.

Ah want tae be him, I'd said, pointing at the television set as Marc Bolan glittered and glammed his way through 'Ride a White Swan'.

My father's disgust was evident. Fucken typical, he'd said; my ma chastising him for the festive profanity.

'Wee poofter' was thrown in for good measure.

George! she shouted, and the route map to a battering was set. It was just a question of which one of us would be on the receiving end.

Ah've asked Suzy tae marry me.

Inky informed me of his plans in my tiny bedroom in early 1979. He'd just turned nineteen. A little more than eighteen months older than me. But stronger, physically and psychologically, and infinitely more mature.

What? I said. Surprised, but *not* surprised if that makes any sense.

She said aye, he told me. Ah want you tae be ma best man.

Fuck me. When? I asked him.

1985, he replied.

And I laughed because it seemed ridiculous for someone so young and from our background to have their early adult life mapped out so clearly.

What if she dumps ye? I said.

I knew she wouldn't though. Guys with solid prospects like Inky didn't get dumped. Young working-class lassies had stereo-typically domestic priorities back then. Fucking gap years schmoozing around the Andes? Aye, right.

A week after their engagement became official, Inky had taken up his invitation to the Cowcaddens training centre in Cheapside Street. He had his eyes assessed. His height and weight checked. He then underwent chest x-rays before a selection day at the Fire Department HQ in Hamilton. Inky passed the interview with flying colours, a proud George announced, when the envelope containing the job offer was opened by him, and not the person it was addressed to. All that paternal pride building up over two decades itching to be released.

Inky went to Gullane for his residential training. Without his equilibrating influence, the situation he'd left behind worsened. Why was I not more like my brother? Why couldn't I get a proper job? Why couldn't I just fucking grow up? Why didn't I just fuck off? Inky was the pacifier our family needed. I was glad when his stint away was over. Those months as a punchbag were taking their toll.

Inky's subsequent probationary posting was in London Road. He returned to stay at home with us. I can't recall exactly when this was, but it must've been mid eighty-one. Inky had brought home the Bunnymen album, *Heaven Up Here*. I spent so much time playing it, learning the chords to 'Over the Wall', that he told me just to keep it. He was great like that, always giving me stuff of his that he knew I liked but couldn't afford myself.

Inky was responsible. He saved his money. He planned and

prepared, and all the while I courted the disdain of both my parents by messing about with Brian, then Reef. But even when the band started to take off, my parents still couldn't find it in themselves to offer praise. Encouragement only came from my half-brother.

Five years after picking up the *Evening Times* and clipping out the Strathclyde Fire Brigade job advert, Inky passed his final exam first time. He waited until getting a full-time posting on the south-side before arranging his wedding. Then, the week before the band flew to America, he bought a lovely wee first-floor flat. Inky was the only person I knew who had a mortgage. And owning prop-erty outright was something that only rich people like Ronnie Mason did.

With no forward planning whatsoever, I eventually followed my brother's lead and left home. Having little alternative, Anna and I had moved in at Mount Vernon on our return from America in the late summer of 1983. For the first month or so, I was put in Brian's old room. And rather than break my legs, Ronnie let me work off the band's debts by first working in, and then eventually running, one of his betting shops just along from Parkhead Cross. And while he reluctantly accepted that Anna and I were still to-gether, Ronnie insisted on overseeing the legal annulment of our spontaneous American marriage. I was calmly informed of the change to our status one evening – and in the same sentence was asked to pass the salt. I didn't receive, nor did I ask for, any evi-dence of the annulment. This might've been for the best. I didn't have to contend with whatever justification was used. It mattered little to me anyway.

My ex-wife Anna went back to university or college or some-where, studying for a nursing degree. And, over time, we settled into a bearable if claustrophobic routine. Anna and I in her room, dutifully fucking each other in respectful silence to pass the time between my shifts and her lectures. Ronnie ducking in and out, and Brenda, his third wife, keeping so much to herself that weeks could pass without encountering her at all. All things considered, it was still far better than life at my ma and da's place.

In typical fashion, Inky had cultivated a better relationship with my former bandmates than I now enjoyed. I saw Bingo here and there, but she had moved on without a backwards look. Chic and Reef, on the other hand, retained the bitterness forged in Phoenix two years earlier. Both believed I had robbed them of their future. Both now tolerated me solely because I was Inky's brother, and his best man. The organiser of his stag do.

The front door to Inky's flat was open. I should've been there at 1.00pm. I was over an hour late. I can't recall why. It's unimportant except that it led to me hearing Chic, typically louder than he needed to be.

Where *is* that annoying cunt? he said. Jeez, fucken best man, tae.

I now stood at the end of the hall, eavesdropping on the conversation coming from Inky's living room. It was the day of Live Aid. I didn't share the nation's anticipation. I thought it tasteless. The richest people in the world exhorting members of the public to dig deep into already strained domestic budgets to excuse long-term inaction from governments. Meanwhile, the rich people on stage had their profiles raised. Wonder how many artists would've battered down Bob Geldof's door for a slot if they'd had to donate all profits from their rocketing record sales for the year following their performance. Live Aid was certainly momentous, and yet still seemed to stir up some resentments among my former band-mates.

Fucken pish, this. That could've been us oan there, instead ae Nick bastart Kershaw.

I heard Reef's voice but couldn't see him through the crack in the open door.

Aye, an' if ma auntie had baws she'd be ma uncle, said Inky.

Just sayin', said Reef.

Well don't. If it hudnae been for Jamie, none ae you balloons would've been tae America, never mind on *Top ae the Pops*, so shut the fuck up.

Inky always stuck up for me when my so-called mates revisited what they had lost and who they considered was to blame for depriving them of their future.

Cannae help it sometimes, said Chic.

I glimpsed on Inky's glass-topped table the powdery trails that must be emboldening the redundant drummer.

We were aw set back then ... a deal wi' yon Seymour Stein lined up an' everythin'. Then that daft cunt gets his arm cut open an' the game's a fucken bogey.

Christ Almighty, that wis hardly his fault, wis it? said Inky.

Ye get one chance in life – an' that wis oors. Jamie refusin' tae leave an' fly back hame immediately an' deal with the media. That's what fucked us, said Reef.

Auld news, son, said my brother. Move on wi' yer life, for Christ's sake.

Ye watch somethin' like this, an' it really hits ye hard, Inky.

Well, he might be a miserable bastart, but he's still ma brother – and ma best man, so lay off it th' day, right?

Aye. S'pose, said Reef.

Qué será, eh, lads? No' many other cunts in ma Job Centre queue have done a line wi' the wee Madonna, like.

Now this *was* a surprise. Kenny McFadden. Where the fuck had he sprung from? And more importantly, why had Inky allowed him to come on the stag? Kenny had disappeared like snow off a baker's roof when the American dream was dead.

Right, said Inky. Knock the greetin' oan the heid. Talkin' ae which, get these doon ye'se. Ah've got a stag night tae get tae. Ah'll leave Jamie a note on the front door. Tell him we'll get him an' the other yins at Tennents.

I moved swiftly backwards. Before slinking down the tenement's stairs and heading for the comparative safety of the betting shop, I heard my brother shout:

Hey, which one ae you lazy bastarts left the front door open? Were ye'se aw born in Tollcross Park?

Took yer time, eh? Inky said, spotting me.

Sneaking in late, fifty quid down on the Shawfield dogs, and hoping for both failures to go unnoticed despite it being my responsibility for organising the day. He was at the bar completing an order.

He'll get these, he informed the barman, before winking at me.

Ten poun' fifty, son, said the barman.

Can ye add another pint ae lager on, mate, I said.

Aye. That'll be eleven pounds an' fifty-five pence.

I watched him pour as men lined the busy bar two deep, jostling for position and his attention.

Looks like Charlie Nicholas, him, said the barman.

The television above the gantry showed Bono from U2 dancing with a young woman he'd plucked out of the crowd. You had to hand it to the cunt, he was an entertainer. That night at Tiffany's – the last time I saw Brian Mason – the Irish singer was clambering all over the speaker stacks, just one misplaced footing away from breaking his fucking neck. It was exhilarating to watch.

'Member ah told ye they'd be bigger than the Beatles? A familiar voice from behind me. It was Reef.

Aye, ah remember, I said.

Wish that'd been us up there, he said.

It was the theme of the day.

How ye been, Jamie?

Ah'm fine. You?

No' too bad, pal.

We both stared at the screen. Seconds became minutes, and the minutes felt like hours.

Thinkin' ae gettin' another band goin', he said.

Aye. Ah thought ye might. I said this with an edge I hadn't intended.

Whit's that meant tae mean? He was suddenly aggrieved. I knew it wouldn't take much.

Eh? He'd caught me cold. What d'ye mean? I asked him.

Two anxious amateur boxers shadowing each other. Reluctant to land the first punch.

Ye bloody expect me tae hang about waitin' for you tae come tae yer senses then?

Mate, that's the last fucken thing ah expect, I said.

Silence. Staring.

Here's yer change, son. The barman's bell interrupted us. Back to our respective corners. We had nowhere else to go with this. So, he brushed past me. Off to the toilets. And if it hadn't already been, the tone was set for the rest of a tortuous and traumatic day.

We drifted from bar to pub, away from the West End. Knocked back from Henry Afrikas and Cardinal Follies, drawn further back east and closer to where we're from. To where we'll end up. It took three times as long for us to flow from Byres Road to Duke Street than for Phil Collins to appear at Wembley and then across the Atlantic at the John F. Kennedy stadium. Then again, the Genesis singer had more purpose. The original eleven comprised those I've noted, plus Inky's firefighting colleagues and Suzy's brothers, both of whom were paralytic by mid-evening and had either peeled away on their own or were left behind in the drunken debris.

This is a fucken shite stag, said Chic to the others, but loud enough for me to hear.

The boy deserves better, the accusation being levelled. Tequila slammers – and the added pickled mezcal worms for the stag – comprised the evening menu. I held the kitty. I was on the bell.

Drinks passed around one at a time since I still couldn't trust my right hand's grip with the weight of a tray. I was able to pace my own consumption; one to every three of theirs. The performances from London, and then later Philadelphia, were the talk of the town. Tattooed, muscular arms held aloft and around broad Glaswegian shoulders, prompted by the intoxicated spirit of benevolent aid for others less fortunate. There must be an answer, *Let It Be*.

Remember that time Reef fucked Madonna? said Chic as we staggered through the maze of Dennistoun streets, spilling kebab meat – and Inky spilling his stomach contents at regular intervals. Kenny McFadden muttered something unintelligible, and the drunken firemen laughed.

An' just before Jamie fucked all ae us, if memory serves, Reef added, slurring the words.

Fuck off, I said tamely.

The drunken firemen laughed again.

Aye, that wis oor time, said Chic.

He and I less incapacitated than the others.

The time ye fucken snorted Brian, thinkin' it was Charlie? *That* time, ye mean? I countered. Aye, fucken time ae oor lives, pal, right enough.

We were headed somewhere serious.

Is it no' time for you tae be hame wi yer Horlicks an' yer slippers, an' tuckin' in yer snobby missus? asked Chic. Ya borin' cunt, ye!

A fight burst out from the Variety Bar just ahead. It grabbed the attention. The pub was known locally as Shotgun Central. Passers-by could easily get caught in the crossfire. The tension between Chic and I simmered, and we took a strategic right on the corner. We strolled on beyond the packed boozer, down derelict, deserted industrial streets and back towards Inky's place across the river. But I couldn't let the former drummer's slight go.

Borin'? I said.

Whit? he answered.

Ye called me a borin' cunt.

Aye. So? Ye always have been. Her tae.

On the basis ae what?

He pondered this, and then said:

It's yer brother's stag an' ye've done fuck all that yer supposed tae. You're his best man, are ye no'?

Like what? Strip him bollock naked an' superglue his baws tae a lamppost? Somethin' like that ... like what *you'd* dae? I said.

Aye. Somethin' that he'll remember an' have a fucken laugh about for the rest ae his life. Spewin' the fucken worm's a bit tame, mate. Every cunt does that.

Chic had been winding me up all day and it had become impossible to ignore. I glanced at Inky, suspended between his drunken colleagues. Like exhausted soldiers carting a wounded, unconscious comrade off the battlefield. He wouldn't even remember anything we did to him. But with the booze clouding my perspective, Chic's goading made me feel like I'd let my brother down badly. That the night hadn't been special enough. The stag stories the other firefighters had told during the journey east wouldn't be getting a new chapter following this mediocre failure. I'd been a bad choice as best man and, once sober, Inky would realise it too.

Well? Chic said, finger in my chest.

Well whit? Get tae fuck, I said.

Fucken telt ye. Borin'. An' a bastardin' chicken, tae, he said.

Swinging a punch would've been pointless. Plus, that wasn't the way I'd have wanted Inky's stag night to be remembered. I breathed in. Looked down at my shoes. And then up towards the other side of the street. Desperate to fight back.

See that wee truck ower there? I said to Chic.

Whit about it? he answered.

We're gonnae tie Inky tae the back ae it, I said.

An' leave him in it overnight?

Aye.

Christ, ye took yer time, but finally ... the fucken best man has turned up, he said.

It took us almost half an hour. Inky was now strapped with our belts to the metal bar behind the cab. Shirt off, head down, arms stretched out like a crucified Jesus. My heart pounded. The firemen clapped. The former Hyptones drummer baited.

Why don't ye park it doon the street tae? said Chic. Away fae the streetlights where nae cunt can see it. That'd be funnier.

Steal a fucken truck ... without the keys? Aye, aw'right, ya dopey bastard.

Nae fucken trouble tae me, said Chic.

Five minutes later, Chic had broken into it and had wired the engine.

Oan ye go then, he taunted. Dae it, dae it, dae it, dae it, he sang.

The drunken firemen had wandered away. The entertainment was over for them.

I looked over, and Reef shook his head. Kenny McFadden mouthed *don't*. But I did. I climbed into the cab. I rolled down the window. I crunched the gears putting it in first. Handbrake off. I moved it a few feet, arm out of the window. My twisted fingers formed a V-sign.

Dae it, dae it, dae it, dae it.

Jamie, said Reef. Quietly, but I heard him. And I ignored him.

The road ahead was clear. No-one was around. Just a few feet would be enough. Into the darkness.

Dae it, dae it, dae it, dae it ... ya fucken pussy.

Anything to shut that aggravating cunt up.

The vehicle shunted. It moved more. It jerked. I accelerated. My head spun. My heart pounded in my chest. My hand struggled with the grip. I panicked. I couldn't see the road ahead. I couldn't remember which pedal was the brake and which one made it go faster.

Dae it, dae it, dae it, dae it, growing faint.

Careering. Accelerating. And then we were out of road. Sharply down and to the left. Down. And to the left.

There was shouting from behind me. And then nothing. The icy coldness of dirty water rushed into the cab through the open window. And then all went black, and all sound was extinguished.

7

Humility? It may yet become my only virtue.

The worst thing about the aftermath wasn't seeing Inky once he was well enough to leave hospital. It wasn't even watching Suzy as she rolled his wheelchair down a temporary wooden ramp at my parents' house. And it certainly wasn't the inevitable assault from my da, which left me with a depressed eye socket. It was appreciating just how much my momentary recklessness had altered the course of their entire lives. The terrible acknowledgement that I'd destroyed Suzy's chance of a family with the person she'd loved since they were both fourteen. People change so much during that formative decade from their mid-teens to mid-twenties. But the bond between Inky and Suzy had only strengthened. By contrast, Anna and I were merely a sticking plaster for each other's physical and psychological wounds. Arguably still are. My brother and his fiancée were the real thing. A love that endures; that survives. And it now had to survive the loss of his career; of him doing the one job that he'd always dreamed of. And it had to survive them finding a new home, now that his inaccessible first-floor flat was up for sale, before Suzy had even moved in.

On the instruction of Ronnie's solicitor, I stayed clear of my family, and all connected with them, for fear of making his job harder. My defence was a drunken prank gone tragically wrong. No provable *mens rea* – no intent, and therefore no crime, at least in relation to Inky. The lawyer dropped any reference to me acting on the encouragement of others at the scene.

It's of no consequence to the prosecution, he'd said. Plus, it'll play better with the court if you accept sole responsibility.

So I did. A guilty plea to the theft of the vehicle and the accompanying charges of driving with no insurance, no licence, and – obviously – driving while well over the limit. The punishment? A substantial fine, making me even more indebted to Ronnie Mason. A year of cleaning up Dennistoun as part of a community-service chain gang. And a seven-year ban from driving. I received a second battering. This time, a fully anticipated one from Annabelle's da. Punishment for the case drawing the interest of the newspapers and an unwanted media spotlight shining briefly on the Mason empire. It resulted in a spell on a Royal Infirmary ward. But it felt like a more appropriate sanction than the one the judge imposed.

On top of everything else, I was accumulating a significant personal deficit at the bookies I was supposed to be managing for Ronnie. My options were running out.

You're gonnae disappear, son, Ronnie said to me.

It was 1986. My twelve-month community payback order had just been completed. We were out in his car, with two of his associates in the back. Ronnie Mason's business, such as it was, couldn't afford the tabloid spotlight I was drawing. Sat there in the passenger seat, high up on Cathkin Braes, looking north over the city like it was the beginning of a *Taggart* episode, I was briefly reminded of Michael Corleone. His imminent sojourn to Sicily after murdering Sollozzo and the bent police captain, McCluskey, was tactical. A heroic return would be possible for him, but only after the years had passed and the memories had faded. I wouldn't be returning. I knew it was only his daughter's pleading – and my connection with Brian – that saved me from a more permanent disappearance deep down in the surrounding wetlands.

I departed Glasgow with the hundred pounds Ronnie gave me, the clothes I was standing in, and the case containing my Fender Villager twelve-string, the return of which was the only positive to emerge from the ashes of The Hyptones' implosion.

Ronnie Mason played fair by his daughter. Or so it had seemed to me at the time. He reached out. His contacts in London got me employment there. Low-level stuff. Filing and administrative duties for a Bermondsey-based used-car dealership. Followed by more dogsbody duties. But it paid for a room and about enough food to survive. I picked up some things cheaply. A mattress, a standard lamp, the odd chair from a local IKEA. Of course, anything I had – or added to – I subsequently sold to fund the low-volatility slot machines at The Trocadero.

Gambling is the ultimate high. That moment when your number comes up, your unfancied horse noses out in front, a lowly third-division team comes from behind to complete the unlikeliest of seven-game accumulators. There's nothing compares to surfing that dopamine rush. During those initial years away from Glasgow, I was the happiest I'd ever been. The weird paradox of my situation had given me a modicum of independence, without being constantly reminded of the weight of responsibility for the band's break-up. I was out of my father's firing line. And without the painful reminders of what I'd done to my brother. But then – as it always did – my luck turned. The numbers mocked me. Horses as non-starters. Tabs grew into inescapable debts. Gentle reminders given on first-name terms became regular visits to A&E.

My addiction had always been in me. The joy my father experienced in money won more than money earned was unlike any other he demonstrated. His conviviality extended to everyone on these occasions. Where other men's lives were dull and boring, his appeared vital. Exhilarating. Gambling's capacity to change men, to make them become somehow better than they were following a win, excited me. It was intoxicating. It was the only time I recall wanting to be like him. To experience what gave him that pleasure, what made him everybody's pal.

But it's a lonely calling, the bookies, when the gambler's luck turns. A losing streak is like leprosy. You may as well be wearing a bell around your neck. The only person who'll speak to you is your man. Your dealer. Cards, drugs … no difference in that losers always need a facilitator. Someone who won't ever say: quit, you're ahead. Unlike the drugs or the booze, I didn't have to ingest or inject anything. But then neither did I find the oblivion the junkie or alcoholic seeks. Win? Bet again and win more. Lose? Bet again and recover the losses. *Keep going*. The gambling demon couldn't be avoided. When it was hungry, it needed to be fed. Its ravenous appetite grew out of control in London. Win or lose? Fuck it, I don't care. Feed me!

A lot of the time I spent in London up to 1997 is an impenetrable blur. The last five years, particularly, were so redacted as to be indecipherable as my depression mounted. Dislocated and alone, I found no diversion in other things, like going for a walk in the sunshine, the weekly five-a-side football that my new work colleagues invited me to, or the occasional work night out. I found nothing attractive in the new rave music scene, although, paradoxically, I strummed the twelve-string to distract from my irritable restlessness and the interminable boredom. I only found pleasure in satisfying the compulsion to gamble. Keep on until there's nothing left. And then keep going anyway you can.

The final straw came in the first week of September 1997. An entire country – or at least that's how it seemed at the time – wrapped up in a communal state of self-induced grief for a divorced car-crash victim once destined for the throne. This surreal, all-consuming distraction was the perfect opportunity to go back across town. Between a Parisian tunnel and a televised funeral, there were seven days of public semi-consciousness. I stole a car from the Bermondsey lot. I was convinced no-one would care. I was wrong. If only the garage CCTV system had taken the night off to mourn along with the rest of a distracted, dumbfounded population.

At the end, I had nothing. No job, no means of feeding my habit, or myself. Only a permanent limp resulting from the broken legs administered by the Bermondsey boys. Selling the twelve-string gave me four weeks' grace on the rent for my latest digs and then I was on the street. Support-group meetings followed the same script every time: I cried. Everybody else cried. Then we all went back to gambling. All of us pushing our massive personal boulders around an Escher staircase for all eternity, knowing that if we stopped, the boulders would roll backwards and crush us. Only two options remained: find a way back to Glasgow to plead for widespread forgiveness during the season of goodwill; or a step off a shoogly stool and the eternal release of the noose. Which meant there was only one option.

8

For ten years, I had a permanent reminder pinned to a wall in every place I laid my head. A list of names. Those most harmed:

Reef
He was always going to land on his feet, disposition un-dimmed. We hadn't seen each other after my court case. During it, his hair was long and lank. A scruffy, gingerish beard had sprouted half-heartedly.

Bingo
The Hyptones was a phase she was simply passing through. Good luck to her.

Chic
I acknowledge I treated him badly in America and beforehand

because he was an easy target. I regret it now. On tour, Chic was the truest to himself. Straightforward. Uncomplicated. A cunt, though. Undoubtedly still is. But this is a cleansing, isn't it? So he went on the list with the rest of them.

Kenny McFadden
He got to see America. Its arsehole, primarily. But still, undoubtedly a lifetime's achievement for him.

Inky
Harmed physically, yes. But amazingly, his spirit remained unharmed. His unconditional forgiveness hurt me more. It still does. Suzy hates me, no doubt, but I can hardly hold that against her. They are happy. Stronger in their relationship than they might've been otherwise. Who knows?

Anna
Let's come back to her. She deserves more than a footnote.

Brian
He took his own life. I didn't cause it nor prompt it. But I do feel responsible for pushing him out of his band. And – the real reason my nagging conscience has never let go – I stole his song and claimed it as my own. 'Independent State of Mind' was written, complete and with sketchy chord structures included, on paper scribbled by Brian Mason in my room. After his death, I presented it to the band, and Reef particularly, as my own work. I knew it was a great song. That it would be hailed as such by fans and critics alike. And that it would eat away at Reef that he couldn't claim any credit for it. Stealing something so personal to Brian after he was dead is the source of my pain. We might not have appreciated the significance at the time, but its impact and legacy should've been his alone. But I took it and it all but destroyed me.

David F. Ross

The harm he suffered was self-inflicted. But that doesn't mean I'm not entirely without sympathy for what happened. A few years after our conversation on the flight from San Francisco back to the UK, he wrote his account of our US tour. Following Inky's accident, he expanded and updated it to include the trial. The piece was picked up by *The Face* magazine, by which time Madonna was a globetrotting superstar. Inferences in Ross's writing that she'd been involved in drug-taking or supply, and of her Sire recording contract resulting from sexual favours, were promptly seized on by her legal team. Ross and the magazine lost the court action, largely because I failed to substantiate his defence that I'd been willingly interviewed for the initial piece. As I mentioned before, he's a cunt, but stones and glass houses, eh? The temporary joy of knowing that Madonna takes ninety per cent of all royalties from that horrendous Christmas song Ross lives off has long passed. He deserves a break. And I'm doing this at his behest – first and foremost.

I'm glad I kept this list. Life – or what's left of it – is too short to continue such grudges, and, in any case, reparation was always going to be my only route to any kind of internal peace.

9

Everything had become a struggle. Food, drink, health, sanity. It took losing everything to even consider stopping. You can only beat addiction if you do it for yourself. Not for others. But if you hate yourself, if you're ashamed of yourself, then what's the point of stopping at all?

But in mid-December 1997, when I was poised – literally – at the end of my rope, something unexpected happened. Anna*fucking*belle reappeared.

10

She stood on the other side of Croydon Road. Holding a plastic cup. Not begging, obviously. No, statue-like, in the softly falling snowflakes. She was so still, at first I thought she was an apparition. That my tenuous grasp on reality had finally deserted me. A bus halted in the congestion in front of her. But moments later, when the lights changed to green, she was still there. As pleasing to the eye – if not the heart – as ever. Smiling across at me.

How have you been? she asked, as if a sentence or a shrug in response would cover it. She may have tried hard to conceal her shock at my gaunt, haunted shell. But she wasn't that good an actress.

How did ye find me, Annabelle? I asked.

A stupid question since I already knew the answer. Every step of the last ten years was being tracked and logged by her father through his associates in the south. I had disappeared from Glaswegian life, but not from Ronnie Mason's. All my steps out of line. All the baseball-bat beatings. All noted and documented up north, like I was on a life-long probation programme. Still, I wanted to hear her say it.

It's just *Anna* now, she chided. It wasn't too difficult, obviously, she said.

Obviously. I said it with as much sarcasm as I could muster. My creaking, twisted bones might not be helping prop up one of the new bridges over the M74, but they still belonged to Ronnie Mason. And they always would.

Her natural beauty hadn't diminished with the passing years. Even in the early-winter chill her skin glowed like it might on a Caribbean beach. There had been times in the last decade that I'd expected this porcelain face to show. An envoy from the north – whenever I fucked up too seriously for it to go unnoticed back home. The car theft had made it inevitable.

Why are ye here, Anna?

Leaving this unanswered, we walked in silence towards the Victorian bandstand in the park. I saw her noticing the limp, but she said nothing about it.

Innes reached out, she said. I met him and Suzy. He was in hospital for joint rehabilitation, and I bumped into him. First time in years, obviously. He asked if I'd seen you.

I didn't believe her. She wasn't here for him. There was something else.

An' what did ye tell him? I asked her.

I said you were fine. Doing well down in London.

Well, that was a fucken lie, then, eh?

Your brother wanted to know you were okay, that's all.

An' what if ah wasn't? What if he knew that ah was in a worse state than him?

Who would that benefit, Jamie? You? Certainly not him, she said.

We sat in silence. Me, close to self-pitying tears. Her – the sister of my one-time best friend, whom I'd selfishly screwed over, just to wipe the permanent smugness from the face of another friend – edging her hand towards mine. Some old feelings might still be in there, buried but rising slowly to the surface.

He and Suzy, they have a baby now, she said. Quietly, but with such impeccable timing that I started to assume that this was a new form of torture Ronnie Mason had contracted out. Getting his daughter to suffocate me slowly with information about the only person I cared about.

I couldn't speak. She would've noticed my breathing becoming erratic. The exhalations working their way up to a coughing fit. And then the tears did flow, and her hand lifted away from mine; her arm wrapping its way around my back. I shook my head. I breathed in deeply. I wiped the moisture from my eyes.

When ah first came down here, ah used tae bring the guitar here. Play the auld tunes. Made a few quid tae, I said.

Busking? Wow! Did anybody know it was you? she asked.

I laughed, like someone had suddenly tickled me.

Fuck, naebody knows me here. That's one ae the few plusses.

Just thought someone might've recognised you, that's all.

Jeez, Anna, *ah* don't even recognise me these days.

She sipped from the coffee she'd bought at a stand on the edge of the park. I'd said no to the offer of one from her, but it was colder than I imagined it would be and the smell of hers was intoxicating. If it hadn't been for the pains in my legs, I'd have asked her for the money and gone back.

Hey! See where you're sittin'? I said. Pointing and with a serious tone. Right there on *they* steps...

She stiffened.

What ... where? Leaning around and looking back, as if she'd sat on dogshit.

Naw. The steps, I said. That's where Bowie wrote 'Life on Mars'. Right there, on that exact spot where you're sat.

Christ, Jamie.

I laughed. She did too, eventually.

There should be a plaque up somewhere. Greatest fucken song in the English language, an' nothin' around anywhere tae even acknowledge it, I said.

Her hand was back holding mine.

Ye married, then? I asked.

She saw me looking at her left hand.

You don't recognise this?

I didn't.

It's the ring you bought me, remember? At Fisherman's Wharf ... before we went to that little wedding chapel.

Aw Jeez. Aye. Ah do now, I said.

But I still didn't. 1983 seemed a lifetime away. I anticipated her informing me that we were still married. I'd just taken Ronnie's word for granted, after all. I jumped in first.

Christ, are we still...?

Married? she said, laughing a little too much. You think I'd want to spend the rest of my life with one person? Being *married alive*? To *you*?

Aye, aw'right. Ye dinnae need tae labour the point. Fuck sake.

I often wonder what would've happened if we'd all just flown direct to San Francisco, she said. Avoided that ridiculous trek across all those different states.

We both smiled ruefully at the memory.

Aye, fucken Kenny McFadden, eh? Ye seen him kickin' about?

No ... thankfully.

Anna, why are ye *really* here?

It was her turn to breathe in deeply.

I have something to ask you. 'Independent State of Mind' has been selected for an advertising campaign by an American agency, she said.

She sat forwards. Her tone changed. Her vulnerability evaporating like the falling snowflakes landing on a hot car bonnet.

But they need our permission to use it, she added.

I missed the significance of 'our'. Of all the things she might've said, this would have taken me the longest to guess. I suddenly had so many questions. The one that surfaced first was:

What's it advertisin'?

That's your initial response? she said, before stifling a laugh. It's being considered for a major strategy for Apple Computers. A campaign called 'Think Different'.

I ran my fingers across my stubble. Bright lights flashed in my eyes; a migraine arriving suddenly out of nowhere like an unexpected Tube train bursting from the tunnel and screeching alongside the platform. Mind the gap!

Why us? I stuttered, trying to delay its impact.

I'm still not entirely sure, she said. I received a call out of the blue from the agency in New York, asking about rights. Their strategy features well-known creative geniuses. People whose thinking has changed their respective fields for the better.

Like who?

Em, Muhammad Ali, Amelia Earhart, Picasso, Hendrix...

An' Jamie Hewitt? I said sarcastically.

No. Not you, obviously.

Again, the 'obviously'.

They want a piece of music that isn't widely known, she said.

Thanks.

You know what I mean. Something that won't compete with the thinkers. But 'Independent State of Mind' – it fits perfectly with the message of thinking differently.

It was hard to take her seriously. Yet I knew she wouldn't be here otherwise. My head was spinning. I couldn't see the positives.

That'll no' be cheap, then, eh? I stuttered.

What do you mean?

How much'll it cost?

I must admit I was so attuned to bad news where money was concerned that I was momentarily blinded to the windfall financial opportunity Anna was laying out. I remember my da justifying a skelp by saying: Some folk need a good fucken slap. Like an auld telly. It's the only way they get the full picture.

Maybe he was right.

Cost? she said. Irritated, not amused. They pay us, you idiot. They pay to license the music and to secure the rights, whether they use it or not. Twenty-five grand is the initial offer. It could grow depending on whether they use it worldwide.

The palpitations began. I gasped and had to ask her to repeat the figure, which she did. Slower.

Us? I said eventually, but only to establish how wide that reference was, not to challenge it.

She took a deep breath.

Who do you think paid out on all the bills after the eighty-three UK tour was cancelled? Who do you think chased up the revenue on the single? Who do you think cleared the tax, the accountants, the hangers-on?

The most pregnant of pauses. Then she continued.

Who do you think swept up all the fucking shit after you drove your brother into the fucking Clyde? Us, she said. Your creditors.

This hadn't previously occurred to me. Probably because I was too self-absorbed to see it. Meek, mild-mannered Annabelle Mason, my doormat girlfriend – and one-time wife – from fifteen years earlier, was the one controlling me, not her father. It was a startling revelation. I reasoned that if she'd known it was her brother who had written the song that had laid the golden egg, I'd be dead already.

She didn't complete her nursing studies. She foresaw a different type of future; one where controlling music licensing and publishing contracts would be more lucrative. All those amateur Scottish bands drawing widespread attention from the music industry in the early eighties and getting contractually ripped off. They were Annabelle's target market. She went to law school. She specialised in copyright law. She made influential contacts in useful government departments. She learned how to secure, manage and market rights for works of music. And now that opportunity had smiled kindly on her, she had a plan for us. All of us.

11

Contact had been established, and I discovered a higher power's plan for my life. I'm not religious in any way, but I can accept that there's something in the notion of a higher power. I'd hit rock bottom, the point where it was either suicide or survive until the next low. I think, despite everything, I was receptive to the idea of something greater than myself, a line shooting around my brain: *there must be more to life than this*.

Annabelle was gone. Consigned to history. The meekness now merely part of the long game; a manufactured cover story. Anna was the puppet master. Her offer was a one-time deal. Take it or leave it. Leave it, and she'd cut the strings completely, and I'd be a lifeless heap. Nowhere to go but the final checkout. I was in no position to bargain. The meagre royalties from the record, and the previous two, had been accumulating slowly in an account controlled by Anna – the band's registered financial manager. But now, and for the first time since The Hyptones were on *Top of the Pops* in the early eighties, that account was about to be seriously boosted.

In explaining the circumstances of the deal, Anna doled out acronyms like she was narrating the index of the *Lancet*. My brain hurt.

The only one that matters, she said, is PRS.

It stood for Performing Rights Society and had only just been established.

PRS represents its songwriter, composer and music-publisher members' and collects royalties on their behalf whenever their music is played or performed publicly, she said.

How formal and business-like she sounded. I smirked at the briefest of thoughts: David F. Ross, further screwed by Madonna's team of aggressive rights managers, as they took an even bigger slice of his da's legacy.

With a worldwide Apple advertising campaign on the horizon, my song – the one stolen from her dead brother – could accrue multiple thousands of pounds in future plays. She outlined more immediate plans. Following the exposure, the single would be re-issued and repackaged. Perhaps as a double pack with the first two singles. An extra remix. A tacky button badge. A video commissioned. Anna*fucking*belle, indeed.

But there was something else. Something about her being here now that jarred. I couldn't put my finger on it. That steel in her gaze. It chilled me more than the sharpening London frost.

After the modest success of our first two singles, Kenny McFadden had persuaded Ronnie Mason to fund a better studio and a proper sound engineer to produce 'Independent State of Mind'.

The offers'll be floodin' in after the States, he'd said. We'll be beatin' A&R men off wi' big bloody sticks.

Kenny acting like a charity-shop Colonel Tom Parker and Ronnie Mason starting to think he'd be the new Don Arden; common sense was in short supply back then. The band was surviving on handouts from Anna, so nobody opposed any suggestion, regardless of how bizarre or ridiculous it seemed. And the constant refrain of 'Brian would be so proud' burrowed into my brain to the point where it was all I could hear. We were doing it all for Brian, apparently. Living the future that he'd been so tragically denied; no-one prepared to correct the facts.

I couldn't sleep. Couldn't play on stage properly. Started making excuses to miss band commitments and media appointments. Anxiety invaded my every waking thought. A constant panic that somehow, somewhere, Brian Mason had left something behind that would expose my shame. The idea of Brian speaking from beyond the grave was far-fetched. His relationship with his family had been strained, so I felt certain he wouldn't have confided in them. And as for his other friends, the brain-fried junkie squatters he spiked his veins with, well, they couldn't have told you if it was Saturday or Saturn. Nonetheless, the prospect of exposure paralysed me, and it was that more than anything else that caused the band's implosion in 1983.

Now it was resurfacing. Fifteen years of suppressed guilt were about to be uncorked. It was as if Anna could sense it.

She reached into her bag. She brought out a small book. There were colourful flowers on its cover, as painted centuries ago by van Gogh or Gauguin or suchlike. Embossed in the bottom corner, *Diary 1981*.

My heart rate increased. My breathing accelerated. She handed the book to me. A postcard of San Francisco demarked a specific page. I opened it. I read the entry.

8th October 1981:

He was late. I waited in the café, drawing love hearts on the glass, and then watching them disappear in the dripping condensation. I need to rein in my wild imagination. Lower my expectations. But being in love is a habit that's hard to break. Jamie probably sees me as an obligation because of the money. I'm thinking of better times, as I sit here, left on my own.

I waited and waited. He didn't come.

8th October. My birthday. 1981. The night The Clash played Glasgow Apollo, and I ditched her. More followed in the next day's entry:

We fought. I cried. He shouted, 'YES, YES, YES, you heard me. We're fucking done. Leave me on my own.'

I had heard Reef sing these words plenty of times, but only now, faced with the reality of their origin, did I recall screaming them at her. I re-read her diary entries; slack jawed. Bile rising. I hadn't appropriated Brian's lyrics; he'd stolen them from Anna's diary. 'Independent State Of Mind' was about me standing her up. Her calmness now made sense of her willingness to condone my cruel antipathy back in the mid-eighties. All part of her masterplan.

***Independent State of Mind** (Words by Mason. A. – Music by Mason. B.)*

With Brian dead, there was no point in exposing me, because that wouldn't have served the opportunity that the band represented. We got married in San Francisco because she wanted us to. With the band out of the picture, all that remained was any royalties the records might accrue. And although Anna had spent the last decade cultivating a substantial roster of rights, 'Independent State of Mind' was suddenly where the real money-making opportunity lay.

She handed me a magazine clipping.

'A universal song of hope and heartbreak, of what could've been and what still might be. How many current songwriters have Hewitt's ability to coalesce words and music that are simultaneously a cry of pain and a call to arms, depending on the listener's mood? Weller, Costello? And that's it. Truly magnificent.'

Had she expected me to have forgotten it, or was this another twisting of the knife, given what we both now knew? Mark Ellen's glistening review in *Smash Hits* propelled the record up the charts and into the A-lists of the national radio stations. All based on a lie.

My eyes began to well up. Crying once again like a helpless baby. Weeping for the disastrous mess I'd made of my life. For Brian, and the inescapable feeling that I'd driven him to suicide. Chronic guilt is a horrendous condition. Left untreated, it will eat at your worthless insides like a cancer. Logic and rational thinking play little part in keeping it at bay. As far as I was concerned, I'd as good as held Brian's head under the water until it killed him.

I cannae cope wi' this, Anna. Ah'm fucken done, I sobbed.

And I meant it. There was little left to live for.

Ah'm so fucken ashamed, I told her. Brian, Inky. *You!* I wailed. I've let everyone down.

Black clouds grouped at the edge of my vision. Invaders waiting for the order to attack. There might've been stiff competition, but this felt like the worst moment of my life. My lowest ebb. And then I momentarily lost consciousness because when I came to, I was lying on the bandstand steps and Anna was trying to get me to sip from a water bottle.

Are you okay?

Fuck knows.

I blew out and then regulated my breathing as best I could.

Time to let them go for good, Jamie ... the bad times.

Let them go? I said. Are you fucken jokin'? All the shit I've done. To my brother? To yours?

I had to, she said.

That's different. You never...

Never what? she said. Tried to save him? No. You're right. I didn't. And I could've.

What d'ye mean? I asked her.

I was in the house when it happened. I knew Brian was shooting up in the bathroom. He left the door open. I watched him slip under the water. And I only dialled 999 when he'd stopped breathing.

It was her turn to sob, although she kept it under control.

Ye what? I stammered.

Was this an act? It was hard to tell with her. I didn't know whether to fear her or pity her.

We've all got shit to hide, Jamie, she said. Not just you.

And that was that. A shared past to keep hidden. A future to be protected.

She could easily have kept the news about the advertising campaign to herself. And the subsequent rewards it could bring. I was hardly able to contest anything legally, even if I had known how to. The rest of the band would've been similarly ignorant. And, as her evidence had proved, she had a greater claim to being the song's originator than I did. But, she stressed, that wasn't her style.

Everyone deserves a second chance, she said. This is ours. All of us.

So, there we were. Crisp snowflakes falling on the Bowie Bandstand. Brief, concise explanations given by Anna of the future percentages to apply to everyone who'd had an involvement after her majority cut. Me, Reef, Bingo, Kenny. There was even a provision for Inky and Suzy, in the event I wouldn't be that considerate. The only arrangement I questioned was Chic's. Not because I disagreed; just that it seemed unusual that he'd be getting nothing.

No! Fuck him, she said.

Given Chic's consumption of Brian's ashes, Anna wasn't interested in hearing a plea for him. She was trying to be fair, but even reason had its limits. For my part, I regretted my mistreatment of him on the American tour, but I'd never really acknowledged his role in the stag-night catastrophe. Until now.

Fuck him, I echoed.

We were on the same page at last. Common ground. Anna Mason was practised at this. I had to concede it was impressive. She knew how restrictive music contracts were and how lucrative securing the rights could be. I was invited to trust her. What was left to lose?

Papers passed between us for signature. AFB Management livery branding every page. A sharp touch, I had to give her that. I signed, fingers tinged blue, with a silver pen that looked exactly like the one Brian had once threatened me with. The one with which he had written the song that laid the golden egg. I racked my brain, trying to recall what happened to that pen. Surely to fuck *this* wasn't it. What kind of Robert Johnson-type satanic fucking voodoo would that have represented?

She stood, my long-lost wife. My salvation. My higher power. She had in her possession what she'd travelled south for. My soul. She'd be in touch very soon. A bank account, so routinely abused by me over the years, would be bolstered with a modest advance. I was instructed to get cleaned up; *my shit sorted out*. There was work to do. I was an AFB employee now. I was being given a reprieve. It felt like a stay of execution. It had taken losing everything for me to even consider stopping gambling. Or living. As I said, you can only stop if you do it for yourself. Not for others. Well, let's see.

The people's shy, demure princess was dead. A nation of sycophants grieved. I too was numb, and not just from the biting cold. I didn't know what to think. Or feel. I watched her leave. The implications of a new era dawned. I reflected on what I might have learned from the one that had just drawn to a close.

12

JAMIE HEWITT IS...
...sorry

JAMIE HEWITT IS...
...ashamed

JAMIE HEWITT IS...
...depressed

JAMIE HEWITT IS...
...tired

JAMIE HEWITT IS...
...redundant.

JAMIE HEWITT IS...
...in debt.

JAMIE HEWITT IS...
...lost.

JAMIE HEWITT IS...
...in need of rescue.

JAMIE HEWITT IS...
...leaving London.

JAMIE HEWITT IS...
...dependent on Anna Mason.

JAMIE HEWITT IS...
...heading 'home'.

JAMIE HEWITT IS...
...benefitting from his silence.

JAMIE HEWITT IS...
...lowering his expectations.

JAMIE HEWITT IS...
...giving in to this temptation.

JAMIE HEWITT IS...
...standing at the crossroads.

JAMIE HEWITT IS...
...making deals with the devil.

JAMIE HEWITT IS...
...thankful for small mercies.

JAMIE HEWITT IS...
...still a cunt.

There's no truth, only perspective.

There's no truth, only perspective...

1st October 1983:

Unusually, it's a smell that awakens me. My eyes open, adjusting to the light and the unfamiliar context, but there's no noise. Everything is surprisingly quiet in this house of lost children. But that smell. Freshly baked bread. Coffee. Rich maple syrup ... it reminds me of a happier time, stealing illicit sips from Larry's cognac bottle. I stretch, get up and pull back the curtains. The room I've woken up in is at the rear of Lakeview, an expansive three-story detached house built on a prominent Ingleside peak. The house sits proudly on the corner of Urbano Drive and Corona Street. Craning my neck, I can just see the street sign and the intersection. From the main window, I see children sitting cross-legged in a tight circle in the garden, around the feet of an older woman, who is reading to them from a book. The woman has her back to me, but it's Momma Em and these children are hypnotized by her. The smallest one looks up. The one who ran towards me and hugged my leg when I got here last night. She waves and smiles. Proudly showing off that gap in her mouth where her baby teeth used to be. I laugh and wave back to her.

I acclimatize quickly to these comfortable new surroundings. The intoxicating smells of home-cooked food. The joyful prayers of thanksgiving at every mealtime. Upwards of fourteen clustered around the massive, communal mahogany dining table that is the very heart and soul of this place. Em Bradley – known to everyone in the Ingleside area as Momma Em – welcomed me into her home, as she did all her young houseguests, with open arms. There was no awkwardness. No shame or embarrassment.

Momma Em is adept at making troubled youngsters feel safe and relaxed as they come to terms with the circumstances that have resulted in residential foster care. Brandy told me this in the car. But Brandy didn't come in the house when she dropped me off. I realise now that the arrangement must've been agreed with the older woman weeks before I'd been informed of it. A bedroom with new clothes sized to fit me betrays the pre-planning. That rankled me for a moment but, *hmmm* ... those smells.

Momma Em is immediately strict. Right away, she insists I contact Delphine and Larry to let them know I'm safe and how to get in touch if there is ever a need to. The first call is daunting. Larry answers. He confirms my suspicions. He has lost his job at the bar. Delphine seems pleased to hear from me but spends more time during the call talking to Momma Em; the content of their discussion Em tells me to pay no mind.

There are nine foster children under Momma Em's roof as a crisp fall becomes a cold winter. To earn my keep, I work five days a week, Friday and Saturday being days off. My duties include cleaning and washing, and helping to get the younger children ready for bed. I'm also expected to run errands for Momma Em and her husband, Ben. Where Momma Em is a straight-talking disciplinarian, Ben is a laid-back, free-thinking liberal. He and I get along from the beginning. Ben talks to me about sports. About culture. The arts. Politics. He talks about current affairs, and I find myself sitting cross-legged in front of the fire of an evening when the kids are all in bed, absorbing his wisdom. A favorite subject, which he returns to regularly, is his relationship with Harvey Milk and George Moscone, the previous city mayor.

In 1976, Ben worked in the office of Commissioner Art Agnos. Agnos was elected to the California State Assembly, defeating Harvey Milk in the Democratic primary in the Sixteenth District. But Ben remained cordial with Milk, also becoming friendly with the gay-rights activist Cleve Jones. Only two years after first meeting him, Ben was one of the first on the scene to find Harvey Milk face down on the floor of his office in City Hall, shot five times, including twice in the head. Ben left public service shortly after the assassinations of Harvey Milk and Mayor George Moscone. Ben only ever gets exercised at the nation's servile relationship with the gun lobby.

These capitalist bastards only care about selling weapons, they don't care about keeping America safe, he'll say, before throwing his newspaper down and going for a walk to cool off. It happens often.

I love accompanying Ben on one of his decompressions. I diffuse his anger by posing questions that illicit the response: you know this is the only neighborhood in San Francisco having a marine and bay view? Ben's love for the area of his birth is intoxicating. Unlike me, he has never craved a life on the road. Never considered that the grass might be greener elsewhere. He has a contentment with his environment that I hope to find one day. We stroll down Junipero Serra Boulevard, south of Ocean Avenue, towards the newer Ingleside Terraces: a clean, sunny ramble of large white houses, well-edged lawns and curving streets.

Heading further west, Ben tells wonderful stories about the original Urbano Drive, an oval laid along the lines of the old Ingleside Racetrack, the last venue for racing in San Francisco. My favorites are about Connemara, a legendary greyhound who decided there must be a better world than chasing rabbits in circles. One day at the end of a race he had won, Connemara crossed the finish line and kept going until he reached Laguna Honda, where the University of California-San Francisco is now built. The legend claims Connemara led a pack of wild dogs who terrorized cats, chickens and pigs, and even took out a couple of peacocks in Golden Gate Park. The greyhound, worth several thousand dollars, was never recaptured. Urbano Drive becomes my new running circuit. I always smile at the idea of Connemara breaking free as I round the oval and head back uphill.

On Sunday afternoons, after church, we often walk the five miles uphill to the summit of Mount Davidson. I never tire of Ben recounting the time he was an extra in *Dirty Harry*, in the night-time sequence where Clint Eastwood's cop is ordered to put his nose right up against the cement of the Armenian Genocide memorial cross.

Ben gifts me his camera.

Somethin' that shoots, but never kills, he says.

I put it to very good use on our walks.

I've been living at Lakeview for almost a year now, and following Ben's prompting, I've enrolled to complete high school. The claustrophobia I found intolerable in Humble has gone, despite living with so many more people. Ben has taught me how to drive properly. And I have forged a special bond with the youngest child in the house, little Bunny Menendez. Bunny is five years old and known to all, at her insistence, as Rabbit. There is something bewitching about her. It can be a look or a mannerism, or the way dimples materialize when she smiles. I've learned the heartbreaking histories of the other children, but Momma Em won't disclose details of how Rabbit arrived at Lakeview, other than to confirm that the child hadn't known any other home.

I tell Rabbit bedtime stories, and often she falls asleep in my bed, holding tightly on to my dashboard Elvis. That gets me the rough side of Momma Em's tongue. She insists on routine. Consistency.

It's the only way these children can feel secure, she says.

But little Rabbit pleads to stay in my room and it's hard to disappoint her. The stories that enthuse her most are those involving Jimmy, my daddy, as the hero.

Tell me again about Jimmy and the men that wear the skirts, she demands.

And for her, I describe Jimmy Montgomery, and his friend, Dashboard Elvis, both in kilts, fighting giant spiders and hunting for the Loch Ness Monster in Scotland. And the following day, little Rabbit will draw what she remembers of the story.

I wanna go to Scot-*land*, she'd plead.

You will, someday, I tell her.

Other times, I sing to her. One song is the little girl's favourite.

Sing the special song, Jude!

And I do as she commands: *You gotta make your own kind of music. Sing your own special song. / Make your own kind of music. Even if nobody else sings along.*

Rabbit loves this song so much. She makes me sing it every night. We are growing closer. This is a source of consternation to Momma Em that I struggle to understand. She thinks I should be spending equal amounts of time with all the children. But the others are older and appear more independent. And in any case, their average stay here is around four months. Whatever changes in circumstance move them on little Rabbit isn't subject to. She is a permanent fixture. I don't enquire further, but suspect Rabbit and I are the only two who are not here for our own protection.

I spend time encouraging the child's developing artistic inclinations. I can't claim to understand her creative potential, but that's immaterial at this point. Under my untrained tutelage, Rabbit draws constantly. Animals, buildings, bridges, people. The dashboard Elvis figurine. The little girl creates large drawings, full of detailed content.

It's 1986. One of Rabbit's compositions has been selected for an art competition amongst the local schools. Rabbit's elaborate pencil sketch of a future low-rise San Francisco doesn't win, despite deserving to. The judges admit to their assumption that a young person aged sixteen, not six, is the artist. To correct this, Rabbit's drawing is being hung in the de Young Museum at Golden Gate Park.

Rabbit, Em and Ben are invited to a public ceremony held in the de Young Museum's reception hall by the office of city mayor, Dianne Feinstein. Her administration intends to use Rabbit's drawing as part of their campaign to demonstrate that the new city zoning laws will appease local community concerns; that the mayor's new urban blueprint will create a more varied architectural skyline, increase open space near office buildings and encourage development of shops, restaurants, and other establishments at street level.

Ben has told me that the introduction of large skyscrapers to the city's landscape throughout the previous decades was hugely controversial. Corporate America stretching its steel-and-concrete identity ever upwards, cutting brutal swathes through the South of Market district and displacing the resistant gay and leather communities that had occupied the area since the waterfront development of the Embarcadero in the 1950s.

Ben is not a supporter of the Feinstein administration. He can't forgive the mayor's backing of the Carter-Mondale ticket for the 1980 presidential election, against the Bay Area Democrats support for the doomed campaign led by Senator Ted Kennedy. Despite Em's pleading that this event is for Rabbit, Ben won't be persuaded. I drive Em and Rabbit to the de Young instead.

The mayor is – according to the swarm of PR suits buzzing around anxiously – typically late for the shoot. Bored, I wander the galleries while Em tries to entertain the agitated Rabbit. The art I observe amazes and befuddles in equal measure. Several works of substantial size demonstrate no greater artistic flair than Rabbit's, in my opinion. Eventually, I find myself in a confusing, cellular layout at the top of the building. In contrast to the shallow abstraction of the fine arts below, I mosey into a series of smaller, more contemplative spaces that are positively bursting with color and vitality. These are photographs, not paintings. Real life, not an artificial impression. And their beauty seems to lie in their celebration of ordinary community life, much like the one I have left behind in Humble. Photographs captured not merely by an interested observer passing through, but by someone wholly and emotionally invested in the joy and the pain of their subjects. I don't see them as static images. They're moving, laughing, crying, protesting, loving, singing. Speaking directly to me.

There is an odd image of a man in a girl-scout uniform carrying a sign that reads, *Cookies Not Contras*. Another photo implies parallels between the AIDS quarantine and South African apartheid. A third, entitled *Dancers on Stage, 1984*, illustrates a young woman in a bright-red dress dancing gracefully on the back of a flatbed truck with her male partner. Many have the feel of intimate family shots, but their context makes political points. In these pictures, multi-racial community joy and pride seem like acts of resistance. I can't properly explain why these photographs forge such a personal connection. Why their subjects are summoning me, reaching through my ribcage, gently massaging my heart. They prompt joyous tears, and all this before my gaze falls on the one picture I can't look away from. It magnetizes me, drawing my body toward it like I am on castors.

The photograph depicts a Black woman, mouth open. Laughing, leaning on a metal barricade. Or even singing? On a white card mounted to the left-hand side of the large, square photograph, is typed: *Happyness waiting, 1985*. My febrile imagination convinces me that this woman is my mom's sister. The Happyness of Larry's stories.

I rush to the attendant, panting.

Excuse me, who took these photographs? I stumble.

Janet Delaney, says the attendant. She watches me pull a pen from my satchel and write the name on my hand.

Do you want to buy a catalogue? she adds.

How could I get in touch with her? I ask.

Uh, you could contact her at San Mateo. The college. She teaches class there, I think.

I study the dark-haired woman on the back cover of the catalogue. Determined. Serious. Eyes down, glimpsing sideways into the viewfinder of an old double-lens box camera as if she doesn't entirely trust it. I stare at the image and commit it to memory.

I receive directions on how to find Janet Delaney from the photography lab where she works. After an hour searching the streets of Mission, I chance upon the photographer, framing shots with that same remarkable classic Rolleiflex, documenting beauty in the mundanity of life.

Janet Delaney intimidates me initially. Having plotted the various locations described in the exhibition catalogue, I'd anticipated a serendipitous meeting with my aunt, down in the Castro where the photograph had been taken. But uncertain about how to broach the subject of Happyness and Professor Delaney's connection to her, I immaturely fire out rat-a-tat questions that must make me sound like I'm recruiting for a religious cult.

I am looking for Happyness. Do you know Happyness, miss? Do you know where to find Happyness? Please tell me, I say.

I'm out of breath and I haven't even introduced myself. Janet Delaney is irritated. Her focus is interrupted. Even though her current subject is a crude composition of stained stone, cracked glass and rotted wood, she scolds me for disturbing it. As if it is suddenly shy. As if the human characteristics she was teasing out of it are gone.

But Janet Delaney relents. I tell my tale. She understands enough about this unusual story to be intrigued by the chance that her shot may have connected me with my improbable aunt.

We amble along the streets that form the canvas for her art.

The importance of photography is to connect us to our past. It helps us know who we are, what our identity is. What our future could be, says Professor Delaney.

It feels like I should be taking notes. Janet Delaney directs me, her new student, to pay attention to the improvised theater of the streets. The dynamism of human choreography. She reinforces it with a subtle nod to the right, a casual wave of a hand to the left, an eyebrow raised upwards. Janet Delaney uses large-format equipment specifically – she informs me – because the slower, more considered process allows her to capture the color, the life, the details of her composition.

I stop looking and begin to observe. A large gray bird pecking furiously at an unidentifiable roadkill carcass. A curly-haired, barefoot child playing alone in the gutter. A line of bedraggled, emaciated men, some displaying the tell-tale lesions of what will eventually kill them. They wait for soup from an impromptu kitchen. A painted slogan: *God Has Forsaken Us*, and under it in different hand, *Fucking Queers!* Down an alley, the scattered evidence of an enclave of homeless people. These communities are growing and expanding in the Castro and Tenderloin districts. Not merely those displaced by President Reagan's brand of conservatism, but also those still reeling from the AIDS crisis. I become acutely aware of how easily this could've been my existence. Selling blowjobs and unprotected sex down the backstreets merely to survive. Just like the young woman on her knees in Phoenix. My encounters since leaving Humble have been fortunate to say the least.

We walk west along 18th Street. Past stores called Moby Dick and Hand Job. Up the gradual incline of Hartford Street with its colorful timber houses lining each side. Less remarkable

Painted Ladies than the venerated ones of Steiner Street, but embellished with dusty reds, pinks and purples, and everything fashionably loud in between. Downhill on 19th Street and taking a right, we reach Castro Street. The photographer gestures towards a vacant store. 575 is the number above the door.

That was Castro Camera, she says.

Harvey Milk's place? I ask.

Harvey Milk was a good photographer. He sold cameras and film from here. But his real talent was in connecting people. People using their lens to make a difference to society, she says.

It is obvious that this place carries huge significance for Janet Delaney. As it did for Ben.

I snap Janet Delaney, framed in the shop frontage, with Ben's Minolta Maxxum, which he has all but relinquished, so often is it strapped around my neck.

I wanna see those, says Janet Delaney, smiling.

Together, we can't find Happyness. But in photography, I've found something else. I've carried Jimmy Montgomery's picture with me since leaving Humble. That and his letter are the only things I have to even acknowledge his existence. I stole the Polaroid camera because I wanted a record of my experiences, good *and* bad. And the photograph of the guitarist taken with it carries a power that I can't fully explain. I've been drawn to photography but hadn't ever considered applying to study the subject.

Not until now.

Professor Delaney is prepared to offer a testimonial in return for a few summer months of my shadowing assistance. My mentor thinks the photographs I take of those participating in the first AIDS Walk in Golden Gate Park in July show real promise. My grade average is good enough, but her personal recommendation will help me get accepted.

For interview, I am asked to bring an image that means something important to me, and to articulate what the personal significance is. And why only a photograph can hold that meaning. I bring two: the magazine cover shot of my father, the soldier, and the polaroid of the guitarist from the Scottish band that I took four years ago in Phoenix, Arizona, on the night several lives took a different direction.

I talk enthusiastically about them and after a week's deliberation, confirmation is there, in the form of a notice pinned up in the college foyer.

In this fall semester of 1987, the enrolment list for the Associate in Arts Degree with a Major in Photography at the College of San Mateo, San Francisco includes the following freshmen students:
Anderson, *Michael J.*
Angier, *Garlan C.*
Arnold, *Lois A.*
Berensmeier, *Lou S.*
Berry, *D. Bruce*
Clemens, *Gregory*
Donner, *Maurice J.*
Frassetti, *Eric*
Galindo, *Mary Lloyd*
Griffiths, *Robert W.*
Kowerski, *Eva Mae.*
Martinez, *Jacqueline*
Montgomery, *Judithea.*
Odum, *Ernest L.*
Roach, *Betty R.*
Suebert, *Linda K.*
Yoshimura, *Tadao*
Young, *Andrew D.*
Zimmerman, *Robert D.*
Course tutor: Professor Janet Delaney.

I am in.

I enter my first semester at the College of San Mateo with a greater sense of purpose than I have had for some time. In fact, the only time I recall being so determined to achieve something was when I left Texas. Everyone else in Humble seemed to have moved on from the death and tragedy, leaving me alone with a grief I didn't understand and didn't feel entitled to. The decision to leave it all behind, once made, provided me with a second chance. It gave me a second family. I have a past, but it's in the past. In the years since arriving at Lakeview, contact with the indignant Delphine and the impuissant Larry has become sporadic. Birthdays and Thanksgiving are the only occasions on which I reach out. And it is always on me to do so.

This is my future: for three lecture-critique hours and three lab hours per week, I worship at the lectern of Janet Delaney. I am introduced to basic black-and-white photographic skills and equipment. I learn precise methods of negative developing, printing and finishing the photograph. I spend as much time in the dark room as I do in the light. My classmates nickname me Contessa Dracula. I graduate to experimental techniques, all the while building a strong portfolio. Constructing a new identity.

My first eighteen months at college are the happiest time of my life so far. Whilst Em continues to keep me at arm's length emotionally, Ben loves me like I'm his own granddaughter. He encourages me to be driven, independent, resilient. Able to stand up for myself.

Other children continue to pass through our lives, some more damaged than others. Some more challenging than others. None of them connect intuitively with me like Rabbit does. Rabbit is constantly by my side when she's not at school. I know what's she's thinking. What she'll say, sometimes before she says it. The synergy between us makes me think fate has driven us together – as if *she* is my lost relative and not Happyness.

That first night, when Brandy dropped me off, I couldn't have imagined remaining at Lakeview for what will be five years this summer. Now I can't ever imagine leaving. I think of Brandy and Matt regularly, and of how grateful I am to have encountered them. They excavated a confidence I didn't know was buried deep inside me. But Brandy was right. Matt was her responsibility, and I had a life to live, as selfish as that might sound. All of which makes what happened next so devastating because it was so avoidable.

It's early morning on a crisp Sunday in February 1988. There are only five foster children at Lakeview and Momma Em has decided to take them all to an extended church service. Ben, despite protestations that began days ago, has gone too. The house is quiet. Only Rabbit and I are home. She has a fever and I leapt at the opportunity to babysit. I don't care for the gospels. The Reverend Libero is a fearsome performer. He pushes the literal interpretation of heaven and hell and of salvation and damnation. Forgiveness doesn't regularly feature. The Jews killed Christ and the Catholics are in thrall to a mysterious tyrant in Rome, he preaches with scientific certainty. It can be entertaining at times, the fire-and-brimstone act. If you're in the right mood, that is. But it's time wasted, in my opinion, especially today when I have an ulterior motive. The phone rings. I know who is calling. I glance at Rabbit. She doesn't look up from her position, slumped in a bean bag, hypnotized by whatever is on television, drawing pad across her knees.

Hey, I say as I answer the phone, as coolly as I can muster, despite my heart beating faster.

Hey, he replies. Can you come over? It's important, dude.

The caller is Shaun. A couple of years younger than me, but he is the first boy to show interest in me since AJ Carter. I'm flattered, and my priorities are skewed because of it. And she is such a dependable child. I tell her to stay where she is, and she does. If that sounds like an animal's unquestioning obedience to a master, I don't mean it to, but honestly, she is so quiet and self-absorbed in her drawing at times that you'd forget she was even there. And in any case, I was regularly left home alone at her age.

I didn't need to go out. It could've waited. It wasn't important. Shaun only wanted to borrow money from me for tickets to Aerosmith at the Concord Pavilion. My heart sinks, and deep down I am fearful my selfishness will be discovered. Momma Em returning early, perhaps, and the heat that will bring, and I start to run homewards, along Urbano Drive.

The first thing I see is wisps of smoke polluting the perfectly blue sky. Too much of it, and too dark and thick to be a garden bonfire or barbecue. I round the corner, and my heart is in my mouth. The source of the smoke must be in our street. Now I start to panic. I slow past the biggest of the white Ingleside houses, and then I see Lakeview.

It's on fire.

The flames are being doused by the hoses from three fire trucks. I don't think of Rabbit, I think of myself. And my first reaction is to run, run, run away like Connemara, and never stop running until no-one can find me. But I don't. I need to face the music although I already know it's over. In one horrendous moment of selfish misjudgement.

The blaze started on the top floor. In my room. Only little Rabbit was in the house when the Fire Department arrived. They were alerted by a neighbor concerned at the darkening smoke escaping from an upper window. I don't know what to say. There really is nothing to say. I left her alone in the house. It's immaterial that I was only gone for half an hour. The damage was done the second I took the phone call. The instant that I decided to leave her alone, watching *Little Clowns of Happytown*.

I had gone to meet a boy. A demanding, impatient teenager. Why it couldn't have waited until later in the day when everyone had returned from worship, I hadn't thought to ask. And I didn't question him. I just went out. And I locked Rabbit inside. Desperate to salvage something, I lie. To Momma Em, to Ben, to the emergency services. I tell Momma Em and the police officers that I'd gone out to get medicine for her fever, even though I know where it is kept in the kitchen. And I am forbidden from giving any of the children medicine, in any case.

There are no excuses. Nothing I can say to come back from this now. Poor old Ben tries to placate his wife with a plea on my behalf. *At least no-one...* But we both know Momma Em's fury is entirely justified. Died? she yells at him, as if he was complicit. That's what Ben meant to say, to try, as he always does, to temper. To repair. But this breakage is beyond him. Beyond any fixing. In addition to Rabbit's terrible injuries – she suffers second-degree burns to her right arm from hand to shoulder, to her neck and up to her face – the fire has ripped a huge hole in the top of the house. The entire household will need to be relocated until the Fire Department and the insurance assessors carry out their investigations into the cause. It transpires that a faulty adaptor sparked the blaze. But that makes no difference to my punishment. There will be no appealing my sentence. The contractors first make safe and then slowly make good. But I can't remain under her repaired roof. Nor in San Francisco. The future for me lies elsewhere. We are always moving on, if not always moving forwards.

Three times in my life to this point, I've felt the pull of white male attraction. Three times, consecutively, a trauma resulted. Is this mere coincidence? Am I a magnet for such chaos?

There's no such thing as random coincidence, Momma Em would regularly say.

Nothing is incidental. We shape events more than they shape us. These are the last words she says to me.

I confide in Janet Delaney. With nowhere else to turn, I move in with her for a few days. Despite my inexcusable act, she musters some sympathy. She convinces me my eye is good and that I don't need a graduation ceremony to demonstrate that. She has a trip to New York City coming up. She invites me to accompany her. I tell Ben. But I don't ask his opinion before accepting Janet's offer. I've already put him in an invidious position. He wants to offer forgiveness but that can only be unilateral. For his wife, I have become simply an employee fired from a job for the grossest of misconduct. No references. No severance pay.

I try to return the camera, but Ben tells me to keep it, convinced I'll make better use of it. He also gives me money I don't deserve. Forces me to accept it. Makes me promise to return one day to see Rabbit, knowing, I suspect, deep down that I won't. That I'd always be too ashamed.

My frizzy hair was voluminous and 'Donna Summer'-long before the fire. I'd cultivated sufficient self-confidence during my latter years at Lakeview to let it grow. To become female. To let myself be noticed more. After the fire, I cut it all off. I throw away the make-up that I've flirted with since AJ Carter first encouraged it. I return to baggy jeans and boots. I slope back into the androgynous shadows. I guess it feels safer there. Not specifically female. Not particularly Black. Unspecific. Ordinary.

Existence for most people is ordinary. Mundane. Forgettable. Paradoxically, these are the folds that Janet Delaney has encouraged me to roll back and examine. Our lives are invariably punctuated by the memorable circumstances, or in my experience, unusual occurrences. It is on these fortuitous events that lives pivot. Back in Humble, AJ Carter colorized the dusty sepia. In San Francisco, Janet Delaney lit the bohemian flame. In New York, I would be open to all possibilities. I am determined not to look back with contrition, but to live posing questions to which the only appropriate response can be YES!

PART THREE:

Jude – Another New York Trilogy

(Act i) 1988–1995

It's early in 1988, five weeks since the fire that disfigured Rabbit. I'm shivering in the jump seat of a chilly DHL cargo-plane cockpit. It's the red-eye flight headed for JFK International Airport. We left at midnight and will arrive on the East Coast in the early hours of the morning. My first time airborne and I'm tired and excited – and trembling at every unexpected shudder of the fuselage. Tightly gripping the tiny dashboard Elvis in my coat pocket as if idolatry will guarantee our safety. Janet Delaney works – when occasion demands – as a courier, delivering last-minute packages across the continent. It provides her with regular opportunities to travel cheaply to the greatest and most dramatic urban canvas in America. Her hand has reached over to my forearm so many times that she has now left it there – reassurance that all will be well. For the duration of the flight *and* the uncertain months ahead, I hope.

We're in the city delivering her package. Obligation complete, Janet Delaney is here to photograph people and places. We head downtown to Seaport. Janet has an old university friend living in an apartment block overlooking the East River. Her friend's name is Erin Pressley. Different spelling, Janet quickly points out, as if I've automatically assumed Erin is a relative. We'll stay with Erin until Janet returns to San Francisco and, once again, I must face a future in an unfamiliar city alone. We head out onto the brutally cold Manhattan streets. Both of us moving in a wintery, sleep-deprived daze. She takes shots of New Yorkers on the Rolleiflex. And I observe and listen. She talks of a calmer, more intimate kind of photography, which seems at odds with the intensity of the city and the livewire energy of its citizens. I miss her when she leaves.

Ben's money buys me a month's grace on Erin's lumpy sofa.

Four tough weeks that put our fledgling relations under strain. Janet Delaney's friend is patient with me, but her daily queries about my plans begin to rankle. I fear that Erin is reporting on my lack of progress, and fearing any problems with Janet's mentorship, I'm driven towards the classifieds. Five weeks after arriving in Manhattan, I secure a stockgirl's job at Bloomingdales.

I leave Erin's apartment promising to stay in touch. The relief apparent in her goodbyes and good-lucks translates. Erin is the only person I know in a tightly packed population of almost one and a half million, but she will not expect to see me again.

The bohemian life I've imagined is out there waiting for me. I move from Manhattan to Queens and into the dank, squalid residence of a co-worker named Hennessey. Hennessey showed me the ropes during my first week in the store, and I took an instant liking to him. He seems desperate for company of any kind. His uncle, in tight with the tenants' association, reluctantly pulled strings to get him this piece of public housing on 62nd Drive and 108th Street. It was, he tells me, a hotly contested patch of the borough seventeen years earlier, when it was first designated for low-income habitation by the New York Housing Authority. By his own admission, Hennessey struggles with the upkeep of the place. The paint and paper peels from every surface, and wintry drafts blow determinedly through windows that have long lost their seals. Piles of ash fill several saucers, none from the same crockery family. Taped over a huge hole in the drywall is a poster of a sportsman: Kenny Dalglish, Hennessey informs me, a soccer player from the Glasgow Celtic. They were his pa's favorite team and since his pa's now dead, Hennessey has taken up the cause.

Hope to go and see them play some day, he tells me, wrapping his pa's beloved Celtic scarf around his neck. It's all he has left of him.

His desperation for a roommate to share the $30 a week rent has been as pressing as my need to become one. The apartment consists of one main room with one narrow bed. Hennessey says he'll sleep on a metal folding chair and that I can have the bed. He is just grateful to have someone to talk to. But, although this may sound weird, I feel like I've known him forever, rather than a few days.

We can share, I tell him.

I immediately pin the magazine cover featuring my dad and my polaroid of the Scottish guitarist to a wall over my side of the bed, as I have done in every place that I've laid my head since the night in Phoenix. I tell him that it means I intend to stay.

You're marking your territory, he says.

Hennessey – in all the time I spend with him, I never know his first name – is a young, wiry boy of Irish descent. He has the same pale skin and fairness of hair as Jimmy Montgomery, another transatlantic immigrant. I don't consider this a maladaptive fixation, part of a latent Electra complex, until years later when a therapist, in the aftermath of a painful break-up, raises it.

Hennessey introduces me to the weed he has been illegally growing on a tiny south-facing terrace. He is shy and awkward, and although he doesn't confess to it, I can tell that he is, like me, a virgin. Weeks pass and we grow closer and more intimate. His initial attempts at intercourse on the bed we share are endearingly tender, if a little unintentionally painful. Eventually, without a television between us, we get high and fuck regularly to pass long evenings cheaply. His confidence and dexterity improve with the practice, but I find sex with him neither pleasant nor unpleasant. Hennessy, to his credit, is always grateful. Never forceful.

For a year, this becomes our routine:

Monday to Saturday, we rise early. Take the short walk across 63rd to the Rego Park subway. Catch the yellow R-line to Lexington Avenue, invariably standing for the fifty-minute journey. Wash in the warm water of the store's staff restroom. Start work in the stockroom at 8.00am. Take lunch separately, me wandering the bustling metropolis, wide-eyed and with camera primed. In the afternoon, log, locate and distribute more stock around this horizontally organized city of commercialism. We clock off together and head back east. We eat, invariably beans or rice or, when the hunger pangs drive us to it, stolen lamb chops from the Cohen Kosher Meat Market on 108th.

On Sundays, I venture out. I wander, observing as Janet Delaney has taught me to. I take pictures of the local demographic. By my reckoning, the white faces outnumber the Black by around three to one, other than when the Mets are home at Shea Stadium. Only the slow, imperceptible shift of the seasons affects the time we spend outside of our twelfth-floor eyrie.

In January 1989, Hennessey loses his job, and the routine changes. He offers little detail regarding his apparent redundancy, yet it seems odd to me that the post-Christmas downturn has only claimed my roommate as its sole victim. I later find out that Hennessey was caught selling his homemade pot on the premises and was immediately fired.

I consider the change in our circumstances as a cue to look for somewhere else to live, but only once Hennessey can support himself. He believes the best route to self-sufficiency is in the manufacture and local retailing of his grass. I find this unlikely for several reasons: although far from a connoisseur – I don't indulge as fully as he does; I can't handle the paranoia it induces – I know Hennessey's pungent product isn't top of the range. Also, his price point will need to be low to attract the locals. And even if he succeeds, I fear his profits will go up in his own smoke. Most significantly, Hennessey lacks the necessary muscle to sustain the life of a drugs kingpin.

I take a second job, waiting evening tables at a fifties diner out near La Guardia Airport off Grand Central Parkway. The hourly rate is poor, but the tips are good. The restaurant's proximity to the Rikers Island Bridge ensures a clientele comprised of lawyers and gangsters with business on the island. The ability to turn a deaf ear to the chatter is well rewarded.

My extra income keeps Hennessey afloat – until the spring

when I leave him, and Queens. I gift him my dashboard Elvis, hoping, against logic, that it will favor him, as if it's a captured leprechaun. I take up residence in a low-rise Brooklyn loft space with two young women and an extravagantly gay man. The eldest of the three is Monique, a free-spirited artist of indeterminate age. Monique has a magnetic personality. She dresses in outlandish hippy clothing and is the centre of attention in any situation. But I like her a lot, and I sense that the feeling is mutual. The apartment is ostensibly hers, paid for by a middle-aged Italian who frequents the diner where we both work. Monique happily plays the part of paramour, acknowledging the many benefits it brings her, including courtesy cabs between our Bushwick neighborhood and the diner for our shifts. Although she brags that she doesn't need my share of the rent, she takes it. Regardless, it seems that, once again, I have fallen favorably at the feet of fate. The other female is Andrea Patullo, or Andi, as she prefers. Andi arrived in the city from upstate with dreams of becoming the next Madonna. She met Alessandro at a dance casting. They hit it off. That was six years ago. She sings. She plays guitar – left-handed like Jimi – and sends weekly cassettes to East Coast record labels. Despite many rejections, her optimism is undimmed. I take to Andi like a duck to water. Her relentless positivity is a boon. Puerto Rican Alessandro is a freelance make-up artist. He talks with a deeply sonorous and elongated pronunciation, as if he's rehearsing for *Phantom of the Opera* on the Broadway stage as opposed to his actual job of dressing the faces for it. His 'wall' in the apartment is lined with framed opening-night posters signed by the production's stars: Michael Crawford, Sarah Brightman, and Judy Kaye. Mine, by contrast, simply has my regular companions – my father, and the Scottish guitarist – although they are now supplemented by a snap taken of Hennessey as he looked skywards at a passing jet, which I managed to frame perfectly in the top right of the shot. I will certainly miss Hennessey, but Brooklyn represents progress.

I am welcomed warmly by all. There is an underlying tension between Monique and Andi, I observe, but I put it down to an initial possessiveness over me which I'm certain will pass once I become part of the sparse furniture. For the first time in my twenty-two years, I feel cool – simply for being in the orbit of interesting and creative people. Everybody I encounter, whether out on the sidewalks or on the unlit stairways, or on the cold industrial landings, has a smile and an interesting story to tell. I snap regularly, and gradually, I build a portfolio of diverse characters. The natural light filtering into the apartment is dramatic, and my series of monochromatic portraits are marked by the depth it helps me to capture. These willing subjects with time on their hands – the impoverished artists, the out-of-work musicians, the bit-part actors – all stimulated, as I am, by our shared environment.

It transpires that our building is owned by Monique's Italian *dolce papa*. He visits regularly, not only to see her and to view her canvases, propped up in the high-ceilinged space, but also to look out for his property. It's also the perfect cover for his criminal activities. I don't witness any of this, but I know from the Italian's polite warnings about seeing nothing and saying nothing that it happens. In return, we have rent stabilization protection. And right now, that's a good deal. Knickerbocker Avenue, where we are, suffered the consequences of the 1977 city blackout and the resulting riots more obviously than other parts of the borough. It's taken over a decade for property owners like the Italian to address obligations to bring buildings up to code and become eligible for a valuable Certificate of Occupancy for residential use. Most ratcheted up the rent to unaffordable levels. But the Italian hasn't.

I am living well at this point in my life. I've become accustomed to the orchestra of sirens and the periodic percussion of local gunfire. There is a bathroom with a door we can lock. Curtains drape luxuriously from rope tied to steel columns, allowing each of us to have a bit of personal space. The Italian has installed a long galley-type kitchen, and the intoxicating smells from Ales-sandro's exuberant cooking ensures there's a stream of visitors dropping by, and a constant hospitable buzz. Although some visit purely to trade in the Italian's produce. I'm earning, photograph-ing, contented, and, wrapped up in our little commune, not feeling obliged to consider those I have left behind in Humble or San Francisco, or more recently, in Queens.

It's September 1989.

Hey girl, says Andi. I got a couple of passes for a gig across the river tonight. Fancy comin'?

She already knows I'll come.

Sure, I say.

It's a Wednesday night and there's nothing doing otherwise. Besides, I have a later start in the store tomorrow due to the Thurs-day night stocktake.

Who's playing? I ask.

The B-52s, she says. It's at Radio City Music Hall.

Sounds good, I tell her, although I don't really know much of the band's music beyond the recent 'Love Shack' single, which has been a staple of MTV and the hip-radio station playlists for the last few months. However, it's a night out with my closest girl-friend. Andi and I shared a recent drunken sexual encounter, and no morning-after regret followed it. It has drawn us closer. We are careful to keep any manifestation of this closeness from Monique.

Cool, says Andi.

Baz – from her band – knows the singer from the support artists, and he can get us on the guest list.

We catch the L-line train at Myrtle-Wyckoff and head to Man-hattan early, as instructed by Baz. Half an hour later, we're walking up 6th Avenue, my arm looped through hers. The warmth from her body and the smell of her perfume makes me pull her closer.

The drummer in Andi's band meets us outside the venue. Although I now feel like an adopted New Yorker, the bright lights of this vertical city still take my breath away. It's as diametrically opposed to my Humble beginnings as it seems possible to get. Floodlights illuminate the darkening sky like we're attending a Hollywood premiere, or Commissioner Gordon is summoning Batman. I don't often photograph buildings as principal subjects, but on this occasion the beautiful Art Deco corner demands to be center stage.

Hey man, we're on the Love Tractor list, says Baz to the door attendant. It's under Stone. There's four, but one's already in.

Wristbands are strapped, identifying us as – for the purpose of tonight – VIPs. It prompts the same buzz of excitement I had at my first-ever concert, at the Razzle Rodeo Club in Phoenix nearly seven years earlier.

Up here, says Andi.

And instead of being out front in the stalls of this cavernous shell, we head to stage right.

Hi, we're Love Tractor. It's great to be here in New York City, at the famous Radio City Music Hall.

The band's singer is from the south, although not Texas.

Athens, Georgia, confirms Andi. Same as the B-52s. And REM, she adds.

And they are good. Very good. Although I spend more time snapping the audience, which is gradually growing in anticipation of the headliners. And then something remarkable happens. I remember Delphine shuddering once and saying that someone had just walked over her grave. That's exactly how I feel right then.

Thanks. This is a song we love. I hope we can do it justice, says the singer. And he strums familiar chords.

I've never heard any Love Tractor songs before tonight, but then, those lyrics...

Love hearts on the glass, dripping condensation
Your wild imagination, my lowered expectation

A habit hard to break, becomes an obligation
Think of better times, but just leave me on my own

He sings them serenely. And I can't believe it. Immediately I'm back there in Phoenix. Brandy screaming. Matt covered in blood. The polaroid on my wall.

A sad situation, a desperate generation
(An independent state of mind)
And we're different now. Opposite directions
(An independent state of mind)

The words still reach right into my soul. Andi can't understand why I'm suddenly crying. Why I am so upset.

I'm not, I tell her.

But she doesn't believe me. She leads me backstage to a quieter space. She kisses my cheek and wipes the tears from my face with her sleeve. We hear the appreciative cheers as the band finish their support slot. The four members of Love Tractor squeeze past us. One of them sees me.

You okay, miss? he asks.

Yeah, she's just a bit... says Andi on my behalf. Tailing off because she's not exactly sure what I'm just a bit of.

It's fine, I say through the sobs. Feeling tiny and foolish, like a little child who's dropped her lollipop in the dirt.

We don't normally make our audience cry, says the singer.

I look up. He's smiling. I smile too to reassure him and Andi that I really am fine.

That song, 'Independent State of Mind', I say. It means a lot to me. I just wasn't expecting to hear it tonight.

Ah, says the singer. We love that song too. The Hyptones. Great bunch of guys. We met them here in the city. Couldn't understand a word they said, mind you. He smiles. Shame what happened to them. Such a brilliant song, he says.

What do you mean? I ask.

Uh, the thing in Phoenix, and the breakdown, he says. I'm Mike, by the way. Mike Richmond.

He extends a hand, which he has politely wiped on his T-shirt first.

Jude, I respond. And this is Andi. She's in a band too.

Really? That's great, says Mike.

He ushers us into a packed dressing room, where I recognize the headliners from the scattered merchandise that's lying around.

Great set, guys, says a beautiful woman with an extraordinary mane of bright-red hair. It's Kate Pierson. I'll later be introduced to her after I fail to take a surreptitious photograph.

Cheers, Kate, says Mike.

The B-52s are getting ready to go on. Love Tractor sign T-shirts and programs and posters that bear their name.

I was there that night, I say to Mike. In Phoenix.

Jeez. Really? he says. He looks amazed. Wait there a second, he says.

He goes to a bag and rifles around in it. He brings out a magazine. *The Face*, from May earlier this year. Its glossy cover is folded and torn. The gurning cover star is the actor Dennis Quaid as Jerry Lee Lewis in a new biopic. Mike from Love Tractor hands it to me, just as an older man smoking a cigar draws him away.

I flick through the contents, not sure what he intends me to find. It's a British publication and most of the features involve people I've never heard of. But there's one about Mike Tyson and a model, and one that interests me about Robert Mapplethorpe. And then, right at the end, there it is.

'Ballad of the Band – the Tragic Story of The Hyptones,' by David F. Ross.

I take in the pictures first. There's a color shot of the band on the set of a TV show. There's a picture of the 'Independent State of Mind' record sleeve. A ticket stub from the night of the Razzle Rodeo Club concert. And then, on the final page of the feature, there's a blurred polaroid shot taken from inside the venue. I'm scanning the text for any references but before I reach the end...

Sorry about that, says Mike from Love Tractor. Promoters,

man. Every question sounds like a threat, y'know? He laughs. *Do you want some?* He was just asking about sugars for the coffee, but it felt like he was offering to break my legs.

This article, that's me, I stutter, pointing at the photograph.

Wow! Really? That's incredible, says Mike. Look, I'm gonna go catch the band. You can keep the magazine, he says, handing me a bright-yellow B-52s *Cosmic Thing* tour T-shirt.

Good luck with your band, he says to Andi before heading back to the stage.

I study every word of the story on the train home. I'm referred to, but obviously not named in the text. It chills me to see it all written down. The night Brandy and Matt's future changed. The night the guitarist's – Jamie Hewitt is his name – future changed. And me at the center of it all. Would I be here now, in New York, if we hadn't heard their song on the radio? I unfold the T-shirt and pull it on over my coat. Andi merely smiles. She knows little of my past.

I am wearing this yellow T-shirt, faded and holed though it is from five years of washing and moth consumption, when I next encounter Hennessey. I can't be sure it's him. But that makes no difference since he immediately knows it's me.

Fuck, Jude! The patron saint of lost causes. How the hell are ya? he says cheerily.

I see his dirty green-and-white scarf. He lifts a jaunty cap pulled to one side, and there are feathers in his filthy hair. I half expect a pigeon to fly out like it was part of a vaudevillian magic act. His face is smeared black. His eyes, once smiling, are different; from then, and to each other. He looks dreadful. At least twenty pounds lighter, and he didn't have that to spare. Ragged clothes hang from his fragile frame. When he stands, I can see bony ribs through a child's Mickey Mouse T-shirt stretched tightly over them.

He is in a bad place, literally and figuratively. I come across him sleeping rough in the shadows of an abandoned gas station on Avenue B and 2nd, down on the Lower East Side. He is sheltered under a sheet of corrugated metal bent out from the shed that I'm here to photograph. A plastic bag full of personal paraphernalia that has been doubling as a pillow contains the little dashboard Elvis Presley. I'm amazed he still has it. It's missing a lower leg. It hasn't brought him the luck I'd hoped it would.

What ya doin' way down here? he says, articulating the exact words that I'm thinking.

I'm here on a shoot, I tell him, and as I breathe in, I catch his rotten smell. I work hard not to gag.

Yeah? he says. All the way here to take me picture?

He smiles and it looks painful. Teeth missing and rotten. Faint Irish brogue dripping out past bloody gums. He looks and sounds like the singer from that band he liked; the one who sang 'The Broad Majestic Shannon', which he played constantly on the cassette player I got him for his birthday. I start to ask him how he's been but catch myself. Instead...

So, what you up to, J? asks Hennessey.

He speaks slowly. High or exhausted? It's hard to tell.

Working, I say.

He's surprised at this.

Capturing the Alphabet City vibe and specifically the 2B Art Space before it disappears, I tell him.

Motherfuckers, he snarls.

He's most likely referring to the developers planning to demolish the casual, relaxed buzz of creativity that exists inside the old industrial warehouse. Fires burn in metal drums tended to by those warming their hands over them. There's the woodpecker tap-tapping of a sculptor's hammer as he chisels a concrete block.

I notice the blowtorch of a young smith scorching a steel sheet. The 2B attracts rebels and rule breakers, artists and poets, sculptors, and anarchists. It's also an occasional home to the Bowery 'bums', who now include Hennessey in their growing number. The juxtaposition of the arty and the displaced, with a commercial wrecking ball imminent, is an angle the *Village Voice* will be expecting from me. It's a good story. A good new gig for me. Pictures and words. I salve my conscience with what I've taken from Janet Delaney. I'm not an observer sitting on the sidelines. I live here. I'm on the inside of the picture. I'm on the side of my subject.

To Rudy Giuliani, the newly elected Republican Mayor, the 2B is just another scary, unregulated piece of the city to be wiped away in his relentless clean-up campaign. Another place of authenticity deemed too dangerous and unprofitable to be permitted to exist. Like a lazy, disobedient student, not currently reaching full potential. I reconsider my brief and begin snapping my former bedmate against the wild, guerrilla graffiti backdrop. Hennessey poses as best he can until I tell him not to. He calls out to a downtrodden colleague; a fellow panhandler in a wheelchair who, hand out and without introduction, angrily yells back:

How's about some dough, Joe?

This is Avery, says Hennessey. Don't mind him, he calls everybody Joe.

Hi, Avery, I say. Can I take your picture?

He grunts. His hand extends further. I pull out five bucks and snap while he adjusts himself. Urine drips a trail from the underside of his chair as he rolls away from us.

Poor fucker, says Hennessey, without irony. Walked off the platform at Lafayette. Train was slowing so it didn't kill him. Better for him if it had. Lost his legs and stuck in that chair. And now he's not allowed to pan down there anymore.

Jesus, Hennessey, I say, not able to stop myself any longer. That's brutal.

He's at the crackpipe, too. It's tough for him, he says.

And you? I ask.

I'm off the junk now. I got the needle phobia. Not just AIDS. From way back, he says. Besides, I've got too much livin' to do. He tries to laugh but it degenerates into a guttural cough that sounds like his insides erupting.

What the fuck happened to you, Hennessey? I whisper.

He continues the cough and then winces. Whatever's going on inside of him isn't trivial.

The weed, man. Caused me a few problems up in the projects after you left. He tries to laugh again, as if it's nothing really. It was me own doin', I guess, he says.

The gangs? I ask.

This time just a rueful smile.

No. Me uncle. And me brutal fucken cousins.

He shakes his head.

They ran the blocks. Said I was bringing the 'hood down. Drawing heat from the cops. So, they hobbled me. Couldn't pay for the treatment. Apartment had gone when I got out of the rehab. He shrugs. This street ain't so bad, he says. Some good people here. We look out for each other. I sleep in the back of the 2B when it gets too cold, an' they serve us soup there. Good, good people here, he repeats. He sighs. Dunno what'll happen to us soon.

Your eye? I inquire. He smiles. I snap him up close.

A punch. A hefty left hook, he says. Pupil's fucken dilated. I can't see out of it good ... but hasn't done David Bowie any harm, yeah? Pull up a chair, he says, kicking over a small, rusting oil drum for me.

He slumps back down, grimacing. He has nowhere to be. All the time in the world. So, I tell him my tale. Just two old friends catching up...

❦

In the years since I last saw Hennessey, I've moved in the opposite social direction from him. Up in the world. I now feel like a real native New Yorker. Monique's Italian bought some of my pictures, along with Monique's art, and together we self-funded a small gallery showing in the West Village. A few paid pieces in the *East Village Eye* resulted in offers to freelance for the *Voice*. My writing, limited though it was, supported my photographs. My articles drew the occasional favorable comment. Eventually, I could afford to give up the diner, although I retained a promoted position at Bloomingdales. But Andi and I moved out of the Bushwick loft. The locale was rapidly descending into gangland turf wars. Old sneakers dangled on power lines over every street, signaling the location of a crack house or a prime drug-dealing spot. And it was becoming harder to ignore the Italian's often-violent visitors. But that wasn't the catalyst. There was a major falling-out with Monique. She was frequently wired; she'd become increasingly paranoid and hateful with it.

What you doin' with her, girlfriend? she'd say to me, referring to the relationship I had with Andi.

You're becomin' more white than nigger! Sheddin' your skin, just like the rest. You Black ... or you white? Ain't nothin' in between. No coffee-crème mulattos allowed in here, bitch. Pick a side, she challenged.

There was no coming back from the subsequent fight. That night, Andi and I were gone. A month after we left The Well, Monique was dead. Raped and murdered, and her body found discarded on waste ground on the edge of the Jackie Robinson Parkway. Monique had been caught transferring narcotics into Rikers Island. Alessandro was certain the Italian had ordered the sanction, convinced that she would rat him out as part of a plea bargain. It was made to look like a common assault. An unlucky hooker who picked the wrong john.

It occurred to me then that the free cab rides we enjoyed to and from the restaurant were trafficking more than just us.

Monique was a sweet soul, it's true, but always a little too easily drawn to the wild side.

Requiescat in pace, my darling.

We didn't go to the funeral. That was five years ago, back in 1992.

Andi and I now live on East 1st Street, in the Bowery. We left Queens with next to nothing, but the junk stores and thrift shops of the Lower East Side provide ample opportunity to supplement our meagre possessions. The front door of the apartment opens into the tiny kitchen. The bathtub is in the kitchen too. Privacy is at a premium. Over to the left, a small living space looks out onto evening sunlight when the weather plays ball. In the space between is an elevated platform – the bed. We go outside and down the hall to use – or queue for – a little water-closet toilet which no-one deems it their responsibility to clean. There is no ventilating window either. It's a quarter of the size of the Italian's Bushwick loft' and our building is a place of congregation for a squatting guild of artisans. But Andi likes it because of the area's proximitous association with the Ramones and Blondie and Television and the CBGB's fraternity. And I like it because I really like *her*. Emotionally and physically. The sex between us is invariably instigated by Andi, but always welcome. Despite an innate shyness, I become more adventurous on the occasions that she returns from rehearsals with a couple of wraps for us.

You blossom like a Texas flower on coke, she regularly tells me.

I live around here now, I say to Hennessy as I finish bringing him up to speed. Can I buy you a tea when I'm done? I ask him.

Sure, he says. If I'm still here.

And I'm not sure if he means in this location or this consciousness.

He leans closer.

Make me look cool, Jude, he pleads.

The dirty corrugations on his face are the equal of those he is surrounded by. He looks twenty years older than he is. I turn away because I don't want to cry in front of him. I'll weep for him later, and for Avery, and for every other poor soul facing eviction from the wasteland of the street. The only place they can call home. I spend the day prioritizing the inhabitants over their habitation, determined to pay tribute to their struggle.

Instead of a tea, I give him money and take off my old B-52s T-shirt, since he says how much he likes the color. I'm left in my bra and a thin jacket, but it'll fit him better than the one he's wearing. I promise I'll return and that I'll look out for him until Giuliani's crackdown on the street people, the minor offenders and the squeegee men, forces them all to move on. My track record on maintaining past contacts isn't good. But this is one commitment I intend to keep.

Here, he says as I'm about to leave. He hands me the dashboard Elvis. I'd just been lookin' after him for ya, until the next time we met. It brought me luck, he says.

And seeing my puzzled expression, he adds...

He brought you back to me.

I return to Andi and spend a grateful night in the safe, warm cocoon between her thighs.

(Act ii) 1995–2001

My editors at the *Village Voice* anticipate a photo essay in line with the brief – which I provide. But rather than atmospheric images of the 2B art district, I offer photographs of thirteen men, their names chalked on boards held in front of them. I entitle the photos 'Thirteen More Wanted Men' as a tribute to the large, controversial mural created by Andy Warhol for the New York State Pavilion at the 1964 World's Fair at Flushing Meadows, next to where Hennessey and I had lived. Warhol's brief then was to depict 'something to do with New York'. I decide to use it as an influence to explore man's place in a shrinking, changing world that prioritizes consumerism over humanism. I'm finding my voice, and its uniqueness is down to my personal connection to the subject. Janet Delaney taught me well. The text supports their struggle.

My article – 'The Low Expectations of The Bowery Bums' – is printed in the *Village Voice* in early 1996. My encounter with Hennessey shifted its focus towards an aspect that those who have never experienced homelessness won't be able to grasp. There may not be heating, or running water, or a front door that can be locked, but street people are part of a living community. They look out for each other, respecting the value of their meagre belongings or fortuitous finds. And they are as attached to the routines of their environment as those with a roof over their head. Hennessey, and Avery, and Ziggy Flatiron, and the rest of the Bowery Bums, don't want sympathy. They don't want disdain either. They simply want to be left alone in the courageous, characterful, complex, creative, mean streets they call home.

The piece, with its direct challenge to Rudy Giuliani to stop hammering the hot-dog vendors, the jaywalkers, and the homeless community, prompts conflict with the mayor's office. Shortly afterwards, the decision is taken to switch the *Voice* to a free, alternative weekly after years of the paper carrying a cover price. It may unintentionally hasten the eviction of those who populate the 2B Art Space. Rents increase by 900% in the aftermath of publication.

But more significantly for me, this article leads to an approach from a Madison Avenue advertising agency. They are offering me a year's contract. Where I lacked formal qualifications, I had the gallery-show reviews, Janet Delaney's endorsement, and the controversy of the *Voice* article demonstrating that I 'thought differently'; a key attribute at the Camel/De Souza agency. It is a real turning point for me. I initially feel embarrassed to have profited from Hennessey's encounter, especially since it has left him even more homeless, so to speak. I also worry about the uncredited paraphrasing of lyrics from the 'Independent State of Mind' record that I used in the piece, but Andi urges me to accept the offer. So, I do.

I say a fond farewell to Bloomingdales – and all who sold in her – in the fall of ninety-six. I'm not yet thirty. I am salaried, and on a full-term contract for the first time in my working life. I am being paid $21,000 a year as a junior art director at the Camel/De Souza agency. Everyone who works here is a director of something, it seems.

My early work for them is sporadic. Stock photography aimed at high-profile campaigns for Ford and Coca-Cola. Sketch ideas and concepts for other stock exchange-listed companies that do little other than illustrate my inexperience. None of my work is used.

Andi and I move again. Once again, at her insistence. This time, to a rent-controlled basement apartment of a brownstone in the West Village. I find it ironic that the gay bohemian vibe of Christopher Street is more obviously gentrified – the *after* of Giuliani's clean-up campaign – than the *before* of Bowery. But I do as I am told.

We move in on a night of city-wide celebration in late October. The New York Yankees have defeated the Atlanta Braves to win their first World Series in eighteen years. I head out late into spirited Greenwich Village streets that feel faintly reminiscent of the Times Square victory celebrations captured by Alfred Eisenstaedt in 1945. I pray for the happenstance of a Yankees fan embracing and kissing a total stranger, but I don't encounter anything that memorable.

It's July 1997. A regular job is a challenge. I don't fit easily into the kind of incubator where the juniors burst to impress and jostle with each other to catch a senior eye. The corporate 'we' preaches collaboration but it's rarely on show. And in any case, teamwork requires a level of discipline and compromise that is alien to my freelancing background. To compound this, my appearance, my southern twang, my unconventional route to this job, all mark me as an outlier, a social climber, one to be sidelined and, if necessary, devoured by the pack. It feels like I'm back in Humble High. Uncertain of myself and lacking the confidence to contribute. This claustrophobic office environment is like a strange laboratory melting pot where the Caucasians dominate. Survival of the fittest. Unsurprisingly, I say as little about outside interests as I can get away with.

Pick a side!

Monique's challenge rattles around my aching skull. Perhaps this is what she meant. Maybe it wasn't about personal attraction to a white woman, but the city's bifurcation on grounds of race and class. Black or white, nothing in between.

Which side are you on, Jude?

Months in and still finding my feet, I'm called into one of four internal teams to be briefed on a major assignment. Ten years prior, the agency lost the Apple Computer business account. Since then, Apple's fortunes have suffered. Original founder Steve Jobs left to form NeXT. Last year, NeXT was bought by Apple Computer. Our bosses in Manhattan and Los Angeles view this as an opportunity for Jobs to make up for the agency getting screwed over in the past. The agency will be pitching against three competitors for a major Apple campaign, and Jobs is expected to be heavily involved.

This is massive news, Jude, says Herman.

Herman is another junior art director. There is an army of us here on Madison Avenue. He is a Stanford graduate and Ivy League-keen. He is bemused by my indifference.

Just another job ... or *Jobs*, I say. Herman doesn't laugh. He's a serious fellow.

There's no time to script a long, written-out strategy or to storyboard a detailed creative brief, says an impossibly exuberant account director who has flown in from Los Angeles.

We gotta figure out how to get Apple back on track, and fast. List the strengths and weaknesses in their market, he says, as the entire studio scribbles every word.

Look for uniqueness. Look for shock. Look for impact, we are told.

A room full of junior creatives simmers in anticipation of being the one that provides the spark. One potential strategy is outlined – simple monochrome photographs of revolutionary people and events. Black-and-white headshots are my milieu. For the first time since arriving at the agency, I'm in control of an output. Over the course of a week in which I barely leave the studio, we – me, Herman and five others who've rarely worked together before – sketch out ideas for ads involving a photograph I've sourced of Albert Einstein. Someone else has a photo of Gandhi. Rosa Parks features. Muhammad Ali. Another carries the famous photo of flowers placed in gun barrels during the protest against the Vietnam War. Our team has tacked photos, images, sketches, phrases to every wall surface in our corner of the room. The approaches taken by other teams are, to my mind, mediocre and forgettable. A management review of interim work is under way, and it is not progressing constructively. The pressure is getting to everyone in the agency.

Who the fuck's this guy? an abrupt senior colleague asks, glancing at my snap of Hennessey from the *Village Voice* piece. He fingers an elastic band that's holding his long, black, shiny hair in a preposterous ponytail. No-one answers. My colleagues turn to look at me. The sly stare of blame.

Was this you? he asks.

I don't answer initially. He's not letting it go.

Hey, Daisy Duke, I'm speaking to you.

It's no-one, I say defensively.

Why the fuck's he up here then?

It's the style of the photograph, I stammer. I think it might be—

Well, don't *think!* I'm interrupted. We don't pay you to think. He's a bum. Get it down from there. You *think* we're gonna present Steve fucking Jobs with a campaign that features some hobo cunt who's never even seen a computer before?

I stare, motionless.

Well? he says impatiently.

I am an example being made to the other juniors.

Get your thumb out your butt, sweetheart! he shouts.

I unpin Hennessey, removing him from the gallery of geniuses.

Hey, don't worry about him, says Herman once the critics have moved on. He's an asshole. Even some of the higher-ups think so. I've heard them.

It's cool, I tell him.

But it isn't. Affronted and close to tears, I take a sharpie and write *THINK!* in the wall space vacated by Hennessey's portrait, above a scribbled representation of the Apple logo. I leave the studio aggrieved and exhausted. A jumper on the line closes the subway to my neighborhood. Rather than waiting, I walk home in the hope that it clears my head. It doesn't. Back at our basement, Andi is entertaining.

Hey honey, she says.

She's drunk. Her arms have a life of their own. They drape around me before I can get my jacket off. This is an uninhibited show for two equally drunk strangers. Empty bottles litter the floor.

Who's this? I ask in a stressed, exasperated husband-from-the-sixties tone.

Well, she giggles, this is Bobbie, and over there ... that's Jackie.

The cuteness of their names is lost on me.

We met over at the auditions with R. Kelly. I *love* them, she slurs.

The door opens behind me. Another guest.

An' this is—

Barbie? I say, interrupting her.

She now knows I'm furious. Three identikit white models toss their backcombed hair and raise melodramatic eyebrows at the row that's brewing.

Well, no, sugar ... *not* Barbie. This is, em, Mindy.

Hi, I say. Sullen and uncooperative and I know I'm at fault but it's a runaway train and there's no brakeman. I pull away from Andi's uncoordinated arms.

Look, everybody, I'm sorry, but I've had a real shit day at work. I'm beat. Another time, yeah?

That's the signal for them to leave. But they don't. They double down. Another bottle gets opened. It's them or me. But I have no place else to go.

Yeah, we've all been there, girlfriend, says Bobbie or Jackie.

The attempt at sisterhood solidarity falls on its ass. My irritation increases. I'm uncomfortable around people, is the way Andi will explain my behavior to them tomorrow. And, in a sense, she'll be right. Photography offers engagement but at a distance. I have few friends. Andi, Hennessey and, when he can be bothered, Alessandro. That's about it. There's no-one from my past. Only the present. There's no-one from work. But I've carefully cultivated this isolation. I take lunch at my desk, or out in Central Park photographing people. When I get too exhausted to continue, I go home. My co-workers hit the bars. They stopped inviting me months ago.

Been where, exactly? I ask.

My arms are folded and I'm suddenly aware of the tension rising up my body. The one called Mindy makes the mistake of putting her hands on my shoulders. There's a head-tilt. Condescension alert.

Girl, kick off those sneakers and chill, she says.

You know how you reach for hurtful sentences that you don't really mean? But you do it to start an argument, or end one? No? You *don't* do that? Really? Well, I do.

I'm fucking sick of being talked down to by talentless, privileged white people! I scream.

The air goes out of the room. I see the three guest backing singers look at me closely. Studying me intently. My recessive white genes. My blue eyes. My short blonde hair. My ever so slightly non-Caucasoid nose. Andi's hands cover her face.

What the fuck, Jude? she utters from behind them.

You know I'm Black, right? No? You weren't aware? Fuck, that's a pity. We could've had a party game. Guess what race she is. I bet you'd never get it.

Jude, that's enough, shouts Andi.

Tears are welling in her eyes and her mascara is running. She still looks pretty, but we're past the point of no return.

But ... Black people don't have freckles, says Mindy, and it's almost funny the naive way she says it. It's the kind of thing close friends laugh at years later: *Remember when Mindy first met Jude, and she said...* as we're preparing to be each other's bridesmaids.

We should go, whispers Bobbie or Jackie.

Probably best, I say firmly.

They shimmy past and kiss their hostess. I hear one offering to call later. Probably concerned that the Black woman will resort to type and murder the white one.

The fight, when it comes, is a relief for both of us.

You've been absolutely fucking intolerable since you've been with that agency, she says.

That agency that *you* persuaded me to join, I counter.

I can't do this anymore, she says. She's spinning out. Clothes are being thrust into a holdall.

Do what, exactly? Swan about the apartment getting loaded with the white Supremes.

Well, it's more fun than being with you, these days, she yells.

Okay, why not spend *all* your time with them then? I'm sure R. Kelly's got a few spare bedrooms up in Long Island.

Fuck off, Jude! she screams.

You're quite happy when my job, which you hate, pays the rent, and buys alcohol for you and your friends, I scream back.

This is unfair. My earnings are regular, hers have been sporadic. But she's been doing profitable session work of late. And now there's this R. Kelly American tour in the offing. Things should be great for us. Both working, both contributing. But we reach for words that will harm most when we are upset, and often, the trigger for it masks a bigger underlying issue.

It's not your job that I hate, she says, before leaving.

A slammed door is a full stop.

I slump on the beanbag. Staring out my basement window high up into the night sky. A full moon illuminates the edge of the room, catching me in the narrow field of its spotlight. I've never reached for the racial epithets before. It's the first time I've felt a pressure to establish racial clarity. I still don't know if I identify with being Black or white, one more than the other. Or why it's even important to do that. But suddenly, it's consuming me. I'm exhausted but I can't sleep. Starving, but I can't eat. And a realization emerges as dawn breaks. The naive positivity that I carried with me from Humble has morphed into something different.

I'm saying YES! but only to other people's desires for me:

Moving to Lakeview: Brandy
Moving in with Hennessey: Hennessey*
Sex with Hennessey: Hennessey*
Moving out of the Brooklyn loft: Monique
Lesbianism: Andi*
Moving to the Lower East Side: Andi
Accepting the agency job offer: Andi
Moving to the West Village: Andi

*I shouldn't imply that these were coercive. I was a willing participant, if not the instigator.

I return to the agency early the next morning. I still don't know where Andi has gone, and my stupid pride prevents me from trying to find out. The realization that I may be incapable of love, that I sabotage happiness, hits me hard. I catch sight of myself in the glass of the reception's doors. It's unlikely that my disheveled state will be noticed. Many of the younger creatives and interns do all-nighters when a big campaign deadline is coming up. When I reach the board room, there is a buzz of activity and it's all focused on my team's corner. One of the L.A. directors is pontificating over a clipboard. His manner makes it hard to determine whether he's pleased or angry.

This...! *This* is brilliant, I hear him say.

Pleased it is, then. Through gaps in the suits, I see him pointing at the place where Hennessey's photograph was pinned. At my sketch of the Apple logo. At the word *THINK!*

It's *so* different. This is genius. Who is the author of this piece? He asks, and before Herman can speak, the pony-tailed asshole puts his hand up and tells everyone it was him.

The *Think Different* campaign is in full swing. *Different* has been added in L.A. *Think Different* is interesting. It may be grammatically clumsy but attaching those words to some of the world's most different-thinking people is simplistic genius, the essence of every successful advertising campaign in history.

The campaign focus shifts to the West Coast, to Palo Alto and to the office of Apple CEO, Steve Jobs. The computer mastermind is taking a central role in the development of the ads. He was previously unconvinced about television as the right medium. The pony-tailed asshole is no longer with the agency. He moved on. He's the type that moves on every six months or so. He's the type with an eye constantly on other opportunities. He's the type who times the jump before an internal appraisal finds him out. He's the type of asshole that prospers in the advertising fraternity. Male, white, slimy used-car-salesman style, and no fucking substance whatsoever. I write *Fuck You Asshole!* in his leaving card and depart the building before he opens it.

I'm less involved in the Apple campaign now, but my remaining contribution is to compile a list of potential music tracks to reinforce the message. It's a slim reward for my earlier input being attributed to the ponytailed asshole, but I suck it up. I hear a song on the radio one morning. It has a chorus that goes:

Come on, come on, come on little rabbit,
Show me where you got it 'cause I know you got a habit.

It strikes an immediate chord with me, but I'd struggle to explain the relevance to my colleagues. So, naturally, I suggest 'Independent State of Mind' as an early choice. I argue that it reinforces a unique way of thinking, an independence. A celebration of the crazy ones. The misfits. The rebels. The troublemakers.

I scan copies of David F. Ross's 'Ballad of the Band' article and send a memo to everyone in the promo team, with '<u>It Doesn't Get Much Crazier Than This</u>' underlined as its subject heading. I conceal my own involvement in the final craziness and the notion takes root, over predictable alternatives from the standard MTV star roster. I promote the notion that the music should support the idea of different or independent thinking, but without the track being so well known that it competes with the associated twelve geniuses. After all, John Lennon and Bob Dylan and Jimi Hendrix are among the chosen ones. Wouldn't it be odd, I successfully assert, for a Michael Jackson or a Madonna track to play underneath them? The Hyptones record gets promoted to the next round. And I am instructed to pursue rights for its potential use. I start with the writer David F. Ross, and the contact details listed in *The Face* magazine. Calls are made.

Weeks pass with no obvious progress. Then a call comes through to the office for me. It's from an organization based in Scotland called AFB Management, who look after the rights to 'Independent State of Mind'. Eventually, the deal is done. My song choice gets green-lit. And I feel a sense of atonement, in knowing that Jamie Hewitt's band will reap the benefits of Apple's global reach, regardless of what they are doing now.

The Millennium comes and goes. We survive it. Planes don't fall out of the sky. No-one is reported dead because of a catastrophic computer failure. I celebrate the survival of our species alone. One postcard – from, ironically enough, Houston – is the extent of any contact from Andi:

Hi. Hope you're okay. Tour is tough. RK is a fucking sexist asshole!
Don't say I told you so.
  We should speak. Happy New Years.
  Andi x

That was nine months ago. We haven't spoken. The postcard is still on the fridge door, held in place by an 'I ♥ NY' magnet.

I head out for a regular catch-up with Hennessey. His posture is as poor as it was when I photographed him, but his complexion has improved with a roof regularly over his head. And he has bulked up too. For eighteen months, I've been giving him a part of my salary. He declined to begin with, but I persisted. He'd earned it. Those photographs for the *Voice* opened doors for me, even if I sometimes wish they'd remained closed. He deserved part of the reward, and I was only too happy to share it with him.

How's things, buddy? I ask.

I'm tip-top, doll, says Hennessey.

We sit on the grass at Battery Park. His choice of location. I take his photograph, as I do regularly. He doesn't look at the lens or pose. He knows the drill.

Never mind me, he says. How's the new place?

It's good, I say. Nice to have an outlook.

And it is. I'm still in the Village but on the third floor of a block on the corner of Bedford and 7th. It's tiny, but I don't have to share my claustrophobia.

The basement was fine, but it was too dark, I say.

Yeah, the darkness, I know, he says, and we both wrinkle rueful smiles from the corners of our mouths. The darkness that drove Andi away. Not the lack of daylight.

An' what 'bout you? he asks.

I'm fine, I say, with downward emphasis.

Don't sound like it, he says.

And he's right. I'm in a bind. After two years, I'm as essential to Camel/De Souza as a whiteboard, or a graphics card or, yes, an iMac. We're the spokes that the efficiency of the wheel is based on. But we're just spokes. Ordinary and unremarkable. Taken for granted until one of us breaks and then anger is the response.

Jesus, it's just a job, Hennessey. At least I've got one, I say, and it sounds like a jibe at him, which I'm about to correct when...

So have I, he says.

And it's uttered so matter-of-factly that I almost miss it.

A job, he says to reinforce.

What?

I got a job, he repeats.

Really? where?

Over there, he says.

He is nodding towards the financial district, and I can't help but laugh. But he isn't joking.

I'm gonna be a janitor, he says, as proudly as an expectant father.

Honestly?

I can't quite believe it, given everything he's been through.

Yeah, he says. That's why I wanted to bring you here. I'm gonna be involved in some big world trade. He laughs. Well, cleaning up after it.

I'm so happy for him, I lean over and hug him, and slowly, we overbalance, and I land on top of him. We hold the embrace until I feel his cock hardening underneath me. I don't acknowledge it as it will embarrass him.

I simply say, That's so amazin', Hennessey. Now you'll have to tell me your first name.

Guess, he says, just like he has every other time I've asked him.

You still behavin' yourself at the shelter? I ask him.

Sure, he says, between mouthfuls of meatball sub.

You made any friends?

Some.

Any *girl*-friends?

No. He swallows and looks down.

Doesn't pay to get too close to folks on Skid Row. They usually ain't about for too long, y'know? he says.

You sure? I ask, pointlessly. But Hennessey senses my desire to unload.

You got somethin' to tell *me*? he asks.

I rub my hand across my face and sigh in a where-do-I-fucking-start manner.

Jeez, where do I fucking start, I say, confirming the full extent of the awkwardness I've gotten myself into with a high-maintenance married client. It's doubtful Hennessey can offer anything other than a non-judgmental ear but right now, that's exactly what's needed.

For six months, I've been gettin' in deeper and deeper with this client, I tell him.

What d'you mean, deeper? he asks.

Another sigh. Another melodramatic wipe of my sweating brow.

Sex? he asks. He already knows the answer.

It's worse than that, I tell him. She's been payin' me for it.

She? He seems surprised at this, like Andi was just a phase I'd grow out of. Or maybe I'm just overly attuned to any negative inferences today.

Her name's Astrid Atard. She commissioned my agency for a freelance shoot, havin' seen some of my earlier pictures in *Aperture* magazine. She said I had a unique eye for capturing sadness and hope simultaneously.

You do, says Hennessy, wryly.

I was flattered. Those photographs were from a time when I was struggling financially, but I think they were amongst my best work, I say.

Always better to get the excuses in first, I've learned.

She's one of these bored Hamptons housewives with too much time on her hands and far too much money, I tell him, laying the seeds of blame.

So, what was the job? he asks. He has turned himself round to face me, becoming more curious by the sentence.

My brief was to capture her in a series of disparate contexts over a three-month period for the opening night of a photographic gallery her financier husband was funding in her name.

Fuck, Jude ... imagine havin' money to burn on shit like that.

Yeah, but she wanted to be photographed up in the projects ... above 110th or up in Prospect Heights. I mean, fuck, Hennessey: a white woman in a fur coat and me wanderin' after her with an expensive camera around my neck. I think I'm tough enough, but, Jesus...

What about the sex? He says this in a way that implies he'd like to extract a tasty bone or two from my miserable carcass.

More sighing, but I figure he's earned a morsel.

Well, since you ask ... The first time we had sex was on a tiny rowboat off Shinnecock Bay. I was drunk. She lay back, an arm above her head. She waved to a friend on the shore while she guided my fingers to her pussy with the other hand. Afterwards, we ate cold cuts and then I threw up over the side.

Holy fuck, he says. And we both laugh loudly at the absurdity.

She invited me to a party held in an expensive apartment on the Upper East Side, hosted by a woman named Luna, one of her friends, I continue.

Jeez, the high life, huh?

I shake my head.

She's there, lordin' it over everyone even though it's not her party. 'Jude ... over here,' she shouts, snappin' her fingers. 'Jude, doll, take a photograph of us. We're celebrating.' These five women – four white, one Black person – pose. Bonnie, the Black woman, she seems as uneasy as me. This Luna, she has one of these new mobile telephones with in-built point-and-shoot cameras. I've never seen one before. I take some photos of them with it. None of them passes the bar. In all of them, Astrid's face is like a lemon-suckin' rodent.

I bet, he says.

'Oh no, look at your face, Bonnie, Jude's made you look *so* haggard,' says Astrid. 'Those lines.' Fucking shakin' her head. 'Maybe this one?' and she holds it up to the others, an' I can tell from Bonnie's reaction that it's one where I've managed to cut her out of the shot. 'This is the best one. It's a shame you're not in it though, Bonnie. And that's from a professional photographer too,' fucking Astrid jokes, tut-tuttin', and laughin' at me. 'I might need to rethink your rate.'

What a bitch, says Hennessey.

I left early tellin' nobody, but before I did, I whispered to Bonnie, 'Your friend Astrid, she's a cunt!'

Ha Ha, good for you, says Hennessey. He applauds.

I saw Astrid one more time, a few nights after the party. She was in a rage and cracked a bottle of expensive Champagne off my forehead because of Bonnie's gossipy tattle, I say.

Fuck, Jude, you've gotta get out of that viper's nest, Hennessey says.

I know, I tell him.

I have become a prostitute. I'm ashamed of myself, and of the way I allowed Astrid's money to pollute me. I shudder when I think of Janet Delaney and what she would say if she knew. And if – as she has threatened – Astrid Atard reports my less-than-exemplary conduct to my employers.

I could lose my job, Hennessey, I say.

You won't, he says, and despite him having no basis on which to make that assertion, I briefly believe him. I leave for home, grateful that he's in my life and feeling that in this city of five boroughs and eight million people, Hennessey might be the only one I need.

This thought carries me uptown to my apartment. When I get there, a card has been taped to my door. The words on it read:

I'M COMING FOR YOU AND YOU WON'T KNOW WHEN

❦

I now send regular letters to Lakeview. I enquire after Rabbit. That is always the purpose of my correspondence. Pleasantries, yes. Updates, yes. But it is always about Rabbit. How she is doing in school. If she is still drawing and painting. If she is happy. The replies – from Ben, obviously – are sporadic, but they confirm that he's been calling my mom and Larry and letting them know I am fine. When I get the call that morning, I know it is because Ben has passed on my number even though I asked him not to.

Hey, Jude. It's Larry. Your mom's sick, he says.

Straight to the point, from which I can gauge the seriousness. I look at my watch. 6:52am.

I think you should come home, sweetheart, he says.

I'm blindsided.

Uh, I've got work, I reply.

It's an instinctive reaction to buy time. Time Delphine clearly doesn't have. For all the obscure conditions that could've claimed her, it's a common one that has snuck up undetected. Pancreatic adenocarcinoma: the worst of the cancer variations, as I understand. A truly rapid onset with no obvious symptoms that Larry has been aware of. She has either kept them hidden or was as shocked as he was four weeks ago when a sudden stomach pain and unexplained weight loss found their cause. Either way, she has days. A week or so at most. At least she won't be suffering the extended ignominy of the typical poverty-stricken, terminally ill American. Larry won't see it this way, of course. In the future, he'll appreciate the speed of the journey from diagnosis to deathbed.

Come home, Jude, he says. Softly but firmly.

Okay.

It's 8.00am. I call the agency. A receptionist answers. I get through to someone in Human Resources.

A week off at such short notice isn't ideal, Jude, but since it's a close relative…

I look through my current client contacts. An early-morning meeting will have to be cancelled. I am due to photograph the new World Trade Center artist-in-residence on an upper floor of 1 WTC. The agency is hoping to commission original artwork for an airline campaign. The artist is Scottish. I'd been looking forward to talking to her about her background. And taking shots of the city as it wakes, from the highest point above it. And there would've been the bonus of catching up with Hennessey over a coffee in his new place of work.

I call to reschedule. The Scottish artist's number rings out. It's still early. An impossibly beautiful Manhattan fall morning. The most mesmerizing blue sky. Unseasonably humid, too. I open the window fully to take it in. Breathing in deeply; the calmness before the emotional storm of Humble. I take a shower and after some breakfast, decide that I'll address the issue of booking a flight to Houston. I walk into the kitchen still wrapped in a towel. I pour coffee. I take a bagel from the basket and pick at it. I look out again to the developing bustle on 7th Avenue. It's 8.42am.

I call the artist's number. Again, it rings out. This time, I leave a message:

Hi there, it's Jude Montgomery here. We were due to meet this morning but I'm really sorry. I've had some personal news from home, and I'll have to reschedule. I'll try to catch you again later. Hopefully, we can rearrange for later in September.

I don't say 'bye'. And I don't hang up either. A large bang over to my right startles me. It sounds more like a train wreck than an RTA. I rush over to the window. Whatever has just occurred shocks people in the street below. They point. Upwards. Their hands cover their mouths. I remember the reactions on the day of the shooting at Humble High. This is similar. Drivers get out of their cars. They step forwards, doors left wide open. Motors idling. As if they can't quite believe what they are witnessing.

What's happenin'? I shout down from my building.

No-one hears or acknowledges me. I turn the television on.

CNN morning anchor, Carol Lin, is speaking over a startling image.

...This just in. You are looking at obviously a very disturbing live shot there. That is the World Trade Center, and we have uncon-firmed reports this morning that a plane has crashed into one of the towers...

I look at the clock. It's 8.48am. My meeting with the artist was to be on the 110th floor of the north tower. I'm close to the screen. Hoping for some clue as to what tower the grey smoke is billowing from.

Which tower is it? I shout at the screen.

My breathing is escalating. What one does Hennessey work in? The artist won't be at work that early. Creative people sleep late and work to their own clock, don't they?

In minutes, flames are witnessed. A commercial jet? No-one onboard can have survived this.

Jesus fucking Christ!

I stagger backwards. I reach for my bag. The long lens that I hardly ever use pokes out. I changed it last night in preparation for the city shots from the top of the World Trade Center. I stuff rolls of film in the side pocket. I pull on my sneakers and head out.

Out in the street, there's an air of quiet disbelief. I snap ran-domly and without properly focusing. People react to what is happening. And even before I round the corner to see what they are looking at for myself, I know that this is something tragic and historic I am witnessing.

The tower, when it finally comes into view down 7th Street, takes the air out of me. I lift the lens, and as I press to take the shot, a second plane smashes into the middle of the other tower. It's 9.03am.

Hennessey! I call out his name and know nothing will ever be the same again.

Two planes hitting the Twin Towers isn't a coincidence. It can no longer be a calamitous accident.

Oh my God, we're under attack! someone yells.

The shock of earlier turns to panicked screaming. All around me, people scour the skies, looking through the drifting, darkening smoke. We are staring, many of us through tears, fearful of more planes. The first tower hit is damaged near the top. The second tower is visibly holed closer to the center. The impact on the latter looks greater. A bigger airplane perhaps. I'm running, unaware of when I started, towards downtown. Sirens now drown out the cacophony of other insistent sounds. I reach the junction of Varick Street and West Broadway. I stop, out of breath, unable to run like I once did. Still panting, I instinctively lift the camera again. I focus closely on the first tower hit.

It looks like it could collapse any second, I hear from over my shoulder.

Unthinkable minutes ago, it now seems inevitable that it will. The top of the building explodes, like a faulty firecracker. And I stare at it through the viewfinder. I press. And I press. And the structure suddenly tears apart. And I press. And the insides of it burst out in millions of tiny pieces. And I press. And the screams from all around me intensify. And I press. I focus again. Closer. Papers fly out of the gaping wound like confetti. Tiny dots fall straight down from the top. I focus closer. The dots are shaped like humans. The dots *are* human beings. Jumping out of a burning building a hundred stories above the city. Jumping for their families. Jumping because identification *might* be possible that way. I zoom in tight on one. A Black woman, in a smart business suit and white blouse. I can see her so clearly. She is floating effortlessly. Calm, relaxed, resigned to dying. I press repeatedly. Twelve shots in the short time it takes for her life to end. And it seems like everything is frozen in time except this monument to Western free-market capitalism collapsing right in front of us. And I press. It feels wrong to be recording such a catastrophic loss on film. Of life, surely. Of lifestyle, certainly. Of liberty? Well, that depends on what this is we are witnessing. Like Janet Delaney taught me,

I don't look away. I'm an invading onlooker at the scene of a terrible accident. All I can do is press. And it's not like the Bowery Bums. I'm removed from this. A voyeur merely filming, not emotionally entangled. Not yet at least.

In minutes, the mushroom cloud of dust and debris is rolling towards us. It engulfs the street before us, like a brutalist urban sandstorm.

Run, lady. Fucking run for it!

A man's face yelling straight into mine breaks the spell the fog has over me. It's almost upon us. I'm unable to move. Rooted to the spot, waiting for it to hit. I'm pulled down. Dragged along. Under a vehicle. The white noise of this concrete avalanche is astonishing. I can't hear. Everything turns black. The brilliant sunshine of that beautiful September morning has been extinguished. This is the Dust Age.

The first sounds I can distinguish are glass breaking and a voice desperately calling through the blackness. It sounds like I am underwater. I crawl out from this impromptu shelter. I feel around for my savior, but there's no-one close to me. I make my way towards the despairing voice. There is a faint glow ahead. I follow it. It guides me to a deli. Inside, firefighters, police officers and a few others stumble around. They cough out mouthfuls of mud. They pour bottles of water over their faces. They catch intermittent breaths.

You okay, miss? someone asks.

I can't tell if it's a man or a woman. We are all coated in dusty gray. Like we've crawled from an ash-filled pit.

Yeah. I think so, I say, and my throat feels like sandpaper has been drawn across it. The person – I think it's a woman: stoutly built, and with a deep, croaky Joan Rivers accent – pours cold water on my face. I reel from the shock of it.

Be careful, she says. That looks real nasty.

I put my hand to my forehead and feel the wetness. I look at my fingers. Whatever it is, it's dark and thick against the gray. I sniff the rusty-iron odor. My head is cut; but then so is everyone else's. I brush it off, feeling for my camera. I can't determine if it's damaged or not. I drip some of the bottled water across the lens and wipe it clean. And I press again.

Outside, the neighborhood is still engulfed in the dust cloud's darkness. But another sudden dull, booming sound makes me run again. This time, away from the carnage. My running stops quickly. My windpipe feels like it is constricting, preventing air getting in or breath getting out. 7th Street is an exodus of fellow survivors slowly making their way out of the smoke and towards the daylight. Everyone is completely powdered. Everyone is bleeding from some source. Nevertheless, it's remarkable how calm and quiet we have become as shock takes hold. We just silently, slowly make our way to safety. I catch myself whispering – Don't be at work, don't be at work, don't be at work – over and over and over.

I pray that he's sick. I pray that he missed a train. I pray to the Lord God Almighty – whom I've never called on for favors before – that some divine intervention has stopped Hennessey from being one of those damned, doomed souls who jumped from thirteen hundred feet to avoid being incinerated by twenty thousand gallons of aviation fuel.

The voices inside the apartment surprise me. They are coming from the television, which I must've left on. Rudy fucking Giuliani is being interviewed. I turn the volume down. I'm exhausted. Filthy. Smeared in the grit and the dirt and the dust and the ash of what feels like a cremated city. I burst into tears for the umpteenth time in a few hours. I can't order my thoughts. I have no idea what to do next. I suddenly want to get out of the city, to head south, away from this destruction. But I can't until I know Hennessey – and the artist I was due to meet – are safe. And I need to shake a terrible thought; that Astrid Atard might have perished, saving me from future disciplinary action. I need answers. My phone beeps. I'd left it on the table in the rush to leave. Sixteen missed messages. None from those I'm currently concerned about. Fourteen are from Larry. One is from Ben. One is from Andi.

🐾

Sun rises on the twelfth. I haven't slept. It wasn't a nightmare. It really happened. The streets are empty. Downtown from 14th Street the police patrol relentlessly. I venture out, with camera. Dumbfounded by the eerie silence, punctuated only by a speeding ambulance. Staggered by the extent of the devastation, these monumental structures rendered to rubble. Dumbstruck by the carcass of twisted, ragged steel around what is now being referred to in the media as Ground Zero. A rib cage ripped open, exposing the city's ischaemic heart.

For two desperate days, I pace the detritus-ridden streets of downtown Manhattan, searching for clues of Hennessey. But all I find is hundreds and hundreds of bereft people hunting cluelessly, like me. I have pictures of him, from the Think Different! times. Black-and-white mugshot photographs; Hennessey, once again, a wanted man. I visit the local hospitals, showing his picture to sad shakes of the head. I become convinced that he is wandering the streets, dazed and confused, and unaware of who he is or what has just happened to him. Some kind people I show the photo to ask his name, but I can only say 'Hennessey'. An address? I burble that...

He has a new place ... over in The Bronx, but I don't know where. He hasn't told me. He wants to wait until he's fixed it up better before I visit...

I paste the contact sheets to walls, trees, store windows, subway signs – any public surface where the tape will adhere. Hennessey is a tiny part of a massive collage of pain. Some pictures bear medical or dental records to help identify the corpses. But most of the images just tell personal stories. The children that are without a parent. The wives missing a husband. The brothers, the sisters, the uncles, the aunts. Each poster registers a pain that is impossible to describe. Many of the missing are smiling in these photographs. The juxtaposition of happiness and loss is devastating. Another one of Janet Delaney's lessons: there is a truth in photography that is multi-layered.

The devastating pleas record just how loved these people are, as if acknowledging this will make the crucial difference between finding them and not. It's an excruciating gallery of tragedy, pinned along street after street. Many of these pictures will remain in place after all reasonable hope is gone. Nobody will remove them. Nobody will desecrate these memories. They are obituaries-in-waiting for those that won't return. Hennessey now joins them, this growing army of missing soldiers. All lost in action. My heart breaks for all of them. I photograph as many of these homemade homages as I can.

Three days later, I'm on an overnight Amtrack from Penn Station. It was the first one available. The closure of North American airspace has now been lifted, but I can't deny the apprehension I have about boarding a plane right now, despite the substantial increases in security that will be in place. Locking the stable door after the horse has bolted is not reassuring me.

It takes more than two days to get to Houston. Two days of listening to fearful, fevered conversations in a hot, cramped economy-class compartment. Manhattan is in ruins. The dead number into the thousands. Hundreds more remain unaccounted for. The attack on the World Trade Center is our generation's Pearl Harbor. That's the consistent view. For the more vocal passengers among us, those responsible for the outrage in New York range from the Russians, the Muslims – or towelheads, as they are referenced – and the Democrats.

A fight breaks out as our train nears New Orleans. Not, unsurprisingly, down to anyone mounting a defense in support of these groups, but because a Black man, travelling alone, shakes his head when the burly, red-faced southerner opposite him yells, We gotta nuke all these commie bastards!

Our nation's questionable foreign policy is one thing, but raw emotions always boil over when our perceived freedoms are threatened on our own soil. We're a nation of aggressors. With a natural impulse to reach for a weapon as a means of control. As a mechanism to win an argument. To prove a point. To fight back.

My mom died about eight hours after I boarded the train. I'd forgotten to charge the battery for my phone, compounding this by forgetting to take the charger with me. Larry's face when I glimpse it on the concourse of Houston station tells me all I need to know. I'm ever so slightly relieved, I have to admit. I don't possess the emotional depth for a deathbed atonement, and I suspect Delphine would've preferred it this way too. A flight from New York would've given us a few hours at most, but what could that time have achieved? My mom stopped being a mom decades ago. She considered me plain, ordinary, unremarkable. A reflection of herself. A mirror held up to her own low worth and self-hate. If she ever had any pride in me, she kept it well hidden. All I could offer would've been regret for the way her life – and our relationship – turned out. Is that really the last thing someone wants to hear before slipping away into the vast nothingness?

I cried in Larry's arms, but more for him. For *his* loss, rather than my own.

There's definitely no place like home. Depressingly, nothing has changed. Except for the advancing disrepair, everything inside is exactly as I remember it. The little wooden cross in the backyard commemorates Gonzo. The old dog's bones are buried in the spot where he drew his last breath.

He just dragged his fat ass outside one afternoon, lay down in the dirt and died, says Larry. It was his time.

I'm relieved Larry didn't consider a similar resting place for Delphine. She will be in a small cemetery a half hour's walk away.

There's five of us inside the tiny timber-clad chapel on the edge of the burial grounds. A neighbor who looked in on Delphine when Larry was away, and a woman at the rear, dressed in black and wearing a thick veil. I make a mental note to speak to her afterwards.

Meantime, an elderly Black minister attempts to rouse us as only a gospel-loving brother can. But he's no Al Sharpton. I mouth 'Delphine' to him when his memory betrays him. He doesn't use notes. Presumably, they get in the way of the pontificating. It's over quickly. The extraordinary details of my momma's early life don't feature. Larry doesn't want them to.

We go outside, 'The Sun Ain't Gonna Shine Anymore' still playing from the small cassette player. The woman in black has gone, and I curse myself for not being sharper; for shaking hands with the minister and for indulging his polite small talk. And this only intensifies when I see a new bouquet at the edge of the grave as we walk behind the coffin. I reach down and see the hand-written note:

You were the best of us! God bless.

H. x

I look for her.

Jesus, Larry, look.

What, Jude?

This!

There is no-one around us apart from the minister and the four staff members who've lifted my mom's simple coffin from the back of the flatbed truck we walked behind.

It must be her sister, Larry. Happyness, the one you told me about, remember? I almost met her in San Francisco. I've seen a photograph. We gotta go, Larry. She can't be far. C'mon, Larry let's…

Desperation is making me hyperventilate.

Jude, your momma ain't even in the ground yet, Larry says.

But Larry, it's her sister!

He sighs, and then puts an arm around me.

Jude, I'm so sorry, girl.

What for?

He pauses. The minister is watching us. Looking for a sign that we're ready to lay her to rest. But I'm not ready. Not yet.

Larry? What's goin' on?

He clears his throat. Uh, that thing I told you about her sisters … I made that up, he tells me.

And it draws the wind straight out of me. I cough to encourage some airflow. I don't know whether to cry or to slap him.

What the fuck do you mean? I shout, and the five-man burial team stop in their tracks.

I … um. Uh, I jus' … I wanted you to care. Think differently about her, he says. The tears well up in his eyes. He's a broken man. And despite my rage at him, I can't help but console him.

We sit on a polished stone bench with no back to it. Our posture must look awkward. The graveside breakdown aside, Larry is looking better than when I first arrived over a week ago. His face remains wrinkled and ridged, but there's a clarity about his eyes that suggests he's managed to sleep for the first time in a while. His dark hair is streaked with silvery gray, but, still in the suit he hasn't been seen out of since the burial, he portrays a distinguished mourner. One who wears grief well, if that isn't a ridiculous notion.

Y'know, I went to the store th'other day an' came out with four different kinds of toothpaste. I bought tins of tomatoes, an' I don't even like 'em, says Larry. I stayed up til three in the mornin' watchin' a documentary on Jim an' Tammy Faye, for Chrissake!

It's only been a few days, yet he doesn't recognize himself.

Grief makes you crazy, I tell him. He just slowly nods.

My momma's grave, newly filled with soil, is just aways over to our left. Only thirty feet or so. When we speak, it's in hushed tones, like we used to out on the porch, and it almost makes me smile to think it's because we don't want her to hear what we're saying.

She might not have shown it, but she always loved you, girl, he says, barely above a whisper.

She didn't, Larry, I say.

Not angrily, just realistically sanguine. No point in glossing over the facts of it.

Don't be unkind, now, he says.

He's a good man. He always has been. I hope she knew how lucky she was in having him by her side.

I'm not, I tell him. And I'm not upset about your wild cover stories either, although I was. We all just gotta get through shit...

I feel myself slipping back into the exaggerated southern twang of a good ole' boy.

Larry smiles.

She said some wicked things, Jude, it's true. But she didn't mean it. She'd so much pain wrapped up tight. That was her way of lettin' it out, is all.

I remember a fight once, I say, can't even recall what it was about, but she ended it by remindin' me that she almost died givin' birth, as if that was somehow my fault. As if her inability to conceive afterwards was my doin'. Part of a devious masterplan cast in the womb.

I laugh at the absurdity of it. Larry doesn't.

Well, I wasn't around back then, but I know she never blamed you, Jude.

His defense of her is unstinting.

She had such low expectations for me though, I say.

This time I'm not laughing.

In school – and even at track meets. She wouldn't come close to those when I was attendin' Humble High. I know adults have their own shit goin' on, but you need to put that aside sometimes for your kids.

I see him nodding slowly.

It's part of the responsibility of havin' them, I say.

She was a complicated woman, your momma, he says. But I loved her all the same.

I reach out and touch his hand. If he really means it, he must give me something. All I want is a glimmer to hang on to. Something that helps me understand her and the complex relationship we shared. And then unexpectedly, he provides it.

There's a reason she didn't go to your track meets, he says. Your first day at Humble High?

I feel myself turning round to face him.

She walked with you to school, he says.

I acknowledge this.

You got closer to the gates, an' she dropped off an' walked way behind you?

I remember that, I tell him. I was upset because I needed her there with me that day. But she backed away. She left me on my own, Larry.

He shakes his head slowly.

She didn't want you to be embarrassed by her, he says. All those privileged white kids … your momma didn't want you disadvantaged on your first day.

Those 'coffee-crème' jibes from fellow students, the hateful references to 'the help', the jokes about my speed being ethnically stereotypical. The *Black* cross I thought I was bearing alone.

Was she right? Would it have been much, much worse if Delphine had been at my side? If she'd been up in the bleachers shouting my name? If she'd been in the front row applauding the day AJ Carter and I received our medals? If she'd drawn attention to a poor Black family skirting around the edges of a lauded southern institution for the predominantly white? At least the 'what are you?' question would've been redundant. A side would've been picked. It matters little now. I should keep the past inside my notebooks. It's the only place where it makes any sense.

I hug Larry in the George Bush Intercontinental Airport car park. Both of us know it's for the final time. We don't labor it, and there's no forced sentimentality.

Take care of yourself, Jude, he says. I'm sorry, he says yet again. Try an' enjoy life more. Life's for the living, honey.

You too, Larry, I reply.

And with that, my tiny circle loses yet another member.

There's a bizarre protest ongoing. Geriatric and wheelchair-bound veterans have chained themselves to the railings around the terminal. The target of their protest is unclear, but I, and others behind me, get heckled and cussed at as we pass them. Inside and out, airport security officials outnumber passengers. It takes longer to get from the concourse through the numerous personal checks and onto the flight than between take-off and landing. It's ten days since the Twin Towers fell. A surreal atmosphere pervades everything. An entire nation emerging from a brief period of hibernation, stunned and suspicious of what the awakening will bring.

Back in Manhattan, there's better news. A switchboard operator from the agency calls, and I panic – the agency never calls. In the time it takes to transfer the call to Beth Haim, my line manager, I rehearse the mitigation it would take to counter Astrid

Atard's accusations. But if she is coming for me, it's not today. The purpose of Beth's call is to offer condolences and make sure I'm okay to return to work. And also to say that Vanessa, the artist I was due to meet, has survived despite being on the ninety-first floor of the North Tower when the first plane hit.

She'd gone in early to her studio around 6.00am to paint the sunrise, says Beth. It's unbelievable. She nipped down to the lobby to get a juice at 8.30am. She came back up and was coming out of the elevator at her floor when ... BAM!

Holy shit, I say.

Yeah, Beth says. It's a goddam miracle.

I hope for a similarly miraculous tale about my friend, Hennessey. God knows there are lots emerging. The *New York Times* has a supplement dedicated to them. I find one that hits me in the gut. Every word of it:

> *Republican Senator, Devlin Carter had an incredible escape from the tragedy. The 57-year-old Texan was due at a breakfast meeting at the Windows of the World restaurant on the 106th and 107th floors of 1 World Trade but arrived early for it. The Senator went into the LensCrafters store in the lobby on the off chance that a pair of broken spectacles could be fixed while he waited. He was extraordinarily lucky; the store had just opened and had a vacancy. He waited half an hour to get his glasses fixed during which the first plane hit ten floors below where he should have been.*

I hope Devlin Carter deserved his good fortune. I hope the trauma of losing a son so young made him a better person in the intervening years. And I hope his close shave with death will create empathy for others where little evidence of it previously existed.

(Act iii) From Then to Now

I knew deep down that he was dead even as I added his picture to the rest of the lampposts. Life had never cut him much of a break before. It seemed inevitable that wouldn't change when he needed it most. Some people are just destined to be in the wrong place at the wrong time.

Six months after the disaster, I receive confirmation. Hennessey's remains have been identified using a comparison to the record held in New York-Presbyterian Hospital, in Queens, where he was treated following the beating from his relatives. I am his designated 'emergency contact'. In the months that follow, survivor stories describe a maintenance man wearing a bright yellow T-shirt as a mask against the thickening dust cloud. Despite his slightness of frame, he summoned the strength from somewhere to force open an escape door. He yelled 'Just keep going!' to several people before heading upwards to look for more trapped survivors to help, minutes before the North Tower collapsed.

Hennessey wasn't an ordinary man.

The telephone calls begin around the end of March 2002. Several a day. No-one speaks on the other end. Only heavy breathing before I hang up. Until one call in the middle of the night begins with the muffled threat: 'I'm going to fucking kill you, black bitch!' It seems inevitable that it's Astrid Atard. She'd gradually receded to the back of my mind for over a year.

NYPD officers come, but not to my aid. They come because Astrid has accused me of stealing her jewelry, a fur coat and now a Persian cat. This is their third call-out to my apartment. The third occasion she has wasted police time. The officers are as irritated as me. I'm informed that this is a pattern of behavior, but since Julian Atard is 'balls deep with Giuliani' their hands are tied. They must be seen to be investigating. The most senior cop suggests I leave town for a while, until she gets me out of her system. Until she moves on to some other victim, is what they mean. This seems highly unlikely, I consider, since she has waited eighteen months for this. Astrid Atard is a woman who'll be plotting retribution for a grudge as she draws her last breath.

Regardless, I take the advice.

A road trip south, away from all the emotional heartache of the city and the unpredictable chaos of a high-maintenance stalker, is in order.

I excite myself by making vague plans that will probably never happen for a book of photographs that celebrate the American hinterland. No publishing house is likely to accept the pitch, but that doesn't matter. It's the very idea of escaping the city that is sustaining me.

The drive south is languorous, as befits my cautious driving. I have no real destination in mind. My subconscious is navigating. I discover exactly what I expect to find. A huge transformation in rural America from when I initially crossed it eighteen years ago. Pictures of animals locked away in industrial prisons, vacant farmlands, bankrupt towns, hunched, destitute workers, and all the while, the sense that a resurgent political far right is building power in the countryside. It is a new heart of darkness. An introverted country, hidden away from the metropolitan spotlight, reconstituting itself along America's traditional lines of race, poverty, and commercial advantage. I photograph numerous protests and several riots as I pass from city to city. There is no obvious common driver for the anarchy, except anger. From Harrisburg to

Huntington, from Tupelo to Tulsa, from Stillwater to Santa Rosa. If one place voices fury at Bush's abandonment of them, the next targets Clinton's legacy in ignoring their plight. When it's not our political leaders in the firing line, it's the Black people, or the Hispanics, or the Muslims. I am making a visual record of a country living in perpetual fear of the *other*. Rage is the only constant.

I photograph so many dispiriting things in this tableau of middle America, that it's almost a relief to find myself back in the familiar streets of Wickenburg. Little has changed, and in my mind's eye I see Brandy, hot donuts in her hands, running along the street to get out of the rain and back to us. It was for Matt's birthday. He'd have been twenty-four, I think.

And just because I told myself I would, I return to Frontier Street.

I press the buzzer.

Hello?

Um, hi ... is this Mrs Forde?

Yes, is the reply. She sounds anxious. As if she doesn't get many unexpected callers.

Hello, Mrs Forde. I don't think you'll recall but I briefly lived upstairs. It was a long time ago now. My name's Jude Montgomery.

There's a silence.

I came here in 1983. With Brandy and Matt.

Oh! she says. And then the lock releases. And I go back in time.

Brandy died at the beginning of 2000. But her wild, untamed spirit was extinguished years earlier. She had remained here and dealt with the consequences of that night at the Razzle Club, as she promised me she would. No blame apportioned.

Just the roll of the dice, Jude. Be lucky. Make us proud – the last words she said to me before I sullenly stomped up to Momma Em's door without even saying goodbye. How I've wished I could take back that moment every single day since.

I'm very sorry, my dear, Mrs Forde says, pouring me a tea. It was terrible at the end. Brandy couldn't look after herself, ne'er mind that poor boy. She just wore out, she did. Working all hours. I tried to tell her, he needs full-time care, I said. But I couldn't help, not with my hip being so. And she wouldn't call her folks...

She sees me crying.

Oh dear, let me get you somethin' for that.

I drive to the care home but once there, I can't go in. Instead, I walk around back to peer through the painted fence into the garden, hoping to recognize him. I wait for thirty minutes or so, and eventually, a man is wheeled out into the sunlight. He is wrapped up against the cold but I'm sure it's Matt. That greying quiff, that sparkle in the eye. I wave and imagine a goofy smile in response. But if it is him, there's nothing there. It's almost too much.

I knew Rabbit was Brandy's daughter from my very first weeks at Lakeview. The same quirky mannerisms, the determination to do things perfectly. A sideways look when she was amused. And those eyes, alluring and mischievous and loving, all at the same time. It wasn't my place to say back then. And Em closed down any of my questions about Rabbit's background. For whatever reason, Brandy had been erased from her daughter's life. And now she's gone. It seems so unfair. All of it.

I call from the care home's parking lot, but only after composing myself.

Momma Em? Hi, it's Jude. I breathe in deeply. I'm really sorry to have to tell you, but Brandy's dead.

I know, Jude, she says softly.

It takes me by surprise.

You know? Oh, I say. Uh ... when did you, um...

I hear her sigh, like she's just picked up an unwanted call from an aluminum siding salesman.

Uh, last year, she says.

It seems like I've caught her out.

But ... you didn't think to call me?

No. I didn't, Jude. We thought it was for the best.

The *best*, I say.

My voice is rising.

How could it be for the best? She was my friend.

Jude, you only knew her for a couple of months, twenty years ago. Get some perspective.

I'm sobbing now. Barely able to speak.

Is Ben there?

Ben is out right now, she says, with the coldness of someone protecting a mob boss from an Internal Revenue Service rep.

Does Rabbit know? I ask.

Em doesn't immediately answer, and I know from this that she doesn't.

I'm in Wickenburg, I say. I can be there in twelve hours or so. Will I come home, Em?

This isn't your home, she says. It hasn't been since...

The fire is the unsaid end of that sentence.

Don't you think poor Rabbit has been through enough? she adds, pouring peroxide into my open wound.

This stops me in my tracks. I have nothing to offer in response.

Goodbye, Jude.

The call ends.

Driving back east, I feel so totally and utterly alone. All bridges burnt. The only person I could call a friend entombed under 250,000 tons of steel and concrete. I sob uncontrollably, and the idea of shutting my eyes and letting the vehicle roll left across the highway into the path of an oncoming truck is only prevented by the pain and suffering it would cause another innocent family.

❦

My return to Manhattan brings the not-unexpected news that I have been fired from Camel/De Souza. Astrid Atard kept her promise. I surprise myself by viewing this as an early release from a jail sentence. Better to consider that Astrid has done me a favour, rather than become mired in the notion that she has won. Feeling freed, I immerse myself in freelance work, and for the following few years, things stabilize and gradually improve.

❦

It's not until 2005 that my 9/11 photographs gain any acclaim. A Chelsea gallery puts on a show and there is good coverage – and some positive reviews, one in the *New York Times*. My trip across America did finally turn into a publication – a monograph entitled *American Hinterland*. I still get a steady stream of royalties from it.

Out of the blue, most likely in response to the *NYT* coverage, Janet Delaney reaches out. She composed the introduction for the book but it was following the publisher's approach to her, not mine. I haven't spoken to her in years although I'm delighted to hear from her now. A short-term teaching position has opened at the New York Institute of Photography. Janet recommends me for the position, which, following an unusual and prolonged interview, I am offered. The NYIP is moving exclusively into home-study courses, but to supplement revenue they are retaining one face-to-face class. The course forces me to reread my college notes, which is more enjoyable than I thought it would be. The fire at Lakeview meant I dropped out of Janet Delaney's class, so I didn't complete my formal training. But I allay any anxieties about my fitness for the role by reminding myself that I have gleaned all I needed to learn about taking good pictures through trial and error, out in the field.

I settle in quickly and enjoy the structure of a regular day that doesn't have the pressure of the private sector. I compose lectures on Richard Avedon, photographic art in the service of advertising, and the early process of employing an iodine-sensitized silver plate and mercury vapor – otherwise known as a daguerreotype photograph. My class subscription grows quickly, and it seems that I have finally found a calling that suits my unsociable lifestyle and my fitful relationship with a schedule.

August brings the welcome news that a gallery show at MoMA will feature three of my photographs. A crassly titled exhibition, *Capturing Disaster,* is to run for two months up to Thanksgiving. I pick up a copy of *Time Out*, reading it on the train to my class. Coverage of the exhibition I'll be part of is sparse, but in the 'Coming Soon' section there is this:

> *At the age of only twenty-seven, Bunny Menendez, the San Franciscan artist known as Rabbit, has taken the art world by storm. Largely self-taught, she is redefining portraiture and the nude, producing art of extraordinary honesty and vitality. Her subjects are unique and resist traditionally accepted notions of beauty. Rabbit challenges our understanding of ourselves and our place in a culture where the pursuit of flawless perfection has become the American Curse. She is a painter who emerges once in a generation. MoMA is honored to present the first full exhibition of Rabbit's career. Don't miss it.*
> *From October 31ˢᵗ – February 28ᵗʰ.*

The first thing I notice, apart from the vastness of the canvases, is the thickness of the paint. As if it was applied with a trowel rather than a brush. I wonder if injury has forced this less dexterous technique upon her. Then, as I examine the paintings, I begin to feel as if I am intruding on her intimacy. It makes me uneasy at first, but Rabbit has captured the strength and fragility of the human body in every one of these artworks. Particularly the self-portraits. I stare, breathless, at abstracted images of the woman who was the little girl I once knew. Her work is genuinely breath-taking.

I stand at the back as the opening speeches are made by various top-level members of MoMA management, and their sponsors. Trying to remain inconspicuous as I scan the heads in the crowd for a sign of her. I don't know what she looks like now. Rabbit's paintings of herself have her facing away, presumably to fix the gaze on parts of her body the viewer might initially be uncomfortable looking at. Is she the small, shaven-headed woman with the full-length black sari? Or the tall, statuesque, mini-skirted redhead over to the right? Or the sallow skinned...

Ladies and gentlemen, honored guests, friends of MoMA, please welcome ... Rabbit.

And there she is. None of those I'd guessed. She is small, and reassuringly ordinary. Shoulder-length black hair that has surely been dyed. She is wearing army boots, turned-up bleached jeans, and a long white sweatshirt that has had one sleeve ripped off, putting her extensively scarred arm on show.

Uh ... um, hello. Thank you all for coming. I'm, uh, not used to speaking in public. So, um ... uh, I'm gonna keep this short. As you can see, my body is imperfect ... and for as long as I can remember, I have been fascinated by our society's perception of my imperfection. Of all imperfections. Um, why people will sometimes stare when I leave my arm exposed like it is now. Or recoil from a person missing a limb. Or, um, feel uneasy talking to a person with a visible curving scar from a neurological operation. The subjects I paint have imperfections that aren't detractions. In most cases, they are the evidence of survival, and that is, uh, surely life-affirming.

The assembled group applauds.

So, can I just thank MoMA, and its sponsors ... Angelique, my agent, Em and Ben, my momma and pop, and again, you all for coming. I hope the exhibition positively challenges your perceptions. Thank you.

Glasses are raised and more applause follows. Music plays: 'Make Your Own Kind of Music' by Cass Elliot, and I wilt. I am tearful. The enormity of what she has achieved in such a short time hits home. I stand at the back of the hall, in the shadows, watching her move uncomfortably between pretentious people desperate to shake her hand or have a catalogue signed. There are even those who ask for a photograph with her.

She doesn't know I'm here. I've been in two minds for the weeks leading up to this opening as to whether to approach her or not. I decide to leave. All these years and I still can't face up to the psychological and physical harm I caused her. It's enough for me to have witnessed her happy and enjoying this success. I turn and thread my way through the bodies towards the lift.

Jude? Is that you? I hear as the doors slide closed behind me.

Two days later, I notice a Twitter DM notification. It's from Rabbit:

Hi Jude. I saw you at my show opening the other night. Why didn't you say hello?

The message was sent fourteen hours ago. I'm not a regular user of social media. I dip in to observe, rarely to participate. But I know enough about the currency of Twitter to realise what the lack of an immediate response can imply. She'll think I'm deliberately avoiding contact, which, weirdly, is the exact opposite of what I crave. I just don't have the tools. Tentative, distanced communications are the best way to start.

Rabbit, I'm sorry. I had a deadline to file. Your show was amazing. I'm so so pleased for you.

I send this and then stare at the words, analyzing them. Three dots appear under my message, jumping up and down in sequence. My heart rate increases. She is reading.

Thank you. I'm glad you liked the work. How are you?

I'm well. Living quietly as always. Are you still in New York?

No, I had to fly back east right after the show. I didn't know you were in town. We should've met up. There's a lot of time to catch up on. X

I notice the kiss. It seems significant.

How's Momma Em, Ben? Are there still lots of kids running around. Jx?

They're fine. No more kids though. They've retired from fostering. It was getting too much for them. Em told me you'd been around California a couple of years ago. But you'd been too busy to make it to Lakeview.

There's no kiss this time. That also seems significant. Maybe she's angry with me. I don't know how to respond. I desperately wanted to see her then, but Em prevented it. I walk away from my phone. Twenty minutes pass before I type…

I really wanted to come and see you. To speak to you. To tell you things.

An almost equal gap and then …

Oh. What things?

It's like these are coded messages, and a team of FBI analysts are deciphering them before permitting a response. This last one especially. My heart is beating furiously as I weigh the consequences of what I'm preparing to type. She should know about her mom. Em should've told her. I'm rattled at her lying to Rabbit about me. Why say anything at all? I'm torn between a responsibility to keep Brandy's memory alive and appreciating the sadness it will cause Rabbit. But she has a right to know what a vibrant, inspiring soul her mother was. I'm certain it's where she gets her creative spark. My heart is racing ahead of my brain. I should ask her for her number. I should call her and talk to her.

But I don't know how I'd say the words. So instead, I carelessly write...

Rabbit, I desperately wanted to see you, but Em prevented it. I was visiting the place where your mom and I stayed for a couple of months before I came to Lakeview. Your momma was the most alive person I'd ever met. She made me the person I am today. She died five years ago and I'm so sorry I didn't tell you more about her before now.

I attach a photo of Brandy I have stored on my phone, and the scan of a drawing she did of me while we were in Wickenburg.

There are no bouncing dots this time. An hour passes. Nothing. Two hours. Three.

I turn the phone off and go to bed, tears in my eyes.

In the morning, I wake to...

FFS I can't believe you just told me that on fucking Twitter!!!

Three days later, Rabbit unfollows me.

Even though I'm working, I can't help but get caught up in the buzz of the multitudes flooding towards Central Park. I am excited to be on the inside of the story, not detached, not simply observing. I'm photographing the determined faces of those convinced that change is almost upon us. And I've picked a side. The Black in the streets outnumbers the white, as would be expected for a campaign rally eagerly anticipating our country's first ever Black President. No-one will take it for granted; the history of Black America is not one characterized by positivity. But the polls are favorable, and I'm sharing the mood of optimism. I've been commissioned to photograph the event, which will involve speeches, music, and – it has been rumored – an unscheduled appearance by the candidate himself.

YES WE CAN T-shirts are everywhere. *YES.* That word, the positivity of it is carrying these believers – me amongst them –

along on a tidal wave of anticipation for better, more equal times ahead. Even the shape the word makes on the lips of those chanting is uplifting. I hear celebratory music carried on the breeze from the Central Park stage long before it is in sight. My camera is trained on the audience more than the stage, though, just as it was twenty years earlier when Love Tractor and the B-52s played at Radio City and I was with Andi. I pick out beautiful Black people and white people, smiling, kissing, hugging in the twilight as if their time truly has come. It's a swaying, grooving melting pot of life, stretching as far as my lens can zoom. And it feels, briefly, like a vision of the America so many have died for or suffered in pursuing.

Darkness falls over the city. The emotions build towards the final act, Stevie Wonder. From the edge of the stage, I zoom in on a woman. Mixed race too, perhaps, her features like mine, her face full of exhausted joy, wet with tears. Her expression suggests she still somehow can't comprehend that this is happening, and she is witnessing it. Where other artists have appeared solo and acoustic, the Motown superstar has brought along a band and backing singers. I'm eye level with the stage but I've spent the whole evening facing the people watching it. I don't notice the three women to the left of his keyboard until a chorus makes me turn, and standing there, alongside Stevie Wonder, is Andi Patullo, *my* Andi. She wears her hair longer, in dreadlocks, unbelievably, and she has put on a little weight since I last saw her, but she carries it well. She looks healthy and happy, and my heart swells with pride for her when she takes a lead vocal on 'Signed, Sealed, Delivered'. Andi makes it into an ode to change and to new tomorrows.

Well, hello stranger, she says.

She leans in to kiss me on both cheeks. There's no animosity, no bitterness after the way we parted. I'm heartened since I deserve both.

Can't believe it, Andi, I tell her. That was incredible. You look phenomenal.

Ah, Jude, sweetie ... thank you. An' right back atcha.

She takes my arm and leads me deep backstage, to the performers' green room. My lanyard pass doesn't extend to this area, but Andi clears it and I'm suddenly sat on a sofa with her.

It's so good to see you, Jude, she says.

We clink glasses.

You've been busy, I say.

Yeah, things are goin' really well just now, she replies. I moved to L.A. a few years ago. It's a weird vibe there, and I miss Manhattan, but Ash loves it.

Ash, her new girlfriend/boyfriend/manager? I avoid enquiring for now.

So, *this* is a huge gig, then.

Yeah, Ash knows Stevie, an' he's been supportin' Barack at events for a few months. This isn't his normal tourin' band, but I got in when he reached out for session singers, she says, and then shrugs sweetly as if still struggling to accept she is deserving of this golden ticket.

Hey, Andi. A deep, familiar New Jersey voice.

Hi, Bruce, says Andi, with a cute little wave. We both watch him stroll across the room and pick up a beer from a long table that's heaving with bottles.

Wow, that's...

Yeah, Ash is producin' his new album, she says. He hopes there might be a session job for me, but I dunno ... Patti usually covers all the female vocals.

Wow, I say again, feeling like it's the only word I know.

She was always a good singer but her journey from the night of the break-up fight to here is astonishing. First-name terms with world superstars and politicians? I'm not sure if I'm bursting with jealousy or pride, but either way, I'm hiding it behind a frozen, wow-shaped mouth.

Ah, here he comes ... Ash! Over here. She beckons him, and he responds, briefly accepting an exaggerated air kiss from the Black-Eyed Peas singer, Fergie, as he passes her. He's young, tall, heavily tattooed. He very closely resembles the actor Owen Wilson, but without the crooked nose.

Hey, she says.

She kisses him on the lips and loops her arm around his waist. I see her fingers slip into the back pocket of his jeans.

This is Jude, one of my oldest friends from NYC.

Hey, Jude, says Ash. You gotta be a musician with that name.

And he sounds like Owen Wilson too.

The anti-freeze kicks in and slowly my facial muscles start to function again.

Uh. Hi there. Um, no. Sorry. No musicality at all, I'm afraid, I stammer.

Jude is a brilliant photographer, says Andi. She's won lots of awards for her work.

That so? says Ash. Cool.

His hippy influence has prompted her dreadlocks, I suspect. They probably surf together. He looks around, perhaps not wishing to miss someone more famous or interesting.

Really great to meet you, Jude. Andi talks about you all the time, he says to me, and then to her, I gotta catch Stevie, babe. Back soon.

He kisses her and touches his forefingers to his mouth before flicking the kiss they hold in my direction.

Well, I say, smiling, He seems—

I know, Andi interrupts. Fucking gorgeous!

And we both laugh and all the anguish of the past is suddenly behind us. Twenty years ago, I'd regularly wake sweating in the middle of the night because of some night terror, and Andi would reach over and pull me into the nook of her body, and whatever fears I was holding on to would disappear, at least for a while. Nowadays, those nightmares are less frequent, but when they do occur, I often still expect her arm to curl over from behind me to make it better.

She isn't ever coming back to my bed, but that's okay. It's definitely pride, not jealousy. Had she stayed, I'd undoubtedly have held her back.

Look, Andi, I'm really sorry for the way we left it when we broke up. I behaved terribly an'...

She puts her hands on my shoulders and stops me.

Jude ... I've missed you. I really want us to be friends again. Let's leave the past where it should stay, eh?

Sure, I say.

I hug her. She hugs me back, and it feels to me like the safest place in the world right now. It saddens me that I never told her I loved her. Not that it would've made a difference to where we are now, but these were words that I could somehow never say. To Andi. To Hennessey. To Brandy. To Rabbit. I knew I loved them, but something always stopped me from telling them. I told AJ Carter I loved him when I didn't even know what it meant. And he died the next day. I had cursed him.

My routine is now firmly established and indifferent to the workday/weekend cycle the rest of the working city is a slave to. I'm independent and self-sufficient, and while there's the occasional relapse when I wish I had someone to share personal fears with, I'm now so used to my own company that anyone breaching it would swiftly be resented, in the same way that Erin Pressley once resented my occupation of her space when I first arrived in New York. The ways in which we are set run deep indeed. The only time away from this rigid circadian rhythm came four years ago in the summer of 2010, when I spent six months on the West

Coast. Not, as you might've presumed, vacationing at the Malibu home of Andi, Ash and their lovely children. Predictably, I haven't seen Andi since the night of the concert for Obama in Central Park in 2008. There's no point in making promises or commitments that you know you'll break.

I decided to recuperate from a double mastectomy by renting a small house on Coldwater Canyon Drive, in West Hollywood. Rosario, the lovely Spanish woman who kept the house – and me, on occasion – clean and spotless, was my only companion. Surprisingly, the consistent warmth prompted a sense of relaxation that felt almost weightless. Although the novelty of it would fade, the hazy glow and shimmering skies, the perpetual dance of the palm trees, explained why so many of the rich and famous choose to hide away in those leafy, elevated canyons. The house sat close to the bottom of a heavily guarded incline that led up to the fortified hilltop home of veteran actor, Charlton Heston. Using the NRA dollar to defend himself rather than the Second Amendment was always Mr Heston's priority, Rosario would say. She wasn't a fan. My contract conditions at Cooper Union – where I had recently been tenured – permitted the sabbatical on reduced pay. And an enticing publishing advance for a future memoir of sorts – the unstructured basis of which you are now reading – paid for the rental.

There isn't much to be said about the cancer that led to this pleasant change in circumstances. It was detected fortuitously early. A screening programme at CU had a low initial student uptake so female staff were encouraged to set an example. I told no-one about the diagnosis. I paid for the necessary surgery and follow-up blasts of therapy that Delphine couldn't have even dreamt of, and I didn't think twice about it. When the subject of breast reconstruction was raised, I immediately said no. Only the mirror would see the scars, I told my consultant. But the physical ones are always easier to live with than the emotional ones. When the bandages were removed, I appreciated what it must have meant for Rabbit and her art on the opening night of her MoMA exhibition.

Four years on, I'm still here. On Earth. Alive. In Manhattan, in early 2014. Despite its mission, the cancer has not returned. It knows the inhospitable hostess it would encounter if it did. I'm fifty-five years old. I live the comfortable, uncomplicated and boring life of a single woman of modest means. Without the financial motivation to do so, it's a deepening middle-age groove sliding unremarkably to the grave. I own, rather than rent, an apartment on the Lower East Side a mere baseball pitch away from the building Andi and I lived in when we first crossed the East River. That's gone now of course. My real estate resulted from the widespread community destruction I once famously wrote about. I am reminded of this every time an assessment of my career appears in the newspapers or online.

Who said Americans don't appreciate irony?

Beyond the disappointment in myself, the only stress I deal with is the stretched patience of a publisher, whose already generous deadline expired a year ago. My stated excuse for this is a desire to address my Scottish roots, of which I still know little. But until this year, the opportunity hasn't presented itself.

But now it has. I'm freelancing for *The New Yorker,* and the piece will cover the annual Tartan Day Parade. Words and pictures. It's another dream commission for me. The Parade has come a very long way since the first, in 1999. Back then, two pipe bands and a small but spirited group of Scottish-Americans – an adjective I now use to describe my own nationality – walked from the British Consulate to the United Nations. It has since grown to include thousands of participants, and this year, as part of the Scottish delegation, Anna Mason. Ms Mason and I have some shared history, although she may not recall it as clearly as I do.

It's the morning of the parade and despite not drawing the crowds of the St Patrick's Day equivalent, a sizable Scottish contingent is assembling on 6th Avenue as I pass en route to an early breakfast appointment with her. I reach the destination – The Algonquin on West 44th Street – half an hour ahead of schedule. I am handed a free complimentary copy of *The New Yorker* as I go into the lobby. I take it, thinking that it will advertise me to Anna Mason.

I take a tea when it is offered, and sit in a luxurious high-backed armchair that is the very epitome of Gilded Age opulence. Oddly, half an hour of it and my back starts to hurt in a way that it never did when lounging on the broken rocking chair with the missing rocker that propped open the shutter door back in Humble.

Ah, sorry. Are you okay? A man wearing a kilt has tripped over my bag and is apologizing for it.

It's me who should be sorry, I say. I shouldn't have left that lyin' there.

No harm done; he says with a warm smile.

Are you here for Tartan Day? I ask, needlessly.

The man laughs and twirls the kilt in a manner of which Stan Laurel would've been proud.

Aye. They better not have moved it! My name's Andy, he says. Andy Scott.

Andy Scott ... a Scot from Scotland?

What're the chances, eh?

I'm Jude, I tell him, and, without prompt, my father was a Scot.

Oh, right, where from?

A place in Glasgow called Govan, I say.

Wow, me too, he says. Have you been over?

Uh, no ... not yet, I say. Hopin' to. Tryin' to find out more about him. I'm a journalist, I tell him, although I'm not really; not in the sense of those who once lunched here at the famous round table in the main hall.

I'm a sculptor, says Andy Scott. A modern-day Clydeside welder.

He says this quickly, and I struggle to decipher it, until he senses my confusion and repeats it slowly.

My maquettes are featuring in the parade, well, not on the march, but the route passes where they're installed.

He shows me a photograph of them: two extraordinary horse heads made of small steel shards, glinting in the sunshine on plinths at Bryant Park. They are impossibly beautiful. Solidly powerful and transparently fragile. The sight of them takes my breath away.

They're astonishing.

They're Kelpies … mythical shape-shiftin' creatures that roam the lochs an' streams of Scotland…

It's the type of story I used to tell Rabbit. I imagine her drawings of his Kelpies.

…An' drown people. He laughs as he says this. You should come an' see the *real* ones.

Ms Montgomery? A young woman's voice. I turn away from the sculptor.

Yes, I say, nervously.

I'm Ms Mason's assistant. The appointments are running late but she has asked me to show you up to the Oak Room.

I wish the sculptor well and tell him I'll be watching for his Kelpies on the march route. He hands me a note on which he has written an address.

If you ever make it over to Glasgow, they'll help you with your search, he says.

Upstairs, Anna Mason is waiting. She is seated, monarch-like, against the dark wood-paneled rear wall of the Oak Room. Her posture is unusual, sitting knees up, back curved, her body shaped like a question mark. It seems like the entire Scottish delegation is based here. TV crews with hand-held cameras jostle from one person to the next. Photographers – like me – wait in line for access to their subject. Anna Mason, for her part, looks calm and unflustered. Staring into the middle-distance. Contemplating the future, perhaps. These will be momentous months ahead for her, I suspect, regardless of the outcome of the vote in her homeland.

Eventually, I am at the front of the queue. I have been officially allocated fifteen minutes, although there is no-one waiting behind me now.

Hello, Ms Mason, how are you today? I ask, setting my light meter against her flawless skin.

I'm very well, Ms... She leans to look more closely at my pass. Montgomery. Sorry, she says. I don't have my contacts in yet.

Are you enjoyin' Manhattan?

I am, very much. There's a real buzz about the parade, this year. Have you visited the city before? I ask.

Yes. Many times. But this time feels – I don't know ... monumental, somehow.

I think I know what you mean. My father was Scottish, an' I definitely feel part of the parade this year.

Was he now? she says.

I can sense her studying my features. Trying to work out the genealogy. I save her the trouble.

I'm mixed race. My momma was from Haiti, originally. Jimmy Montgomery, my daddy, was from Glasgow.

Oh, just like me, she says.

Perfect teeth are displayed as she smiles warmly at the connection we've made.

She poses professionally. The faintest hint of steely determination. I snap, and she maintains the gaze even as the flash lights up her face.

I'd love to come to Glasgow. To work on a feature, I tell her.

Then, Jude, you must, I insist, she says.

She reaches into her bag and hands me a card.

Contact Mary on this number, and we can continue getting acquainted in Scotland.

My allotted time is ending. I have the photos I need. I begin packing my equipment away.

Y'know, I know all about The Hyptones too, I tell her. You used to be their photographer, I add, expecting this to prompt further warmth, but instead, she stands. The smile fades. Her eyes narrow as if suddenly convinced she has been set up.

I'm not here to talk about them, she warns.

I see her looking around. Trying to catch the eye of someone who will excuse her without a scene having to be made.

Oh, I'm sorry ... it's just that I've followed them since Phoenix...

I really need to go, I'm very sorry, she says.

Before she brushes past me, I hold out my Polaroid snap of Jamie Hewitt.

I just wondered how he was now, Ms Mason ... I used to work on Madison Avenue. In advertising ... at the Camel/De Souza agency.

She puts her hand to her face. Not in a shocked way; more pondering.

I was part of the team that selected 'Independent State of Mind' for the Apple campaign. We spoke about it once; you probably don't remember, I tell her.

And for the briefest of moments, it looks like she'll relax. That she'll associate me with the surprising call that changed the band's fortunes. I don't want her praise. And I'm not after her gratitude. I just want to ensure the campaign's money made a difference to them. Had given them a better future than *The Face* article prophesied. But instead, she looks like she's been caught in a lie. She takes my arm and gently pulls me to one side.

Look, Ms Montgomery, that was a million years ago. The band represented a very difficult period in my life. My brother was dead, my father was being investigated, and the band was an emotional wrench, not to mention a financial disaster. I wasn't just their photographer, I was Jamie Hewitt's girlfriend; I was the one left to sort out the mess for decades afterwards.

Oh, I understand, I do. This isn't a hack piece, Ms Mason, I'm genuinely interested in what became of them.

I see her looking around.

This is *not* on the record, she warns, a finger raised but not pointing. If you print it, we'll sue.

I find myself nodding, shocked at the determined aggression of her words.

Jamie isn't in a good place. He hasn't been for years. He's too fragile to go through it all again.

But you *do* know where he is.

Jesus Christ, are you not listening? I'm trying to protect him; don't you understand that?

Well, uh, protect him from what? I stammer.

It seems I've stumbled on something. Her pleading eyes aren't drawing the support of her minions, who seem too preoccupied by the haggis canapes and the whisky miniatures to come to her aid.

Jamie Hewitt is an addict. He owed tens of thousands of pounds in gambling debts. He had to disappear. AFB Management supported him through rehab in London and helped him get his life back on track. He now just wants to be left in peace.

She is quietly raging. A consummate, polished, professional politician pressurized; losing her composure, as many politicians do, because of an inability to escape or outrun their past.

I'm leaving, she says.

Thank you, Ms Mason. I'll call about the appointment in Scotland.

She shoots me a glacial backwards glance that withdraws the invitation.

Later that day, I am at home in the Village. It's a sublimely beautiful evening. One where I really notice the lengthening daylight hinting at the promise of brighter days to come. The parade has infused me with its optimism and positivity. And it has offered an unlikely focus. Anna Mason was like a tiny Boadicea, next to the rotund grinning Grand Marshal. She wasn't smiling. She didn't wave. Our conversation prior to it would've been the reason. The majority of those watching her from sidewalks would see a serious female politician on the cusp of a monumental period for her country. A female who knew that while frivolity displayed by a male counterpart might be described as charisma, in the world as it stands, unguarded outbursts of emotion from a woman wouldn't be considered a display of empathy, but evidence she is too physiologically unpredictable for the high-pressure world of powerful men.

Yes, Anna Mason is a fascinating subject. My conversation with her was intriguing – I replay it in my mind as I examine the down-loaded shots. The sense of something being held back would be difficult for any photographer to ignore. I'm drawn to her. It's the eyes. Always the eyes. Every tiny crease in the corners of them. Every slow, subtle closing of the lid to buy time. To allow composure to be regained. Whatever these tells conceal, she is practiced at them. A veteran. Whatever pain she is hiding, she's been hiding it for a long time.

In the weeks that follow my meeting with Anna Mason, I regu-larly reflect on the idealistic, teenage dreams that drove me from Humble to here – thoughts that had begun in the rarefied atmos-phere of Los Angeles during my cancer recuperation. I think on how those dreams had been blunted by my social inadequacies. Slowly erased by a growing awkwardness around people. As the years passed, I'd all but buried those hopes of an exciting, vibrant, bohemian life, dismissing them as youthful naivete. But this was simply a defence against the reality that I was squandering the op-portunity I had taken so many risks as a sixteen-year-old to create. The rigid, predictable routine of my life that my current employ-ment sustains is gradually losing its appeal. I think back to the colder, poorer times with Hennessey in Queens, or with Andi and Monique in Brooklyn, and of how much happier I was then. When I had nothing. When I took chances. When I trusted my instincts about people, about sex. Risky decisions that the staid, middle-aged me would otherwise consider insane. I'm experiencing a curious mix of despondency and motivation, and it's this that seems to prompt me to rediscover the fearless young woman that I used to be.

Life is for the living: a cliched, bumper-sticker phrase Larry bade me goodbye with as I prepared to leave Houston for the last time. Having given it no thought previously, I now recall him saying it like it happened yesterday. Larry's big, furrowed brow as he uttered the words. Imploring me to act. To draw joy from life before something unexpected derails it. Suddenly, it's all I can think about.

I scrabble around in an inch of the undisturbed dust of my least-used closet. They're hidden here, out of sight, out of mind. Those scribbled notebooks full of hope and spunky attitudes.

I wipe clean the white board in my small office. Blue handwritten notes for lecture prompts that have been there for years disappear, leaving a blank canvas. Soon, it is covered by so many names and places and Post-its, and the collected totems of my past, that it resembles the beginnings of a bounty-hunter's mission. I sit back and stare at it, this story of a life. This curious jigsaw-puzzle collage challenging me. There is *The Face* magazine article. The blurred photograph of Jamie Hewitt. Photocopies of Hennessey's 'most wanted' mugshot from the Bowery Bums piece. My AAA 'Obama For President' event press pass. The address given to me by the Scottish sculptor. Anna Mason's Scottish parliamentary office phone number. A 'get well soon' card from Andi, urging me to visit her and Ash in Malibu for Thanksgiving. Jimmy Montgomery's faded, folded *Life* cover picture. A postcard of Rabbit's 'Self Portrait #9' bought from the MoMA Gallery giftshop.

Above the rest, dashboard Elvis hangs from a hook. A breeze

from an open window swivels the figure, and its dancing pelvis makes me laugh. My (almost) constant companion. Maybe it's time to pass him on for good.

The brief interaction with Anna Mason has lit a fire inside of me I considered long extinguished. She has connected my past with my future. It could be the unresolved desire to discover more about Jimmy Montgomery; to identify any attributes inherited from him that might help me understand who I am and what shapes my attitudes. Or maybe it's the more basic need to apologize to Rabbit and atone for the hurt I've caused her. Whichever it is, I'm consumed by the notion that these fragments will somehow piece together across the Atlantic, in Glasgow, where my father was born and where Rabbit now works, painting and teaching fine art in the city's art school.

I am still saying YES, but this time, I mean it. And it's on my terms. I draft spirited emails to my press and media contacts, pitching a detailed feature on Anna Mason, the face of Scottish Independence. I tease extra interest by outlining a potential parallel thread: an investigation into why she is so intent on concealing an aspect of her past. I have money saved and a sudden determination to leave this far-too-comfortable zone. To travel outside of my continent for the first time. To go to the small country that holds the secrets to my origins; a place that might answer that 'what?' question that has plagued me my entire life. And all this in a city currently home to Rabbit. Which cannot be a coincidence.

The take-up has been slow. These things happen. It appears that my former editors have either changed job, retired, or died. I haven't had a written piece published in years. My name has dropped out of journalistic circles, the assumption perhaps being that I too have gravitated toward the less stressful academic life. In addition, the Scottish Independence vote is still four months away and foreign politics rarely registers here in America, unless it involves Russia or China, or our troops invading somewhere. My initial enthusiasm remains undimmed though. It's just a matter of time. And then, in May, there is a news item that does take hold.

The television is on in the corner of my room. CNN, as is, for me, normal:

'A major fire has torn through a famous school of art in Glasgow, Scotland. The world-renowned building is a landmark in the city and is considered one of the nation's most beautiful architectural creations. The extent of the damage remains unclear, but according to eyewitnesses, the entire west wing has been lost, including Charles Rennie Mackintosh's famous library.'

My God! *Rabbit's* School of Art. I immediately panic. The report doesn't confirm if there were casualties, but instead shifts to the Glaswegian architect's influence on Frank Lloyd Wright in the early twentieth century. I look at the clock, still early evening in San Francisco.

The phone rings and rings and rings. With only the two of them in the house now, I give it time.

Hello?

Momma Em?

Yes ... who is this?

It's Jude.

Her sigh is audible. The passage of time has not mellowed her.

Ben! she shouts away from the phone. It's for you.

She doesn't tell him even though I hear him ask who's calling.

Hullo?

Hi, Ben ... it's Jude.

Hey, sweetheart. Is everything okay with you?

Yeah, Ben. I'm fine. Have you spoken to Rabbit? Did you see the reports of the fire in Glasgow?

Yes, Jude. She just called. An hour or so ago. She's fine. A little bit in shock but no-one was hurt.

Oh, thank God.

I feel myself exhaling. Poor Rabbit. All that therapy and then to be faced with the trauma of yet another fire.

She's shook up, but you know Rabbit... he says.

But I don't. Not anymore. I have no idea how she'll cope. I haven't seen or spoken to Rabbit in over five years.

Her only concern was for her team, he says. They're all worried about the students and the work they'll have lost.

Should I call her, Ben?

It's his turn to sigh now.

Jude, sweetheart, I'd leave it for a while.

I'm certain he just means *leave it*, full stop. But those five years have gnawed away. My younger self was determined to move forwards, no regrets, no looking back, despite the collateral damage. This is the one instance where I can't.

I take Ben's advice and make him a promise that I won't call her unannounced. I tell him about my intentions to travel to Scotland, though. Reluctantly, he gives me Rabbit's new contact details, but administers a warning for me to tread very carefully.

If she won't see you, don't force it, Jude. She doesn't deserve that, he says.

I won't, I tell him. Thank you, Ben.

Jude ... you take care of yourself, he says, and there's a finality to it that saddens me.

He's an old man. He's stood by me all these years, even though it must have caused strained relations with his wife. Even the most doggedly independent of people need someone they can turn to in times of self-doubt. For all the time I've known him, Ben has been mine. He won't be there forever.

Goodbye, Jude, he says.

And that's all there is.

My flight departs early tomorrow morning. Six hours, give or take, to London and then a shuttle to Glasgow. I'm packed and prepared. Have been for weeks. Passport and visa all in order. I reached out to Andi to ask if she would be my designated 'next of kin'. My initial reservations over Ash have, I'm happy to say, been unfounded. He has taken good care of her, and their three young children. With all that sorted, there's only one thing left for me to do.

I'll miss this year's memorial service, the first I haven't attended. I've decided to wait until my return in October before visiting the new 9/11 Memorial Museum. It opened a few weeks ago in May. I watched on TV as President Obama gave an address during the dedication ceremony. I couldn't sit still. I paced the room during the broadcast as if his words might contain new information. As if they might somehow change history. My heart rate increased as the names of the dead scrolled alphabetically towards the Hs. And then he was there. Briefly. So painfully brief. On my television screen. In my room. Breaking my heart again.

The yellow B-52s T-shirt I gave to Hennessey is one of the museum artifacts, and I'm afraid of how badly it will affect me when I finally see it. He wore it under his uniform that day. Used it as a mask. Then untied it from his face to stem the blood from an injured woman. She was subsequently pulled from the rubble with it still wrapped around her head.

As I walk downtown, I think about the times we spent together. The ways we entertained ourselves in his old apartment in Queens. The corny jokes he told, the Irish music he played. The time he twisted an ankle dancing on a table too rickety even for his modest weight. Me pushing him around Flushing Meadow in a shopping cart so he could deal his weed until the ankle could sustain him. Us walking for miles and miles one hot Saturday to find a soccer match where the Glasgow Celtic were playing, on a tour of the States. We couldn't afford a ticket, so we just sat outside and listened to the noise. Him lying back ecstatic, eyes closed, scarf around his neck, imagining he was in the crowd. I think of the mix of sheer joy and abject despair I felt when I discovered him again in the Bowery, but saw the state he was in. The feeling that he'd kept himself alive simply for the purpose of returning that dashboard Elvis I'd given him. I think of the variety of methods I employed to get him to accept part of my salary. Telling him he was my muse and I couldn't work creatively if I felt the muse wasn't recompensed, and him saying 'Jude, if you're prepared to go to the lengths of making up that bullshit then, yeah ... wire the money to my accountant's office and my PA will handle the transactions' as he wrapped countless elastic bands around the toe of his sneaker to limit the snow getting in through its flapping sole. And I remember his pride at becoming a janitor at 'the greatest building in the world ... well, one of 'em, at least'. That uniform. He never took it off.

I stroll around the new gardens. Despite the numbers, it is noticeably quiet. Even the birds are respectful. It's an astonishingly affecting place. Two enormous sunken pools of reflection, exactly where the towers stood, the absence of structure, the inverse of traditional memorial devices, surrounded by swamp white oak trees. A field of serenity in the busiest city in the world. The faintest sound of falling water. There is affirmation of life all around.

I kiss my fingers and touch each of the letters on the bronze parapet. Rather than leave the dashboard Elvis to an uncertain fate – I have other plans for him – I place the stem of a white rose in the 'O' of his first name:

MILO HENNESSEY

I click on my iPod and his favorite song plays, blocking out all distractions:

There's no pain, there's no more sorrow. They're all gone, gone in the years, babe.

Cheeks sodden, I decide to leave the memorial to the tourists.

I won't ever visit again. I don't want to be reminded of what I've lost, I want to remember what I had, and what I'll always have. Life is for the living.

PART FOUR:

Mother Glasgow

25th July 2014:

I push the trolley awkwardly through the door marked *ARRI-VALS*. The progress of passengers resembles a pedestrian demolition derby, there are so many wonky wheels. Once through the swishing doors, I maneuver left, out of the slipstream of the front runners. I glance briefly at the excited reunions and then press on, heading for the airport's cab stand. The queue stretches full along the front of the terminal. It reduces slowly, a ratio of one occupant per cab. As I near the front, several impatient people behind request that I share mine with them. I politely decline.

The black cab snails its way eastward along a congested freeway towards the city center. It's very hot, sunny; not what I'd antici-pated at all. There's a big *PEOPLE MAKE GLASGOW* sign on the gable of an old Victorian block. I smile. A similar banner fronted the Tartan Day Parade back in Manhattan. My cab crosses the River Clyde. I read, 'Glasgow's current symbiotic relationship with the river is represented by high-tech, metal-and-glass build-ings facing the water, and old industrial tower cranes punctuating the spaces in between', from an architectural guidebook purchased while delayed in London. The quayside is vibrant and full of people moving, singing, dancing, like there's a carnival on.

Here for the Games, hen? asks my driver.

Oh ... oh, no. No, I'm here on some personal business, I reply.

Yer here at the right time, then. S'been meltin' here for weeks noo, he says.

I don't respond this time. He catches my eye from his rear-view.

Roastin' hot, like, ye know? he says.

I'm used to the heat. I'm from Texas.

Taps aff aw the time ower there, ah'll bet?

Hmm, I say, unsure what I have just affirmed. The remainder of the journey is conducted in silence.

I will be in Glasgow for a few months. This small, self-catering aparthotel in Miller Street – one of the few with availability during the Commonwealth Games – will be my base for the duration. There are now several reasons for my journey. There's the hope of an in-depth feature on Anna Mason, in the run-up to the referendum on the eighteenth of September. This vote has been a very long time coming for the Scottish people. It has been framed by those leading the pro-independence campaign as a once-in-a-generation opportunity. But I see trepidation in the eyes of those making such proclamations: their chance has finally arrived, and they might well be destined to blow it. All indications are that it will be a close-run thing.

I'm also determined to follow up the loose ends of the Hyptones story, and Ms Mason's former position as the band's rights manager. With their only hit now soundtracking the Scottish National Party's campaign, it's easy to deduce that her sudden mood swing in Manhattan in April is connected to the use of the song. And, of course, there's her relationship with Jamie Hewitt to dig deeper into.

And I have some personal searching to do. Looking for the young Jimmy Montgomery, or the strands of the lives that created him. But these are side issues. Cover stories. Rabbit is here in Glasgow too. This is my opportunity to address failing her, as a child and an adult, and to consign those past regrets to history and begin again.

28th July 2014:

Hello? Yes, hello, I hope you can assist me. My name's Jude Montgomery. I met with Ms Mason in Manhattan recently and agreed access for a feature ... Oh, sorry, yes, Montgomery ... that's right ... Yes. I'm freelance. I'm sure she'll remember me.

I flick pages on my diary, primed to provide available dates.

Oh, that's ... um, unusual. Could you check? Will I leave you a contact number? Okay. Yes, I'll hold.

This isn't an encouraging start.

2nd August 2014:

I spend a morning walking around various Glasgow locations – Glasgow Green, the Cathedral Quarter, the Merchant City – occasionally stopping to photograph people unaware their picture is being taken. In the early days of doing the same thing in New York, I never considered this a breach of anyone's privacy. The whole point was to observe ordinary people doing ordinary things – their activity enlivening the context of the city. But now, with the internet a free, open, fully accessible gallery, what might appear ordinary is often rendered sinister by the skewed interpretation of a social-media pile-on. Photography retains the same purpose, but its truthfulness is routinely abused. Believe none of what you read and only half of what you see, as Lou Reed once sang.

I make a series of phone calls. I write notes, the phone wedged between shoulder and left ear. My pen scribbles furiously. Too early to say for definite, but things are looking up.

My impromptu city tour reaches George Square. Despite the late-afternoon rainfall, it is awash with excitement. Later this evening, Usain Bolt will compete in the sprint relay final. His appearance is so eagerly anticipated you would be forgiven for thinking he was representing Scotland at Hampden Park rather than Jamaica. I've noted a concerted attempt from the organizers to keep politics out of the event, but I detect the growing swell of patriotism with each passing day.

My phone rings.

Ben? Hi, how are you? Is everythin' okay? I ask.

...

I look at my watch.

It's, em ... nearly five, I say.

...

In the afternoon, yeah.

...

Yeah, gettin' used to it now.

... ...

No. No not yet. I don't want to push her. Hopefully, yeah, in her own time, I say, and then, after another exhortation to tread warily with Rabbit – which is the purpose of this brief call with him – we say 'bye' simultaneously.

10th August 2014:

Hello? My name is Jude Montgomery ... *(click)* Hello? *Hello*? Is there anyone there?

Earlier optimism has ebbed away completely. It's like trying to make customer complaints calls to the Kremlin.

18th August 2014:

I'm blending into the disbelieving crowd. Many carry expensive cameras just like I do. Many are press photographers – I can tell by the way they hold themselves and their equipment. They are poised, trained to see the details that others don't notice, to anticipate a look or a situation that, captured, can say more than five thousand brilliantly crafted words ever could. I sigh deeply, witnessing the perilous state of Glasgow School of Art after the blaze.

The characterless austerity of a new building immediately across Renfrew Street only serves to magnify the loss. Banks of ugly scaffolding overhang the open roof, propping up the shell of Charles Rennie Mackintosh's masterpiece. The gaping holes offer painful glimpses of the substantial internal damage. I feel like a medical student observing my first post-mortem, shocked but unable to tear myself away. I can only imagine how traumatized Rabbit must be having witnessed this tragedy.

I photograph the dying monument, hoping, against logic, that it will survive and rise again. Not only for Rabbit, who taught and exhibited here until the day the flames rose. But for everyone who cares about beauty and imagination and craft. Glasgow is grieving for this broken emblem of its identity. For those seeking to be free of the Union, it seems like a portent for the weeks ahead.

25th August 2014:

Rabbit is 'out of town'. Again.

I visit a gallery that will provide a temporary academic home for the returning Glasgow School of Art students next month. It will also be Rabbit's base, as their fine art tutor, for the foreseeable future. Almost half of the artwork being exhibited here is for public sale, increasing the potential for much-needed income for those who lost work in the fire. Despite Rabbit being elsewhere, my spirits are lifted by the resilience of the young people I meet. The loss of the building has been traumatic for the city, but several of these students have had their entire course portfolio destroyed.

I wander through the exhibition. Some of the artwork displays smoke or minor fire damage. I can imagine Rabbit teaching her students to embrace the blemishes, using her own body to demonstrate that beauty is often found in the most unexpected places. Much of the display is an appropriately defiant stance for young, creative artists. It tugs at my heart and my imagination, inspiring me in the same way as Janet Delaney's photographs of the effervescent Castro community did almost thirty years ago.

I climb narrow, metal stairs to a mezzanine space that has caught my eye from below. There is no-one in the upper gallery. I gaze at the colourful, vibrant canvasses. All are signed 'Rabbit' in their bottom right-hand corners. None are recognizable from the MoMA exhibition. I stop at one that looks a little like me. Unlike the others, it is flattering. The small white card on the right-hand side of the painting reads:

Dashboard Elvis Is Dead 2009
Oil paint on canvas
Courtesy of the artist and the Museum of Modern Art, New York
(Not for sale)

I turn sharply, head swimming. The light turning liquid. A vision of Brandy laughs, peeking out from behind a large white drape. Hide-and-go-seek amongst an artist's studio paraphernalia. Brandy is wearing a white bath towel. Brandy runs around the mezzanine, splattering paint everywhere. The towel quickly becomes a psychedelic riot of color. She picks up pots and throws the paint at the canvases. It's exactly what I think she'd do. And something I'm certain Rabbit would love. I laugh through the tears.

Are you okay, miss? asks a young student. And I continue to laugh.

Yes, I tell him. Yes, I am.

2nd September 2014:

Someone from Rabbit's team informs me that she will be in England for the next week at least. I enquire further, hoping for, but not expecting elaboration. And I'm told that Rabbit is attempting to establish, through agents in London, links between Glasgow School of Art and studios in Hong Kong and Singapore.

I have a week to kill so I head to the location the sculptor Andy Scott pointed me to for information on Jimmy's family. Glasgow's Mitchell Library is another of the city's buildings with a sad story to tell about the ravages of fire. You wouldn't think it to look upon the substantial, classical stone façade, but it had the same fragile and combustible insides as virtually every other Victorian building in Glasgow. Much-loved and lauded structures gutted by fire is an all-too common occurrence in this city, I've found.

There's a special section on family history. It's situated high up the building, and it's very quiet, with only two staff members covering a large floor area. The department is carpeted with a florid, headache-inducing pattern that momentarily transports me back to a three-night stay in a cheap El Paso motel when I first left home. I select a booth and with the cheerful assistance of the older of the couple on duty, I quickly get to work. After a few days of exclusive research through census records, and birth and death and marriage certificates, the mouse doing all the heavy lifting, a picture emerges that brings joy to my heart.

Larry's description of the facts was essentially correct. James Patrick Montgomery, born on 1st April 1949, had a Protestant mother and a Roman Catholic father – not the other way around, as Larry had it. Elspeth, Jimmy's mom, was a cleaner. His father, Brendan, was a shop steward in the Clydeside shipyards. There is little of note resulting from Elspeth's family thread, but there is much to uncover in following Brendan's. Brendan was the last of five children to Helen and Malachy. Jimmy's grandparents lived in Govan, in the same house that Jimmy would be born in. Helen was a campaigning part of the women's movement led by the Scottish political feminist activist Mary Barbour. Barbour organised the Glasgow rent strikes of 1915. Mary, Helen and twenty thousand others, many of whom were women, marched from Govan to George Square in protest at their unscrupulous landlord's conditions. As I read, I feel connected to Helen. I hope she would've been proud of my written articles, especially 'The Low Expectations of the Bowery Bums', and of me speaking up for them. But as I delve further into her life, looking for other recognisable strands, I find them in an unexpected place. Looking for her in a photo archive, I discover her in several shots in folders named 'The Women's Peace Crusade, 1916–1918'. She is there, in sober dress and soft velvet hat bedecked with flowers. Standing alongside Mary Barbour and two female workers at Govan's Harland & Wolff shipbuilding yard during the First World War. And she is there in a serious, posed photograph of the Glasgow branch of the Women's International League for Peace and Freedom.

But it's a photo credit that I almost miss that astonishes me. Several of the pictures were taken by Malachy Montgomery. My great-grandparents from Scotland; an ordinary woman campaigning for those without a voice, and a photographer, recording the struggle for future generations to learn from. I leave this place positively beaming.

17th September 2014:

I lean against a shop window on the corner of Buchanan Street and Bath Street. To my left, in the area surrounding Donald Dewar's statue, there is a massed gathering of pro-independence activists. I've been here for almost two hours. Flash mobs sing a rousing song called 'Caledonia'. It buoys them, and every time there's a slight dip in levels of optimism, someone yells the opening line, and the effect is like helium being blown into an in-flatable cheerleader at the Superbowl. I'm witnessing an unplanned, extended early-evening ceilidh. Those bedecked in the nation's dark blue chant 'yes we can' and 'hope not fear', just like my cohort did in Central Park in 2008, although the mood here is pensive. From the people I've polled, the outcome is on a knife-edge. Even those most desperate for a YES to be returned acknowledge that in most circumstances, the status quo usually prevails.

Across town, the face of the No Campaign, former Labour prime minister, Gordon Brown, is delivering his final speech. I've discovered that he's been something of a forgotten political figure of late, but the Scottish Independence campaign has revived his career. His enthusiastic, Biblical rhetoric has galvanized disparate forces of Conservatives, Liberals, and his own party – so often dia-metrically opposed on every issue – around their common goal: preserving a union that has lasted for three hundred years. There's so much at stake. So much to lose and so much to gain, depending on your perspective. And right at the centre of it all is Anna Mason. The pressure on those slim shoulders must be colossal, because however the cards fall, win or lose, YES or NO, she will be the one charged with forging the way forwards.

I'm watching the final rallying calls. Famous actors – well, famous in their own country, at least – have been joined on stage by the YES Scotland executive and members of groups including Women for Independence, English Scots for YES, and Firefighters for YES. My Glaswegian ancestors would've most certainly been on this stage. YES, is indeed the word on everyone's lips. And we all wait, not for the diminishing possibility of an appearance by First Minister Alex Salmond, but for the more likely contribution from his deputy, Anna Mason.

A cheer rises. Everyone looks towards the elevated platform. A blonde head can be glimpsed bobbing between those keen to extend good wishes or to capture the moment forever in a selfie.

While this plays out, the opening chords of 'Independent State of Mind' strike up over a tannoy. The vocals, when they come, sound distorted, but it matters little. The song lifts the crowd, and they easily drown the singer out, lungs bursting with every word as if the success of this whole campaign depends on them.

YES, YES, YES, we're done, England … Leave us on our own.

Lyrics adapted to suit. I wonder what Jamie Hewitt would make of it.

All I want is, an independent state of mind.
All I need is, an independent state of mind.
You can give me, an independent state of mind.

This final chorus repeats and reverberates, and becomes a determined, defiant chant that Anna Mason can't speak over. I photograph her with the long lens, zoomed in close to see her features. Her make-up is typically perfect. Although her eyes betray an exhaustion that may – regardless of the outcome – border on relief. It's the eyes. Always the eyes.

She raises her arms and pleads with the crowd to allow her to speak. And then, just as she does, everyone's attention is suddenly drawn left.

Haw, Anna*fucken*belle Mason, you've ruined ma fucken life, ya cow!

A man's angry voice. A voice from her past. There's a bald, tattooed head spotted briefly, before black-clad security men drag him away. I train the camera again. Focus. An extreme close-up. The lens captures a formidable woman struggling not to be seen to crumble in front of this crowd. Rather than a speech to echo those of Salmond, or challenge those of Brown, Anna Mason simply raises a weak arm, mouths, *YES*, and turns, escaping the platform, receding into the backstage throng.

Back in the hotel, I scribble spontaneous early-morning feelings about Scotland and my developing relationship with it. To capture the mood of those I've encountered before the result either validates or eradicates it. The desire of many to go it alone feels like my own back in 1983. Not hatefully dismissive of the past, just desiring a different future they'd feel more in control of shaping. I flick through the test photos on my phone, assemble the notes in front of me and start typing.

A NEW STATE OF INDEPENDENCE
By Judithea Montgomery

There are some incontestable certainties about Britain that the Scottish people will wake up to today. Firstly, and most obviously, it's still actually there. As an outside observer to the YES and NO arguments, I might have assumed the physical location of the land mass was going to change; to be anchored further out to sea, making it even harder for the other people to get to. Secondly, the sun will still rise in the east and set in the west. Although – this being Scotland, after all – you may have to take that for granted rather than witness it with your own eyes. Thirdly – and of no interest to you at all, I'm sure – I will have been here in this wonderful country for exactly fifty-six days.

My experiences, attitudes, understanding, perspectives, etc, have changed in that short time. This change, subtle though it may be, has come about through my interactions with people from different walks of life. My profession (photography) is fundamentally about people. At its best, it records, empathizes with and understands social and cultural need. My work seeks to appreciate the values of cohesion and community, regardless of location. It aspires to capture environments that explain the quality (or lack thereof) of people's everyday lives, regardless of ethnicity, class or boundary.

I've been extremely fortunate in my life. I've had the chance to put whatever skills I have in these areas to positive use in many culturally diverse places in the United States of America. Whether it's been in poverty-stricken parts of New York City, or in the various sensitivities of San Francisco, or in the forgotten Mid-West where an irrational fear of the 'other' drives otherwise rational people to violence, photography has provided a common language that tries to understand people and their hopes, fears, dreams, and concerns.

I was born and grew up in a small part of Houston, Texas, commonly and lazily described as 'socially deprived'. While life in Humble remains challenging for many, there's a warmth and richness in the community to echo that of the other places I've been lucky enough to live and work in. Although I didn't appreciate it when I should have, my hometown has intangible values that are a part of my soul and are the essence of the pictures I've taken. During the all-too brief period I've been here, I've seen people in Glasgow communities – not unlike those my forebears originated from – struggle daily with the pressures of simply living and existing. Addressing the unfairness and inequality in such situations should be the principal driver for those in elected positions of power. But sadly, it seems to me, that isn't the case in the United Kingdom of today. Other, more self-interested and parochial priorities now exist, excluding those most in need of prioritising.

I am not a nationalist, very far from it ... more – despite my limited travel experiences – an internationalist. I am suspicious of boundaries, too aware that race or religion or class are often the basis of such exclusion. Too many in Westminster are ideologically opposed to the core philosophy of welfare and equality that rebuilt post-war Britain. However, the 'Britain' of 2014 is an outdated and divided conceit. It certainly isn't

'Great'. A more liberal, left-leaning and federalist desire to share out opportunity equally isn't reflected in an English-national-ist-driven United Kingdom where maximising shareholder profit and promoting low rates of corporate taxation are the apparent priorities.

The people, places, music, literature, arts, and culture that are resolutely international as opposed to solely British, they aren't going anywhere. They'll still be there to thrill and inspire an independent Scotland for the coming generations. I've in-terviewed and discussed the issue with many people in the past few days, and they've all expressed a level of uncertainty about both the immediate future, and about the prospects for the notion of a union. Whether now, or in future years, an inde-pendent Scotland is inevitable, they feel. Both sides of this most divisive of debates will face difficult economic issues and I'd advise anyone to be skeptical of those who would profess – with the certainty of knowing the sun will rise on this Friday morning – to know exactly what awaits Scotland in either scenario.

But I'm a pragmatic thinker and an optimistic dreamer in equal measure. As unlikely as it might seem now, an opportun-ity to help create the type of caring, socially responsible and equal society that I would want to live the remainder of my life in will always exist. For the people of Scotland, it might just be within a smaller context. Their future must become about people. And all people, not just the more privileged few. That's an aspiration worth striving for.

I hope that becomes the unifying ethos of Scotland's brave new world.

Social media is a battlefield in the aftermath. Egos and opinions and reputations lie bloodied on both sides. An impartial observer

– were it even possible to find one – might deduce from the multitude of conspiratorial threads that no side won. And no side lost. Both might be closer to the truth than anyone wants to admit. It's evident that the underlying tensions that brought this vote into being aren't going to suddenly vanish. The inevitability of Scotland being back in this situation within the coming decade has already been suggested by Anna Mason. I'm even more desperate to speak to her now, but even without her suspicions of me, I'd be so far to the back of that queue that I start to conceive a biographical piece composed without her input.

I'm desperate to know what Jamie Hewitt's attitude to his former girlfriend's political rise is. And what the rest of the band think about their song being far more famous than them. I trawl the various social platforms. All I uncover is an unusual story about Charles Chalmers, the band's former drummer. Seven years ago, he was found guilty of serious assault following a break-in at the house of East End businessman, Ronnie Mason. Anna Mason's father. Chalmers was jailed for three years. The only photograph I can find attached to the story makes Chalmers look like the victim of an assault rather than the perpetrator. I have the sense that the band members are all around me – but as elusive as ghosts, hidden away in the folds and crevices of the city. Talking to them would uncover so much.

After an hour of Hyptones-related search words, I find a promising lead on Facebook. It's a locally based account called Bingo's Biscuits, and in the comments connected to a four-year-old post...

Dont talk abut them anymor. No aloud tae. AFB legals. Fuck knows were Jamie is, mate.

Nothing ventured. Nothing gained.

22nd September 2014:

The bar is busy. A group of men are watching a soccer match on a large overhead TV screen. The mood is somber, mournful. It will take a while for the pro-independence pain to subside. I wait, conspicuous for being on my own, but also for not having a drink in front of me. I glance at my watch several times, resolving to give it another ten minutes. I've been here for an hour. Eventually, a woman comes through the saloon-type double doors. The sunlight floods in and creates a glow around her. My interviewee sees me, and after all the text-message negotiations, it finally looks like it's happening. After saying hello to several other people, the woman takes off a wet coat and sits down. We shake hands.

Four seasons in wan day, eh? says the woman.

Hi, I'm Jude Montgomery.

Well, yer persistent, hen, for a Jude Montgomery, ah'll gie ye that. Jist like this bloody weather.

The squeaking doors swing again, and two men rush in.

Fuck sake, man. Pishin' doon again, says one.

I look at the Glaswegian woman sat opposite me. She looks nothing like the bass player from thirty years earlier, what little I can recall of her. Based on the limited archive material available of The Hyptones' all-too brief career, the passage of time hasn't been kind. She carries an additional forty pounds. She is breathing heavily, as if she suffers from asthma. I notice the holes in her tights just above the heel rim of her shoes. The holes aren't new.

I'm sorry about that – all the texts. It's just that I'm runnin' out of time now. I need to go back to New York soon, I say.

Get ye a drink? she asks.

Please, let me, I reply. The least I could do.

Aye, aw'right, since yer twistin' ma arm. Peroni. A pint.

I go to the bar. A heavily bearded man wearing glasses looks me up and down as I pass him. He continues towards our table.

New burd, Bingo? Ye swipe left an' hit the jackpot or somethin'? he says.

Beat it, Bobby. Ah'm workin' here. She's a journalist. It's an interview, aboot the band … now, fuck off or it's a swift phone call tae the benefits office the morra.

The bearded man tuts loudly enough for me to hear him.

Jeezo, man, he says. Nae need tae threaten folk. Just tryin' tae be friendly, an' that.

The man draws me a sharp look as I return with a beer for Bingo McAllister, and a gin and tonic for myself.

Nosy bastart, says Bingo. Hard tae escape aw yer ghosts around here, y'know?

Bingo gulps back a large mouthful.

Cheers, hen, she says and we clink glasses.

Cheers, I respond.

Ye must be missin' the sunshine, then, eh?

Well, I'm gettin' used to copin' without it. I laugh, but mainly at the consistency with which this subject opens a conversation here.

They say the graveyards are fu' ae folk who'd love this bloody weather, says Bingo. Yet tae come across wan, though.

Maybe there's no such thing as bad weather, only inappropriate clothing?

Bingo winks and raises her glass again.

Aye, so ye know yer Connolly, then. Ye'll dae fine here, says Bingo, then suddenly serious she says: So, is this bein' recorded then? Whit's the payment rate?

Still to be negotiated. I smile. OK if I put this on?

I have the phone in my hand, finger poised over record. Bingo shrugs. I put the device on the table and the button goes from white to red.

Can I start by askin' if you still see any of the group?

Naw. We aw drifted apart after … well, y'know, when Inky had his accident an' that. Although, truth be told, it wis done for me when we got back fae the States. We just couldnae look at each other after that, says Bingo.

She takes another huge drink. A refill will be needed soon, and I have barely sipped mine.

Tough times, Bingo adds.

I detect a touch of melancholy.

Did you visit Jamie in London?

Bingo laughs, surprised at the question. I don't clarify how I know he was there. Better to let her assume I'm in possession of more information from Anna Mason than I am.

Nope.

Why not? I ask.

Didnae even fucken know he wis doon there, says Bingo. Listen, him an' me wurnae that close ... ah dunno if ye heard different.

She's probing.

Well, I'm findin' it difficult to get hold of anyone prepared to talk to me, I tell her.

Aye, well, that's the deal we aw signed wi' the AFB, says Bingo. Anna's crowd, she adds.

For the royalties? I ask, hoping I've stumbled into an area of contention by accident.

Well, no' exactly.

Bingo pauses and looks around the pub before lowering her voice.

It wis a one-off payment. A *big* yin, don't get me wrong. But nae questions allowed tae be asked. Nae future payments either. Nae press or media contact permitted, and *absolutely* nae contact wi' Jamie Hewitt.

But you seem happy doin' this, with me? I counter.

No' exactly *happy*, ah'd say, but beggars cannae be choosers, hen. The money's long since ran oot. Ah'll just need tae take my chances.

Wow, I say. It hadn't occurred to me that our meeting could put her in some kind of danger.

Aye, fucken *wow*, says the former bass player.

So, you don't know where any of the band are now? I ask.

Last ah heard, Reef wis dain' a stint oan the cruise ships. A fucken Val Doonican tribute act or some shite like that. Bingo laughs. That's just the cunt's level, tae be honest.

She drains her glass.

But ask aboot. Oot the west end or up Byres Road. Shut yer eyes, throw a stick an' ah guarantee that ye'll hit someb'dy that wis in a band in the eighties. Someb'dy'll have seen him, sure.

And the others? I ask.

Well, Jamie's the fucken invisible man, int' he? An' Chic ... that poor bastart's been in an' oot ae Barlinnie mair times than... Bingo tails off, as if the punchline won't come, but she's merely signaling the bartender.

Haw, Sandy.

She draws a circle over the table with a chubby, nail-bitten finger.

Hope ye don't mind, eh? she says.

Uh, yes, sure, I say.

Same again?

Yeah, I say. About Chalmers...

Look, says Bingo, hand crossing her chest as if about to swat away a large moth. Chic's a prick – an' as well as it rhymin' it's also true. Cunt cannae help himself. He's got a fucken hard-on for the AFB. Convinced she did him ower an' then got him the jail.

For breakin' into her daddy's house?

He broke intae *her* hoose. Lucky he's still got the pins tae wander around wi', tae be honest.

It was Anna's house? But the papers—

Aye, it's hers. Her da's put everythin' in Anna's name. Probably tae keep *him* oot the jail, says Bingo.

Her brief downward look suggests she thinks she has said too much. She gulps down another mouthful.

Look, she says, my advice? Steer clear ae aw ae them. They're aw bampots. If Jamie's disappeared, that's probably why. Safer away oot the road ae the Masons.

I pause and contemplate this, that the AFB may be a small-scale JFK, with Ronnie, her elderly father, in the Joe Kennedy role, pulling all the strings, politics lending a legitimacy to the family name.

And what about the manager? I ask. I was hopin' to speak to him soon.

McFadden? Doubt he'll sing, says Bingo. That yin's definitely still oan the Mason payroll. Fucken landed oan his feet, that cunt, she says. Ah wanted tae kill that bastart after the States ... when he fucked off an' left us aw in that stinkin' van in San Francisco. We might've only been in it for wan night, but still. He made sure he wis aw'right before sortin' oot the flights hame for the rest ae us.

Where could I contact McFadden? I ask.

Ah thought ye'd already know that Kenny McFadden runs the corporate hospitality at Celtic Park, the lucky bastart. If he fell in the Clyde, he'd come oot wi' salmon in his pockets. Swear tae God, says Bingo.

A loud roar reverberates around the bar as a soccer team on the TV scores.

Ya fucken dancer, Bingo – ah've got a century ridin' oan this game, says the bearded man from earlier.

Aye, Bobby. Tell it tae someb'dy that gie's a shite!

Our drinks arrive amid the commotion.

What about Anna Mason? I ask.

Bingo sniggers sarcastically.

Whit, the Big fucken Bamboozle ... the Anna Fucken Belle. She's a dictator. The real power behind the Ronnie Mason empire. She's probably got Jamie chained tae a radiator in her basement – an' a place next tae him set aside for wee Alex Salmond, tae, for him blowin' this vote.

I laugh, but Bingo doesn't. She purses her lips instead.

Look, hen, dinnae be puttin' anythin' like that intae yer story, or ah'll be back in fucken court again … an' ah dinnae have a decent dress for that, y'know what ah mean? she says.

I'm not sure I do, I say.

But that's all I'll get. The interview's over.

24th September 2014:

A day spent calling numbers connected with Anna Mason's constituency office. No-one answers. Taped apologies and redirections that lead nowhere make me feel the pursuit is as pointless as modern electronic banking. A thought occurs that I should simply manufacture a fake interview with the first minister elect. After all, it's not about her government position or the independence vote. I'm now far more interested in her time as CEO of AFB Management. And her relationship with Jamie Hewitt. The truth of that. And what is truth anyway, other than one person's word over another? I dismiss the thought. The world doesn't need any more badly conceived fiction masquerading as fact.

26th September 2014:

I'm late and the concert I've been invited to will soon be over. A phone call to a former editor in Manhattan has taken far longer than anticipated. Access to Anna Mason is being withheld. It's perhaps unsurprising in the aftermath of the defeat. I figured a formal press pass issued by an ex-employer might help, although securing one is looking unlikely. I can't even be sure that Anna Mason will still be in the country. It would be understandable if she'd escaped it for a few weeks simply to avoid the inevitable questions about how different her future leadership will be from that of the newly resigned Alex Salmond.

I climb the stairs and note the names of bands written on each riser. Few register, but David Bowie is a surprising addition to the Barrowland Ballroom's 'ladder' of fame. The hall is only half full, but those crowded in front of the stage, illuminated by the flashing, syncopated spotlights, are creating a noisy atmosphere that belies their numbers. I cross the rear of the ballroom, feeling the bounce of the floor beneath me. I imagine a full house here, and sense why so many I've met since arriving venerate this place – believing it captures the essence of Glasgow. I head towards the bar and order a Coke, just in time to hear the band's final song. A muscular, elongated version, it may be, but those vocals remain familiar. Lyrics that still entrance and inspire.

Stay free. Stay independent. Fuck the union! shouts the singer as the song finishes in a thumping barrage of drums.

God bless ye, Barrowlands ... ah love ye! G'night.

And with that, he's gone, head down, arm raised in salute, fist clenched in a gloved hand like a Black Power icon. I applaud like a long-standing fan although I only caught two songs.

The houselights come up, and the hall loses some of its mystique. I look up and see the chequerboard quilt of acoustic tiles glued to the vaulted ceiling. I lift my phone, change the camera setting and snap the dispersing crowd as a sea of plastic parts at their feet.

Let's go, hen. Drink up, please.

A burly, black-clad man with perspiration coating a shiny bald head ushers me towards the exit.

Um, I'm with the band, I say, lifting a wrist sporting a piece of brightly coloured paper. The security guy smiles.

Aye, that's whit they aw say, love. He points to a corner. Ower there, hen, he says.

Thank you.

I wander across to a series of tables that block access to a door at the side of the stage.

Doon there, just follow the corridor round, I'm instructed.

I reach an oddly shaped back room. I knock politely on the open door. There are far too many people in there for the space. A few are drunk. No-one hears or notices me. I see the singer, catching his eye. He excuses himself from someone shaking his hand.

Jude, yeah? he asks.

Yeah. I hold out a hand, but he moves it aside and hugs me.

Let's go oot an' find somewhere quieter, he says.

The singer ushers me back out to the stage, where we find an unoccupied corner. We sit, watching technicians dismantling the equipment and cleaners brushing up the empty cups.

Thanks for the ticket, I tell him.

Nae sweat. Thanks for comin'. It's good tae see ye again.

Reef Malcolm has never formally met me before. Our phone call a week prior was the first time we had spoken, yet he treats me like an old friend. It's a little disconcerting. I notice the way his fingers move constantly, touching his chin, running through his long, dark, wet hair. Occasionally touching my knee. I decide he's one of those people who is magnetically warm rather than threateningly tactile.

Wow, it looks totally different with the lights and the atmosphere and the crowd gone, I say.

Aye, that's rock 'n' roll in a nutshell, sweetheart, Reef says. It looks glamourous fae the outside, but it's just a façade. A wee bit ae escapism fae the boredom an' the humdrum.

Do you miss the fame?

Nope, he says. Didnae experience that much of it, tae be fair, but fame was like bein' trapped in a luxury asylum. Folk bring ye meals an' drinks, an' only let ye out for an hour a night tae fucken perform like a monkey for folk who are madder than you. Mental bastarts.

I laugh but suspect it's a rehearsed answer he's used plenty of times before.

That's a bit condescendin' to your audience, Reef, I say, still laughing.

Fuck *them* ... that's *me* ah'm talkin' aboot.

You talked a lot about Jamie an' you on the telephone. Have you never been tempted to find out what he's doin' now? I ask him. To see how he is?

Reef sighs.

When the record wis sellin' millions aff ae the Apple advert, ah automatically thought we'd aw get back together. Celebrate the wee bit ae success an' that. Ah think we'd deserved that bit ae luck, like, y'know? Kenny McFadden, our old manager, contacts me an' says that someb'dy fae New York wants tae use 'Independent State of Mind' tae relaunch a new computer. A big worldwide campaign, like. Ah thought McFadden wis jokin', until ah remembered that he always wis a humourless bastart.

Reef runs his fingers through his hair again and swishes it back like a supermodel on a shoot before continuing.

It wis a total fucken bolt fae the blue when that happened. Ah hudnae heard fae him or the rest ae them in years. Of course, he wis just a front for AFB ... Anna's mob.

Were you happy with the deal you got? I ask him.

Jesus, aye. Like ah'd won the bloody lottery. Ah wisnae asked for permission, but as one ae the listed composers, ah got an upfront sum, an' the royalty cheques still drop through the letter-box every six months. Cannae beat that, he says.

Not everyone got the same though? I ponder. I'm reaching here. Trying to join the dots.

Well, naw, but why should they? he replies, dander suddenly up.

But Chic Chalmers didn't receive anythin'. Wasn't that the reason he broke into Anna Mason's house?

This is the basis of a developing thesis. Let's see what Reef makes of it.

Ach ... Chic. Ah don't know aboot him. He wis always a wal-loper, that yin. Him an' Anna never got on, that's true. But he's a junkie ... a smackheid. Ye cannae believe a word *they* tell ye.

Hmm. He's not biting.

And what about Anna? Are you still in contact with her? I ask.

She's in a league ae her own, that yin. Salmond's arrogance lost that vote. He's just a dick, in my opinion. Once he's buggered off, she's gonnae be the top dog, y'know? Independence is just a matter ae time, he says.

How did you feel about them usin' the song for the indepen-dence campaign? I ask him.

Aw adds tae the bank balance, right? Presumably, Jamie's agreed tae it. Ah'm no' gonnae object, am ah? Ye heard that crowd th'night. Defiant.

Does Anna Mason know you're a supporter?

Em, ah'm no', but dinnae print that, eh? Ye can be for indepen-dence without bein' a nationalist, Reef says. And then adds, We had an arrangement.

With her office? I ask.

Naw, wi' her direct, he says. Ah could play the song durin' the gigs, as long as ah wis encouragin' folk tae vote YES, he says. Small price tae pay.

I take some snaps with his permission, and he preens like Jagger has taught band frontmen the world over to.

Do you like her? I ask. Anna, I mean.

He takes a while to mull this over.

Ah like whit she represents, he says. No' the party, though. It's complicated.

An answer without answering.

Wouldnae want tae get on the wrong side ae her, he admits. And it sounds like he speaks from surviving the experience.

So ... Jamie, I begin.

Look, we aw just leave each other alone. Only Anna, an' mibbe Kenny, knows where everybody is noo, but apparently, it wis aw

Jamie's idea to go oor separate ways, Reef says. So, if it's him yer really after ... then McFadden might know. Doubt he'll tell ye though.

How's it goin' with the new band? I ask.

Reef laughs at the question. Like he's relieved we're suddenly onto a subject with less hidden minefields.

It's good. Ah'm constantly fucken knackered, but it's better than bein' a traffic warden.

I smile. I touch his knee this time.

Ah've done aw'right, tae be honest. Ah can think ae worse lives, he says.

No regrets, then? That's not too bad, I conclude.

Aye. Life's good, hen. He stretches. Ah'm glad they did, but Christ knows how they Apple dudes stumbled oan the song ... Ah mean, it's no' like it wis a worldwide smash hit or anythin' like that. We were one-hit wonders ... naebodies in the big scheme ae things. It's just a cool wee tune, nothin' else.

I think it's much more than that, I say.

Reef doesn't hear this because a sudden noise is being made behind him.

Need tae shift, Reef, mate ... ah've got tae lug they amps.

A stage technician brings the chat to a halt.

Aye cheers, pal, says Reef. We stand.

I should go, I tell him. I kiss him on the cheek. Thank you ... for the ticket, for everythin'...

If ye dae see Jamie, tell him ... well, y'know?

Yeah. I will. Goodbye Reef.

28th September 2014:

The phone rings out. Once again. An anonymous female voice politely encourages me to leave a message.

Hi. It's me again. I'm sorry for leaving so many messages, but I really want to see you before I go back to the States. I have so much I need to say. To tell you about. About your mom. And I have something to give you.

It feels like I'm pleading, and that was the last place I wanted to be.

I grip the figurine in my coat pocket and conclude by simply saying, Yes. I do.

2nd October 2014:

The cab driver drops me on London Road.

Best lettin' ye off here, darlin', she says. Ye'd be quicker walkin', time it'll take me tae get through the crowds.

I thank the woman and hand a twenty-pound note through the tiny hole in the Plexiglas that separates us.

Mind yersel, now, the driver says, happy with the tip.

I head towards the stadium, swept along by a wave of green and white, and by visions of Hennessey walking excitedly alongside me.

I listen to the songs and the banter of the fans. How he'd have loved the spectacle. This is my first experience of a football match. It's just a word but 'soccer' somehow doesn't seem right here. It feels like a pilgrimage. That I am here representing him. I take photographs, lots of them, spellbound by the experience.

Inside the stadium, the atmosphere is electric. I'm shown to a hospitality floor. I notice the sign above the door: *The Mason Suite*.

My seat is amongst the guests of a loud, brashly dressed man who has a private box for the match. I'm not introduced to any of them.

How ye doin', hen. Ah'm Matty.

According to the old man sat next to me, this European match against the team from Zagreb has not captured the imagination of the Celtic fans. He points to the closed top tier of the stadium.

Would normally be rammed, that, says Matty.

Despite this, the volume builds towards kick-off. Tens of thousands of supporters, glowing in the floodlights, stood under a green-and-white tapestry of scarves, singing 'You'll Never Walk Alone' up into the dark sky over Glasgow's East End is a spine-tingling moment. I look to my right and it's not Matty I see, it's Hennessey. He raises his scarf high above his head, looking to the heavens, tears in his eyes.

Better than I ever imagined it'd be, doll, he says.

I smile and reach out to hug him. Matty accepts the embrace. He winks and gives me a knowing smile.

It's aw'right, hen. This place'll dae that tae ye, he says, after I apologize.

The fans aren't in their seats for long. Only a few minutes after the match starts and the home team score.

Piece ae piss, says Matty. But his relaxed demeanor changes during the game's second half. I jot down the following:

Holy fuck, Stokes!

Delia, you're a fud!

Ye couldnae kick yer ain arse, Gordon!

Away an' lose some weight, Commons, ya fat bastart, ye!

Celtic hold on to win the match, and Matty relaxes.

Hope ye enjoyed that, he says.

I really did, I tell him. Much more than I thought I would.

That's Paradise for ye. Matty winks. Here, take this, he says, handing me his scarf.

That's you a fan for life now. See ye, hen, he says, heading off to the bar.

I'm left alone in the seats. I photograph coordinated lines of stewards climbing and descending the terraces in unison before a voice startles me.

You must be Ms Montgomery ... the *New Yorker*?

I turn to see a stout, smiling man wearing a dark-green blazer with a crest on the breast pocket.

Ah see ye came prepared, he says, motioning to the scarf around my neck.

Oh, that, yes ... Kenny?

Aye, love. Kenny McFadden, at yer service. D'ye enjoy that?

I didn't quite follow the rules, but I had a guide who helped me, I say.

Good stuff, says Kenny.

A roar goes up over Kenny's shoulder.

Is that Rod Stewart over there? I ask him.

Aye. Ah'll maybe introduce ye later. He'll be pished, nae doubt, but he's a charmer, y'know?

You enjoy it here? I ask as Kenny sits alongside me.

Christ, who widnae? They're ma team, like. Heart an' soul. He taps the badge on his jacket.

They were aw Celtic fans tae, y'know, The Hyptones. This is where Jamie an' Brian first came up wi' the idea ae bein' in a band. They could play ... the music, y'know, but they were shite in the beginnin' ... apart fae Jamie. That boy wis a natural, says Kenny.

How did you know them back then?

Ah wis a scout – for Celtic. Lookin' for young players. Ah first spotted Brian scorin' goals for fun for his school team in the seventies. He'd've been aboot twelve. Cocky wee bastard, even then. Three years later, him an' Jamie were playin' in a youth team ah managed. But ye could tell their minds were oan other things. Music mainly, but lassies tae, he says, smiling.

Was he good ... Jamie, I mean? I ask.

At fitba? Aye, an' he knew it tae. He coulda played for the first team. But he loved the music more, y'know. The Ramones, The Clash, The Jam. Him an' Brian just drifted away fae the game. Jamie was easy goin' but Brian was hard work at the end. Bingo was Chic's pal. Chic wis just an arsehole ... still is, as far as ah know.

But he had a drum set. Cannae remember where Reef came fae. He might've been Anna Mason's pal. Reef was a good-lookin' kid, an' fucken full ae himself. A natural frontman.

Kenny laughs and shakes his head.

Ah put two an' two th'gither. Spotted an opportunity, he says.

They were great though, weren't they? They could've been *really* great, I suggest.

Ach. Aye, for about ten minutes ... an' then the flame blew oot. They blamed me. *Qué séra.* Thing is, it's no' always business that ruins it. Sometimes bands have one, mibbe two great ideas, if they're lucky. An' then they run out ae inspiration. It becomes a job, a pain in the arse just like every other yin. An' that's usually when they split up. Or when they should. Just bad timin' that it happened when it did, he says.

But you left them in the States, I say.

I see an eyebrow rise.

Darlin', it wis every man for himself back then.

Kenny stands to shake someone's hand then sits down again.

No' proud ae myself for that, but at least ah've made up for it since. They're aw doin' okay now. Except for Chic, but that's aw doon tae him, naebody else.

I don't update him regarding Bingo McAllister's status.

Do you know where Jamie is? I ask.

Kenny draws air in through his teeth before blowing it out again.

Ach. Ah don't know, love.

He pauses and looks around before whispering: Ah made a promise.

Too whom, I ask.

Kenny McFadden starts to answer but stops himself.

Do you even have a contact number? I ask, too forcefully. I must sound like a private detective.

Look, hen, he just wants tae be left in peace. Don't get me wrong, he's as grateful as the rest ae us tae whoever it wis that decided tae stick their song in that commercial – ye can put *that* in the piece you're doin' – but he'll no' see ye tae talk aboot it directly.

Someone knocks on the glass, trying to gain Kenny's attention.

Listen, miss, ah'll need tae go ... Gerard Butler's waitin' for me.

Kenny stands and lifts a hand before turning away. But he stops before reaching the door. He turns, looks at me directly, pauses, and then sighs. He writes something on a piece of paper, and walks back, handing it to me. It's a telephone number.

For Christ's sake, don't let Anna Mason know ah gie'd ye this, eh? Good luck tae ye. Ah hope it aw works oot for Jamie, wherever the hell he is now, he says.

We shake hands, and then Kenny McFadden is gone, lost in the celebrating crowds.

I sit again. I look out at the empty stadium seats. Two tiny groundsmen fork the grass pitch. They look like small birds pecking at it, dwarfed by the structures surrounding them. I reach for my phone.

Hi, hello ... Reef? Yeah, it's Jude. Jude Montgomery. Sorry to call so late but I have somethin' for you.

4th October 2014:

I meet with the writer David F. Ross. He has suggested the Necropolis as a meeting place. High up among the tiered contours of gravestones overlooking the city. He is an awkward and pensive man. A loner, by his own admission. I tell him that I understand solitude, that I've also had to become comfortable with my own company.

It's a fruitless venture though. Mr Ross has no insight to offer me. And no information other than a possible last-known address for Chic Chalmers. He won't trade it without a reciprocal offer though. Even though it's doubtful I'll follow up on the Chalmers connection, I give him Jamie Hewitt's phone number, the one I received from Kenny McFadden. I've left numerous messages on its voicemail, and it already feels like yet another dead end. Mr Ross tells me he already had it, and we part, both no doubt wishing we'd put the thirty minutes to better use.

8th October 2014:

I leave the coffee shop. Eileen and her friend, Sadie, are long gone. The bustle of the early-evening rush hour has died down. It's dark outside but at least the rain has abated, and the wind has lessened. My phone vibrates in my hand, and I answer it.

Hello, Jude.

I don't recognise the caller's number. Nor, at first, the accent, so unexpected is the call.

It's Rabbit.

Oh my God, I say.

The emotion is rising, and I have to work hard to suppress it for fear of it quickly overwhelming me.

Did you just pick up my message? I ask, trembling.

Hmm. How have you been? Rabbit asks.

Her mood is hard to decipher, still, she's here, calling, reaching out, and that's all that matters.

Uh, yeah ... I've been fine. Desperate to reach you, I say.

Um, things have been kinda tough lately, with the aftermath of the fire an' all, says Rabbit.

I can imagine, I say.

There's a pause. It feels awkward.

Listen, Rabbit, I'm leavin' next week. Returnin' to the States. I really want to—

Yes, says Rabbit. I'll see you.

My eyes well up.

I have meetings and classes in the afternoon but how about lunch tomorrow? she says.

Oh, yes, I say. God, yes ... thank you.

I'll text you, says Rabbit.

Okay.

And with that, she's gone. No declarations of love or regret or forgiveness. That can wait until we are facing each other, I guess.

I hail a passing cab. It veers into the sidewalk, forcing me to move sharply to prevent it being taken by an aggressive man convinced he flagged first.

Do you take a card? I ask.

Sure. Where tae, love?

I read out the address given to me by David F. Ross:

33 Petershill Court, Petershill Drive, please.

The towers at the Red Road Flats – you sure about that?

I hesitate before saying, Yes.

The driver swings the car around and we head off to the East End.

Dashboard Elvis Is Dead

by David F. Ross

'D'ye want me tae wait here, hen?' The driver senses Jude's unease. Her exhilaration at receiving Rabbit's call has gone.

'Would you?'

'Aye, nae problem. Need tae keep the meter runnin' though.'

The orange sodium at the base of these monumental towers makes everything seem scarier. A fog has also descended. Only the blinking red lights at the top give any indication of the scale of these desolate high-rise structures. The towers were once testament to the social experiments of the late sixties. Humans as lab rats, stacked in the sky in poorly built concrete boxes. Now, they stand as tombstones. Fit only for impoverished students or those desperately seeking refuge from genocidal dictatorships. Or Chic Chalmers. *Beggars can't be choosers.* The towers are on borrowed time already. As part of the renewal legacy of the Commonwealth Games, their demolition has been announced. They have less than a year.

Jude considers leaving Chic out of the story. Considers simply walking away from this forgotten foreign wasteland and not looking back. But his perspective on Anna Mason *is* the story, Jude imagines. Her ruthless retribution, his imprisonment; that's what she's hiding. Jude shakes herself, reminded of dark nights in Queens, or Brooklyn, or of the time on 2nd Avenue when she faced down a gang demanding money from her and Andi. Although it's easier to be feisty when you're young and surer of your environment.

A group of youngsters veer out of the misty shadows. One holds a large dog, straining against its rope leash like Gonzo used to. Once upon a time she could've easily outrun the males. Maybe even the dog. Not anymore.

'Help ye there, darlin'?' one says.

'Help ye oot yer scants, he means,' says another. They all laugh.

'Whit ye got in the bag?'

'Lookin' tae buy some smack, hen?'

'...Or tae get a smack?'

'*Smack ma bitch up*! Hahaha, man ... fucken landit, ya cunt.'

The dog barks angrily at Jude, and the youngsters laugh in unison.

'Tyson's efter a bone!'

'Haw-haw, he said *boner*!'

'Much furra blow job then?'

'Fuck, Daz, she's too auld, man. Her teeth'd faw oot while she's suckin' yer boaby!'

Jude moves past without acknowledging them. Avoids eye contact. She smells the beer breath and the pungent weed that recalls Hennessey. It helps to remind herself that she lived for years in the brutal urban projects of the New York boroughs. Young pack-males on the margins are the same the world over. Full of peer-pressurised, toxic bravado. At least Glaswegian ones don't carry guns.

'Gaun, ya fucken asylum seekin' hoor, ye! Awa' back tae yer ain bit.' The last insult from the pack, irritated that Jude hasn't responded to their baiting. They move on. The threat diminishes.

The doors at the base of Chic's tower are broken, the electric cables that once secured entry ripped out and hanging lifeless from their box. The putrid stench of urine is unbelievable. Holes in the plastered concrete range in size from sledgehammer to bullet. On a wall, barely decipherable against the graffiti, Jude snaps an old sign. It reads:

Advice to new students:
Don't use the ice-cream vans.
Don't buy drugs from anyone in the area.
Don't borrow money in the area.
Stay out of the pubs.
Stay out of the bookies.
KEEP TO YOURSELF.

Jude presses the lift button, fearing an encounter on the stairs more. The doors screech open, and once inside, she fears them not opening again. She distracts herself from what's waiting above by thinking of Hennessey and of the time he headed into the depths of the Lower East Side looking for dime-bagged heroin. His lowest ebb, he'd said. He'd climbed a crumbling ten-storey slum to the ninth floor. The elevator was out. The staircase, dark and smelly, and littered with semi-conscious junkies. He held an old harmonica in his pocket like it was a gun and he was Sam Spade. He and Jude had laughed as he described reaching the dealer's sliding hatch cut low down into a metal-plated door and handing over his ten bucks to an elderly Filipino dwarf in return for one bag of Colombian brown.

Thinking of Hennessey brings the faintest of nervous smiles. How he'd laugh if he could see her now. Shivering with anxiety inside a derelict Glaswegian tower block, fingering the plastic dashboard Elvis Presley figure in her pocket to make it look like a weapon. They've been through a lot together, Jude and Elvis. He's been her guardian angel, and briefly, Hennessey's. Tomorrow, Jude will present him to Rabbit. He'll be a lasting connection between the two of them and Brandy.

The doors open. Jude shudders. The man's there. Waiting for her. A dying fluorescent light flickers. It hurts her eyes. When on, it illuminates scores of discarded hypodermic needles on a shiny bed of burnt foils. When off, only the green of a fire-exit sign above a door with a smashed glass panel prevents total darkness.

The green catches him. He looks ill. The fluorescent strobes and he looks worse.

'Chic?' Jude asks. She now wishes she'd walked back to the taxi after the encounter with the young team outside.

'Got the money?' Chic barks. He is wired, and aggressive with it.

'Can I ask you a few questions first?'

'Fucken money!'

Jude clutches her bag tightly under her arm.

'That prick Ross said ye'd pay me!'

Jude has nothing to bargain with. The Buchanan Street busker got the last of the folding kind. Chic Chalmers doesn't look like he'll accept a bank transfer.

'Yes, I will. But look, I just want to ask about Anna Mason. I think I saw you—'

'Dinnae start wi' that fucken devious cunt, right. Money. *Now*!'

This was a big mistake. Jude steps back and presses the lift button behind her. Chic Chalmers hears the gears ratcheting and leaps forwards. He grabs for Jude's bag. Jude's hand rises instinctively. No-one will hear her, but she summons all her rage and screams. She grips Elvis Presley tightly and drags him down Chic's face. Elvis's tiny pointing finger at the end of his extended right arm punctures the pallid skin. It draws blood. The flickering light catches Chic's crumpled face. The fluid bag under his eye is ripped open. The blood runs freely. The crease of his eyelid is torn back. He yells in pain. Jude shrieks, preparing to redeploy the plastic king of rock an' roll. Chic attempts a punch. His fist misses Jude's cheek. She pushes him backwards onto the lift's metal door frame. His back catches a projecting panel. The jagged edge cuts him through the shirt and she sees the fury. His hand reaches into a pocket. They are like dancers in a strobe-lit industrial nightclub. She advances. The green doesn't catch the glint of the blade and she walks onto it, almost gracefully. There's no pain. No panic. Not yet. By the time the light stutters on again, she's down. A discarded syringe has jabbed her face but the warm wetness around her stomach is more worrying. Chic grabs for the bag. She has fallen on it, but her resistance is waning. He rolls her over. She hears him say, 'Sorry. Ah'm fucken sorry, right!' She screams again, this time, not because of the knife wound. But because the needle has gone right through her cheek.

The lift doors open. Chic stumbles inside. He holds her bag with one hand and his torn face with the other. Jude smells his stale sweat and retches.

'Don't leave me here,' she yells. She throws out a foot. The only pain she feels is from the lift doors shutting on her ankle. They force her lower leg to form an odd angle. The metal releases her and Chic aims a kick. He connects at the second attempt. A jolt ratchets up her leg. A bone broken, most likely.

'Fuck sake. This is your fucken fault!' shouts Chic.

Jude lifts a hand, pleading. But the doors rattle shut, and he's gone. She screams for help, but these towers are on the condemned list. Few residents remain, and those that do will be unlikely to venture out of boarded-up, locked doors to help a stranger. No-one is coming. Even the taxi driver will have given up and driven back to the city centre. She will probably die here. In this piss-stinking hellhole. With a migraine from that fucking light. And it might take hours for her to bleed out. But she can't raise herself. Try as she might, she can't move. Her leg has given out. She is weakening. Burning up one minute, freezing cold the next. The dark stains of her blood grow.

That's a lot of blood, she thinks.

She wonders how little a person could survive on.

Time of death? Who knows? Her watch has stopped. Its face broke when she fell.

Rabbit will think Jude has let her down yet again. Andi will get the phone call. She's her designated next-of-kin. There are contact details for Ben too. Rabbit will forgive her then, once the whole story is known.

She is struggling to keep her eyes open now. Her throat is dry. From a scream to a whisper. She holds the bloodied, broken figure close to her and mumbles:

'Through all trials an' tribulations, we will travel every nation ... with our plastic Elvis we'll go far.' She coughs and winces.

If only she'd been a better person. If only she'd told those that mattered that she loved them. Then she might've been more loved in return.

Her eyes are closed. Lids heavier than stacked grocery bags from Edgar Vane's store. She couldn't open them if her life depended on it, ironically enough. She wonders how long she's been here, in Purgatory. No matter now. This is it. The end. She thinks about what happens after death. About where she'll go next. She hopes AJ Carter will be there.

She whispers, 'Bloomingdales.'

And her heart stops beating.

'Hey, is this real, or is this just a ride?'
—Bill Hicks

Postscript

I had two encounters with Jude Montgomery: one by transatlantic telephone call in 1997, and the other in person, in Glasgow in 2014. Both encounters, brief though they were, had dramatic and devastating outcomes. The writing of this book is my attempt to rationalise, explain and atone for my part in these events.

In early October of 2014, I received a call from Jude. Despite the uniqueness of her accent, I didn't immediately recall her as the person who'd contacted me seventeen years earlier, looking for information about or contact details for The Hyptones, the Scottish band I had written articles about. When she reached me in 1997, I immediately assumed hers was merely another in a lengthening line of legal strong arms attempting to protect the interests of the 'Material Girl'. But Jude quickly explained that her interest was in tracking down whoever held the media rights for the song 'Independent State of Mind'. Her marketing agency was interested in using the song for a high-profile campaign, which, if sanctioned, would be very lucrative for the band and their management. I reached out to a company called AFB Management, after discovering it was run by Anna Mason (who featured briefly in my long-read feature, 'Ballad of the Band').

When the campaign was a worldwide success, I was genuinely delighted for Jamie Hewitt, feeling, perhaps undeservedly, that my writing had performed some beneficial part. I doubt he'd have acknowledged it, but that didn't matter to me. The ends justified the means.

Perhaps inspired by the song's renewed application in 2014 as the anthem of the YES vote for Scottish Independence, I signed up. I painted my face blue and white. I campaigned around the west of Scotland with the other recruits. And I was distraught when the vote was lost. So I was at a very low ebb when Jude Montgomery called me for a second time. She explained her background and her involvement in my article about the band. I was astonished. We agreed to meet. My memory of the conversation we shared as we walked around the upper inclines of the Necropolis won't be exact, but what follows is the substance as I now recall it:

4th October 2014:

'Hi there. Lovely to finally meet you,' she says. She extends a gloved hand, backed up by a warm smile.

'Yeah, you too. This your first time in Glasgow?' I ask.

'It is ... first time in Scotland.'

'You managed to see more than just the city?'

'Well, not really,' she says, and I detect the regret. 'I managed Edin-*boro* but not the Highlands, which I'm sad about. Maybe next time.'

'So, how can I help you, Jude?' I ask.

'I'm not entirely sure you can,' she replies. 'I flew over from the States a few months ago, a bit unsure about why. It wasn't really a vacation, and I'm not workin' on a commission. I guess I wanted to see someone who was once very close to me, and I figured that researchin' The Hyptones' song and its use in the independence referendum would provide the justification.'

'Or a cover story?' I suggest.

'That's very perceptive of you,' she says, smiling.

'And has it?'

'No, not exactly.' She laughs.

We climb to the peak and look over the city sprawling in front of us. It's cold but clear and you can see all the way to the mouth of the Clyde.

'It's really beautiful, here,' she says.

I find myself nodding in agreement, as if it's new information, although I come here almost every weekend. We simply watch for a while, hypnotised as the metropolis goes about its business below us. Like the invited guests of St Mungo, sat on a Glaswegian Mount Olympus.

'The Necropolis has a mythical status for Glaswegians,' I tell her. 'It's the seed of the city, but it's also a place where lots of local gangsters are said to have met a violent end.' She doesn't respond to this, and I feel a bit foolish; like a dull tour guide losing the attention of his audience.

'I had hoped you might know how to contact Chic Chalmers,' Jude says, coming straight to the point.

'Em ... well. I'm not sure I should be—'

'Apart from Jamie Hewitt, he's the only person involved with the band that I haven't managed to speak to,' she says. 'I'm flyin' home in a week, an' this is probably my last opportunity.' I don't respond immediately. I suspect she knows I have what she needs. 'Please, David,' she says. 'This is a great, positive story. I see it as the natural continuation to your piece.' She's imploring me now, one journalist to another, although I'm not that, and arguably never have been. But the instincts remain. It's always about the story, right? The story is the thing, and it's not a story until all the angles have been covered.

'Y'know, Jude, I never really wanted this. I wanted to write novels, but I just wasn't good enough. Creative enough. I've got too little imagination for anything other than joining the obvious dots between facts. That's how *The Face* article got me into so much trouble.' I draw several deep breaths, as if this admission has taken a lot out of me.

'Why not do it, then?' she says, as if it was the simplest thing in the world. 'I'm writing a memoir at the moment.'

'Yeah. Fuck. How's that going?'

'It's difficult, sure, but important to me too, y'know? I'm not so organised, though. It's all recorded on tapes from an old dicta-tion machine.' She opens her bag to let me look inside.

'Jesus, you carry them with you. No copies?'

She shakes her head and then laughs, acknowledging the madness of this.

'I'll transcribe them sometime. Soon, when I'm back in New York.' She looks at me like a tutor does a disconsolate student. 'C'mon David ... you should do it. I've seen your writing. It's good. What you got to lose?'

Some people rise to a challenge. Some people shrivel in the face of one.

'I feel that I can't move on until I square everything with Jamie Hewitt. I've no idea where he is ... or if he's even still alive! Christ, I've had the longest sustained period of writer's block in history, and he's the reason why.' I laugh at the ridiculousness of this, but it still crumples me inside to admit this failure. I catch her smiling. Her sympathy is not what I need.

'I can maybe help you, then,' she says. 'I have his number. I give you Jamie, and you give me Chic.' She laughs again. The absurdity of us swapping the details of forgotten Scottish musicians of the early eighties as if they were Cold War spies and access to them could bring down a corrupt government. After a time, I agree to this arrangement, despite having a creeping feeling of dread about it.

'Look, you need to be really careful with Chic,' I warn her. 'He's a bit bloody ... unhinged. He contacted me a few years ago, after he came out of prison. Wanted me to write his story. "The fucken truth an' nuthin' but," he said. About how Anna Mason had shafted him. Made sure he got nothing from the Apple campaign royalties. He claimed he had evidence that Anna Mason got him arrested and sent down for breaking into her house and seriously assaulting her. Chalmers says he was invited there to discuss a po-tential settlement, and that she'd been battered by someone else prior to him getting there. Probably a set-up by her own security people. He's a dangerous man, Jude. You'd be best avoiding him,' I tell her. But I sense the fearlessness of the journalist rising. I can see the fire in her eyes. I've just made her pursuit of him more attractive, not less. I reluctantly trade Chic Chalmers' last-known address and contact details for Jamie Hewitt's telephone number.

'So, you mentioned meeting someone close to you earlier. How did that go?' I ask her as we're about to say our goodbyes.

She shrugs. 'Ask me next week, before I go home,' she says with a wry smile. 'She's finally agreed to meet me.'

'Good luck,' I tell her. 'And safe travels.'

And with that she's gone. Off to seek the final piece of the jigsaw, at an address I have provided her with. Off to meet Chic Chalmers. The man who would kill her two days later.

I called Jamie Hewitt repeatedly that evening. When he finally answered, he sounded tired, depressed even. I was surprised he stayed on the call after I told him who I was. But I spoke quickly. Tried to get past the sincere apologies and the regret for the hurt I might have caused him. He said little. But we remained connected, and our conversation lasted for a little under an hour. He let me know that Reef Malcolm had been in touch. He knew Jude Montgomery was in town. I told her she had been behind the decision for 'Independent State of Mind' to be used in the Apple campaign. He wasn't aware of this. Didn't seem overly grateful, but I think that was just his way.

At the end of the call, he admitted to his guilt over several things: toxic relationships and bad decisions leading him to his current state. But mostly he talked about his character flaws. I asked him where he was staying. He wouldn't tell me. I gave him my address in the unlikely event that I might be able to help him in future. I suggested that he might find it cathartic to talk to someone about his pain, his addiction. Or at least to write the reasons for it down if he felt unable to talk to articulate them in person.

Two years later, I received a package in the post. Inside was a colour photograph of David Bowie, who had died the week before, and sheafs of lined paper. The first line, written in red biro was:

Hello. My name is Jamie. And I'm a cunt!

It's June 2020. A top-floor tenement flat in Dennistoun is being cleared following the death of its elderly tenant, Mrs Eileen Chalmers. During the clearance, a false plasterboard panel is found in an internal cupboard. Since a new boiler system is to be fitted in the flat, the panel is ripped out. In the space behind, the workers discover a woman's bag, and inside it, a camera, a recording device, a box of tapes and a series of notepads. Further investigation determines them to belong to the American photographer and journalist, Jude Montgomery.

Chic Chalmers, former drummer with The Hyptones, a Scottish band from the eighties whose song 'Independent State of Mind' was the theme for Anna Mason's rise to power as first minister, is serving a minimum of eighteen years in prison for the murder of Ms Montgomery. Eileen Chalmers is Chic's mother.

Less than a week later, this story breaks. The tapes contain fragments of autobiographical accounts of Jude Montgomery's Texan childhood and her early adult life in San Francisco and New York. But there are also scribbled notes from an October 2014 telephone call between the American woman and Scotland's first minister, Anna Mason. As a result, the discovery becomes national news and is also broadcast in the United States.

The following day, Jamie Hewitt's body is found floating in shallow water near the rocky western edge of Gigha, a remote island off the west coast of Kintyre in Scotland. The island has a population of 158 people. Those interviewed claim to have had no idea that Jamie Hewitt had lived amongst them since the late nineties. Jamie Hewitt's death would later be reported as misadventure.

At the end of a week in which these news items rocked me, First Minister Anna Mason shocked the entire country by resigning from her position.

I can't know with any certainty what Jude Montgomery's tapes contained, beyond the bare bones of the memoir she said she was writing. She had told me that the death of her high-school boyfriend in a mass shooting was the catalyst for the trajectory of her entire life from that point on.

I can only imagine the torment Jamie Hewitt went through in the years before his death, sketched out in the folder full of handwritten confessions he sent me.

It's purely my conjecture that Anna Mason's resignation was connected to the discovery of Jude's tapes and the subsequent death of Anna's former boyfriend, Jamie Hewitt. But given their tangled history, surely these events are too closely linked to be pure coincidence.

I took Jude's advice. I discovered my own creativity in another person's voice. Hers.

This book lacks something that might be expected of it: the tying up of loose ends. But that isn't my job. It's yours. I'm passing over the responsibility. You might speculate that Jude Montgomery and Anna Mason did in fact have a meeting prior to Jude's murder, and that, during it, Jude recorded Anna confirming that she and Jamie felt equally responsible for her brother Brian's death. Anna might also, in this recording, have alluded to her exploitation of the band's publishing rights, uncontested by any of the members of The Hyptones. If Anna suspected the tapes found in

Chic Chalmers' mother's flat included the details of this conversation, her political position would've been untenable.

You might also consider Jamie Hewitt's death as suspicious, and not the misadventure verdict that was recorded. If Ronnie Mason feared his lifelong dealings were about to be exposed, he might act in a way that removed all potential threats. Were that the case, however, you might ask why Jamie Hewitt survived as long as he did. I'd answer that simply: despite everything, Anna Mason still really loved him. She never married after Jamie, and there is no evidence of relationships with other people. Hers was the most heartbreaking of all loves ... the love that isn't reciprocated. It would've been uncomfortable for Ronnie, but as long as Jamie was well out of the picture, everything would've been manageable. High-risk stakes for Anna Mason given her political stature, but a situation that she'll have felt she still had control of.

To further this theory of Mason family control, I'd also pose this question: if the discovery of Jude Montgomery's tapes and notebooks were so public, why has their content never yet been published? Powerful people have many ways of maintaining that power.

In the end, the truth doesn't matter ... only your perspective does.

I read of Jude Montgomery's death in a small column buried away deep inside the *Glasgow Herald*. The suspected murder of a renowned American photographer and journalist should've been bigger news. Media outlets seemed preoccupied with the first days of Anna Mason's leadership of her party and her rule as first minister. For the days and weeks following, I hid myself away in my flat, fearing and anticipating the call from the police, but it never came. I reasoned that unless Jude had written or recorded anything of our brief meeting, investigators wouldn't have known we'd met nor that I had provided her with Chalmers' address. I don't know why I didn't volunteer this information. Anxiety? Fear? The terrible realisation that I was implicated? That I'd be extracted from the security of my anonymity? That the shallowness of my own life would be exposed during the inevitable trial? I don't know. One of those decisions, and who knows if they are ever for the best.

Over the course of two miserable weeks in March 2015, during which it rained every day, I sat in the back row of Glasgow Sheriff Court's public benches. Once again, I don't know why I did. Guilt, perhaps. Curiosity, most certainly. Charles Chalmers was on trial for the murder of Judithea Montgomery. I felt that I owed it to Jude to see justice being delivered for her. To find out more about her life and her achievements. Or maybe just to relieve myself a little of the enormous burden I was carrying.

Chalmers' not-guilty plea was based on a flimsy defence that the woman's death was an accident, occurring during a drug deal that had gone wrong. Only character witnesses called to speak for the defence were presented to the court. They included a social worker, a probation officer, and a shifty youth who claimed that an American woman approached him for drugs outside the Red Road flats on the night she died. The accused's mother, Eileen Chambers, and her close friend, Sarah Docherty, both testified under oath to having encountered the same American woman in a city-centre café on the afternoon of her death.

'She was right there, tryin' tae phone her dealer in front ae us,' Eileen Chambers told the court.

'It's just incredible that it turned oot tae be Charlie she wis callin',' said Sarah Docherty.

The prosecution made short work of this unlikely coincidence, and of Chalmers' plea. He was sentenced to life with no possibility of parole before 2033. But during the proceedings, I learned nothing of Jude's background that couldn't be found online. No-one was called to defend her honour. It was as if her life and her death were being conveniently erased. This only multiplied the disgust I had for myself and magnified the regret that I hadn't gone to the police earlier.

❦

Who knows where the inspiration to be creative comes from? I spent fruitless decades searching for the creative spark to compose writing that mattered. Words and sentences that tackled human frailty at the same time as lifting the spirit. Disposable fluff pieces for lifestyle magazines offered me little in the way of fulfilment. I craved the freedom of the fiction writer. No need for painstaking research. Of making all the facts align with the permissions to publish them.

We live in the Age of Information. Everything you could ever conceivably want to find out about a person, famous or not, is available in only a few clicks. But how much of it can we trust? Aside from the time of birth and the date of death, the truth of an incident or an occurrence – or even the story of a life – is wrapped up in the telling and the perspective of the teller.

As I sat on those unforgiving wooden benches, listening to im-plausible excuses, fabricated solely to salvage something from a desperate criminal's wasted life, I started to imagine the life he had taken. I sketched out a tragic story of lonely, damaged individuals; of the hopes and dreams and fears and regrets that Jude's killing would leave unrealised. Of how ordinary people – strangers – exist in extraordinary times, until random acts and coincidental occurrences throw them together, and the direction of their lives are forever altered and entwined. I felt compelled to tell Jude's story because no-one else was doing it.

But that's just a necessary legal disclaimer. And most of the time, patently not true. It was necessary because I could ill-afford to revisit the Madonna machinations – a perpetuity for which I'm still contractually bound by a form of inhibitory *omerta*.

A question directly asked of my previous writing, '*Ballad of the Band*': 'Is this fiction masquerading as fact? Or fact dressed up as fiction?' The difference between fiction and nonfiction is whether the content is invented or factual, isn't it? But once again, who is the arbiter of the facts? Whose truth can we fully rely on? During a radio interview in the latter part of 1983, Jamie Hewitt said:

'We didn't know what was happening – even as it was happening to us.'

Those at the epicentre of an old story often recall it in a way that paints a favourable picture or reinforces a certain perspective. Eventually there's no truth. Only perspective.

I am complicit in the tragic events that this book concludes with. Not only did I provide Jude Montgomery with the address of her killer, but I also alerted him that she was coming. That he should trust her to tell his story and that she would pay for his information. I completely underestimated the depths to which Chic Chalmers had fallen, and that ignorance cost a life.

Just like my father before me, I have no understanding of happiness, how to recognise it nor how to cultivate it. His solution was to end his life. Although similar thoughts have often crossed my mind, I lack the courage for that. I have no idea what the future holds for me, but it won't include writing. This is Jude Montgomery and Jamie Hewitt's book, not mine. It may not soar with the lasting and memorable majesty of 'Independent State of Mind' or paint as vivid a picture of the human struggle as *Hinterland*, but this story salutes them. Two people who deserve to be remembered, not least for the positive impact they had on the people around them. It is the very least I owe them.

Why do we write? Often, it's just to fill the time before death, nothing more.

David F. Ross
December 2022

Acknowledgements

Dashboard Elvis Is Dead began life as a screenplay prompted by a story told to me by Robert Hodgens. It has grown – as initial creative seeds often do – into something completely different and more expansive in its ambition. But I remain grateful to Bobby for his friendship and for the kernel of an idea that just wouldn't let go.

Thanks also to Ken McCluskey, Lawrence Donegan, Karen Allison, Stephen Cameron and Dakota Farmer, and to Mike Richmond, *Love Tractor*, Janet Delaney, and Andy Scott for their time, and for allowing me to fictionalise them.

Thanks to Karen Sullivan, West Camel, Anne Cater, Cole Sullivan and all at the Orenda Books Dream Factory. I'll never take your faith in me for granted.

And finally, to Elaine, Nathan, and Nadia.
Here's another one for that shoogly table leg.

The Inspirations

Red Eye To New York by Janet Delaney.
(Published by MACK Books, 2021)

New York, by Lou Reed
(On Sire Records, 1989)

The New York Trilogy, by Paul Auster.
(Published by Faber & Faber, 1987)

The Wizard of Oz
(Produced by Metro-Goldwyn-Mayer. Directed by Victor
Fleming. 1939)

On The Road, by Jack Kerouac
(Published by Viking Press, 1957)

Great Expectations, by Charles Dickens
(Published by Chapman & Hall, 1861)

A Rake's Progress, by William Hogarth, 1732-1734

Xstabeth, by David Keenan
(Published by White Rabbit Books, 2020)

Scabby Queen, by Kirstin Innes
(Published by 4th Estate, 2020)

And the work of Andy Warhol, Jenny Saville, Lucien Freud,
Mary Ellen Carroll, and of course, Madonna.

The Music

State of Independence, by Donna Summer
(Written by Vangelis and Jon Anderson) Available on Polydor
Records, 1981

O Superman, by Laurie Anderson
(Written by Laurie Anderson) Available on Warner Brothers, 1981

She's Gone, by Hall & Oates
(Written by Daryl Hall & John Oates) Available on Atlantic
Records, 1973

Hey Jude, by The Beatles
(Written by Lennon and McCartney) Available on Apple
Records, 1968

Whitey on The Moon, by Gil Scott-Heron
(Written by Gil Scott-Heron)
Available on Flying Dutchman/RCA Records, 1970

America, by Simon & Garfunkel
(Written by Paul Simon) Available on Columbia Records, 1968

Eight Miles High, by The Byrds
(Written by Clark, McGuinn, Crosby) Available on Columbia
Records, 1966

Come Fly with Me, by Frank Sinatra
(Written by Sammy Cahn and Jimmy van Heusen)
Available on Capitol Records, 1958

Born to Run, by Bruce Springsteen
(Written by Bruce Springsteen) Available on Columbia Records, 1975

Sara, by Bob Dylan
(Written by Bob Dylan) Available on Columbia Records, 1976

Chelsea Hotel #2, by Leonard Cohen
(Written by Leonard Cohen) Available on Columbia Records, 1974

Holiday, by Madonna
(Written by Curtis Hudson and Lisa Stevens) Available on Sire Records, 1983

Ain't No Love in the Heart of the City, by Bobby 'Blue' Bland
(Written by Price and Walsh) Available on Dunhill Records, 1974

Highland Sweetheart, by Love Tractor
(Written by Richmond, Cline, Wellford, Swartz) Available on DB Records, 1983

By the Time I Get to Phoenix, by Glen Campbell
(Written by Jimmy Webb) Available on Capitol Records, 1967

Brandy (You're A Fine Girl), by Looking Glass
(Written by Elliot Lurie) Available on Epic Records, 1972

On the Way Home, by Buffalo Springfield
(Written by Neil Young) Available on Atco Records, 1968

Queen Bitch, by David Bowie
(Written by David Bowie) Available on RCA Records, 1971

Over The Wall, by Echo & The Bunnymen
(Written by Sergeant, McCulloch, Pattinson, de Freitas) Available on Korova Records, 1981

Make Your Own Kind of Music, by Cass Elliot
(Written by Barry Mann and Cynthia Weil) Available on Dunhill Records, 1969

The Broad Majestic Shannon, by The Pogues
(Written by Shane McGowan) Available on Island Records, 1988

Love Shack, by the B-52's
(Written by Pierson, Schneider, Strickland, Wilson) Available on Reprise Records, 1989

66, by the Afghan Whigs
(Written by Greg Dulli) Available on Columbia Records, 1998

Dirty Blvd, by Lou Reed
(Written by Lou Reed) Available on Sire Records, 1989

Signed, Sealed, Delivered, I'm Yours, by Stevie Wonder
(Written by Garrett, Wonder, Wright, Hardaway) Available on Motown Records, 1970

You Get What You Give, by New Radicals
(Written by Alexander and Nowels) Available on MCA Records, 1998